Wild Wings
A Romance of Youth

Margaret Rebecca Piper

Contents

WILD WINGS
A ROMANCE OF YOUTH

BY

Margaret Rebecca Piper

CHAPTER I
MOSTLY TONY

A mong the voluble, excited, commencement-bound crowd that boarded the Northampton train at Springfield two male passengers were conspicuous for their silence as they sat absorbed in their respective newspapers which each had hurriedly purchased in transit from train to train.

A striking enough contrast otherwise, however, the two presented. The man next the aisle was well past sixty, rotund of abdomen, rubicund of countenance, beetle-browed. He was elaborately well-groomed, almost foppish in attire, and wore the obvious stamp of worldly success, the air of one accustomed to giving orders and seeing them obeyed before his eyes.

His companion and chance seat-mate was young, probably a scant five and twenty, tall, lean, close-knit of frame with finely chiseled, almost ascetic features, though the vigorous chin and generous sized mouth forbade any hint of weakness or effeminacy. His deep-set, clear gray-blue eyes were the eyes of youth; but they would have set a keen observer to wondering what they had seen to leave that shadow of unyouthful gravity upon them.

It happened that both men--the elderly and the young--had their papers folded at identically the same page, and both were studying intently the face of the lovely, dark-eyed young girl who smiled out of the duplicate printed sheets impartially at both.

The legend beneath the cut explained that the dark-eyed young beauty was Miss Antoinette Holiday, who would play Rosalind that night in the Smith College annual senior dramatics. The interested reader was further enlightened to the fact that Miss Holiday was the daughter of the late Colonel Holiday and Laura LaRue, a well known actress of a generation ago, and that the daughter inherited the gifts as well as the beauty of her famous mother, and was said to be planning to follow the stage herself, having made her debut as the charming heroine of "As You Like It."

The man next the aisle frowned a little as he came to this last sentence and went back to the perusal of the girl's face. So this was Laura's daughter. Well, they had not lied in one respect at least. She was a winner for looks. That was plain to be seen even from the crude newspaper reproduction. The girl was pretty. But what else did she have beside prettiness? That was the question. Did she have any of the rest of it--Laura's wit, her inimitable charm, her fire, her genius? Pshaw! No, of course she hadn't. Nature did not make two Laura LaRue's in one century. It was too much to expect.

Lord, what a woman! And what a future she had had and thrown away for love! Love! That wasn't it. She could have had love and still kept on with her career. It was marriage that had been the catastrophe--the fatal blunder. Marriage and domesticity for a woman like that! It was asinine--worse--criminal! It ought to have been forbidden by law. And the stubbornness of her! After all these years, remembering, Max Hempel could have groaned aloud. Every stage manager in New York, including himself, had been ready to bankrupt himself offering her what in those days were almost incredible contracts to prevent her from the suicidal folly on which she was bent. But to no avail. She had laughed at them all, laughed and quit the stage at six and twenty, and a few years later her beauty and genius were still--in death. What a waste! What a damnation waste!

At this point in his animadversions Max Hempel again looked at the girl in the newspaper, the girl who was the product of the very marriage he had been cursing, LaRue's only daughter. If there had been no marriage, neither would there have been this glorious, radiant, vividly alive young creature. Men called Laura LaRue dead. But was she? Was she not tremendously alive in the life of her lovely young daughter? Was it not he, and the other childless ones who had treated matrimony as the one supreme mistake, that would soon be very much dead, dead past any resurrection?

Pshaw! He was getting sentimental. He wasn't here for sentiment. He was here for cold, hard business. He was taking this confounded journey to witness an amateur performance of a Shakespeare play, when he loathed traveling in hot weather, detested amateur performances of anything, particularly of Shakespeare, on the millionth of a chance that Antoinette Holiday might be possessed of a tithe of her mother's talent and might eventually be starred as the new ingenue he was in need of, afar off, so to speak. It was Carol Clay herself who had warned him. Carol was wonderful--would always be wonderful. But time passes. There would come a season when the public would begin to count back and remember that Carol had been playing ingenue parts already for over a decade. There must always be youth--fresh, flaming youth in the offing. That was the stage and life.

As for this Antoinette Holiday girl, he had none too much hope. Max Hempel never hoped much on general principles, so far as potential stars were concerned. He had seen too many of them go off fizz bang into nothingness, like rockets. It was more than likely he was on a false trail, that people who had seen the girl act in amateur things had exaggerated her ability. He trusted no judgment but his own, which was perhaps one of the reasons why he was one of the greatest living stage managers. It was more than likely she had nothing but a pretty, shallow little talent for play acting and no notion under the sun of giving up society or matrimony or what-not for the devilish hard work of a stage career. Very likely there was some young galoot waiting even now, to whisk Laura LaRue's daughter off the stage before she ever got on.

Moreover there was always her family to cope with, dyed in the wool New Englanders at that, no doubt with the heavy Puritan mortmain upon them, narrow as a shoe string, circumscribed as a duck pond, walled in by ghastly respectability. Ten to one, if the girl had talent and ambition, they would smother these things in her, balk her at every turn. They had regarded Ned Holiday's marriage to Laura a misalliance, he recalled. There had been quite a to-do about it at the time. Good God! It had been a misalliance all right, but not as they reckoned it. It had not been considered suitable for a Holiday to marry an actress. Probably it would be considered more unsuitable for a Holiday to *be* an actress. Suitable! Bah! The question was not whether the career was fit for the girl, but whether the girl could measure up to the career. And irascibly, unreasonably indignant as if he had already been contending in argument with legions of mythical, over-respectable Holidays, Max Hempel whipped his paper open to another page, a page that told of a drive somewhere on the western front that had failed miserably, for this was the year nineteen hundred and sixteen and there was a war going on, "on the other side." Oh, typically American phrase!

Meanwhile the young man, too, had stopped staring at Antoinette Holiday's pictured face and was staring out of the window instead at the fast flying landscape. He had really no need anyway to look at a picture of Tony. His head and heart were full of them. He had been storing them up for over eight years and it was a considerable collection by now and one in which he took great joy in lonely hours in his dingy little lodging room, or in odd moments as he went his way at his task as a reporter for a great New York daily. The perspicuous reader will not need to be told that the young man was in love with Tony Holiday--desperately in love.

Desperately was the word. Slight as Max Hempel's hope may have been that Laura LaRue's daughter was to prove the ingenue he sought, infinitely slighter was Dick Carson's hope of ever making Tony his wife. How could it be otherwise? Tony Holiday was as far above him in his own eyes as the top of Mount Tom was high above the onion beds of the valley. The very name he used was his only because she had given it to him. Dick Nobody he had been. Richard Carson he had become through grace of Tony.

Like his companion the young man went back into the past, though not so far a journey. As vividly as if it were but yesterday he remembered the misery of flesh and spirit which had been his as he stowed himself away in the hay loft in the Holiday's barn, that long ago summer dawn, too sick to take another step and caring little whether he lived or died, conscious vaguely, however, that death would be infinitely preferable to going back to the life of the circus and the man Jim's coarse brutality from which he had made his escape at last.

And then he had opened his eyes, hours later, and there had been Tony--and there had been chiefly Tony ever since, for him.

If ever he amounted to anything, and he meant to amount to something, it would be all due to Tony and her Uncle Phil. The two of them had saved him in more ways than one, had faith in him when he wasn't much but a scarecrow, ignorant, profane, unmoral, miserable, a "gutter brat" as some one had once called him, a phrase he had never forgotten. It had seemed to brand him, set him apart from people like the Holidays forever. But Tony and Doctor Phil had shown him a different way of looking at it, proved to him that nothing could really disgrace him but himself. They had given him his chance and he had taken it. Please God he would make himself yet into something they could be proud of, and it would all be their doing. He would never forget that, whatever happened.

A half hour later the train puffed and wheezed into the station at Northampton. Dick Carson and Max Hempel, still close together, descended into the swarming, chattering crowd which was delightfully if confusingly congested with pretty girls, more pretty girls and still more pretty girls. But Dick was not confused. Even before the train had come to a full stop he had caught sight of Tony. He had a single track mind so far as girls were concerned. From the moment his eyes discovered Tony Holiday the rest simply did not exist for him. It is to be doubted whether he knew they were there at all, in spite of their manifest ubiquity and equally manifest pulchritude.

Tony saw him, too, as he loomed up, taller than the others, bearing resistlessly down upon her. She waved a gay greeting and smiled her welcome to him through the throng. Max Hempel, close behind, caught the message, too, and recognized the face of the girl who smiled as the original of the newspaper cut he had just been studying so assiduously. Deliberately he dogged the young man's heels. He wanted to get a close-up view of Laura LaRue's daughter. She was much prettier than the picture. Even from a distance he had made that out, as she stood there among the crowd, vivacious, vivid, clad all in white except for the loose coral-hued sweater which set off her warm brunette beauty and the slim but charmingly rounded curves of her supple young body. Yes, she was like Laura, like her and yet different, with a quality which he fancied belonged to herself and none other.

Almost jealously Hempel watched the meeting between the girl and the youth who up to now had been negligible enough, but suddenly emerged into significance as the possible young galoot already mentally warned off the premises by the stage manager.

"Dick! O Dick! I'm *so* glad to see you," cried the girl, holding out both hands to the new arrival. Her cheeks were flushed, her eyes shining. She looked quite as glad as she proclaimed.

As for the young man who had set down his suitcase and taken possession of both the proffered hands, there wasn't the slightest doubt that he was in the seventh heaven of bliss wherever that may be. Next door to Fool's Paradise, Max Hempel hoped somewhat vindictively.

"Just you wait, young man," he muttered to himself. "Bet you'll have to, any-way. That glorious young thing isn't going to settle down to the shallows of mat-rimony without trying the deep waters first, unless I'm mightily mistaken. In the meantime we shall see what we shall see to-night." And the man of power trudged away in the direction of a taxicab, leaving youth alone with itself.

"Everybody is here," bubbled Tony. "At least, nearly everybody. Larry went to a horrid old medical convention at Chicago, and can't be here for the play; but he's coming to commencement. Of course, Granny isn't able to travel and Aunt Margery couldn't come because the kiddies have been measling, but Ted is here, and Uncle Phil--bless him! He brought the twins over from Dunbury in the car. Phil Lambert and everybody are waiting down the street. Carlotta too! To think you haven't ever met her, when she's been my roommate and best friend for two years! And, oh! Dicky! I haven't seen you myself for most a year and I'm so glad." She beamed up at him as she made this rather ambiguous statement. "And you haven't said a word but just 'hello!' Aren't you glad to see me, Dicky?" she reproached.

He grunted at that.

"About a thousand times gladder than if I were in Heaven, unless you hap-pened to be sitting beside me on the golden stairs. And if you think I don't know how long it is since I've seen you, you are mightily mistaken. It is precisely one mil-lion years in round numbers."

"Oh, it is?" Tony smiled, appeased. "Why didn't you say so before, and not leave me to squeeze it out of you like tooth-paste?"

Dick grinned back happily.

"Because you brought me up not to interrupt a lady. You seemed to have the floor, so to speak."

"So to speak, indeed," laughed Tony. "Carlotta says I exist for that sole purpose. But come on. Everybody's crazy to see you and I've a million things to do." And tucking her arm in his, Tony marshaled the procession of two down the stairs to the street where the car and the old Holiday Hill crowd waited to greet the newest comer to the ranks of the commencement celebrants.

With the exception of Carlotta Cressy, Tony's roommate, the occupants of the car are known already to those who followed the earlier tale of Holiday Hill[1].

---

1 The earlier experiences of the Holidays and their friends are related in "The

First of all there was the owner of the car, Dr. Philip Holiday himself, a married man now, with a small son and daughter of his own, "Miss Margery's" children. A little thicker of build and thinner of hair was the doctor, but possessed of the same genial friendliness of manner and whimsical humor, the same steady hand held out to help wherever and whenever help was needed. He was head of the House of Holiday now for his father, the saintly old pastor, had gone on to other fields and his soldier brother Ned, Tony's father, had also gone, in the prime of life, two years before, victim of typhus, leaving his beloved little daughter, and his two sons just verging into manhood, in the care of the younger Holiday.

As Dick and the doctor exchanged cordial greetings, the latter's friendly eyes challenged the young man's and were answered. Plainly as if words had been spoken the doctor knew that Dick was keeping faith with the old pact, living up to the name the little girl Tony had given him in her impulsive generosity.

"Something not quite right, though," he thought. "The boy isn't all happy. Wonder what the trouble is. Probably a girl. Usually is at that age."

At the wheel beside the doctor was his namesake and neighbor, Philip Lambert. Phil was graduating, himself, this year from the college across the river, a sturdy athlete of some note and a Phi Beta Kappa man as well. Out of a harum-scarum, willful boyhood he had emerged into a finely tempered, steady young manhood. The Dunbury wiseacres who had been wont to shake their heads over Phil's youthful escapades and prophesy a bad end for such a devil-may-care youngster now patted themselves complacently on the back, as wiseacres will, and declared they had always known the boy would turn out a credit to his family and the town.

On the back seat were Phil's sisters, the pretty twins, Charley and Clare, still astonishingly alike at twenty, as they had been at twelve, and still full of the high spirits and ready laughter and wit that had made them the life of the Hill in the old days. Neither looked a day over sixteen, but Clare had already been teaching two years in a Dunbury public school and Charley was to go into nurse's training in the fall.

Larry, the young doctor, as Dunbury had taken to calling him in distinction from his uncle, was not yet arrived, as Tony had explained; but Ted, her younger brother, was very much on the scene, arrayed in all the extravagant niceties of

---

House on the Hill."

modish attire affected by university undergraduates. At twenty, Ted Holiday was as handsome as the traditional young Greek god and possessed of a godlike propensity to do as he liked and the devil take the consequences. Already Ned Holiday's younger son had acquired something of a reputation as a high flier among his own sex, and a heart breaker among the fairer one. Reckless, debonair, utterly irresponsible, he was still "terrible Teddy" as his father had jocosely dubbed him long ago. Yet he was quite as lovable as he was irrepressible, and had a manifest grace to counterbalance every one of his many faults. His soberer brother Larry worried uselessly over Ted's misdeeds, and took him sharply to task for them; but even Larry admitted that there was something rather magnificent about Ted and that possibly in the end he would come out the soundest Holiday of them all.

There remains only Carlotta to be introduced. Carlotta was lovely to look upon. A poet speaks somewhere of a face "made out of a rose." Carlotta had that kind of a face and her eyes were of that deep, violet shade which works mischief and magic in the hearts of men. As for her hair, it might well have been the envy of any princess, in or out of the covers of a book, so fine spun was it in texture, so pure gold in color, like the warm, vivid shimmer of tropical sunshine. She lifted an inquiring gaze now to Dick, as she held out her hand in acknowledgment of the introduction, and Dick murmured something platitudinous, bowed politely over the hand and never noticed what color her eyes were. A single track mind is both a curse and a protection to a man.

"Carlotta **would** come," Tony was explaining gaily, "though I told her there wasn't room. Let me inform you all that Carlotta is the most completely, magnificently, delightfully spoiled young person in these United States of America."

"Barring you?" teased her uncle.

"Barring none. By comparison with Carlotta, I am all the noble army of saints, martyrs and seraphim on record combined. Carlotta is preordained to have her own way. Everybody unites to give it to her. We can't help it. She hypnotizes us. Some night you will miss the moon in its accustomed place and you will find that she wanted it for a few moments to play with."

Philip Lambert had turned around in his seat and was surveying Carlotta rather curiously during this teasing tirade of Tony's.

"Oh, well," murmured Carlotta. "Your old moon can be put up again when I am through with it. I shan't do it a bit of harm. Anyway, Mr. Carson must not be told such horrid things about me the very first time he meets me, must he, Phil? He might think they were true." She suddenly lifted her eyes and smiled straight up into the face of the young man on the front seat who was watching her so intently.

"Well, aren't they?" returned the young man addressed, stooping to examine the brake.

Carlotta did not appear in the least offended at his curt comment. Indeed the smile on her lips lingered as if it had some inner reason for being there.

"Hop in, Tony," ordered Ted with brotherly peremptoriness. "Carlotta, you are one too many, my love. You will have to sit in my lap."

"I'm getting out," said Phil. "I'm due across the river. Want Ted to take the wheel, Doctor?"

"I do not. I have a wife and children at home. I cannot afford to place my life in jeopardy." The doctor's eyes twinkled as they rested a moment on his youngest nephew.

"Now, Uncle Phil, that's mean of you. You ought to see me drive."

"I have," commented Dr. Holiday drily. "Come on over here, one of you twinnies, if Phil must go. See you to-night, my boy?" he turned to his namesake to ask as Charley accepted the invitation and clambered over the back of the seat while the doctor took her brother's vacated post.

Phil shook his head.

"No. I was in on the dress rehearsal last night. I've had my share. But you folks are going to see the jolliest Rosalind that ever grew in Arden or out of it. That's one sure thing."

Phil smiled at Tony as he spoke, and Dick, settling himself in the small seat beside Ted, felt a small barbed dart of jealousy prick into him.

Tony and Phil were obviously exceedingly good friends. They had, he knew, seen much of each other during the past four years, with only a river between. Phil was Tony's own kind, college-trained, with a certified line of good old New England ancestry behind him. Moreover, he was a darned fine fellow--one of the best, in fact. In spite of that hateful little jabbing dart, Dick acknowledged that. Ah well, there was more than a river between himself and Tony Holiday and there always would be. Who was he, nameless as he was, to enter the lists against Philip Lambert or any one else?

The car sped away, leaving Phil standing bareheaded in the sunshine, staring after it. The mocking silver lilt of Carlotta Cressy's laughter drifted back to him. He shrugged, jammed on his hat and strode off in the direction of the trolley car.

Dick Carson might just as well have spared himself the pain of jealousy. Phil had already forgotten Tony, was remembering only Carlotta, who would never deliberately do a mite of harm to the moon, would merely want to play with it at her fancy and leave it at her whim for somebody else to replace, if anybody cared to take the pains. And what was a moon more or less anyway?

CHAPTER II
WITH ROSALIND IN ARDEN

Of course it is understood that every graduating class rightfully asserts, and is backed up in its belief by doting and nobly partisan relatives and blindly devoted, hyperbolic friends, that *its* particular, unique and proper senior dramatics is the most glorious and unforgettable performance in all the histrionic annals of the college, a thing to make Will Shakespeare himself rise and applaud from his high and far off hills of Paradise.

Certainly Tony's class knew, past any qualms of doubt, and made no bones of proclaiming its conviction that there never had been such a wonderful "As You Like It" and that never, so long as the stars kept their seats in the heavens and senior classes produced Shakespeare--two practically synonymous conditions--would there ever be such another Rosalind as Tony Holiday, so fresh, so spontaneous, so happy in her acting, so bewitchingly winsome to behold, so boyish, yet so exquisitely feminine in her doublet and hose, so daring, so dainty, so full of wit and grace and sparkle, so tender, so merry, so natural, so all-in-all and utterly as Will himself would have liked his "right Rosalind" to be.

So the class maintained and so they chanted soon and late, in many keys, "with a hey and a ho and a hey nonino." And who so bold or malicious, or age cankered as to dispute the dictum? Is it not youth's privilege to fling enthusiasm and superlatives to the wind and to deal in glorious arrogance?

It must be admitted, however, in due justice, that the class that played "As You Like It" that year had some grounds on which to base its pretensions and vain-glory. For had not a great stage manager been present and applauded until his palms were purple and perspiration beaded his beak of a nose? Had he not, as the last curtain, descended, blown his nose, mopped his brow, exclaimed "God bless my soul!" three times in succession and demanded to be shown without delay into the presence of Rosalind?

As we know already, the great stage manager had not come over-willingly or over-hopefully to Northampton to see Tony Holiday play Rosalind. Indeed, when it had been first suggested that he do so, he had objected violently and remarked with conviction that he would "be da--er--*blessed* if he would." But he had come and he had been blessed involuntarily.

For he had seen something he had not expected to see--a real play, with real magic to it, such magic as all his cunning stage artifice, all the studied artistry of his fearfully and wonderfully salaried stellar attachments somehow missed achieving. He tried afterwards to explain to Carol Clay, his favorite star, just what the quality of the magic was, but somehow he could not get it into words. It wasn't exactly wordable perhaps. It was something that rendered negligible the occasionally creaking mechanism and crudeness of stage business and rendition; something compounded of dew and sun and wind, such as could only be found in a veritable Forest of Arden; something elusive, exquisite, iridescent; something he had supposed had vanished from the world about the time they put Pan out of business and stopped up the Pipes of Arcady. It was enchanting, elemental, genuine Elizabethan, had the spirit of Master Skylark himself in it. Maybe it was the spirit of youth itself, immortal youth, playing immortal youth's supreme play? Who knows or can lay finger upon the secret of the magic? The great stage manager did not and could not. He only knew that, in spite of himself, he had drunk deep for a moment of true elixir.

But as for Rosalind herself that was another matter. Max Hempel was entirely capable of analyzing his impressions there and correlating them with the cold hard business on which he had come. Even if the play had proved a greater bore than he had anticipated, the trip from Broadway to the Academy of Music would still have been materially worth while. Antoinette Holiday was a genuine find, authentic star stuff. They hadn't spoiled her, plastered her over with meaningless mannerisms. She was virgin material--untrained, with worlds to learn, of course; but with a spark of the true fire in her--her mother's own daughter, which was the most promising thing anybody could say of her.

No wonder Max Hempel had peremptorily demanded to be shown behind the scenes without an instant's delay. He was almost in a panic lest some other manager should likewise have gotten wind of this Rosalind and be lurking in the wings even now to pounce upon his own legitimate prey. He couldn't quite forget either the tall young man of the afternoon's encounter, his seatmate up from Springfield. He wasn't exactly afraid, however, having seen the girl and watched her live Rosalind. The child had wings and would want to fly far and free with them, unless he was mightily mistaken in his reading of her.

Tony was still resplendent in her wedding white, and with her arms full of roses, when she obeyed the summons to the stage door on being told that the great manager wished to see her. She came toward him, flushed, excited, adorably pretty. She laid down her roses and held out her hand, shy, but perfectly self-possessed.

"'Well, this is the Forest of Arden,'" she quoted. "It must be or else I am dreaming. As long as I can remember I have wanted to meet you, and here you are, right on the edge of the forest."

He bowed low over her hand and raised it gallantly to his lips.

"I rather think I am still in Arden myself," he said. "My dear, you have given me a treat such as I never expected to enjoy again in this world. You made me forget I knew anything about plays or was seeing one. You carried me off with you to Arden."

"Did you really like the play?" begged Tony, shining-eyed at the praise of the great man.

"I liked it amazingly and I liked your playing even more amazingly. Is it true that you are going on the stage?" He had dropped Arden now, gotten down to what he would have called brass tacks. The difference was in his voice. Tony sensed it vaguely and was suddenly a little frightened.

"Why, I--I don't know," she faltered. "I hope so. Sometime."

"Sometime is never," he snapped. "That won't do."

The Arden magic was quite gone by this time. He was scowling a little and thrust out his upper lip in a way Tony did not care for at all. It occurred to her inconsequentially that he looked a good deal like the wolf, in the story, who threatened to "huff and puff" until he blew in the house of the little pigs. She didn't want her house blown in. She wished Uncle Phil would come. She stooped to gather up her roses as if they might serve as a barricade between her and the wolf. But suddenly she forgot her misgivings again, for Max Hempel was saying incredible things, things which set her imagination agog and her pulses leaping. He was offering her a small role, a maid's part, in one of his road companies.

"Me!" she gasped from behind her roses.

"You."

"When?"

"To-morrow--the day after--next week at the latest. Chances like that don't go begging long, young lady. Will you take it?"

"Oh, I wish I could!" sighed Tony. "But I am afraid I can't. Oh, there is Uncle Phil!" she interrupted herself to exclaim with perceptible relief.

In a moment Doctor Holiday was with them, his arm around Tony while he acknowledged the introduction to the stage manager, who eyed him somewhat uncordially. The two men took each the other's measure. Possibly a spark of antagonism flashed between them for an instant. Each wanted the lovely little Rosalind on his own side of the fence, and each suspected the other of desiring to lure her to the other side if he could. For the moment however, the advantage was all with the doctor, with his protecting arm around Tony.

"Holiday!" muttered Hempel. "There was a Holiday once who married one of the finest actresses of the American stage--carried her off to nurse his babies. I never forgave that man. He was a brute."

Tony stiffened. Her eyes flashed. She drew away from her uncle and confronted the stage manager angrily.

"He wasn't a brute, if you mean my father!" she burst out. "My mother was Laura LaRue."

"I know it," grinned the manager, thoroughly delighted to have struck fire. The girl was better even than he had thought. She was magnificent, angry. "That's why I'm here," he added. "I just offered this young person a part in a practically all-star cast, touring the West. Do you mind?" he challenged Doctor Holiday.

"I should mind her accepting," said the other man tranquilly. "As it is, I am duly appreciative of the offer. Thank you."

"What if I told you she had accepted?" the wolf snapped.

Tony saw the swift shadow cloud her uncle's face and hated the manager for hurting him like that.

"I didn't," she protested indignantly. "You know I wouldn't promise anything without talking to you, Uncle Phil. I told him I couldn't go."

"But you wanted to," persisted the wolf, bound to get his fangs in somewhere.

Tony smiled a little wistfully.

"I wanted to most awfully," she confessed, patting her uncle's arm to take the sting out of her admission. "Will you ask me again some day?" she appealed to the manager.

He snorted at that.

"You'll come asking me, young lady, and before long, too. Laura LaRue's daughter isn't going to settle down to being either a butterfly or a blue-stocking. You are going on the stage and you know it. No use, Holiday. You won't be able to hold her back. It's in the blood. You may be able to dam the tide for a time, but not forever."

"I don't intend to dam it," said the doctor gravely. "If, when the time comes, Tony wishes to go on the stage, I shall not try to prevent her. In fact I shall help her in every way in my power."

"Uncle Phil!" Tony's voice had a tiny catch in it. She knew her grandmother would be bitterly opposed to her going on the stage, and had imagined she would have to win even her uncle over by slow degrees to the gratifying of this desire of her heart. It had hurt her even to think of hurting him or going against him in any way--he who was, "father and mother and a'" to her. Dear Uncle Phil! How he always understood and took the big, broad viewpoint!

The manager grunted approval at that. His belligerency waned.

"Congratulate you, sir. That's spoken like a man of sense. Evidently you are able to see over the wall farther than most of the witch-ridden New Englanders I've met. I should like the chance to launch this Rosalind of yours. But don't make it too far off. Youth is the biggest drawing card in the world and--the most transient. You have to get in the game early to get away with it. I'll start her whenever you say--next week--next month--next year. Guarantee to have her ready to understudy a star in three months and perhaps a star herself in six. She might jump into the heavens overnight. Stranger things have happened. What do you say? May I have an option on the young lady?"

"That is rather too big a question to settle off hand at midnight. Tony is barely twenty-two and she has home obligations which will have to be considered. Her grandmother is old and frail and--a New Englander of the old school."

"Too bad," commiserated the manager. "But never mind all that. All I ask is that you won't let her sign up with anybody else without giving me a chance first."

"I think we may safely promise that and thank you. Tony and I both appreciate that you are doing her a good deal of honor for one small school girl, eh Tony?" The doctor smiled down at his flushed, starry-eyed niece. He understood precisely what a big moment it was for her.

"Oh, I should think so!" sighed Tony. "You are awfully kind, Mr. Hempel. It is like a wonderful dream--almost too good to be true."

Both men smiled at that. For youth no dream is quite too extravagant or incredible to be potentially true. No grim specters of failure and disillusionment and frustration dog its bright path. All possibilities are its divine inheritance.

"Mr. Hempel, did you know my mother?" Tony asked suddenly, with a shadow of wistfulness in her dark eyes. There were so few people whom she met that had known her mother. It was as if Laura LaRue had moved in a different orbit from that of her daughter. It always hurt Tony to feel that. But here was one who was of her mother's own world. No wonder her eyes were beseeching as they sought the great manager's.

He bowed gravely.

"I knew her very well. She was one of the most beautiful women I have ever seen--and one of the greatest actresses. Your father was a lucky man, my dear. Few women would have given up for any man what she gave up for him."

"Oh, but--she loved him," explained Laura LaRue's daughter simply.

Again Hempel nodded.

"She did," he admitted grimly. After all these years there was no use admitting that that had been the deepest rub of all, that Laura had loved Ned Holiday and had never, for even the span of a moment, thought of caring for himself. "I repeat, your father was a very lucky man--a damnably lucky one."

And with that they shook hands and parted.

It was many months before Tony was to see Max Hempel again and many waters were to run under the bridge before the meeting came to pass.

Outside in the car, Ted, Dick and the twins waited the arrival of the heroine of the evening. The three latter greeted her with a burst of prideful congratulation; the former, being merely a brother, was distinctly cross at having been kept waiting so long and did not hesitate to express his sentiments fully out loud. But Doctor Holiday cut short his nephew's somewhat ungracious speech by a quiet reminder that the car was here primarily for Tony's use, and the boy subsided, having no more to say until, having deposited the occupants of the car at their various destinations, he announced to his uncle with elaborate carelessness that he would take the car around to the garage.

But he did not turn in at the side street where the garage was. Instead he shot out Elm Street, "hitting her up" at forty. There had been a reason for his impatience. Ted Holiday had important private business to transact ere cock crow.

Tony lay awake a long time that night, dreaming dreams that carried her far and far into the future, until Rosalind's happy triumph of the evening almost faded away in the glory of the yet-to-be. It was characteristic of the girl's stage of development that in all her dreams, no lovers, much less a possible husband, ever once entered. Tony Holiday was in love with life and life alone that wonderful June night. As Hempel had shrewdly perceived she was conscious of having wings and desirous of flying far and free with them ere she came to pause.

She did remember, in passing however, how she had caught Dick's eyes once as he sat in the box near the stage, and how his rapt gaze had thrilled her to intenser playing of her part. And she remembered how dear he was afterward in the car when he held her roses and told her softly what a wonderful, wonderful Rosalind she was. But, on the whole, Dick, like most of the rest of the people with whom she had held converse since the curtain went down upon Arden, seemed unimportant and indistinct, like courtiers and foresters, not specifically named among the *dramatis personae*, just put in to fill out and make a more effective stage setting.

Dick, too, in his room on Greene Street, was wakeful. He sat by the window far into the night. His heart was heavy within him. The gulf between him and Tony had suddenly widened immeasureably. She was a real actress. He hadn't needed a great manager's verdict to teach him that. He had seen it with his own eyes, heard it with his own ears, felt it with his own heart. He had worshiped and adored and been made unutterably sad and lonely by her dazzling success, glad as he was that it had come to her. Tony would go on in her shining path. He would always lag behind in the shadows. They would never come together as long as they both lived. She had started too far ahead. He could never overtake her.

If only there were some way of finding out who he was, get some clue as to his parentage. He only knew that the man they called Jim, who had kicked and beaten and sworn at him with foul oaths until he could bear it no longer, was no kin of his, though the other had claimed the authority to abuse him as he abused his horses and dogs when drink and ugliness were upon him. If only he could find Jim again after all these years, perhaps he could manage to get the truth out of him, find out what the man knew of himself, and how he had come to be in a circus troupe. Yet after all, perhaps it was better not to know. The facts might separate him from Tony even more than he was separated by his ignorance of them. As it was, he started even, with neither honor nor shame bequeathed him from the past. What he was, he was in himself. And if by any miracle of fortune Tony ever did come to care for him it would be just himself, plain Dick, that she would love. He knew that.

The thought was vaguely comforting and he, too, fell adreaming. Most of us foiled humans learn to play the game of make-believe and to find such consolation as we may therein. Often and often in his lonely hours Dick Carson had summoned Tony Holiday to his side, a Tony as bright and beautiful and all adorable as the real Tony, but a dream Tony, withal, a Tony who loved him even as he loved her. And in his make-believe he was no longer a nameless, impecunious cub reporter, but a man who had arrived somewhere, made himself worthy, so far as any mere man could, of the supreme gift of Tony's caring.

To-night, too, Dick played the game determinedly, but somehow he found its consolation rather meager, as cold and remote as the sparkle of the June stars, millions of miles away up there in the velvet sky, after having sat by the side of the living, breathing Tony and, looking into her happy eyes, known how little, how very little, he was in her thoughts. She liked him to be near her, he knew, just as she liked her roses to be fragrant, but neither the roses nor himself was a vital necessity to her. She could do very well without either. That was the pity of it.

At last he got up and went to bed. Falling into troubled sleep he dreamed that he and Tony were wandering, hand in hand, in the Forest of Arden. From afar off came the sound of music, airy voices chanting:

"When birds do sing, hey ding a ding Sweet lovers love the spring."

And then somebody laughed mockingly, like Jacques, and somebody else, clad in motley like Touchstone, but who seemed to speak in Dick's own voice, murmured, "Ay, now am I in Arden, the more fool I."

And even with these words the forest vanished and Tony with it and the dreamer was left alone on a steep and dusty road, lost and aching for the missing touch of her hand.

But later he woke to the song of a thousand birds greeting the new day with full-throated joy. And his heart, too, began to sing. For it was indeed a new day--a day in which he should see Tony. He was irrationally content. Of such is the kingdom of lad's love!

CHAPTER III
A GIRL WHO COULDN'T STOP BEING A PRINCESS

In the lee of a huge gray bowlder on the summit of Mount Tom sat Philip Lambert and Carlotta Cressy. Below them stretched the wide sweep of the river valley, amethyst and topaz and emerald, rich with lush June verdure, soft shadowed, tranquil, in the late afternoon sunshine. They had been silent for a little time but suddenly Carlotta broke the silence.

"Phil, do you know why I brought you up here?" she asked. As she spoke she drew a little closer to him and her hand touched his as softly as a drifting feather or a blown cherry blossom might have touched it.

He turned to look at her. She was all in white like a lily, and otherwise carried out the lily tradition of belonging obviously to the non-toiling-and-spinning species, justifying the arrangement by looking seraphically lovely in the fruits of the loom and labor of the rest of the world. And after all, sheer loveliness is an end in itself. Nobody expects a flower to give account of itself and flower-like Carlotta was very, very lovely as she leaned against the granite rock with the valley at her feet. So Phil Lambert's eyes told her eloquently. The valley was not the only thing at Carlotta's feet.

"I labored under the impression that I did the bringing up myself," he remarked, his hand closing over hers. "However, the point is immaterial. You are here and I am here. Is there a cosmic reason?"

"There is." Carlotta's voice was dreamy. She watched a cloud shadow creep over the green-plumed mountain opposite. "I brought you up here so that you could propose to me suitably and without interruption."

"Huh!" ejaculated Phil inelegantly, utterly taken by surprise by Carlotta's announcement. "Do you mind repeating that? The altitude seems to have affected my hearing."

"You heard correctly. I said I brought you up here to propose to me."

Phil shrugged.

"Too much 'As You Like It,'" he observed. "These Shakespearean heroines are a bad lot. May I ask just why you want me to propose to you, my dear? Do you have to collect a certain number of scalps by this particular rare day in June? Or is it that you think you would enjoy the exquisite pleasure of seeing me writhe and wriggle when you refuse me?"

Phil's tone was carefully light, and he smiled as he asked the questions, but there was a tight drawn line about his mouth even as he smiled.

"Through bush, through briar, Through flood, through fire"

he had followed the will o' the wisp, Carlotta, for two years now, against his better judgment and to the undoing of his peace of mind and heart. And play days were over for Phil Lambert. The work-a-day world awaited him, a world where there would be neither space nor time for chasing phantoms, however lovely and alluring.

"Don't be horrid, Phil. I'm not like that. You know I'm not," denied Carlotta reproachfully. "I have a surprise for you, Philip, my dear. I am going to accept you."

"No!" exclaimed Phil in unfeigned amazement.

"Yes," declared Carlotta firmly. "I decided it in church this morning when the man was telling us how fearfully real and earnest life is. Not that I believe in the real-earnestness. I don't. It's bosh. Life was made to be happy in and that is why I made up my mind to marry you. You might manage to look a little bit pleased. Anybody would think you were about to keep an appointment with a dentist, instead of having the inestimable privilege of proposing to me with the inside information that I am going to accept you."

Phil drew away his hand from hers. His blue eyes were grave.

"Don't, Carlotta! I am afraid the chap was right about the real-earnestness. It may be a fine jest to you. It isn't to me. You see I happen to be in love with you."

"Of course," murmured Carlotta. "That is quite understood. Did you think I would have bothered to drag you clear up on a mountain top to propose to me if I hadn't known you were in love with me and--I with you?" she added softly.

"Carlotta! Do you mean it?" Phil's whole heart was in his honest blue eyes.

"Of course, I mean it. Foolish! Didn't you know? Would I have tormented you so all these months if I hadn't cared?"

"But, Carlotta, sweetheart, I can't believe you are in earnest even now. Would you marry me really?"

"*Would* I? *Will* I is the verb I brought you up here to use. Mind your grammar."

Phil clasped his hands behind him for safe keeping.

"But I can't ask you to marry me--at least not to-day."

Carlotta made a dainty little face at him.

"And why not? Have you any religious scruples about proposing on Sunday?"

He grinned absent-mindedly and involuntarily at that. But he shook his head and his hands stayed behind his back.

"I can't propose to you because I haven't a red cent in the world--at least not more than three red cents. I couldn't support an everyday wife on 'em, not to mention a fairy princess."

"As if that mattered," dismissed Carlotta airily. "You are in love with me, aren't you?"

"Lord help me!" groaned Phil. "You know I am."

"And I am in love with you--for the present. You had better ask me while the asking is good. The wind may veer by next week, or even by tomorrow. There are other young men who do not require to be commanded to propose. They spurt, automatically and often, like Old Faithful."

Phil's ingenuous face clouded over. The other young men were no fabrication, as he knew to his sorrow. He was forever stumbling over them at Carlotta's careless feet.

"Don't, Carlotta," he begged again. "You don't have to scare me into subjection, you know. If I had anything to justify me for asking you to marry me I'd do it this minute without prompting. You ought to know that. And you know I'm jealous enough already of the rest of 'em, without your rubbing it in now."

"Don't worry, old dear," smiled Carlotta. "I don't care a snap of my fingers for any of the poor worms, though I wouldn't needlessly set foot on 'em. As for justifications I have a whole bag of them up my sleeve ready to spill out like a pack of cards when the time comes. You don't have to concern yourself in the least about them. Your business is to propose. 'Come, woo me, woo, me, for now I am in a holiday humor and like enough to consent'"--she quoted Tony's lines and, leaning toward him, lifted her flower face close to his. "Shall I count ten?" she teased.

"Carlotta, have mercy. You are driving me crazy. Pretty thing it would be for me to propose to you before I even got my sheepskin. Jolly pleased your father would be, wouldn't he, to be presented with a jobless, penniless son-in-law?"

"Nonsense!" said Carlotta crisply. "It wouldn't matter if you didn't even have a fig leaf. You wouldn't be either jobless or penniless if you were his son-in-law. He has pennies enough for all of us and enough jobs for you, which is quite sufficient unto the day. Don't be stiff and silly, Phil. And don't set your jaw like that. I hate men who set their jaws. It isn't at all becoming. I don't say my dear misguided Daddy wouldn't raise a merry little row just at first. He often raises merry little rows over things I want to do, but in the end he always comes round to my way of thinking and wants precisely what I want. Everything will be smooth as silk, I promise you. I know what I am talking about. I've thought it out very carefully. I don't make up my mind in a hurry, but when I do decide what I want I take it."

"You can't take this," said Philip Lambert.

Carlotta drew back and stared, her violet eyes very wide open. Never in all her twenty two years had any man said "can't" to her in that tone. It was a totally new experience. For a moment she was too astounded even to be angry.

"What do you mean?" she asked a little limply.

"I mean I won't take your father's pennies nor hold down a pseudo-job I'm not fitted for, even for the sake of being his son-in-law. And I won't marry you until I am able to support you on the kind of job I am fitted for."

"And may I inquire what that is?" demanded Carlotta sharply, recovering sufficiently to let the thorns she usually kept gracefully concealed prick out from among the roses.

Phil laughed shortly.

"Don't faint, Carlotta. I am eminently fitted to be a village store-keeper. In fact that is what I shall be in less than two weeks. I am going into partnership with my father. The new sign **Stuart Lambert and Son** is being painted now."

Carlotta gasped.

"Phil! You wouldn't. You can't."

"Oh yes, Carlotta. I not only could and would but I am going to. It has been understood ever since I first went to college that when I was out I'd put my shoulder to the wheel beside Dad's. He has been pushing alone too long as it is. He needs me. You don't know how happy he and Mums are about it. It is what they have dreamed about and planned, for years. I'm the only son, you know. It's up to me."

"But, Phil! It is an awful sacrifice for you." For once Carlotta forgot herself completely.

"Not a bit of it. It is a flourishing concern--not just a two-by-four village shop--a real department store, doing real business and making real money. Dad built it all up himself, too. He has a right to be proud of it and I am lucky to be able to step in and enjoy the results of all his years of hard work. I'm not fooling myself about that. Don't get the impression I am being a martyr or anything of the sort. I most distinctly am not."

Carlotta made a little inarticulate exclamation. Mechanically she counted the cars of the train which was winding its black, snake-like trail far down below them in the valley. It hadn't occurred to her that the moon would be difficult to dislodge. Perhaps Carlotta didn't know much about moons, after all.

Phil went on talking earnestly, putting his case before her as best he might. He owed it to Carlotta to try to make her understand if he could. He thought that, under all the whimsicalities, it was rather fine of her to lay down her princess pride and let him see she cared, that she really wanted him. It made her dearer, harder to resist than ever. If only he could make her understand!

"You see I'm not fitted for city life," he explained. "I hate it. I like to live where everybody has a plot of green grass in front of his house to set his rocking chair in Sunday afternoons; where people can have trees that they know as well as they know their own family and don't have to go to a park to look at 'em; where they can grow tulips and green peas--and babies, too, if the lord is good to 'em. I want to plant my roots where people are neighborly and interested in each other as human beings, not shut away like cave dwellers in apartment houses, not knowing or caring who is on the other side of the wall. I should get to hating people if I had to be crowded into a subway with them, day after day, treading on their toes, and they on mine. Altogether I am afraid I have a small town mind, sweetheart."

He smiled at Carlotta as he made the confession, but she did not respond. Her face gave not the slightest indication as to what was going on in her mind as he talked.

"I wouldn't be any good at all in your father's establishment. I've never wanted to make money on the grand scale. I wouldn't be my father's son if I did. I couldn't be a banker or a broker if I tried, and I don't want to try."

"Not even for the sake of--having me?" Carlotta's voice was as expressionless as her face. She still watched the train, almost vanishing from sight now in the far distance, leaving a cloud of ugly black smoke behind it to mar the lustrous azure of the June sky.

Phil, too, looked out over the valley. He dared not look at Carlotta. He was young and very much in love. He wanted Carlotta exceedingly. For a minute everything blurred before his gaze. It seemed as if he would try anything, risk anything, give up anything, ride rough shod over anything, even his own ideals, to gain her. It was a tense moment. He came very near surrendering and thereby making himself, and Carlotta too, unhappy forever after. But something stronger held him back. Oddly enough he seemed to see that sign ***Stuart Lambert and Son*** written large all over the valley. His gaze came back to Carlotta. Their eyes met. The hardness was gone from the girl's, leaving a wistful tenderness, a sweet surrender, no man had ever seen there before. A weaker lad would have capitulated under that wonderful, new look of Carlotta's. It only strengthened Philip Lambert. It was for her as well as himself.

"I am sorry, Carlotta," he said. "I couldn't do it, though I'd give you my heart to cut up into pieces if it could make you happy. Maybe I would risk it for myself. But I can't go back on my father, even for you."

"Then you don't love me." Carlotta's rare and lovely tenderness was burned away on the instant in a quick blaze of anger.

"Yes I do, dear. It is because I love you that I can't do it. I have to give you the best of me, not the worst of me. And the best of me belongs in Dunbury. I wish I could make you understand. And I wish with all my heart that, since I can't come to you, you could care enough to come to me. But I am not going to ask it--not now anyway. I haven't the right. Perhaps in two years time, if you are still free, I shall; but not now. It wouldn't be fair."

"Two years from now, and long before, I shall be married," said Carlotta with a sharp little metallic note in her voice. She was trying to keep from crying but he did not know that and winced both at her words and tone.

"That must be as it will," he answered soberly. "I cannot do any differently. I would if I could. It--it isn't so easy to give you up. Oh, Carlotta! I love you."

And suddenly, unexpectedly to himself and Carlotta, he had her in his arms and was covering her face with kisses. Carlotta's cheeks flamed. She was no longer a lily, but a red, red rose. Never in her life had she been so frightened, so ecstatic. With all her dainty, capricious flirtations she had always deliberately fenced herself behind barriers. No man had ever held her or kissed her like this, the embrace and kisses of a lover to whom she belonged.

"Phil! Don't, dear--I mean, do, dear--I love you," she whispered.

But her words brought Phil back to his senses. His arms dropped and he drew away, ashamed, remorseful. He was no saint. According to his way of thinking a man might kiss a girl now and then, under impulsion of moonshine or mischief, but lightly always, like thistledown. A man didn't kiss a girl as he had just kissed Carlotta unless he had the right to marry her. It wasn't playing straight.

"I'm sorry, Carlotta. I didn't mean to," he said miserably.

"I'm not. I'm glad. I think way down in my heart I've always wanted you to kiss me, though I didn't know it would be like that. I knew your kisses would be different, because *you* are different."

"How am I different?" Phil's voice was humble. In his own eyes he seemed pitifully undifferent, precisely like all the other rash, intemperate, male fools in the world.

"You are different every way. It would take too long to tell you all of them, but maybe you are chiefly different because I love you and I don't love the rest. Except for Daddy. I've never loved anybody but myself before, and when you kissed me I just seemed to feel my *meness* going right out of me, as if I stopped belonging to myself and began to belong to you forever and ever. It scared me but--I liked it."

"You darling!" fatuously. "Carlotta, will you marry me?"

It was out at last--the words she claimed she had brought him up the mountain to say--the words he had willed not to speak.

"Of course. Kiss me again, Phil. We'll wire Daddy tomorrow."

"Wire him what?" The mention of Carlotta's father brought Phil back to earth with a jolt.

"That we are engaged and that he is to find a suitable job for you so we can be married right away," chanted Carlotta happily.

Phil's rainbow vanished almost as soon as it had appeared in the heavens. He drew a long breath.

"Carlotta, I didn't mean that. I can't be engaged to you that way. I meant--will you marry me when I can afford to have a fairy princess in my home?"

Carlotta stared at him, her rainbow, too, fading.

"You did?" she asked vaguely. "I thought--"

"I know," groaned Phil. "It was stupid of me--worse than stupid. It can't be helped now I suppose. The damage is done. Shall we take the next car down? It is getting late."

He rose and put out both hands to help her to her feet. For a moment they stood silent in front of the gray bowlder. The end of the world seemed to have come for them both. It was like Humpty Dumpty. All the King's horses and all the King's men couldn't restore things to their old state nor bring back the lost happiness of that one perfect moment when they had belonged to each other without reservations. Carlotta put out her hand and touched Philip's.

"Don't feel too badly, Phil," she said. "As you say, it can't be helped--nothing can be helped. It just had to be this way. We can't either of us make ourselves over or change the way we look at things and want things. I wish I were different for both our sakes. I wish I were big enough and brave enough and fine enough to say I would marry you anyway, and stop being a princess. But I don't dare. I know myself too well. I might think I could do it up here where it is all still and purple and sweet and sacred. But when we got down to the valley again I am afraid I couldn't live up to it, nor to you, Philip, my king. Forgive me."

Phil bent and kissed her again--not passionately this time, but with a kind of reverent solemnity as if he were performing a rite.

"Never mind, sweetheart. I don't blame you any more than you blame me. We've got to take life as we find it, not try to make it over into something different to please ourselves. If some day you meet the man who can make you happy in your way, I'll not grudge him the right. I'm not sure I shall even envy him. I've had my moment."

"But Phil, you aren't going to be awfully unhappy about me?" sighed Carlotta. "Promise you won't. You know I never wanted to hurt the moon, dear."

Philip shook his head.

"Don't worry about the moon. It is a tough old orb. I shan't be too unhappy. A man has a whole lot of things beside love in his life. I am not going to let myself be such a fool as to be miserable because things started out a little differently from what I would like to have them." His smile was brave but his eyes belied the smile and Carlotta's heart smote her.

"You will forget me," she said. It was half a reproach, half a command.

Again he shook his head in denial.

"Do you remember the queen who claimed she had Calais stamped on her heart? Well, open mine a hundred years from now and you'll read *Carlotta*."

"But won't you ever marry?" pursued Carlotta with youth's insistence on probing wounds to the quick.

"I don't know. Probably," he added honestly. "A man is a poor stick in this world without a home and kiddies. If I do it will be a long time yet though. It will be many a year before I see anybody but you, no matter where I look."

"But I am horrid--selfish, cowardly, altogether horrid."

"Are you?" smiled Phil. "I wonder. Anyway I love you. Come on, dear. We'll have to hurry. The car is nearly due."

And, as twilight settled down over the valley like a great bird brooding over its nest, Philip and Carlotta went down from the mountain.

CHAPTER IV
A BOY WHO WASN'T AN ASS
BUT BEHAVED LIKE ONE

Baccalaureate services being over and the graduates duly exhorted to the wisdom of the ages, the latter were for a time permitted to alight from their lofty pedestal in the public eye and to revert temporarily to the comfortable if less exalted state of being plain every day human girls.

While Philip and Carlotta went up on the heights fondly believing they were settling their destinies forever, Tony had been enjoying an afternoon *en famille* with her uncle and her brother Ted.

Suddenly she looked at her watch and sprang up from the arm of her uncle's chair on which she had been perched, chattering and content, for a couple of hours.

"My goodness! It is most four o'clock. Dick will be here in a minute. May I call up the garage and ask them to send the car around? I'm dying for a ride. We can go over to South Hadley and get the twins, if you'd like. I'm sure they must have had enough of Mt. Holyoke by this time."

"Car's out of commission," grunted Ted from behind his sporting sheet.

"Out of commission? Since when?" inquired Doctor Holiday. "It was all right when you took it to the garage last night."

"I went out for a joy ride and had a smash up," explained his nephew nonchalantly, and still hidden behind the newspaper.

"Oh Ted! How could you when you know we want to use the car every minute?" There was sharp dismay and reproach in Tony's voice.

"Well, I didn't smash it on purpose, did I?" grumbled her brother, throwing down the paper. "I'm sorry, Tony. But it can't be helped now. You'd better be thankful I'm not out of commission myself. Came darn near being."

"Oh Ted!" There was only concern and sympathy in his sister's exclamation this time. Tony adored her brothers. She went over to Ted now, scrutinizing him as if she half expected to see him minus an arm or a leg. "You weren't hurt?" she begged reassurance.

"Nope--nothing to signify. Got some purple patches on my person and a twist to my wrist, but that's all. I was always a lucky devil. Got more lives than a cat."

He was obviously trying to carry matters off lightly, but never once did he meet his uncle's eyes, though he was quite aware they were fixed on him.

Tony sighed and shook her head, troubled.

"I wish you wouldn't take such risks," she mourned. "Some day you'll get dreadfully hurt. Please be careful. Uncle Phil," she appealed to the higher court, "do tell him he mustn't speed so. He won't listen to me."

"If Ted hasn't learned the folly of speeding by now, I am afraid that nothing I can say will have much effect. I wonder--"

Just here the telephone interrupted with an announcement that Mr. Carson was waiting downstairs. Tony flew from the phone to dab powder on her nose.

"Since we can't go riding I think I'll take Dick for a walk in Paradise," she announced into the mirror. "Will you come, too, Uncle Phil?"

"No, thank you, dear. Run along and tell Dick we expect him back to supper with us."

The doctor held open the door for his niece, then turned back to Ted, who was also on his feet now, murmuring something about going out for a stroll.

"Wait a bit, son. Suppose you tell me first precisely what happened last night."

"Did tell you." The boy fumbled sulkily at the leaves of a magazine that lay on the table. "I took the car out and, when I was speeding like Sam Hill out on the Florence road, I struck a hole. She stood up on her ear and pitched u--er--*me* out in the gutter. Stuck her own nose into a telephone pole. I telephoned the garage people to go after her this morning. They told me a while ago she was pretty badly stove up and it will probably take a couple of weeks to get her in order." The story came out jerkily and the narrator kept his eyes consistently floorward during the recital.

"Is that all?"

"What more do you want?" curtly. "I said I was sorry, if that is what you mean."

"It isn't what I mean, Ted. I assume you didn't deliberately go out to break my car and that you are not particularly proud of the outcome of your joy ride. I mean, exactly what I asked. Have you told me the whole story?"

Ted was silent, mechanically rolling the corner of the, rug under his foot. His uncle studied the good-looking, unhappy young face. His mind worked back to that inadvertent "u--er--*me*" of the confession.

"Were you alone?" he asked.

A scarlet flush swept the lad's face, died away, leaving it a little white.

"Yes."

The answer was low but distinct. It was like a knife thrust to the doctor. In all the eight years in which he had fathered Ned's sons, both before and since his brother's death, never once to his knowledge had either one lied to him, even to save himself discomfort, censure or punishment. With all their boyish vagaries and misdeeds, it had been the one thing he could count on absolutely, their unflinching, invariable honesty. Yet, surely as the June sun was shining outside, Ted had lied to him just now. Why? Rash twenty was too young to go its way unchallenged and unguided. He was responsible for the lad whose dead father had committed him to his charge.

Only a few weeks before his death Ned had written with curious prescience, "If I go out any time, Phil, I know you will look after the children as I would myself or better. Keep your eye on Ted especially. His heart is in the right place, but he has a reckless devil in him that will bring him and all of us to grief if it isn't laid."

Doctor Holiday went over and laid a hand on each of the lad's hunched shoulders.

"Look at me, Ted," he commanded gently.

The old habit of obedience strong in spite of his twenty years, Ted raised his eyes, but dropped them again on the instant as if they were lead weighted.

"That is the first time you ever lied to me, I think, lad," said the doctor quietly.

A quiver passed over the boy's face, but his lips set tighter than ever and he pulled away from his uncle's hands and turned, staring out of the window at a rather dusty and bedraggled looking hydrangea on the lawn.

"I wonder if it was necessary," the quiet voice continued. "I haven't the slightest wish to be hard on you. I just want to understand. You know that, son, don't you?"

The boy's head went up at that. His gaze deserted the hydrangea, for the first time that day, met his uncle's, squarely if somewhat miserably.

"It isn't that, Uncle Phil. You have every right to come down on me. I hadn't any business to have the car out at all, much less take fool chances with it. But honestly I have told you all--all I can tell. I did lie to you just now. I wasn't alone. There was a--a girl with me."

Ted's face was hot again as he made the confession.

"I see," mused the doctor. "Was she hurt?"

"No--that is--not much. She hurt her shoulder some and cut her head a bit." The details came out reluctantly as if impelled by the doctor's steady eyes. "She telephoned me today she was all right. It's a miracle we weren't both killed though. We might have been as easy as anything. You said just now nothing you could say would make me have sense about speeding. I guess what happened last night ought to knock sense into me if anything could. I say, Uncle Phil--"

"Well?" as the boy paused obviously embarrassed.

"If you don't mind I'd rather not say anything more about the girl. She--I guess she'd rather I wouldn't," he wound up confusedly.

"Very well. That is your affair and hers. Thank you for coming halfway to meet me. It made it easier all around."

The doctor held out his hand and the boy took it eagerly.

"You are great to me, Uncle Phil--lots better than I deserve. Please don't think I don't see that. And truly I am awfully ashamed of smashing the car, and not telling you, as I ought to have this morning, and spoiling Tony's fun and--and everything." Ted swallowed something down hard as if the "everything" included a good deal. "I don't see why I have to be always getting into scrapes. Can't seem to help it, somehow. Guess I was made that way, just as Larry was born steady."

"That is a spineless jellyfish point of view, Ted. Don't fool yourself with it. There is no earthly reason why you should keep drifting from one escapade to another. Get some backbone into you, son."

Ted's face clouded again at that, though he wasn't sulky this time. He was remembering some other disagreeable confessions he had to make before long. He knew this was a good opening for them, but somehow he could not drive himself to follow it up. He could only digest a limited amount of humble pie at a time and had already swallowed nearly all he could stand. Still he skirted warily along the edge of the dilemma.

"I suppose you think I made an awful ass of myself at college this year," he averred gloomily.

"I don't think it. I know it." The doctor's eyes twinkled a little. Then he grew sober. "Why do you, Ted? You aren't really an ass, you know. If you were, there might be some excuse for behaving like one."

Ted flushed.

"That's what Larry told me last spring when he was pitching into me about--well about something. I don't know why I do, Uncle Phil, honest I don't. Maybe it is because I hate college so and all the stale old stuff they try to cram down our throats. I get so mad and sick and disgusted with the whole thing that I feel as if I had to do something to offset it--something that is real and live, even if it isn't according to rules and regulations. I hate rules and regulations. I'm not a mummy and I don't want to be made to act as if I were. I'll be a long time dead and I want to get a whole lot of fun out of life first. I hate studying. I want to do things, Uncle Phil--"

"Well?"

"I don't want to go back to college."

"What do you want to do?"

"Join the Canadian forces. It makes me sick to have a war going on and me not in it. Dad quit college for West Point and everybody thought it was all right. I don't see why I shouldn't get into it. I wouldn't fall down on that. I promise you. I'd make you proud of me instead of ashamed the way you are now." The boy's voice and eyes were unusually earnest.

His uncle did not answer instantly. He knew that there was some truth in his nephew's analysis of the situation. It was his uneasy, superabundant energy and craving for action that made him find the more or less restricted life of the college, a burden, a bore and an exasperation, and drove him to crazy escapades and deeds of flagrant lawlessness. He needed no assurance that the boy would not "fall down" at soldiering. He would take to it as a duck to water. And the discipline might be the making of him, prove the way to exorcise the devil. Still there were other considerations which to him seemed paramount for the time at least.

"I understand how you feel, Ted," he said at last. "If we get into the war ourselves I won't say a word against your going. I should expect you to go. We all would. But in the meantime as I see it you are not quite a free agent. Granny is old and very, very feeble. She hasn't gotten over your father's death. She grieves over it still. If you went to war I think it would kill her. She couldn't bear the strain and anxiety. Patience, laddie. You don't want to hurt her, do you?"

"I s'pose not," said Ted a little grudgingly. "Then it is no, Uncle Phil?"

"I think it ought to be no of your own will for Granny's sake. We don't live to ourselves alone in this world. We can't. But aside from Granny I am not at all certain I should approve of your leaving college just because it doesn't happen to be exciting enough to meet your fancy and means work you are too lazy and irresponsible to settle down to doing. Looks a little like quitting to me and Holidays aren't usually quitters, you know."

He smiled at the boy but Ted did not smile back. The thrust about Holidays and quitters went home.

"I suppose it has got to be college again if you say so," he said soberly after a minute. "Thank heaven there are three months ahead clear though first."

"To play in?"

"Well, yes. Why not? It is all right to play in vacation, isn't it?" the boy retorted, a shade aggressively.

"Possibly if you have earned the vacation by working beforehand."

Ted's eyes fell at that. This was dangerously near the ground of those uncomfortable, inevitable confessions which he meant to put off as long as possible.

"Do you mind if I go out now?" he asked with unusual meekness after a moment's rather awkward silence.

"No, indeed. Go ahead. I've had my say. Be back for supper with us?"

"Dunno." And Ted disappeared into the adjoining room which connected with his uncle's. In a moment he was back, expensive panama hat in one hand and a lighted cigarette held jauntily in the other. "I meant to tell you you could take the car repairs out of my allowance," he remarked casually but with his eye shrewdly on his guardian as he made the announcement.

"Very well," replied the latter quietly. Then he smiled a little seeing his nephew's crestfallen expression. "That wasn't just what you wanted me to say, was it?" he added.

"Not exactly," admitted the boy with a returning grin. "All right, Uncle Phil. I'm game. I'll pay up."

A moment later his uncle heard his whistle as he went down the driveway apparently as care free as if narrow escapes from death were nothing in his young life. The doctor shook his head dubiously as he watched him from the window. He would have felt more dubious still had he seen the boy board a Florence car a few minutes later on his way to keep a rendezvous with the girl about whom he had not wished to talk.

CHAPTER V
WHEN YOUTH MEETS YOUTH

Three quarters of an hour later Ted was seated on a log, near a small rustic bridge, beneath which flowed a limpid, gurgling stream. On a log beside him sat a girl of perhaps eighteen years, exceedingly handsome with the flaming kind of beauty like a poppy's, striking to the eye, shallow-petaled. She was vividly effective against the background of deep green spruces and white birch in her bright pink dress and large drooping black hat. Her coloring was brilliant, her lips full, scarlet, ripely sensuous. Beneath her straight black brows her sparkling, black eyes gleamed with restless eagerness. An ugly, jagged, still fresh wound showed beneath a carefully curled fringe of hair on her forehead.

"I don't like meeting you this way," Ted was saying. "Are you sure your grandfather would have cut up rough if I had come to the house and called properly?"

"You betcher," said his companion promptly. "You don't know grandpa. He's death on young men. He won't let one come within a mile of me if he can help it. He'd throw a fit if he knew I was here with you now. We should worry. What he don't know won't hurt him," she concluded with a toss of her head. Then, as Ted looked dubious, she added, "You just leave grandpa to me. If you had had your way you would have spilled the beans by telephoning me this morning at the wrong time. See how much better I fixed it. I told him a piece of wood flew up and hit me when I was chopping kindling before breakfast and that my head ached so I didn't feel like going to church. Then the minute he was out of the yard I ran to the 'phone and got you at the hotel. It was perfectly simple that way--slick as grease. Easiest thing in the world to make a date. We couldn't have gotten away with it otherwise."

Ted still looked dubious. The phrase "gotten away with it" jarred. At the moment he was not particularly proud of their mutual success in "getting away with it." The girl wasn't his kind. He realized that, now he saw her for the first time in daylight.

She had looked all right to him on the train night before last. Indeed he had been distinctly fascinated by her flashing, gypsy beauty, ready laughter and quick, keen, half "fresh" repartee when he had started a casual conversation with her when they chanced to be seat mates from Holyoke on.

Casual conversations were apt to turn into casual flirtations with Ted Holiday. Afterward he wasn't sure whether she had dared him or he had dared her to plan the midnight joy ride which had so narrowly missed ending in a tragedy. Anyway it had seemed a jolly lark at the time--a test of the mettle and mother wit of both of them to "get away with it."

And she had looked good to him last night when he met her at the appointed trysting place after "As You Like It." She had come out of the shadows of the trees behind which she had been lurking, wearing a scarlet tam-o'-shanter and a long dark cloak, her eyes shining like January stars. He had liked her nerve in coming out like that to meet him alone at midnight. He had liked the way she "sassed" him back and put him in his place, when he had tried impudently enough to kiss her. He had liked the way she laughed when he asked her if she was afraid to speed, on the home stretch. It was her laugh that had spurred him on, intoxicated him, made him send the car leaping faster and still faster, obeying his reckless will.

Then the crash had come. It was indeed a miracle that they had not both been killed. No thanks to the rash young driver that they had not been. It would be many a day before Ted Holiday would forget that nightmare of dread and remorse which took possession of him as he pulled himself to his feet and went over to where the girl's motionless form lay on the grass, her face dead white, the blood flowing from her forehead.

Never had he been so thankful for anything in his life as he was when he saw her bright eyes snap open, and heard her unsteady little giggle as she murmured, "My, but I thought I was dead, didn't you?"

Game to her fingertips she had been. Ted acknowledged that, even now that the glamour had worn off. Never once had she whimpered over her injuries, never hurled a single word of blame at him for the misadventure that had come within a hair's breadth of being the last for them both.

"It wasn't a bit more your fault than mine," she had waived aside his apologies. "And it was great while it lasted. I wouldn't have missed it for anything, though I'm glad I'm not dead before I've had a chance to really live. All I ask is that you won't tell a soul I was out with you. Grandpa would think I was headed straight for purgatory if he knew."

"I won't," Ted had promised glibly enough, and had kept his promise even at the cost of lying to his uncle, a memory which hurt like the toothache even now.

But looking at the girl now in her tawdry, inappropriate garb he suffered a revulsion of feeling. What he had admired in her as good sport quality seemed cheap now, his own conduct even cheaper. His reaction against himself was fully as poignant as his reaction against her. He was suddenly ashamed of his joy ride, ashamed that he had ever wished or tried to kiss her, ashamed that he had fallen in with her suggestion for a clandestine meeting this afternoon.

Possibly Madeline sensed that he was cold to her charms at the moment. She flashed a shrewd glance at him.

"You don't like me as well to-day as you did last night," she challenged.

Caught, Ted tried half-heartedly to make denial, but the effort was scarcely a success. He had yet to learn the art of lying gracefully to a lady.

"You don't," she repeated. "You needn't try to pretend you do. You can't fool me. You're getting cold feet already. You're remembering I'm just--just a pick-up."

Ted winced again at that. He did not like the word "pick-up" either, though to his shame he hadn't been above the thing itself.

"Don't talk like that, Madeline. You know I like you. You were immense last night. Any other girl I know, except my sister Tony, would have had hysterics and fainting fits and lord knows what else with half the excuse you had. And you never made a bit of fuss about your head, though it must have hurt like the deuce. I say, you don't think it is going to leave a scar, do you?"

He leaned forward with genuine concern to examine the red wound.

"I think it is more than likely. Lot you'll care, Ted Holiday. You'll never come back to see whether it leaves a scar or not. See that bee over there nosing around that elderberry. Think he'll come back next week? Not much. I know your kind," scornfully.

That bit into the lad's complacency.

"Of course, I care and of course, I'll come back," he protested, though a moment before he had had not the slightest wish or purpose to see her again, rather to the contrary.

"To see whether there is a scar?"

"To see you," he played up gallantly.

Her hard young face softened.

"Will you, honest, Ted Holiday? Will you come back?"

She put out her hand and touched his. Her eyes were suddenly wistful, gentle, beseeching.

"Sure I'll come back. Why wouldn't I?" The touch of her hand, the new softness, almost pathos of her mood touched him, appealed to the chivalry always latent in a Holiday.

He heard her breath come quickly, saw her full bosom heave, felt the warm pressure of her hand. He wanted to put his arm around her but he did not follow the impulse. The code of Holiday "noblesse oblige" was operating.

"I wish I could believe that," Madeline sighed, looking down into the water which whirled and eddied in white foam and splash over the rocks. "I'd like to think you really wanted to come--really cared about seeing me again. I know I'm not your kind."

He started involuntarily at her voicing unexpectedly his own recent thought.

"Oh, you needn't be surprised," she threw at him half angrily. "Don't you suppose I know that better than you do. Don't you suppose I know what the girls you are used to look like? Well, I do. I've watched 'em, on the street, on the campus, in church, everywhere. I've even seen your sister and watched her, too. Somebody pointed her out to me once when she had made a hit in a play and I've seen her at Glee Club concerts and at vespers in the choir. She is lovely--lovely the way I'd like to be. It isn't that she's any prettier. She isn't. It's just that she's different--acts different--looks different--dresses different from me. I can't make myself like her and the rest, no matter how I try. And I do try. You don't know how hard I try. I got this dress because I saw your sister Tony wearing a pink dress once. I thought maybe it would make me look more like her. But it doesn't. It makes me look more **not** like her than ever, doesn't it?" she appealed rather disconcertingly. "It's horrid. I hate it."

"I don't know much about girls' dresses," said Ted. "But, now you speak of it, maybe it would be prettier if it were a little--" he paused for a word--"quieter," he decided on. "Do you ever wear white? Tony wears it a lot and I think she looks nice in it."

"I've got a white dress. I thought about putting it on to-day. But somehow it didn't look quite nice enough. I thought--well, I thought I looked handsomer in the pink. I wanted to look pretty--for you." The last was very low--scarcely audible.

"You look good to me all right," said the boy heartily and he meant it. He thought she looked prettier at the moment than she had looked at any time since he had made her acquaintance.

Perhaps he was right. She had laid aside for once her mask of hard boldness and was just a simple, humble, rather pathetic little girl, voicing secret aspirations toward a fineness life had denied her.

"I say, Madeline," Ted went on. "You don't--meet other chaps the way you met me to-day, do you?" Set the blind to lead the blind! If there was anything absurd in scapegrace Ted's turning mentor he was unconscious of the absurdity, was exceedingly in earnest.

"What's that to you?" She snapped the mask back into place.

"Nothing--that is--I wouldn't--that's all."

She laughed shrilly.

"You're a pretty one to talk," she scoffed.

Ted flushed.

"I know I am. See here, Madeline. You're dead right. I ought not to have taken you out last night. I ought not to have let you meet me here to-day."

"I made you--I made you do both those things."

Ted shook his head at that.

"A man's to blame always," he asserted.

"No, he isn't," denied Madeline. "A girl's to blame always."

They stared at each other a moment while the brook tinkled through the silence. Then they both laughed at the solemnity of their contradictions.

"But there isn't a bit of harm done," went on Madeline. "You see, I knew that first night on the train that you were a gentleman."

"Some gentlemen are rotters," said Ted Holiday, with a wisdom beyond his twenty years.

"But you are not."

"No, I'm not; but some other chap might be. That is why I wish you would promise not to go in for this sort of thing."

"With anybody but you," she stipulated.

"Not with anybody at all," corrected Ted soberly, remembering his own recent restrained impulse to put his arm around her.

"Well, I don't want to--at least not with anybody but you. I never did it before with anybody. Honest, Ted, I never did."

"That's good. I felt sure that you hadn't."

"Why?"

He grinned sheepishly and stooped to break off a dry twig from a nearby bush.

"By the way you didn't let me kiss you," he admitted. "A fellow likes that in a girl. Did you know it?" He tossed away the twig and looked back at the girl as he asked the question.

"I thought they liked--the other thing."

"They do and they don't," said Ted, his paradox again betraying a scarcely to be expected wisdom. "But that is neither here nor there. What I started out to say was that I'm glad you don't make a practice of this pick-up business. It--it's no good," he summed up.

"I know." Madeline nodded understanding of the import of his warning. She was far too handsome and too prematurely developed physically to be devoid of experience of the ways of the opposite sex. Like Ophelia she knew there were tricks in the world and she liked frank Ted Holiday the better for reminding her of them. "I won't do it," she promised. "That is, unless you don't ever come back yourself. I don't know what I'll do then--something awful, maybe."

"I'll come fast enough. I'll come to-morrow." he added obeying a sudden impulse, Ted fashion.

"Will you?" The girl's face flushed with delight. "When?"

"To-morrow afternoon. I can't dodge the ivy stuff in the morning. Will four o'clock do all right?"

"Yes. Come here to this same place."

"I say, Madeline, can't I come to the house? I hate doing it like this."

"No, you can't. If you want to see me you'll have to do it this way. It's lots nicer here than in the house, anyway."

Ted acquiesced, since he had no choice, and rose, announcing that it was time to go now.

"We don't have to go yet. I told Grandpa I was going to spend the evening with my friend, Linda Bates. He won't know. We can stay as long as we like."

"I am afraid we can't," said Ted decidedly. "Come on, my lady." He held out both hands and Madeline let him draw her to her feet, though she was pouting a little at his gainsaying of her wishes.

"You may kiss me now," she said suddenly, lifting her face to his.

But Ted backed away. The code was still on. A girl of his own kind he would have kissed in a moment at such provocation, or none. But he had an odd feeling of needing to protect this girl from herself as well as from himself.

"You had more sense than I did last night. Let's follow your lead instead of mine," he said. "It's better."

"But Ted, you will come to-morrow?" she pleaded. "You won't forget or go back on your promise?"

"Of course, I'll come," promised Ted again readily.

Five minutes later they parted, he to take his car, and she to stroll in the opposite direction toward her friend Linda's house.

"He is a dear," she thought. "I'm glad he wouldn't kiss me, so there," she said aloud to a dusty daisy that peered up at her rather mockingly from the gutter.

An automobile horn honked behind her. She stepped aside, but the car stopped.

"Well, here is luck. Where are you going, my pretty maid?" called a gay, bold voice.

She turned. The speaker was one Willis Hubbard, an automobile agent by profession, lady's man and general Lothario by avocation. His handsome dark face stood out clearly in the dusk. She could see the avid shine in his eyes. She hated him all of a sudden, though hitherto she had secretly rather admired him, though she had always steadily refused his invitations.

For Madeline was wary. She knew how other girls had gone out with Willis in his smart car and come back to give rather sketchy accounts of the evening's pleasure jaunt. Her friend Linda had tried it once and remarked later that Willis was some speed and that Madeline had the right hunch to keep away from him.

But it happened that Madeline Taylor was the particular peach that Willis Hubbard hankered after. He didn't like them too easy, ready to drop from the bough at the first touch. All the same, he meant to have his way in the end with Madeline. He had an excellent opinion of his powers as a conquering male. He had, alas, plenty of data to warrant it in his relations with the fair and sometimes weak sex.

"What's your hurry, dearie?" he asked now. "Come on for a spin. It's the pink of the evening."

But she thanked him stiffly and refused, remembering Ted Holiday's honest blue eyes.

"What are you so almighty prunes and prisms for, all of a sudden? It's the wrong game to play with a man, I can tell you, if you want to have a good time in the world. I say, Maidie, be a good girl and come out with me to-morrow night. We'll have dinner somewhere and dance and make a night of it. Say yes, you beauty. A girl like you oughtn't to stay cooped up at home forever. It's against nature."

But again Madeline refused and moved away with dignity.

"Your grandfather will never know. You can plan to stay with Linda afterward. I'll meet you by the sycamore tree just beyond the Bates' place at eight sharp--give you the best time you ever had in your life. Believe me, I'm some little spender when I get to going."

"No, thank you, Mr. Hubbard. I tell you I can't go."

He stared at the finality of her manner. He had no means of knowing that he was being measured up, to his infinite disadvantage, with a blue eyed lad who had stirred something in the girl before him that he himself could never have roused in a thousand years. But he did know he was being snubbed and the knowledge disturbed his fond conceit of self.

"Highty tighty with your 'Mr. Hubbards'! You will sing another tune by to-morrow night. I'll wait at the sycamore and you'll be there. See if you won't. You're no fool, Maidie. You want a good time and you know I'm the boy to give it to you. So long! See you to-morrow night." He started his motor, kissed his hand impudently to her and was off down the road, leaving Madeline to follow slowly, in his dust.

CHAPTER VI
A SHADOW ON THE PATH

Across the campus the ivy procession wound its lovely length, flanked by rainbow clad Junior ushers immensely conscious of themselves and their importance as they bore the looped laurel chains between which walked the even more important Seniors, all in white and each bearing an American Beauty rose before her proudly, like a wand of youth.

At the head of the procession, as president of the class, walked Antoinette Holiday, a little lady of quality, as none who saw her could have helped recognizing. Her uncle, watching the procession from the steps of a campus house, smiled and sighed as he beheld her. She was so young, so blithe-hearted, so untouched by the sad and sordid things of life. If only he could keep her so for a little, preserve the shining splendor of her shield of innocent young joy. But, even as he thought, he knew the folly of his wish. Tony would be the last to desire to have life tempered or kept from her. She would want to drain the whole cup, bitter, sweet and all.

Farther back in the procession was Carlotta, looking as heavenly fair and ethereal as if she had that morning been wafted down from the skies. Out of the crowd Phil Lambert's eyes met hers and smiled. Very sensibly and modernly these two had decided to remain the best of friends since fate prevented their being lovers. But Phil's eyes were rather more than friendly, resting on Carlotta, and, underneath the diaphanous, exquisite white cloud of a gown that she wore, Carlotta's heart beat a little faster for what she saw in his face. The hand that held her rose trembled ever so slightly as she smiled bravely back at him. She could not forget those "very different" kisses of his, nor, with all the will in the world, could she go back to where she was before she went up the mountain and came down again in the purple dusk. She knew she had to get used to a strange, new world, a world without Philip Lambert, a rather empty world, it seemed. She wondered if this new world would give her anything so wonderful and sweet as this thing that she had by her own act surrendered. Almost she thought not.

Ted, standing beside his uncle, watching the procession, suddenly heard a familiar whistle, a signal dating back to Holiday Hill days, as unmistakable as the Star Spangled Banner itself, though who should be using it here and why was a mystery. In a moment his roving gaze discovered the solution. Standing upon a slight elevation on the campus opposite he perceived Dick Carson. The latter beckoned peremptorily. Ted wriggled out of the group, descended with one leap over the rail to the lawn, and made his way to where the other youth waited.

"What in Sam Hill's chewing you?" he demanded upon arrival. "You've made me quit the only spot I've struck to-day where I had room to stand on my own feet and see anything at the same time."

"I say, Ted, what train was Larry coming on?" counterquestioned Dick.

"Chicago Overland. Why?"

"Are you sure?"

"Of course I am sure. He wired Tony. What in thunder are you driving at? Get it out for Pete's sake?"

"The Chicago Overland smashed into a freight somewhere near Pittsburgh this morning. There were hundreds of people killed. Oh, Lord, Ted! I didn't mean to break it to you like that." Dick was aghast at his own clumsiness as Ted leaned against the brick wall of the college building, his face white as chalk. "I wasn't thinking-- guess I wasn't thinking about much of anything except Tony," he added.

Ted groaned.

"Don't wonder," he muttered. "Let's not let her get wind of it till we have to. Are you sure there--there isn't any mistake?" Ted put up his hand to brush back a refractory lock of hair and found his forehead wet with cold perspiration. "There's got to be a mistake. Larry--I won't believe it, so there!"

"You don't have to believe it till you know. Even if he was on the train it doesn't mean he is hurt." Dick would not name the harsher possibility to Larry Holiday's brother.

"Of course, it doesn't," snapped Ted. "I say, Dick, is it in the papers yet?"

"No, it will be in an hour though, as soon as the evening editions get out."

"Good! Dick, it's up to you to keep Tony from knowing. She is going to sing in the concert at five. That will keep her occupied until six. But from now till then nix on the news. Take her out on the fool pond, walk her up Sunset Hill, quarrel with her, make love to her, anything, so she won't guess. I don't dare go near her. I'd give it away in a minute, I'm such an idiot. Besides I can't think of anything but Larry. Gee!" The boy swept his hand across his eyes. "Last time I saw him I consigned him to the devil because he told me some perfectly true things about myself and tried to give me some perfectly sound advice. And now--I'm damned if I believe it. Larry is all right. He's got to be," fiercely.

"Of course, he is," soothed Dick. "And I'll try to do as you say about Tony. I'm not much of an actor, but I guess I can carry it through for--for her sake."

The little break in the speaker's voice made Ted turn quickly and stare at the other youth.

"Dick, old chap, is it like that with you? I didn't know."

Ted's hand went out and held the other's in a cordial grip.

"Nobody knows. I--I didn't mean to show it then. It's no good. I know that naturally."

"I'm not so sure about that. I know one member of the family that would be mighty proud to have you for a brother."

The obvious ring of sincerity touched Dick. It was a good deal coming from a Holiday.

"Thank you, Ted. That means a lot, I can tell you. I'll never forget your saying it like that. You won't give me away, I know."

"Sure not, old man. Tony is way up in the clouds just now, anyway. We are all mostly ants in our minor ant hills so far as she is concerned. Gee! I hope it isn't this thing about Larry that is going to pull her down to earth. If anything had to happen to any of us why couldn't it have been me instead of Larry. He is worth ten of me."

"We don't know that anything has happened to Larry yet," Dick reminded.

"I say, Ted, they must have got the ivy planted. Everybody's coming back. Tony is lunching with me at Boyden's right away, and I'll see that she has her hands full until it is time for the concert. You warn Miss Carlotta, so she'll be on guard after I surrender her. I'm afraid you will have to tell your uncle."

"I will. Trot on, old man, and waylay Tony. I'll make a mess of things sure as preaching if I run into her now."

Tony thought she had never known Dick to be so entertaining or talkative as he was during that luncheon hour. He regaled her with all kinds of newspaper yarns and related some of his own once semi-tragic but now humorous misadventures of his early cub days. He talked, too, on current events and world history, talked well, with the quiet poise and assurance of the reader and thinker, the man who has kept his eyes and ears open to life.

It was a revelation to Tony. For once their respective roles were reversed, he the talker, she the listener.

"Goodness me, Dick!" she exclaimed during a pause in what had become almost a monologue. "Why haven't you ever talked like this before? I always thought I had to do it all and here you talk better than I ever thought of doing because you have something to say and mine is just chatter and nonsense."

He smiled at that.

"I love your chatter. But you are tired to-day and it is my turn. Do you know what we are going to do after luncheon?"

"No, what?"

"We are going to take a canoe out on your Paradise and get into a shady spot somewhere along the bank and you will lean back against a whole lot of becoming cushions and put up that red parasol of yours so nobody but me can see your face and then--"

"Dicky! Dicky! Whatever is in you to-day? Paradise, pillows and parasols are familiar symptoms. You will be making love to me next."

"I might, at that," murmured Dick. "But you did not hear the rest of my proposition. And then--I shall read you a story--a story that I wrote myself."

"Dick!" Tony nearly upset her glass of iced tea in her amazement at this unexpected announcement. "You don't mean you have really and truly written a story!"

"Honest to goodness--such as it is. Please to remember it is my maiden effort and make a margin of allowance. But I want your criticism, too--all the benefit of your superior academic training."

"Superior academic bosh!" scoffed Tony. "I'll bet it is a corking story," she added unacademically. "Come on. Let's go, quick. I can't wait to hear it."

Nothing loath to get away speedily before the newsboys began to cry the accident through the streets, Dick escorted his pretty companion back to the campus and on to Paradise, at which point they took a canoe and, finally selecting a shady point under an over-reaching sycamore tree, drifted in to shore where Tony leaned against the cushions, tilted her parasol as specified at the angle which forbade any but Dick to see her charming, expressive young face and commanded him to "shoot."

Dick shot. Tony listened intently, watching his face as he read, feeling as if this were a new Dick--a Dick she did not know at all, albeit a most interesting person.

"Why Dick Carson!" she exclaimed when he finished. "It is great--a real story with real laughter and tears in it. I love it. It is so--so human."

The author flushed and fidgeted and protested that it wasn't much--just a sketch done from life with a very little dressing up and polishing down.

"I have a lot more of them in my head, though," he added. "And I'm going to grind them out as soon as I get time. I wish I had a bigger vocabulary and knew more about the technical end of the writing game. I am going to learn, though--going to take some night work at the University next fall. Maybe I'll catch up a little yet if I keep pegging away."

"Catch up! Dick, you make me so ashamed. Here Larry and Ted and I have had everything done for us all our lives and we've slipped along with the current, following the line of least resistance. And you have had everything to contend with and you are way ahead of the rest of us already. But why didn't you tell me before about the story? I think you might have, Dicky. You know I would be interested," reproachfully.

"I--I wasn't talking much about it to anybody till I knew it was any good. But I--just took a notion to read it to you to-day. That's all."

It wasn't all, but he wanted Tony to think it was. Not for anything would he have betrayed how reading the story was a desperate expedient to keep her diverted and safe from news of the disaster on the Overland.

He escorted Tony back to the campus house at the latest possible moment and Carlotta, in the secret, pretended to upbraid her roommate for her tardiness and flew about helping her to get dressed, talking continuously the while and keeping a sharp eye on the door lest some intruder burst in and say the very thing Tony Holiday must not be permitted to hear. It would be so ridiculously easy for somebody to ask, "Oh, did you hear about the awful wreck on the Overland?" and then the fat would be in the fire.

But, thanks to Carlotta, nobody had a chance to say it and later Tony Holiday, standing in the twilight in front of College Hall's steps, sang her solo, Gounod's beautiful Ave Maria, smiled happily down into the faces of the dear folks from her beloved Hill and only regretted that Larry was not there with the rest--Larry who, for all the others knew, might never come again.

After dinner Ted rushed off again to the telegraph office which he had been haunting all the afternoon to see if any word had come from his brother, and Doctor Holiday went on up to the campus to escort his niece to the informal hop. He had decided to go on just as if nothing was wrong. If Larry was safe then there was no need of clouding Tony's joy, and if he wasn't--well, there would be time enough to grieve when they knew. By virtue of his being a grave and reverend uncle he was admitted to the sacred precincts of his niece's room and had hardly gotten seated when the door flew open and Ted flew in waving two yellow telegraph blanks triumphantly, one in each hand, and announcing that everything was all right--Larry was all right, had wired from Pittsburgh.

Before Tony had a chance to demand what it was all about the door opened again and a righteously indignant house mother appeared on the threshold, demanding by what right an unauthorized male had gone up her stairway and entered a girl's room, without permission or escort.

"I apologize," beamed Ted with his most engaging smile. "Come on outside, Mrs. Maynerd and I'll tell you all about it." And tucking his arm in hers the irrepressible youth conveyed the angry personage out into the hall, leaving his uncle to explain the situation to Tony.

In a moment he was back triumphant.

"She says I may stay since I'm here, and Uncle Phil is here to play dragon," he announced. "She thought at first Carlotta would have to be expunged to make it legal, but I overruled her, told her you and I had played tiddle-de-winks with each other in our cradles," he added with an impish grin at his sister's roommate. "Of course I never laid eyes on you till two years ago, but that doesn't matter. I have a true tiddle-de-winks feeling for you, anyway, and that is what counts, isn't it, sweetness?"

Carlotta laughed and averred that she was going to expunge herself anyway as Phil was waiting for her downstairs. She picked up a turquoise satin mandarin cloak from the chair and Ted sprang to put it around her bare shoulders, stooping to kiss the tip of her ear as he finished.

"Lucky Phil!" he murmured.

Carlotta shook her head at him and went over to Tony, over whom she bent for an instant with unusual feeling in her lovely eyes.

"Oh, my dear," she whispered. "I wish I could tell you how I feel. I'm so glad-- so glad." And then she was gone before Tony could answer.

"Oh me!" she sighed. "She has been so wonderful. You all have. Ted--Uncle Phil! Come over here. I want to hold you tight."

And, with her brother on one side of her and her uncle on the other, Tony gave a hand to each and for a moment no one spoke. Then Ted produced his telegrams one of which was addressed to Tony and one to her uncle. Both announced the young doctor's safety. "Staying over in Pittsburgh. Letter follows," was in the doctor's message. "Sorry can't make commencement. Love and congratulations," was in Tony's.

"There, didn't I tell you he was all right?" demanded Ted, as if his brother's safety were due to his own remarkably good management of the affair. "Gee! Tony! If you knew how I felt when Dick told me this morning. I pretty nearly disgraced myself by toppling over, just like a girl, on the campus. Lord! It was fierce."

"I know." Tony squeezed his hand sympathetically. "And Dick--why Dick must have kept me out in Paradise on purpose."

"Sure he did. Dick's a jim dandy and don't you forget it."

"I shan't," said Tony, her eyes a little misty, remembering how Dick had fought all day to keep her care-free happiness intact. "I don't know whether to be angry at you all for keeping it from me or to fall on your necks and weep because you were

all so dear not to tell me. And oh! If anything had happened to Larry! I don't see
how I could have stood it. It makes us all seem awfully near, doesn't it?"

"You bet!" agreed Ted with more fervor than elegance. "If the old chap had
been done for I'd have felt like making for the river, myself. Funny, now the scare
is over and he is all safe, I shall probably cuss him out as hard as ever next time he
tries to preach at me."

"You had better listen to him instead. Larry is apt to be right and you are apt to
be wrong, and you know it."

"Maybe it is because I do know it and because he is so devilish right that I damn
him," observed the youngest Holiday sagely, his eyes meeting his uncle's over his
sister's head.

It wasn't until he had danced and flirted and made merry for three consecutive
hours at the hop, and proposed in the exuberance of his mood to at least three different charmers whose names he had forgotten by the next day, that Ted Holiday
remembered Madeline and his promise to keep tryst with her that afternoon. Other
things of more moment had swept her clean from his mind.

"Thunder!" he muttered to himself. "Wonder what she is thinking when I
swore by all that was holy to come. Oh well; I should worry. I couldn't help it. I'll
write and explain how it happened."

So said, so done. He scribbled off a hasty note of explanation and apology which
he signed "Yours devotedly, Ted Holiday" and went out to the corner mail box to
dispatch the same so it would go out in the early morning collection, and prepared
to dismiss the matter from his mind again.

Coming back into his room he found his uncle standing on the threshold.

"Had to get a letter off," murmured the young man as his uncle looked inquiring. He turned to light a cigarette with an air of determined casualness. He didn't
care to have Uncle Phil know any more about the Madeline affair.

"It must have been important."

"Was," curtly. "Did you think I was joy riding again?"

"No, I heard you stirring and thought you might be sick. I haven't been able to
get to sleep myself."

Seeing how utterly worn out his uncle looked, Ted's resentment took quick,
shamed flight. Poor Uncle Phil! He never spared himself, always bore the brunt of

everything for them all. And here he himself had just snapped like a cur because he suspected his guardian of desiring to interfere with his high and mighty private business.

"Too bad," he said. "Wish you'd smoke, Uncle Phil. It's great to cool off your nerves. Honest it is! Have one?" He held out his case.

Doctor Holiday smiled at that, though he declined the proffered weed. He understood very well that the boy was making tacit amends for his ungraciousness of a moment before.

"No, I'll get to sleep presently. It has been rather a wearing day."

"Should say it had been. I hope Aunt Margery doesn't know about the wreck. She'll worry, if she knew Larry was coming east."

"I wired her this evening. I didn't want to take any chance of her thinking he was in the smash."

Ted laid down his cigarette.

"You never forget anybody do you, Uncle Phil?" he said rather soberly for him.

"I never forget Margery. She is a very part of myself, lad."

And when he was alone Ted pondered over that last speech of his uncle's. He wondered if there would ever be a Margery for him, and, if so, what she would think of the Madelines if she knew of them.

CHAPTER VII
DEVELOPMENTS BY MAIL

After the family had reassembled on the Hill the promised letter from Larry arrived. He was staying on so long as his services were needed. The enormous number of victims of the wreck had strained to the uttermost the city's supply of doctors and nurses, and there was more than enough work for all. The writer spared them the details of the wreck so far as possible; indeed, evidently was not anxious to relive the horrors on his own account. He mentioned a few of the many sad cases only. One of these was the instant death of a famous surgeon whose loss to the world seemed tragic and pitifully wasteful to the young doctor. Another was the crushing to death of a young mother who, with her two children, had been happily on their way to meet the husband who had been in South America for a year. Larry had made friends with her on the train and played with the babies who reminded him of his small cousins, Eric and Hester, Doctor Philip's children.

A third case he went into more fully, that of a young woman--just a mere girl in appearance though she wore a wedding ring--who had received a terrible blow on the base of her brain which had driven out memory entirely. She did not know who she was, where she was going, or whence she had come. Her physical injuries, otherwise, were not serious, a broken arm and some bad bruises, nothing but what she would easily recover from in a short time; but, for all her effort, the past remained as something on the other side of a strange, blank wall.

"She tries pitifully hard to remember, and is so sweet and brave we are all devoted to her. I always stop and talk to her when I go by her. She seems to cling to me, rather, as if I could help her get things back. Lord knows I wish I could. She is too dainty and fragile a morsel of humanity to be left to fight such a thing alone. She is a regular little Dresden shepherdess, with the tiniest feet and hands and the yellowest hair and bluest eyes I ever saw. Her husband must be about crazy, poor chap, not hearing from her. I suppose he will be turning up soon to claim her. I hope so. I don't know what will become of her if he does not.

"It is late and I must turn in. I don't know when I shall get home. I don't flatter myself Dunbury will miss me much when it has you. Give everybody my love and tell Tony I am awfully sorry I couldn't get to commencement. I guess maybe she is glad enough to have me alive not to mind much. I'm some glad to be alive myself."

The letter ended with affectionate greetings to the older doctor from his nephew and junior assistant. With it came another epistle from the same city from an old doctor friend who had watched Philip Holiday, himself, grow up, and had immediately set his eye on the younger Holiday, when he had discovered the relationship.

"You have a lad to be proud of in that Larry of yours," he wrote. "He is on the job early and late, no smart Alecness, no shirking, no fool questions, just there on the spot when you want him with cool head, steady nerves and a hand as gentle as a woman's. I like his quality, Phil. Quality shows up at a time like this. He is true Holiday, through and through, and you can tell him I said so when you see him."

The doctor smiled, well pleased at this tribute to Ned's son and this letter, like Larry's, he handed to his wife Margery to read.

The thirties had touched "Miss Margery" lightly. She was still slim and girlish-looking. In her simple gown of that forgetmenot blue shade which her husband particularly loved she seemed scarcely older than she had on that day, some eight years earlier, when he had found her giving a Fourth of July party to the Hill youngsters, and had begun to lose his heart to her then and there. It was not by shedding care and responsibility, however, that she had kept her youth. It was by no means the easiest thing in the world to be a busy doctor's wife, the mother of two lively children and faithful daughter to an invalid and rather "difficult" mother-in-law, as well as to care for a big house and an elastic household, which in vacation time included Ned Holiday's children and their friends. Needless to say she did not do any painting these days. But there is more than one way of being an artist, and of the art of simple, lovely, human living Margery Holiday was past mistress.

"Doesn't sound much like 'Lazy Larry' these days, does it?" she commented, giving the letters back to her husband. "I know you are proud of Doctor Fenton's letter, Phil. You ought to be. It is more than a little due to you that Larry is what he is."

"We are advertised by our loving wives," he misquoted teasingly. "I have always observed that the things we approve of in the younger generation are the fruit of seeds we planted. The things we disapprove of slipped in inadvertently like weeds."

The same mail that brought Larry's letter brought one also to Ted from Madeline Taylor, a letter which made him wriggle a little internally, and pull his forelock, as was his habit when things were a bit perturbing.

Madeline had gone to bed that Sunday night after her meeting with Ted in the woods, full of the happiest kind of anticipations and shy, foolish, impossible dreams. Her mind told her it was the rankest of nonsense to dream about Ted Holiday, but her heart would do it. She knew the affair with Ted had begun wrong, but she couldn't help hoping it would come out beautifully right. She couldn't help making believe she had found her prince, a bonny laddie who liked her well enough to play straight with her and to come again to see her.

She meant to try so hard, so very hard, to make herself into the kind of girl he was used to and liked. She cut out the picture of Tony Holiday that Max Hempel and Dick Carson had studied that day on the train. She studied it even harder and hid it away among her very special treasures where she could take it out and look at it often and use it as a model. She even snatched her hitherto precious earrings from their pink cotton resting place and hurled them as far as she could into the night. She was very sure Tony Holiday did not wear earrings, and she was even surer she had seen Ted's eyes resting disapprovingly on hers. The earrings had to go. They had gone.

The next afternoon she had waited for a while patiently by the brook. The distant clock struck the half hour, the three quarters, the full hour. No Ted Holiday. By this time her patience had long since evaporated and now blazed into blind rage. Ted had forgotten his promise, if indeed he had ever meant to keep it. He was with those other girls--his kind. Maybe he was laughing at her, telling them how "easy" she had been, how gullible. No, he wouldn't! He would be ashamed to admit he had had anything to do with her. Men did not boast of their conquest of one kind of girl to another. She had read enough fiction to know that.

In any case she hated Ted Holiday with a fine fury of resentment. She wanted to make him suffer, even as she was suffering, though she sensed vaguely that men couldn't suffer that way. It was only women who were capable of such fine-drawn torture. Men went free.

From her rage against her recreant cavalier she went on to rage against life built on a man-made plan for the benefit of man. Women were hurt, no matter what they did. Being good wasn't any use. You got hurt all the worse if you were good. It was silly even to try. It was better to shut your eyes and have a good time.

Pursuing this reasoning brought Madeline Taylor to the sycamore tree that night where Willis Hubbard's car waited. She went with Willis, not to please him, not to please herself, but to spite Ted Holiday. She had hinted to Ted she would do something desperate if he failed her. She had done something desperate, but it was herself, not Ted, that had been hurt. She discovered that too late.

The next morning had brought Ted's pleasant, penitent note, explaining his defection and expressing the hope that they might meet again soon, signed hers "devotedly." Poor Madeline! The cup of her regret was very bitter to the taste as she read that letter of Ted Holiday's.

Something of her misery and self-abasement crept into the letter to Ted, together with a passionate remorse for having doubted him and her even more vehement regret for having gone out with Willis Hubbard. The whole complex story of her emotional reactions was of course not written down for Ted's eyes; but he read quite enough to permit him to guess more than he cared to know. Hubbard was evidently something of a rotter. Maybe he was a bit of a rotter himself. If he hadn't taken the girl out joy riding himself she wouldn't have gone with the other two nights later. That was plain to be seen with half an eye and Ted Holiday was man enough to look at the fact straight and unblinking for a moment.

Well! He should worry. It wasn't his fault if Madeline had been fool enough to go out with Hubbard, when she knew what kind of a chap he was. He wasn't her keeper. He didn't see why she had to ask him to forgive her. It was none of his business. And he wished she hadn't begged so earnestly and humbly that he would see her again soon. He didn't want to see her. Yet, down underneath, Ted Holiday had an uneasy feeling he ought to want it, ought to try to make up to her in some way for something which was somehow his fault, even though he did disclaim the responsibility.

Two days later came another letter even more disturbing. It seemed Madeline was going to Holyoke again soon to visit her Cousin Emma and wanted Ted to join her. She was "dying" to see him. He could stay at Cousin Emma's, but maybe he wouldn't like that because there was a raft of children always under foot and Fred, Emma's husband, was a dreadful "ordinary" person who smoked a smelly pipe and sat round in his shirt sleeves. But if he would come and stay at a hotel they could have a wonderful time. She did want to see him so much. Besides, Willis pestered her all the time and said if she went away he would come down in his car every night to see her. So if Ted didn't want her to run around with Willis as he said in his last letter he had better come himself. She didn't like Willis the way she did Ted, though. Some ways she hated him and she wished awfully she hadn't ever had anything to do with him. And finally she liked Ted better than anybody in the world, and would he please, please come to Holyoke, because she wanted him to so very, very much?

And then the postscript. "The cut is going to leave a scar, I am most sure. I don't care. I like it. It makes me think of you and what a wonderful time we had together that night."

Ted read the letter coming up the Hill, and for once forebore to whistle as he made the ascent. His mind was busy. A week of Dunbury calm and sweet do-nothing had sufficed to make him undeniably restless. Madeline's proposal struck him as rather a jolly idea accordingly. After all, she was a dandy little girl, and he owed her a lot for not making any fuss over his nearly killing her. He didn't like this Hubbard fellow, either. He rather thought it was his duty to go and send him about his business. Ted was a bit of a knight, at heart, and felt now the chivalric urge, combining with others less unselfish, to go to the rescue of the damsel and set her free of the false besieger.

Her undisguised admission of her caring for him was a bit disconcerting, although perhaps also a little sweet to his youthful male vanity. Her caring was a complication, made him feel as if somehow he ought to make up to her for failing her in the big thing by granting her the smaller favor.

By the time he had reached the top of the Hill he was rather definitely committed in his own mind to the Holyoke trip, if he could throw enough dust in his uncle's eyes to get away with it.

Arrived at the house he flung the other mail on the hall table and went up-stairs. As he passed his grandmother's room he noticed that the door was ajar and stepped in for a word with her. She looked very still and white as she lay there in the big, old fashioned four-poster bed! Poor Granny! It was awfully sad to be old. Ted couldn't quite imagine it for himself, somehow.

"'Lo, Granny dear," he greeted, stooping to kiss the withered old cheek. "How goes it?"

"About as usual, dear. Any word from Larry?" There was a plaintive note in Madame Holiday's voice. She was never quite content unless all the "children" were under the family roof-tree. And Larry was particularly dear to her heart.

"Yes, I just brought a letter for Uncle Phil. The very idea of your wanting Larry when you have Tony and me, and you haven't had us for so long." Ted pretended to be reproachful and his grandmother reached for his hand.

"I know, dear boy. I am very glad to have you and Tony. But Larry is a habit, like Philip. You mustn't mind my missing him."

"Course I don't mind, Granny. I was just jossing. I don't blame you a bit for missing Larry. He is a mighty good thing to have in the family. Wish I were half as valuable."

"You are, sonny. I am so happy to be having you here all summer."

"Maybe not quite all summer. I'll be going off for little trips," he prepared her gently.

"Youth! Youth! Never still--always wanting to fly off somewhere!"

"We all fly back mighty quick," comforted Ted. "There come the kiddies."

A patter of small feet sounded down the hall. In the next moment they were there--sturdy Eric, the six year old, apple-cheeked, incredibly energetic, already bidding fair to equal if not to rival his cousin Ted's reputation for juvenile naughtiness; and Hester, two years younger, a rose-and-snow creation, cherubic, adorable, with bobbing silver curls, delectably dimpled elbows and corn flower blue eyes.

Fresh from the tub and the daily delightful frolic with Daddy, they now appeared for that other ceremonial known as saying good-night to Granny.

"Teddy! Teddy! Ride us to Granny," demanded Eric hilariously, jubilant at finding his favorite tall cousin on the spot.

"'Es, wide us, wide us," chimed in Hester, not to be outdone.

"You fiends!" But Ted obediently got down on "all fours" while the small folks clambered up on his back and he "rode" them over to the bed, their bathrobes flying as they went. Arrived at the destination Ted deftly deposited his load in a giggling, squirming heap on the rug and then gathering up the small Hester, swung her aloft, bringing her down with her rose bud of a mouth close to Granny's pale cheeks.

"Kiss your flying angel, Granny, before she flies away again."

"Me! Me!" clamored Eric vociferously, hugging Ted's knees. "Me flying angel, too!"

"Not much," objected Ted. "No angel about you. Too, too much solid flesh and bones. Kiss Granny, quick. I hear your parents approaching."

Philip and Margery appeared on the threshold, seeking their obstreperous offspring.

There was another stampede, this time in the direction of the "parents."

"Ca'y me! Ca'y me, Daddy," chirruped Hester.

"No, me. Ride me piggy-back," insisted Eric.

"Such children!" smiled Margery. "Ted, you encourage them. They are more barbarian than ever when you are here, and they are bad enough under normal conditions."

Ted chuckled at that. He and his Aunt Margery were the best of good friends. They always had been since Ted had refused to join her Round Table on the grounds that he might have to be sorry for being bad if he did, though he had subsequently capitulated, in view of the manifest advantages accruing to membership in the order.

"That's right. Lay it to me. I don't believe Uncle Phil was a saint, either, was he, Granny?" he appealed. "I'll bet the kids get some of their deviltry by direct line of descent."

His grandmother smiled.

"We forget a good deal about our children's naughtinesses when they are grown up," she said. "I've even forgotten some of yours, Teddy."

"Lucky," grinned her grandson, stooping to kiss her again. "*Allons, enfants*."

Later, when the obstreperous ones were in bed and everything quiet Philip and Margery sat together in the hammock, lovers still after eight years of strenuous married life and discussed Larry's last letter, which had contained the rather astonishing request that he be permitted to bring the little lady who had forgotten her past to Holiday Hill with him.

"Queer proposition!" murmured the doctor. "Doesn't sound like sober Larry."

"I am not so sure. There is a quixotic streak in him--in all you Holidays, for that matter. You can't say much. Think of the stray boys you have taken in at one time or another, some of them rather dubious specimens, I infer."

Margery's eyes smiled tender raillery at her husband. He chuckled at the arraignment, and admitted its justice. Still, boys were not mystery ladies. She must grant him that. Then he sobered.

"It is only you that makes me hesitate, Margery mine. You are carrying about as heavy a burden now as any one woman ought to take upon herself, with me and the house and the children and Granny. And here is this crazy nephew of mine proposing the addition to the family of a stranger who hasn't any past and whose future seems wrapped mostly in a nebular hypothesis. It is rather a large order, my dear."

"Not too large. It isn't as if she were seriously ill, or would be a burden in any way. Besides, it is Larry's home as well as ours, and he so seldom asks anything for himself, and is always ready to help anywhere. Do you really mind her coming, Phil?"

"Not if you don't. I am glad to agree if it is not going to be too hard for you. As you say, Larry doesn't ever ask much for himself and I am interested in the case, anyway. Shall we wire him to bring her, then?"

"Please do. I shall be very glad."

"You are a wonder, Margery mine." And the doctor bent and kissed his wife before going in to telephone the message to be sent his nephew that night, a message bidding him and the little stranger welcome, whenever they cared to come to the House on the Hill.

And far away in Pittsburgh, Larry got the word that night and smiled content. Bless Uncle Phil and Aunt Margery! They never failed you, no matter what you asked of them.

CHAPTER VIII
THE LITTLE LADY WHO FORGOT

Larry Holiday was a rather startlingly energetic person when he once got under way. The next morning he overruled the "Mystery Lady's" faint demurs, successfully argued the senior doctor into agreement with his somewhat surprising plan of procedure, wired his uncle, engaged train reservations for that evening, secured a nurse, preempted the services of a Red Cap who promised to be waiting with a chair at the station so that the little invalid would not have to set foot upon the ground, and finally carried the latter with his own strong young arms onto the train and into a large, cool stateroom where a fan was already whirring and the white-clad nurse waiting to minister to the needs of the frail traveler.

In a few moments the train was slipping smoothly out of the station and the girl who had forgotten most things else knew that she was being spirited off to a delightful sounding place called Holiday Hill in the charge of a gray-eyed young doctor who had made himself personally responsible for her from the moment he had extricated her, more dead than alive, from the wreckage. Somehow, for the moment she was quite content with the knowledge.

Leaving his charge in the nurse's care, Larry Holiday ensconced himself in his seat not far from the stateroom and pretended to read his paper. But it might just as well have been printed in ancient Sanscrit for all the meaning its words conveyed to his brain. His corporeal self occupied the green plush seat. His spiritual person was elsewhere.

After fifteen minutes of futile effort at concentration he flung down the paper and strode to the door of the stateroom. A white linen arm answered his gentle knock. There was a moment's consultation, then the nurse came out and Larry went in.

On the couch the girl lay very still with half-closed eyes. Her long blonde braids tied with blue ribbons lay on the pillow on either side of her sweet, pale little face, making it look more childlike than ever.

"I can't see why I can't remember," she said to Larry as he sat down on the edge of the other cot opposite her. "I try so hard."

"Don't try. You are just wearing yourself out doing it. It will be all right in time. Don't worry."

"I can't help worrying. It is--oh, it is horrible not to have any past--to be different from everybody in the world."

"I know. It is mighty tough and you have been wonderfully brave about it. But truly I do believe it will all come back. And in the meanwhile you are going to one of the best places in the world to get well in. Take my word for it."

"But I don't see why I should be going. It isn't as if I had any claim on you or your people. Why are you taking me to your home?" The blue eyes were wide open now, and looking straight up into Larry Holiday's gray ones.

Larry smiled and Larry's smile, coming out of the usual gravity and repose of his face, was irresistible. More than one young woman, case and non-case, had wished, seeing that smile, that its owner had eyes for girls as such.

"Because you are the most interesting patient I ever had. Don't begrudge it to me. I get measles and sore throats mostly. Do you wonder I snatched you as a dog grabs a bone?" Then he sobered. "Truly, Ruth--you don't mind my calling you that, do you, since we don't know your other name?--the Hill is the one place in the world for you just now. You will forgive my kidnapping you when you see it and my people. You can't help liking it and them."

"I am not afraid of not liking it or them if--" She had meant to say "if they are at all like you," but that seemed a little too personal to say to one's doctor, even a doctor who had saved your life and had the most wonderful smile that ever was, and the nicest eyes. "If they will let me," she substituted. "But it is such a queer, kind thing to do. The other doctors were interested in me, too, as a case. But it didn't occur to any of them to offer me the hospitality of their homes and family for an unlimited time. Are you Holidays all like that?"

"More or less," admitted Larry with another smile. "Maybe we are a bit vainglorious about Holiday hospitality. It is rather a family tradition. The House on the Hill has had open doors ever since the first Holiday built it nearly two hundred years ago. You saw Uncle Phil's wire. He meant that 'welcome ready.' You'll see. But anyway it won't be very hard for them to open the door to you. They will all love you."

She shut her eyes again at that. Possibly the young doctor's expression was rather more un-professionally eloquent than he knew.

"Tired?" he asked.

"Not much--tired of wondering. Maybe my name isn't Ruth at all."

"Maybe it isn't. But it is a name anyway, and you may as well use it for the present until you can find your own. I think Ruth Annersley is a pretty name myself," added the young doctor seriously. "I like it."

"Mrs. Geoffrey Annersley," corrected the girl. "That is rather pretty too."

Larry agreed somewhat less enthusiastically.

Ruth lifted her hand and fell to twisting the wedding ring which was very loose on her thin little finger.

"Think of being married and not knowing what your husband looks like. Poor Geoffrey Annersley! I wonder if he cares a great deal for me."

"It is quite possible," said Larry Holiday grimly.

He had taken an absurd dislike to the very name of Geoffrey Annersley. Why didn't the man appear and claim his wife? Practically every paper from the Atlantic to the Pacific had advertised for him. If he was any good and wanted to find his wife he would be half crazy looking for her by this time. He must have seen the newspaper notices. There was something queer about this Geoffrey Annersley. Larry Holiday detested him cordially.

"You don't suppose he was killed in the wreck, do you?" Ruth's mind worked on, trying to put the pieces of the puzzle together.

"You were traveling alone. Your chair was near mine. I noticed you because I thought--" He broke off abruptly.

"Thought what?"

"That you were the prettiest girl I ever saw in my life," he admitted. "I wanted to speak to you. Two or three times I was on the verge of it but I never could quite get up the courage. I'm not much good at starting conversations with girls. My kid brother, Ted, has the monopoly of that sort of thing in my family."

"Oh, if you only had," she sighed. "Maybe I would have told you something about myself and where I was going when I got to New York."

"I wish I had," regretted Larry. "Confound my shyness! I don't see why anybody ever let you travel alone from San Francisco to New York anyway," he added. "Your Geoffrey ought to have taken better care of you."

"Maybe I haven't a Geoffrey. The fact that there was an envelope in my bag addressed to Mrs. Geoffrey Annersley doesn't prove that I am Mrs. Geoffrey Annersley."

"No, still there is the ring." Larry frowned thoughtfully. "If you aren't Mrs. Geoffrey Annersley you must be Mrs. Somebody Else, I suppose. And the locket says ***Ruth from Geoffrey***."

"Oh, yes, I suppose I am Mrs. Geoffrey Annersley. It seems as if I must be. But why can't I remember? It seems as if any one would remember the man she was married to--as if one couldn't forget that, no matter what happened. But if there is a Geoffrey Annersley why doesn't he come and get me and make me remember him?"

Larry shook his head.

"Don't worry, please. We'll keep on advertising. He is bound to come before long if he really is your husband. Some day he will be coming up our hill and run away with you, worse luck!"

Ruth's eyes were on the ring again.

"It is funny," she said. "But I can't make myself ***feel*** married. I can't make the ring mean anything to me. I don't want it to mean anything. I don't want to be married. Sometimes I dream that Geoffrey Annersley has come and I put my hand over my eyes because I don't want to see him. Isn't that dreadful?" she turned to Larry to ask.

"You can't help it." Larry tried manfully to push back his own wholly unreasonable satisfaction in her aversion to her presumptive husband. "It is the blow and the shock of the whole thing. It will be all right in time. You will fall on your Geoffrey's neck and call him blessed when the time comes."

"I don't believe he is coming," she announced suddenly with conviction.

Larry got up and walked over to her couch.

"What makes you say that?" he demanded.

"I don't know. It was just a feeling I had. Something inside me said right out loud: 'He isn't coming. He isn't your husband.' Maybe it is because I don't want him to come and don't want him to be my husband. Oh, dear! It is all so queer and mixed up and horrid. It is awful not to be anybody--just a ghost. I wish I'd been killed. Why didn't you leave me? Why did you dig me out? All the others said I was dead. Why didn't you let me *be* dead? It would have been better."

She turned her face away and buried it in the pillow, sobbing softly, suddenly like a child.

This was too much for Larry. He dropped on his knees beside her and put his arms around the quivering little figure.

"Don't, Ruth," he implored. "Don't cry and don't--don't wish you were dead. I--I can't stand it."

There was a tap at the door. Larry got to his feet in guilty haste and went to the door of the stateroom.

"It is time for Mrs. Annersley's medicine," announced the nurse impersonally, entering and going over to the wash stand for a glass.

The white linen back safely turned, Larry gave one swift look at Ruth and bolted, shutting the door behind him. The nurse turned to look at the patient whose face was still hidden in the pillow and then her gaze traveled meditatively toward the door out of which the young doctor had shot so precipitately. Larry had forgotten that there was a mirror over the wash stand and that nurses, however impersonal, are still women with eyes in their heads.

"H--m," reflected the onlooker. "I wouldn't have thought he was that kind. You never can tell about men, especially doctors. I wish him joy falling in love with a woman who doesn't know whether or not she has a husband. Your tablets, Mrs. Annersley," she added aloud.

*   *   *   *   *

"Larry, I think your Ruth is the dearest thing I ever laid eyes on," declared Tony next day to her brother. "Her name ought to be Titania. I'm not very big myself, but I feel like an Amazon beside her. And her laugh is the sweetest thing--so soft and silvery, like little bells. But she doesn't laugh much, does she? Poor little thing!"

"She is awfully up against it," said Larry with troubled eyes. "She can't stop trying to remember. It is a regular obsession with her. And she is very shy and sensitive and afraid of strangers."

"She doesn't look at you as if you were a stranger. She adores you."

"Nonsense!" said Larry sharply.

Tony opened her eyes at her brother's tone.

"Why, Larry! Of course, I didn't mean she was in love with you. She couldn't be when she is married. I just meant she adored you--well, the way Max adores me," she explained as the tawny-haired Irish setter came and rested his head on her knee, raising solemn worshipful brown eyes to her face. "Why shouldn't she? You saved her life and you have been wonderful to her every way."

"Nonsense!" said Larry again, though he said it in a different tone this time. "I haven't done much. It is Uncle Phil and Aunt Margery who are the wonderful ones. It is great the way they both said yes right away when I asked if I could bring her here. I tell you, Tony, it means something to have your own people the kind you can count on every time. And it is great to have a home like this to bring her to. She is going to love it as soon as she is able to get downstairs with us all."

Up in her cool, spacious north chamber, lying in the big bed with the smooth, fine linen, Ruth felt as if she loved it already, though she found these Holidays even more amazing than ever, now that she was actually in their midst. Were there any other people in the world like them she wondered--so kind and simple and unfeignedly glad to take a stranger into their home and a queer, mysterious, sick stranger at that!

"If I have to begin living all over just like a baby I think I am the luckiest girl that ever was to be able to start in a place like this with such dear, kind people all around me," she told Doctor Holiday, senior, to whom she had immediately lost her heart as soon as she saw his smile and felt the touch of his strong, magnetic, healing hand.

"We will get you out under the trees in a day or two," he said. "And then your business will be to get well and strong as soon as possible and not worry about anything any more than if you were the baby you were just talking about. Can you manage that, young lady?"

"I'll try. I would be horrid and ungrateful not to when you are all so good to me. I don't believe my own people are half as nice as you Holidays. I don't see how they could be."

The doctor laughed at that.

"We will let it go at that for the present. You will be singing another tune when your Geoffrey Annersley comes up the Hill to claim you."

The girl's expressive face clouded over at that. She did not quite dare to tell Doctor Holiday as she had his nephew that she did not want to see Geoffrey Annersley nor to have to know she was married to him. It sounded horrid, but it was true. Sometimes she hated the very thought of Geoffrey Annersley.

Later Doctor Holiday and his nephew went over the girl's case together from both the personal and professional angles. There was little enough to go on in untangling her mystery. The railway tickets which had been found in her purse were in an un-postmarked envelope bearing the name Mrs. Geoffrey Annersley, but no address. The baggage train had been destroyed by fire at the time of the accident, so there were no trunks to give evidence. The small traveling bag she had carried with her bore neither initial nor geographical designation, and contained nothing which gave any clew as to its owner's identity save that she was presumably a person of wealth, for her possessions were exquisite and obviously costly. A small jewel box contained various valuable rings, one or two pendants and a string of matched pearls which even to uninitiated eyes spelled a fortune. Also, oddly enough, among the rest was an absurd little childish gold locket inscribed "Ruth from Geoffrey."

She had worn no rings at all except for a single platinum-set, and very perfect, diamond and a plain gold band, obviously a wedding ring. The inference was that she was married and that her husband's name was Geoffrey Annersley, but where he was and why she was traveling across the United States alone and from whence she had come remained utterly unguessable. Larry had seen to it that advertisements for Geoffrey Annersley were inserted in every important paper from coast to coast but nothing had come of any of his efforts.

As for the strange lapse of memory, there seemed nothing to do but wait in the hope that recovered health and strength might bring it back.

"It may come bit by bit or by a sudden bound or never," was Doctor Holiday's opinion. "There is nothing that I know of that she or you or any one can do except let nature take her course. It is a case of time and patience. I am glad you brought her to us. Margery and I are very glad to have her."

"You are awfully good, Uncle Phil. I do appreciate it and it is great to have you behind me professionally. I haven't got a great deal of confidence in myself. Doctoring scares me sometimes. It is such a fearful responsibility."

"It is, but you are going to be equal to it. The confidence will come with experience. You need have no lack of faith in yourself; I haven't. There is no reason why I should have, when I get letters like this."

The senior doctor leaned over and extracted old Doctor Fenton's letter from a cubby hole in his desk and gave it to his nephew to read. The latter perused it in silence with slightly heightened color. Praise always embarrassed him.

"He is too kind," he observed as he handed back the letter. "I didn't do much out there, precious little in fact but what I was told to do. I figured it out that we young ones were the privates and it was up to us to take orders from the captains who knew their business better than we did and get busy. I worked on that basis."

"Sound basis. I am not afraid that a man who can obey well won't be able to command well when the time comes. It isn't a small thing to be recognized as a true Holiday, either. It is something to be proud of."

"I am proud, Uncle Phil. There is nothing I would rather hear--and deserve. But, if I am anywhere near the Holiday standard, it is you mostly that brought me up to it. I don't mean any dispraise of Dad. He was fine and I am proud to be his son. But he never understood me. I didn't have enough dash and go to me for him. Ted and Tony are both more his kind, though I don't believe either of them loved him as I did. But you seemed to understand always. You helped me to believe in myself. It was the best thing that could have happened to me, coming to you when I did."

Larry turned to the mantel and picked up a photograph of himself which stood there, a lad of fifteen or so, facing the world with grave, sensitive eyes, the Larry he had been when he came to the House on the Hill. He smiled at his uncle over the boy's picture.

"You burned out the plague spots, too, with a mighty hot iron, some of them," he added. "I'll never forget your sitting there in that very chair telling me I was a lazy, selfish snob and that, all things considered, I didn't measure up for a nickel with Dick. Jerusalem! I wonder if you knew how that hit. I had a fairly good opinion of Larry Holiday in some ways and you rather knocked the spots out of it, comparing me to my disadvantage with a circus runaway."

He replaced the picture, the smile still lingering on his face.

"It was the right medicine though. I needed it. I can see that now. Speaking of doses I wish you would make Ted tutor this summer. I don't know whether he has told you. I rather think not. But he flunked so many courses he will have to drop back a year unless he makes up the work and takes examinations in the fall."

The senior doctor drummed thoughtfully on the desk. So that was what the boy had on his mind.

"Why not speak to him yourself?" he asked after a minute.

"And be sent to warm regions as I was last spring when I ventured to give his lord highmightiness some advice. No good, Uncle Phil. He won't listen to me. He just gets mad and swings off in the other direction. I don't handle him right. Haven't your patience and tact. I wonder if he ever will get any sense into his head. He is the best hearted kid in the world, and I'm crazy over him, but he does rile me to the limit with his fifty-seven varieties of foolness."

CHAPTER IX
TED SEIZES THE DAY

The next morning Ted strolled into his uncle's office to ask if the latter had any objections to his accepting an invitation to a house-party from Hal Underwood, a college classmate, at the latter's home near Springfield.

The doctor considered a moment before answering. He knew all about the Underwoods and knew that his erratic nephew could not be in a safer, pleasanter place. Also his quick wit saw a chance to put the screws on the lad in connection with the tutoring business.

"I suppose your June allowance is able to float your traveling expenses," he remarked less guilelessly than the remark sounded.

The June allowance was, it seemed, the missing link.

"I thought maybe you would be willing to allow me a little extra this month on account of commencement stunts. It is darned expensive sending nosegays to sweet girl graduates. I couldn't help going broke. Honest I couldn't, Uncle Phil." Then as his uncle did not leap at the suggestion offered, the speaker changed his tack. "Anyway, you would be willing to let me have my July money ahead of time, wouldn't you?" he ingratiated. "It is only ten days to the first."

But Doctor Holiday still chose to be inconveniently irrelevant.

"Have you any idea how much my bill was for repairing the car?" he asked.

Ted shook his head shamefacedly, and bent to examine a picture in a magazine which lay on the desk. He wasn't anxious to have the car incident resurrected. He had thought it decently buried by this time, having heard no more about it.

"It was a little over a hundred dollars," continued the doctor.

The boy looked up, genuinely distressed.

"Gee, Uncle Phil! It's highway robbery."

"Scarcely. All things considered, it was a very fair bill. A hundred dollars is a good deal to pay for the pleasure of nearly getting yourself and somebody else killed, Ted."

Ted pulled his forelock and had nothing to say.

"Were you in earnest about paying up for that particular bit of folly, son?"

"Why, yes. At least I didn't think it would be any such sum as that," Ted hedged. "I'll be swamped if I try to pay it out of my allowance. I can't come out even, as it is. Couldn't you take it out of my own money--what's coming to me when I'm of age?"

"I could, if getting myself paid were the chief consideration. As it happens, it isn't. I'm sorry if I seem to be hard on you, but I am going to hold you to your promise, even if it pinches a bit. I think you know why. How about it, son?"

"I suppose it has to go that way if you say so," said Ted a little sulkily. "Can I pay it in small amounts?"

"How small? Dollar a year? I'd hate to wait until I was a hundred and forty or so to get my money back."

The boy grinned reluctantly, answering the friendly twinkle in his uncle's eyes. He was relieved that a joke had penetrated what had begun to appear to be an unpleasantly jestless interview. He hated to be called to account. Like many another older sinner he liked dancing, but found paying the piper an irksome business.

"Nonsense, Uncle Phil! I meant real paying. Will ten dollars a month do?"

"It will, provided you don't try to borrow ahead each month from the next one."

"I won't," glibly. "If you will--" The boy broke off and had the grace to look confused, realizing he had been about to do the very thing he had promised in the same breath not to do. "Then that means I can't go to Hal's," he added soberly.

He felt sober. There was more than Hal and the house-party involved, though the latter had fallen in peculiarly fortuitous with his other plans. He had rashly written Madeline he would be in Holyoke next week as she desired, and the first of July and his allowance would still be just out of reach next week. It was a confounded nuisance, to say the least, being broke just now, with Uncle Phil turned stuffy.

"No, I don't want you to give up your house-party, though that rests with you. I'll make a bargain with you. I'll advance your whole July allowance minus ten dollars Saturday morning."

Ted's face cleared, beamed like sudden sunshine on a cloudy March day.

"You will! Uncle Phil, you certainly are a peach!" And in his exuberance he tossed his cap to the ceiling, catching it deftly on his nose as it descended.

"Hold on. Don't rejoice too soon. It was to be a bargain, you know. You have heard only one side."

"Oh--h!" The exclamation was slightly crestfallen.

"I understand that you fell down on most of your college work this spring. Is that correct?"

This was a new complication and just as he had thought he was safely out of the woods, too. Ted hung his head, gave consent to his uncle's question by silence and braced himself for a lecture, though he was a little relieved that he need not bring up the subject of that inconvenient flunking of his, himself; that his uncle was already prepared, whoever it was that had told tales. The lecture did not come, however.

"Here is the bargain. I will advance the money as I said, provided that as soon as you get back from Hal's you will make arrangements to tutor with Mr. Caldwell this summer, in all the subjects you failed in and promise to put in two months of good, solid cramming, no half way about it."

"Gee, Uncle Phil! It's vacation."

"You don't need a vacation. If all I hear of you is true, or even half of it, you made your whole college year one grand, sweet vacation. What is the answer? Want time to think the proposition over?"

"No--o. I guess I'll take you up. I suppose I'll have to tutor anyway if I don't want to drop back a class, and I sure don't," Ted admitted honestly. "Unless you'll let me quit and you won't. It is awfully tough, though. You never made Tony or Larry kill themselves studying in vacations. I don't see--"

"Neither Tony or Larry ever flunked a college course. It remained for you to be the first Holiday to wear a dunce cap."

Ted flushed angrily at that. The shot went home, as the doctor intended it should. He knew when to hit and how to do it hard, as Larry had testified.

"Fool's cap if you like, Uncle Phil. I am not a dunce."

"I rather think that is true. Anyway, prove it to us this summer and there is no one who will be gladder than I to take back the aspersion. Is it understood then? You have your house-party and when you come back you are pledged to honest work, no shirking, no requests for time off, no complaints. Have I your word?"

Ted considered. He thought he was paying a stiff price for his house-party and his lark with Madeline. He could give up the first, though a fellow always had a topping time at Hal's; but he couldn't quite see himself owning ignominiously to Madeline that he couldn't keep his promise to her because of empty pockets. Moreover, as he had admitted, he would have to tutor anyway, probably, and he might as well get some gain out of the pain.

"I promise, Uncle Phil."

"Good. Then that is settled. I am not going to say anything more about the flunking. You know how we all feel about it. I think you have sense enough and conscience enough to see it about the way the rest of us do."

Ted's eyes were down again now. Somehow Uncle Phil always made him feel worse by what he didn't say than a million sermons from other people would have done. He would have gladly have given up the projected journey and anything else he possessed this moment if he could have had a clean slate to show. But it was too late for that now. He had to take the consequences of his own folly.

"I see it all right, Uncle Phil," he said looking up. "Trouble is I never seem to have the sense to look until--afterward. You are awfully decent about it and letting me go to Hal's and--everything. I--I'll be gone about a week, do you mind?"

"No. Stay as long as you like. I am satisfied with your promise to make good when you do come."

Ted slipped away quickly then. He was ashamed to meet his uncle's kind eyes. He knew he was playing a crooked game with stacked cards. He hadn't exactly lied--hadn't said a word that wasn't strictly true, indeed. He was going to Hal's, but he had let his uncle think he was going to stay there the whole week whereas in reality he meant to spend the greater part of the time in Madeline Taylor's society, which was not in the bargain at all. Well he would make up later by keeping his promise about the studying. He would show them Larry wasn't the only Holiday who could make good. The dunce cap jibe rankled.

And so, having satisfied his sufficiently elastic conscience, he departed on Saturday for Springfield and adjacent points.

He had the usual "topping" time at Hal's and tore himself away with the utmost reluctance from the house-party, had half a mind, indeed, to wire Madeline he couldn't come to Holyoke. But after all that seemed rather a mean thing to do after having treated her so rough before, and in the end he had gone, only one day later than he had promised.

It was characteristic that, arrived at his destination, he straightway forgot the pleasures he was foregoing at Hal's and plunged whole-heartedly into amusing himself to the utmost with Madeline Taylor. *Carpe Diem* was Ted Holiday's motto.

Madeline had indeed proved unexpectedly pretty and attractive when she opened the door to him on Cousin Emma's little box of a front porch, clad all in white and wearing no extraneous ornament of any sort, blushing delightfully and obviously more than glad of his coming. He would not have been Ted Holiday if he hadn't risen to the occasion. The last girl in sight was usually the only girl for him so long as she *was* in sight and sufficiently jolly and good to look upon.

A little later Madeline donned a trim tailored black sailor hat and a pretty and becoming pale green sweater and the two went down the steps together, bound for an excursion to the park. As they descended Ted's hand slipped gallantly under the girl's elbow and she leaned on it ever so little, reveling in the ceremony and prolonging it as much as possible. Well she knew that Cousin Emma and the children were peering out from behind the curtains of the front bedroom upstairs, and that Mrs. Bascom and her stuck up daughter Lily had their faces glued to the pane next door. They would all see that this was no ordinary beau, but a real swell like the magnificent young men in the movies. Perhaps as she descended Cousin Emma's steps and went down the path between the tiger lilies and peonies that flanked the graveled path with Ted Holiday beside her, Madeline Taylor had her one perfect moment.

Only the "ordinary" Fred, on hearing his wife's voluble descriptions later of Madeline's "grand" young man failed to be suitably impressed. "Them swells don't mean no girl no good no time," he had summed up his views with sententious accumulation of negatives.

But little enough did either Ted or Madeline reck of Fred's or any other opinion as they fared their blithe and care-free way that gala week. The rest of the world was supremely unimportant as they went canoeing and motoring and trolley riding and mountain climbing and "movieing" together. Madeline strove with all her might to dress and act and *be* as nearly like those other girls after whom she was modeling herself as possible, to do nothing, which could jar on Ted in any way or remind him that she was "different." In her happiness and sincere desire to please she succeeded remarkably well in making herself superficially at least very much like Ted's own "kind of girl" and though with true masculine obtuseness he was entirely unaware of the conscious effort she was putting into the performance nevertheless he enjoyed the results in full and played up to her undeniable charms with his usual debonair and heedless grace and gallantry.

The one thing that had been left out of the program for lack of suitable opportunity was dancing, an omission not to be tolerated by two strenuous and modern young persons who would rather fox trot than eat any day. Accordingly on Thursday it was agreed that they should repair to the White Swan, a resort down the river, famous for its excellent cuisine, its perfect dance floor and its "snappy" negro orchestra. Both Ted and Madeline knew that the Swan had also a reputation of another less desirable sort, but both were willing to ignore the fact for the sake of enjoying the "jolliest jazz on the river" as the advertisement read. The dance was the thing.

It was, indeed. The evening was decidedly the best yet, as both averred, pirouetting and spinning and romping through one fox trot and one step after another. The excitement of the music, the general air of exhilaration about the place and their own high-pitched mood made the occasion different from the other gaieties of the week, merrier, madder, a little more reckless.

Once, seeing a painted, over-dressed or rather under-dressed, girl in the arms of a pasty-faced, protruding-eyed roue, both obviously under the spell of too much liquid inspiration, Ted suffered a momentary revulsion and qualm of conscience. He shouldn't have brought Madeline here. It wasn't the sort of place to bring a girl, no matter how good the music was. Oh, well! What did it matter just this once? They were there now and they might as well get all the fun they could out of it. The music started up, he held out his hand to Madeline and they wheeled into the maze of dancers, the girl's pliant body yielding to his arms, her eyes brilliant with excitement. They danced on and on and it was amazingly and imprudently late when they finally left the Swan and went home to Cousin Emma's house.

Ted had meant to leave Madeline at the gate, but somehow he lingered and followed the girl out into the yard behind the house where they seated themselves in the hammock in the shade of the lilac bushes. And suddenly, without any warning, he had her in his arms and was kissing her tempestuously.

It was only for a moment, however. He pulled himself together, hot cheeked and ashamed and flung himself out of the hammock. Madeline sat very still, not saying a word, as she watched him march to and fro between the beds of verbena and love-lies-bleeding and portulaca. Presently he paused beside the hammock, looking down at the girl.

"I am going home to-morrow," he said a little huskily.

Madeline threw out one hand and clutched one of the boy's in a feverish clasp.

"No! No!" she cried. "You mustn't go. Please don't, Ted."

"I've got to," stolidly.

"Why?"

"You know why."

"You mean--what you did--just now?"

He nodded miserably.

"That doesn't matter. I'm not angry. I--I liked it."

"I am afraid it does matter. It makes a mess of everything, and it's all my fault. I spoiled things. I've got to go."

"But you will come back?" she pleaded.

He shook his head.

"It is better not, Madeline. I'm sorry."

She snatched her hand away from his, her eyes shooting sparks of anger.

"I hate you, Ted Holiday. You make me care and then you go away and leave me. You are cruel--selfish. I hate you--hate you."

Ted stared down at her, helpless, miserable, ashamed. No man knows what to do with a scene, especially one which his own folly has precipitated.

"Willis Hubbard is coming down to-morrow night and if you don't stay as you promised I'll go to the Swan with him. He has been teasing me to go for ages and I wouldn't, but I will now, if you leave me. I'll--I'll do anything."

Ted was worried. He did not like the sound of the girl's threats though he wasn't moved from his own purpose.

"Don't go to the Swan with Hubbard, Madeline. You mustn't."

"Why not? You took me."

"I know I did, but that is different," he finished lamely.

"I don't see anything very different," she retorted hotly.

Ted bit his lip. Remembering his own recent aberration, he did not see as much difference as he would have liked to see himself.

"I suppose you wouldn't have taken *your* kind of girl to the Swan," taunted Madeline.

"No, I--"

It was a fatal admission. Ted hadn't meant to make it so bluntly, but it was out. The damage was done.

A demon of rage possessed the girl. Beside herself with anger she sprang to her feet and delivered a stinging blow straight in the boy's face. Then, her mood changing, she fell back into the hammock sobbing bitterly.

For a moment Ted was too much astonished by this fish-wife exhibition of temper even to be angry with himself. Then a hot wave of wrath and shame surged over him. He put up his hand to his cheek as if to brush away the indignity of the blow. But he was honest enough to realize that maybe he had deserved the punishment, though not for the reason the girl had dealt it.

Looking down at her in her racked misery, his resentment vanished and an odd impersonal kind of pity for her possessed him instead, though her attraction was gone forever. He could see the scar on her forehead, and it troubled and reproached him vaguely, seemed a symbol of a deeper wound he had dealt her, though never meaning any harm. He bent over her, gently.

"Forgive me, Madeline," he said. "I am sorry--sorry for everything. Goodby."

In a moment he was gone, past the portulaca and love-lies-bleeding, past Cousin Emma's unlit parlor windows, down the walk between the tiger lilies and peonies, out into the street. And Madeline, suddenly realizing that she was alone, rushed after him, calling his name softly into the dark. But only the echo of his firm, buoyant young feet came back to her straining ears. She fled back to the garden and, throwing herself, face down, on the dew drenched grass, surrendered to a passion of tearless grief.

Ted astonished his uncle, first by coming home a whole day earlier than he had been expected and second, by announcing his intention of seeing Robert Caldwell and making arrangements about the tutoring that very day. He was more than usually uncommunicative about his house-party experiences the Doctor thought and fancied too that just at first after his return the boy did not meet his eyes quite frankly. But this soon passed away and he was delighted and it must be confessed considerably astounded too to perceive that Ted really meant to keep his word about the studying and settled down to genuine hard work for perhaps the first time, in his idle, irresponsible young life. He had been prepared to put on the screws if necessary. There had been no need. Ted had applied his own screws and kept at his uncongenial task with such grim determination that it almost alarmed his family, so contrary was his conduct to his usual light-hearted shedding of all obligations which he could, by hook or crook, evade.

Among other things to be noted with relief the doctor counted the fact that there were no more letters from Florence. Apparently that flame which had blazed up rather brightly at first had died down as a good many others had. Doctor Holiday was particularly glad in this case. He had not liked the idea of his nephew's running around with a girl who would be willing to go "joy-riding" with him after midnight, and still less had he liked the idea of his nephew's issuing such invitations to any kind of girl. Youth was youth and he had never kept a very tight rein on any of Ned's children, believing he could trust them to run straight in the main. Still there were things one drew the line at for a Holiday.

CHAPTER X
TONY DANCES INTO A DISCOVERY

Tony was dressing for dinner on her first evening at Crest House. Carlotta was perched on the arm of a chair near by, catching up on mutual gossip as to events that had transpired since they parted a month before at Northampton.

"I have a brand new young man for you, Tony. Alan Massey--the artist. At least he calls himself an artist, though he hasn't done a thing but philander and travel two or three times around the globe, so near as I can make out, since somebody died and left him a disgusting big fortune. Aunt Lottie hints that he is very improper, but anyway he is amusing and different and a dream of a dancer. It is funny, but he makes me think a little bit once in a while of somebody we both know. I won't tell you who, and see if the same thing strikes you."

A little later Tony met the "new young man." She was standing with her friend in the big living room waiting for the signal for dinner when she felt suddenly conscious of a new presence. She turned quickly and saw a stranger standing on the threshold regarding her with a rather disconcertingly intent gaze. He was very tall and foreign-looking, "different," as Carlotta had said, with thick, waving blue-black hair, a clear, olive skin and deep-set, gray-green eyes. There was nothing about him that suggested any resemblance to anyone she knew. Indeed she had a feeling that there was nobody at all like him anywhere in the world.

The newcomer walked toward her, their glances crossing. Tony stood very still, but she had an unaccountable sensation of going to meet him, as if he had drawn her to him, magnet-wise, by his strange, sweeping look. They were introduced. He bowed low in courtly old world fashion over the girl's hand.

"I am enchanted to know Miss Holiday," he said. His voice was as unusual as the rest of him, deep-throated, musical, vibrant--an unforgettable voice it seemed to Tony who for a moment seemed to have lost her own.

"I shall sit beside Miss Tony to-night, Carla," he added. It was not a question, not a plea. It was clear assertion.

"Not to-night, Alan. You are between Aunt Lottie and Mary Frances Day. You liked Mary Frances yesterday. You flirted with her outrageously last night."

He shrugged.

"Ah, but that was last night, my dear. And this is to-night. And I have seen your Miss Tony. That alters everything, even your seating arrangements. Change me, Carlotta."

Carlotta laughed and capitulated. Alan's highhanded tactics always amused her.

"Not that you deserve it," she said. "Don't be too nice to him, Tony. He is not a nice person at all."

So it happened that Tony found herself at dinner between Ted's friend, and her own, Hal Underwood, and this strange, impossible, arbitrary, new personage who had hypnotized her into unwonted silence at their first meeting.

She had recovered her usual poise by this time, however, and was quite prepared to keep Alan Massey in due subjection if necessary. She did not like masterful men. They always roused her own none too dormant willfulness.

As they sat down he bent over to her.

"You are glad I made Carlotta put us together," he said, and this, too, was no question, but an assertion.

Tony was in arms in a flash.

"On the contrary, I am exceedingly sorry she gave in to you. You seem to be altogether too accustomed to having your own way as it is." And rather pointedly she turned her pretty shoulder on her too presuming neighbor and proceeded to devote her undivided attention for two entire courses to Hal Underwood.

But, with the fish, Hal's partner on the other side, a slim young person in a glittering green sequined gown, suggesting a fish herself, or, at politest, a mermaid, challenged his notice and Tony returned perforce to her left-hand companion who had not spoken a single word since she had snubbed him as Tony was well aware, though she had seemed so entirely absorbed in her own conversation with Hal.

His gray-green eyes smiled imperturbably into hers.

"Am I pardoned? Surely I have been punished enough for my sins, whatever they may have been."

"I hope so," said Tony. "Are you always so disagreeable?"

"I am never disagreeable when I am having my own way. I am always good when I am happy. At this moment I am very, very good."

"It hardly seems possible," said Tony. "Carlotta said you were not good at all."

He shrugged, a favorite mannerism, it seemed.

"Goodness is relative and a very dull topic in any case. Let us talk, instead, of the most interesting subject in the universe--love. You know, of course, I am madly in love with you."

"Indeed, no. I didn't suspect it," parried Tony. "You fall in love easily."

"Scarcely easily, in this case. I should say rather upon tremendous provocation. I suppose you know how beautiful you are."

"I look in the mirror occasionally," admitted Tony with a glimmer of mischief in her eyes. "Carlotta told me you were a philanderer. Forewarned is forearmed, Mr. Massey."

"Ah, but this isn't philandery. It is truth." Suddenly the mockery had died out of his voice and his eyes. "***Carissima,*** I have waited a very long time for you--too long. Life has been an arid waste without you, but, Allah be praised, you are here at last. You are going to love me--ah, my Tony--how you are going to love me!" The last words were spoken very low for the girl's ears alone, though more than one person at the table seeing him bend over her, understood, that Alan Massey, that professional master-lover was "off" again.

"Don't, Mr. Massey. I don't care for that kind of jest."

"Jest! Good God! Tony Holiday, don't you know that I mean it, that this, is the real thing at last for me--and for you? Don't fight it, Mademoiselle Beautiful. It will do no good. I love you and you are going to love me--divinely."

"I don't even like you," denied Tony hotly.

"What of that? What do I care for your liking? That is for others. But your loving--that shall be mine--all mine. You will see."

"I am afraid you are very much mistaken if you do mean all you are saying. Please talk to Miss Irvine now. You haven't said a word to her since you sat down. I hate rudeness."

Again Tony turned a cold shoulder upon her amazing dinner companion but she did not do it so easily or so calmly this time. She was not unused to the strange ways of men. Not for nothing had she spent so much of her life at army posts where love-making is as familiar as brass buttons. Sudden gusts of passion were no novelty to her, nor was it a new thing to hear that a man thought he loved her. But Alan Massey was different. She disliked him intensely, she resented the arrogance of his assumptions with all her might, but he interested her amazingly. And, incredible as it might seem and not to be admitted out loud, he was speaking the truth, just now. He did love her. In her heart Tony knew that she had felt his love before he had ever spoken a word to her when their eyes had met as he stood on the threshold and she knew too instinctively, that his love--if it was that--was not a thing to be treated like the little summer day loves of the others. It was big, rather fearful, not to be flouted or played with. One did not play with a meteor when it crossed one's path. One fled from it or stayed and let it destroy one if it would.

She roused herself to think of other people, to forget Alan Massey and his wonderful voice which had said such perturbing things. Over across the table, Carlotta was talking vivaciously to a pasty-visaged, narrow-chested, stoop-shouldered youth who scarcely opened his mouth except to consume food, but whose eyes drank in every movement of Carlotta's. One saw at a glance he was another of that spoiled little coquette's many victims. Tony asked Hal who he was. He seemed scarcely worth so many of Carlotta's sparkles, she thought.

"Herb Lathrop--father is the big tea and coffee man--all rolled up in millions. Carlotta's people are putting all the bets on him, apparently, though for the life of me I can't see why. Don't see why people with money are always expected to match up with somebody with a whole caboodle of the same junk. Ought to be evened up I think, and a bit of eugenics slipped in, instead of so much cash, for good measure. You can see what a poor fish he is. In my opinion she had much better marry your neighbor up there on the Hill. He is worth a gross of Herb Lathrops and she knows it. Carlotta is no fool."

"You mean Phil Lambert?" Tony was surprised.

Hal nodded.

"That's the chap. Only man I ever knew that could keep Carlotta in order."

"But Carlotta hasn't the slightest idea of marrying Phil," objected Tony.

"Maybe not. I only say he is the man she ought to marry. I say, Tony, does she seem happy to you?"

"Carlotta! Why, yes. I hadn't thought. She seems gayer than usual, if anything." Tony's eyes sought her friend's face. Was there something a little forced about that gaiety of hers? For the first time it struck her that there was a restlessness in the lovely violet eyes which was unfamiliar. Was Carlotta unhappy? Evidently Hal thought so. "You have sharp eyes, Hal," she commented. "I hadn't noticed."

"Oh, I'm one of the singed moths you know. I know Carlotta pretty well and I know she is fighting some kind of a fight--maybe with herself. I rather think it is. Tell Phil Lambert to come down here and marry her out of hand. I tell you Lambert's the man."

"You think Carlotta loves Phil?"

"I don't think. 'Tisn't my business prying into a girl's fancies. I'm simply telling you Phil Lambert is the man that ought to marry her, and if he doesn't get on to the job almighty quick that pop-eyed simpleton over there will be prancing down the aisle to Lohengrin with Carlotta before Christmas, and the jig will be up. You tell him what I say. And study the thing a bit yourself while you are here, Tony. See if you can get to the bottom of it. I hate to have her mess things up for herself that way."

Whereupon Hal once more proceeded to do his duty to the mermaid, leaving Tony to her other partner.

"Well," the latter murmured, seeing her free. "I have done the heavy polite act, discussed D'Annunzio, polo and psycho-analysis and finished all three subjects neatly. Do I get my reward?"

"What do you ask?"

"The first dance and then the garden and the moon and you--all to myself."

Tony shook her head. She was on guard.

"I shall want more than one dance and more than one partner. I am afraid I shan't have time for the moon and the garden to-night. I adore dancing. I never stop until the music does."

A flash of exultancy leaped into his eyes.

"So? I might have known you would adore dancing. You shall have your fill. You shall have many dances, but only one partner. I shall suffice. I am one of the best dancers in the world."

"And evidently one of the vainest men," coolly.

"What of it? Vanity is good when it is not misplaced. But I was not boasting. I *am* one of the best dancers in the world. Why should I not be? My mother was Lucia Vannini. She danced before princes." He might have added, "She was a prince's mistress." It had been the truth.

"Oh!" cried Tony. She had heard of Lucia Vannini--a famous Italian beauty and dancer of three decades ago. So Alan Massey was her son. No wonder he was foreign, different, in ways and looks. One could forgive his extravagances when one knew.

"Ah, you like that, my beauty? You will like it even better when you have danced with me. It is then that you will know what it is to dance. We shall dance and dance and--love. I shall make you mine dancing, *Toinetta mia*."

Tony shrank back from his ardent eyes and his veiled threat. She was a passionate devotee of her own freedom. She did not want to be made his or any man's--certainly not his. She decided not to dance with him at all. But later, when the violins began to play and Alan Massey came and stood before her, uttering no word but commanding her to him with his eyes and his out-stretched, nervous, slender, strong, artist hands, she yielded--could scarcely have refused if she had wanted to. But she did not want to, though she told herself it was with Lucia Vannini's son rather than with Alan Massey that she desired to dance.

After that she thought not at all, gave herself up to the very ecstasy of emotion. She had danced all her life, but, even as he had predicted, she learned for the first time in this man's arms what dancing really was. It was like nothing she had ever even dreamed of--pure poetry of motion, a curious, rather alarming weaving into one of two vividly alive persons in a kind of pagan harmony, a rhythmic rapture so intense it almost hurt. It seemed as if she could have gone on thus forever.

But suddenly she perceived that she and her partner had the floor alone, the others had stopped to watch, though the musicians still played on frenziedly, faster and faster. Flushed, embarrassed at finding herself thus conspicuous, she drew herself away from Alan Massey.

"We must stop," she murmured. "They are all looking at us."

"What of it?" He bent over her, his passionate eyes a caress. "Did I not tell you, *carissima* Was it not very heaven?"

Tony shook her head.

"I am afraid there was nothing heavenly about it. But it was wonderful. I forgive you your boasting. You are the best dancer in the world. I am sure of it."

"And you will dance with me again and again, my wonder-girl. You must. You want to."

"I want to," admitted Tony. "But I am not going to--at least not again to-night. Take me to a seat."

He did so and she sank down with a fluttering sigh beside Miss Lottie Cressy, Carlotta's aunt. The latter stared at her, a little oddly she thought, and then looked up at Alan Massey.

"You don't change, do you, Alan?" observed Miss Cressy.

"Oh yes, I change a great deal. I have been very different ever since I met Miss Tony." His eyes fell on the girl, made no secret of his emotions concerning her and her beauty.

Miss Cressy laughed a little sardonically.

"No doubt. You were always different after each new sweetheart, I recall. So were they--some of them."

"You do me too much honor," he retorted suavely. "Shall we not go out, Miss Holiday? The garden is very beautiful by moonlight."

She bowed assent, and together they passed out of the room through the French window. Miss Cressy stared after them, the bitter little smile still lingering on her lips.

"Youth for Alan always," she said to herself. "Ah, well, I was young, too, those days in Paris. I must tell Carlotta to warn Tony. It would be a pity for the child to be tarnished so soon by touching his kind too close. She is so young and so lovely."

Alan and Tony strayed to a remote corner of the spacious gardens and came to a pause beside the fountain which leaped and splashed and caught the moonlight in its falling splendor. For a moment neither spoke. Tony bent to dip her fingers in the cool water. She had an odd feeling of needing lustration from something. The man's eyes were upon her. She was very young, very lovely, as Miss Cressy had said. There was something strangely moving to Alan Massey about her virginal freshness, her moonshine beauty. He was unaccustomed to compunction, but for a fleeting second, as he studied Tony Holiday standing there with bowed head, laving her hands in the sparkling purity of the water, he had an impulse to go away and leave her, lest he cast a shadow upon her by his lingering near her.

It was only for a moment. He was far too selfish to follow the brief urge to renunciation. The girl stirred his passion too deeply, roused his will to conquer too irresistibly to permit him to forego the privilege of the place and hour.

She looked up at him and he smiled down at her, once more the master-lover.

"I was right, was I not, *Toinetta mia*? I did make you a little bit mine, did I not? Be honest. Tell me." He laid a hand on each of her bare white shoulders, looked deep, deep into her brown eyes as if he would read secret things in their depths.

Tony drew away from his hands, dropped her gaze once more to the rippling white of the water, which was less disconcerting than Alan Massey's too ardent green eyes.

"You danced with me divinely. I shall also make you love me divinely even as I promised. You know it dear one. You cannot deny it," the magically beautiful voice which pulled so oddly at her heart strings went on softly, almost in a sort of chant. "You love me already, my white moonshine girl," he whispered. "Tell me you do."

"Ah but I don't," denied Tony. "I--I won't. I don't want to love anybody."

"You cannot help it, dear heart. Nature made you for loving and being loved. And it is I that you are going to love. Mine that you shall be. Tell me, did you ever feel before as you felt in there when we were dancing?"

"No," said Tony, her eyes still downcast.

"I knew it. You are mine, belovedest. I knew it the moment I saw you. It is Kismet. Kiss me."

"No." The girl pulled herself away from him, her face aflame.

"No? Then so." He drew her back to him, and lifted her face gently with his two hands. He bent over her, his lips close to hers.

"If you kiss me I'll never dance with you again as long as I live!" she flashed.

He laughed a little mockingly, but he lowered his hands, made no effort to gainsay her will.

"What a horrible threat, you cruel little moonbeam! But you wouldn't keep it. You couldn't. You love to dance with me too well."

"I would," she protested, the more sharply because she suspected he was right, that she would dance with him again, no matter what he did. "Any way I shall not dance with you again to-night. And I shall not stay out here with you any longer." She turned to flee, but he put out his hand and held her back.

"Not so fast, my Tony. They have eyes and ears in there. If you run away from me and go back with those glorious fires lit in your cheeks and in your eyes they will believe I did kiss you-."

"Oh!" gasped Tony, indignant but lingering, recognizing the probable truth of his prediction.

"We shall go together after a minute with sedateness, as if we had been studying the stars. I am wise, my Tony. Trust me."

"Very well," assented Tony. "How many stars are there in the Pleiades, anyway?" she asked with sudden imps of mirth in her eyes.

Again she felt on safe ground, sure that she had conquered and put a too presuming male in his place. She had no idea that the laurels had been chiefly not hers at all but Alan Massey's, who was quite as wise as he boasted.

But she kept her word and danced no more with Alan Massey that night. She did not dare. She hated Alan Massey, disapproved of him heartily and knew it would be the easiest thing in the world to fall in love with him, especially if she let herself dance often with him as they had danced to-night.

And so, her very first night at Crest House, Antoinette Holiday discovered that, there was such a thing as love after all, and that it had to be reckoned with whether you desired or not to welcome it at your door.

CHAPTER XI
THINGS THAT WERE NOT ALL ON THE CARD

After that first night in the garden Alan Massey did not try to make open love to Tony again, but his eyes, following her wherever she moved, made no secret of his adoration. He was nearly always by her side, driving off other devotees when he chose with a cool high-handedness which sometimes amused, sometimes infuriated Tony. She found the man a baffling and fascinating combination of qualities, all petty selfishness and colossal egotisms one minute, abounding in endless charms and graces and small endearing chivalries the next; outrageously outspoken at times, at other times, reticent to the point of secretiveness; now reaching the most extravagant pitch of high spirits, and then, almost without warning, submerged in moods of Stygian gloom from which nothing could rouse him.

Tony came to know something of his romantic and rather mottled career from Carlotta and others, even from Alan himself. She knew perfectly well he was not the kind of man Larry or her uncle would approve or tolerate. She disapproved of him rather heartily herself in many ways. At times she disliked him passionately, made up her mind she would have no more to do with him. At other times she was all but in love with him, and suspected she would have found the world an intolerably dull place with Alan Massey suddenly removed from it. When they danced together she was dangerously near being what he had claimed she was or would be--all his. She knew this, was afraid of it, yet she kept on dancing with him night after night. It seemed as if she had to, as if she would have danced with him even if she knew the next moment would send them both hurtling through space, like Lucifer, down to damnation.

It was not until Dick Carson came down for a week end, some time later, that Tony discovered the resemblance in Alan to some one she knew of which Carlotta had spoken. Incredibly and inexplicably Dick and Alan possessed a shadowy sort of similarity. In most respects they were as different in appearance as they were in personality. Dick's hair was brown and straight; Alan's, black and wavy. Dick's eyes were steady gray-blue; Alan's, shifty gray-green. Yet the resemblance was there, elusive, though it was. Perhaps it lay in the curve of the sensitive nostrils, perhaps in the firm contour of chin, perhaps in the arch of the brow. Perhaps it was nothing so tangible, just a fleeting trick of expression. Tony did not know, but she caught the thing just as Carlotta had and it puzzled and interested her.

She spoke of it to Alan the next morning after Dick's arrival, as they idled together, stretched out on the sand, waiting for the others to come out of the surf.

To her surprise he was instantly highly annoyed and resentful.

"For Heaven's sake, Tony, don't get the resemblance mania. It's a disgusting habit. I knew a woman once who was always chasing likenesses in people and prattling about them--got her in trouble once and served her right. She told a young lieutenant that he looked extraordinarily like a certain famous general of her acquaintance. It proved later that the young man had been born at the post where the general was stationed while the presumptive father was absent on a year's cruise. It had been quite a prominent scandal at the time."

"That isn't a nice story, Alan. Moreover it is entirely irrelevant. But you and Dick do look alike. I am not the only or the first person who saw it, either."

Alan started and frowned.

"Good Lord! Who else?" he demanded.

"Carlotta!"

"The devil she did!" Alan's eyes were vindictive. Then he laughed. "Commend me to a girl's imagination! This Dick chap seems to be head over heels in love with you," he added.

"What nonsense!" denied Tony crisply, fashioning a miniature sand mountain as she spoke.

"No nonsense at all, my dear. Perfectly obvious fact. Don't you suppose I know how a man looks when he is in love? I ought to. I've been in love often enough."

Tony demolished her mountain with a wrathful sweep of her hand.

"And registered all the appropriate emotions before the mirror, I suppose. You make me sick, Alan. You are all pose. I don't believe there is a single sincere thing about you."

"Oh, yes, there is--are--two."

"What are they?"

"One is my sincere devotion to yourself, my beautiful. The other--an equally sincere devotion to--*myself*."

"I grant you the second, at least."

"Don't pose, yourself, my darling. You know I love you. You pretend you don't believe it, but you do. And way down deep in your heart you love my love. It makes your heart beat fast just to think of it. See! Did I not tell you?" He had suddenly put out his hand and laid it over her heart.

"Poor little wild bird! How its wings flutter!"

Tony got up swiftly from the sand, her face scarlet. She was indignant, self-conscious, betrayed. For her heart had been beating at a fearful clip and she knew it.

"How dare you touch me like that, Alan Massey? I detest you. I don't see why I ever listen to you at all, or let you come near me."

Alan Massey, still lounging at her feet, looked up at her as she stood above him, slim, supple, softly rounded, adorably pretty and feminine in her black satin bathing suit and vivid, emerald hued cap.

"I know why," he said and rose, too, slowly, with the indolent grace of a leopard. "So do you, my Tony," he added. "We both know. Will you dance with me a great deal to-night?"

"No."

"How many times?"

"Not at all."

"Indeed! And does his Dick Highmightiness object to your dancing with me?"

"Dick! Of course not. He hasn't anything to do with it. I am not going to dance with you because you are behaving abominably to-day, and you did yesterday and the day before that. I think you are nearly always abominable, in fact."

"Still, I am one of the best dancers in the world. It is a temptation, is it not, my own?"

He smiled his slow, tantalizing smile and, in spite of herself, Tony smiled back.

"It is," she admitted. "You are a heavenly dancer, Alan. There is no denying it. If you were Mephisto himself I think I would dance with you--occasionally."

"And to-night?"

"Once," relented Tony. "There come the others at last." And she ran off down the yellow sands like a modern Atalanta.

"My, but Tony is pretty to-night!" murmured Carlotta to Alan, who chanced to be standing near her as her friend fluttered by with Dick. "She looks like a regular flame in that scarlet chiffon. It is awfully daring, but she is wonderful in it."

"She is always wonderful," muttered Alan moodily, watching the slender, graceful figure whirl and trip and flash down the floor like a gay poppy petal caught in the wind.

Carlotta turned. Something in Alan's tone arrested her attention.

"Alan, I believe, it is real with you at last," she said. Up to that moment she had considered his affair with Tony as merely another of his many adventures in romance, albeit possibly a slightly more extravagant one than usual.

"Of course it is real--real as Hell," he retorted. "I'm mad over her, Carla. I am going to marry her if I have to kill every man in the path to get to her," savagely.

"I am sorry, Alan. You must see Tony is not for the like of you. You can't get to her. I wish you wouldn't try."

Dick and Tony passed close to them again. Tony was smiling up at her partner and he was looking down at her with a gaze that betrayed his caring. Neither saw Alan and Carlotta. The savage light gleamed brighter in Alan's green eyes.

"Carlotta, is there anything between them?" he demanded fiercely.

"Nothing definite. He adores her, of course, and she is very fond of him. She feels as if he sort of belonged to her, I think. You know the story?"

"Tell me."

Briefly Carlotta outlined the tale of how Dick had taken refuge in the Holiday barn when he had run away from the circus, and how Tony had found him, sick and exhausted from fatigue, hunger and abuse; how the Holidays had taken him in and set him on his feet, and Tony had given him her own middle name of Carson since he had none of his own.

Alan listened intently.

"Did he ever get any clue as to his identity?" he asked as Carlotta paused.

"Never."

"Has he asked Tony to marry him?"

"I don't think so. I doubt if he ever does, so long as he doesn't know who he is. He is very proud and sensitive, and has an almost superstitious veneration for the Holiday tradition. Being a Holiday in New England is a little like being of royal blood, you know. I don't believe you will ever have to make a corpse of poor Dick, Alan."

"I don't mind making corpses. I rather think I should enjoy making one of him. I detest the long, lean animal."

Had Alan known it, Dick had taken quite as thorough a dislike to his magnificent self. At that very moment indeed, as he and Tony strolled in the garden, Dick had remarked that he wished Tony wouldn't dance with "that Massey."

"And why not?" she demanded, always quick to resent dictatorial airs.

"Because he makes you--well--conspicuous. He hasn't any business to dance with you the way he does. You aren't a professional but he makes you look like one."

"Thanks. A left-hand compliment but still a compliment!"

"It wasn't meant for one," said Dick soberly. "I hate it. Of course you dance wonderfully yourself. It isn't just dancing with you. It is poetry, stuff of dreams and all the rest of it. I can see that, and I know it must be a temptation to have a chance at a partner like that. Lord! Tony! No man in every day life has a right to dance the way he can. He out-classes Castle. I hate that kind of a man--half woman."

"There isn't anything of a woman about Alan, Dick. He is the most virulently male man I ever knew."

Dick fell silent at that. Presently he began again.

"Tony, please don't be offended at what I am going to say. I know it is none of my business, but I wish you wouldn't keep on with this affair with Massey."

"Why not?" There was an aggressive sparkle in Tony's eyes.

"People are talking. I heard them last night when you were dancing with him. It hurts. Alan Massey isn't the kind of a man for a girl like you to flirt with."

"Stuff and nonsense, Dicky! Any kind of a man is the kind for a girl to flirt with, if she keeps her head."

"But Tony, honestly, this Massey hasn't a good reputation."

"How do you know?"

"Newspaper men know a great deal. They have to. Besides, Alan Massey is a celebrity. He is written up in our files."

"What does that mean?"

"It means that if he should die to-morrow all we would have to do would be to put in the last flip. The biographical data is all on the card ready to shoot."

"Dear me. That's rather gruesome, isn't it?" shivered Tony. "I'm glad I'm not a celebrity. I'd hate to be stuck down on your old flies. Will I get on Alan's card if I keep on flirting with him?"

"Good Lord! I should hope not."

"I suppose I wouldn't be in very good company. I don't mean Alan. I mean--his ladies."

"Tony! Then you know?"

"About Alan's ladies? Oh, yes. He told me himself."

Dick looked blank. What was a man to do in a case like this, finding his big bugaboo no bugaboo at all?

"I know a whole lot about Alan Massey, maybe more than is on your old card. I know his mother was Lucia Vannini, so beautiful and so gifted that she danced in every court in Europe and was loved by a prince. I know how Cyril Massey, an American artist, painted her portrait and loved her and married her. I know how she worshiped him and was absolutely faithful to him to the day he died, when the very light of life went out for her."

"She managed to live rather cheerfully afterward, even without light, if all the stories about her are true," observed Dick, with, for him, unusual cynicism.

"You don't understand. She had to live."

"There are other ways of living than those she chose."

"Not for her. She knew only two things--love and dancing. She was thrown from a horse the next year after her husband died. Dancing was over for her. There was only--her beauty left. Her husband's people wouldn't have anything to do with her because she had been a dancer and because of the prince. Old John Massey, Cyril's uncle, turned her and her baby from his door, and his cousin John and his wife refused even to see her. She said she would make them hear of her before she died. She did."

"They heard all right. She, and her son too, must have been a thorn in the flesh of the Masseys. They were all rigid Puritans I understand, especially old John."

"Serve him right," sniffed Tony. "They were rolling in wealth. They might have helped her kept her from the other thing they condemned so. She wanted money only for Alan, especially after he began to show that he had more than his father's gifts. She earned it in the only way she knew. I don't blame her."

"Tony!"

"I can't help it if I am shocking you, Dick. I can understand why she did it. She didn't care anything about the lovers. She never cared for anyone after Cyril died. She gave herself for Alan. Can't you see that there was something rather fine about it? I can."

Dick grunted. He remembered hearing something about a woman whose sins were forgiven her because she loved much. But he couldn't reconcile himself to hearing such stories from Tony Holiday's lips. They were remote from the clean, sweet, wholesome atmosphere in which she belonged.

"Anyway, Alan was a wonderful success. He studied in Paris and he had pictures on exhibition in salons over there before he was twenty. He was feted and courted and flattered and--loved, until he thought the world was his and everything in it--including the ladies." Tony made a little face at this. She did not care very-much for that part of Alan's story, herself. "His mother was afraid he was going to have his head completely turned and would lose all she had gained so hard for him, so she made him come back to America and settle down. He did. He made a great name for himself before he was twenty-five as a portrait painter and he and his mother lived so happily together. She didn't need any more lovers then. Alan was all she needed. And then she died, and he went nearly crazy with grief, went all to pieces, every way. I suppose that part of his career is what makes you say he isn't fit for me to flirt with."

Dick nodded miserably.

"It isn't very pleasant for me to think of, either," admitted Tony. "I don't like it any better than you do. But he isn't like that any more. When old John Massey died without leaving any will Alan got all the money, because his cousin John and his stuck-up wife had died, too, and there was nobody else. Alan pulled up stakes and traveled all over the world, was gone two years and, when he came back, he wasn't dissipated any more. I don't say he is a saint now. He isn't, I know. But he got absolutely out of the pit he was in after his mother's death."

"Lucky for him they never found the baby John Massey, who was stolen," Dick remarked. "He would have been the heir if he could have appeared to claim the money instead of Alan Massey, who was only a grand nephew."

Tony stared.

"There wasn't any baby," she exclaimed.

"Oh yes, there was. John Massey, Junior, had a son John who was kidnapped when he was asleep in the park and deserted by his nurse who had gone to flirt with a policeman. There was a great fuss made about it at the time. The Masseys offered fabulous sums of money for the return of the child, but he never turned up. I had to dig up the story a few years ago when old John died, which is why I know so much about it."

"I don't believe Alan knew about the baby. He didn't tell me anything about it."

"I'll wager he knew, all right. It would be mighty unpleasant for him if the other Massey turned up now."

"Dick, I believe you would be glad if Alan lost the money," reproached Tony.

"Why no, Tony. It's nothing to me, but I've always been sorry for that other Massey kid, though he doesn't know what he missed and is probably a jail-bird or a janitor by this time, not knowing he is heir to one of the biggest properties in America."

"Sorry to disturb your theories, Mr.--er Carson," remarked Alan Massey, suddenly appearing on the scene. "My cousin John happens to be neither a jail-bird nor a janitor, but merely comfortably dead. Lucky John!"

"But Dick said he wasn't dead--at least that nobody knew whether he was or not," objected Tony.

"Unfortunately your friend is in error. John Massey is entirely dead, I assure you. And now, if he is quite through with me and my affairs, perhaps Mr. Carson will excuse you. Come, dear."

Alan laid a hand on Tony's arm with a proprietorial air which made Dick writhe far more than his insulting manner to himself had done. Tony looked quickly from one to the other. She hated the way Alan was behaving, but she did not want to precipitate a scene and yielded, leaving Dick, with a deprecatory glance, to go with Alan.

"I don't like your manner," she told the latter. "You were abominably rude just now."

"Forgive me, sweetheart. I apologize. That young man of yours sets my teeth on edge. I can't abide a predestined parson. I'll wager anything he has been preaching at you." He smiled ironically as he saw the girl flush. "So he did preach,--and against me, I suppose."

"He did, and quite right, too. You are not at all a proper person for me to flirt with, just as he said. Even Miss Lottie told me that and when Miss Lottie objects to a man it means--"

"That she has failed to hold him herself," said Alan cynically. "Stop, Tony. I want to say something to you before we go in. I am not a proper person. I told you that myself. There have been other women in my life--a good many of them. I told you that, too. But that has absolutely nothing to do with you and me. I love you. You are the only woman I ever have loved in the big sense, at least the only one I have ever wanted to marry. I am like my mother. She had many lesser loves. She had only one great one. She married him. And I shall marry you."

"Alan, don't. It is foolish--worse than foolish to talk like that. My people would never let me marry you, even if I wanted to. Dick was speaking for them just now when he warned me against you."

"He was speaking for himself. Damn him!"

"Alan!"

"I beg your pardon, Tony. I'm a brute to-night. I am sorry. I won't trouble you any more. I won't even keep you to your promise to dance once with me if you wish to be let off."

The music floated out to them, called insistently to Tony's rhythm-mad feet and warm young blood.

"Ah, but I do want to dance with you," she sighed. "I don't want to be let off. Come."

He bent over her, a flash of triumph in his eyes.

"My own!" he exulted. "You are my own. Kiss me, belovedest."

But Tony pulled away from him and he followed her. A moment later the scarlet flame was in his arms whirling down the hall to the music of the violins, and Dick, standing apart by the window watching, tasted the dregs of the bitterest brew life had yet offered him. Better, far better than Tony Holiday he knew where the scarlet flame was blowing.

His dance with Tony over, Alan retired to the library where he used the telephone to transmit a wire to Boston, a message addressed to one James Roberts, a retired circus performer.

CHAPTER XII
AND THERE IS A FLAME

When Alan Massey strayed into the breakfast room, one of the latest arrivals at that very informal meal, he found a telegram awaiting him. It was rather an odd message and ran thus, without capitalization or punctuation. "Town named correct what is up let sleeping dogs lie sick." Alan frowned as he thrust the yellow envelope into his pocket.

"Does the fool mean he is sick, I wonder," he cogitated. "Lord, I wish I could let well enough alone. But this sword of Damocles business is beginning to get on my nerves. I have half a mind to take a run into town this afternoon and see the old reprobate. I'll bet he doesn't know as much as he claims to, but I'd like to be sure before he dies."

Just then Tony Holiday entered, clad in a rose hued linen and looking like a new blown rose herself.

"You are the latest ever," greeted Carlotta.

"On the contrary I have been up since the crack of dawn," denied Tony, slipping into a seat beside her friend.

Carlotta opened her eyes wide. Then she understood.

"You got up to see Dick off," she announced.

"I did. Please give me some strawberries, Hal, if you don't mean to eat the whole pyramid yourself. I not only got up, but I went to the station; not only went to the station, but I walked the whole mile and a half. Can anybody beat that for a morning record?" Tony challenged as she deluged her berries with cream.

Alan Massey uttered a kind of a snarling sound such as a lion disturbed from a nap might have emitted. He had thought he was through with Carson when the latter had made his farewells the night before, saying goodnight to Tony before them all. But Tony had gotten up at some ridiculously early hour to escort him to the station, and did not mind everybody's knowing it. He subsided into a dense mood of gloom. The morning had begun badly.

Later he discovered Tony in the rose garden with a big basket on her arm and a charming drooping sun hat shading her even more charming face. She waved him away as he approached.

"Go away," she ordered. "I'm busy."

"You mean you have made up your mind to be disagreeable to me," he retorted, lighting a cigarette and looking as if he meant to fight it out along that line if it took all summer.

Tony snipped off a rose with her big shears and dropped it into her basket. It rather looked as if she were meaning to snip off Alan Massey figuratively in much the same ruthless manner.

"Put it that way, if you like. Only stay away. I mean it."

"Why?" he persisted.

Thus pressed she turned and faced him.

"It is a lovely morning--all blue and gold and clean-washed after last night's storm--a good morning. I'm feeling good, too. The clean morning has got inside of me. And when you come near me I feel a pricking in my thumbs. You don't fit into my present, mood. Please go, Alan. I am perfectly serious. I don't want to talk to you."

"What have I done? I am no different from what I was yesterday."

"I know. It isn't anything you have done. It isn't you at all. It is I who am different--or want to be." Tony spoke earnestly. She was perfectly sincere. She did want to be different. She had not slept well the night before. She had thought a great deal about Holiday Hill and Uncle Phil and her brothers and--well, yes--about Dick Carson. They all armed her against Alan Massey.

Alan threw away his cigarette with an angry gesture.

"You can't play fast and loose with me, Tony Holiday. You have been leading me on, playing the devil with me for days. You know you have. Now you are scared, and want to get back to shallow water. It is too late. You are in deep seas and you've got to stay there--with me."

"I haven't **got** to do anything, Alan. You are claiming more than you have any right to claim."

But he came nearer, towered above her, almost menacingly.

"Because that nameless fool of a reporter with his sanctimonious airs and impeccable morals, has put you against me you want to sack me. You can't do it. Last night you were ready to go any lengths with me. You know it. Do you think I am going to be balked by a miserable circus brat--a mere nobody? Not so long as I am Alan Massey. Count on that."

Tony's dark eyes were ablaze with anger.

"Stop there, Alan. You are saying things that are not true. And I forbid you ever to speak of Dick like that again to me."

"Indeed! And how are you going to prevent my saying what I please about your precious protege?" sneered Alan.

"I shall tell Carlotta I won't stay under the same roof with anybody who insults my friends. You won't have to restrain yourself long in any case. I am leaving Saturday--perhaps sooner."

"Tony!" The sneer died away from Alan's face, which had suddenly grown white. "You mustn't go. I can't live without you, my darling. If you knew how I worshiped you, how I cannot sleep of nights for wanting you, you wouldn't talk of going away from me. I was brutal just now. I admit it. It is because I love you so. The thought of your turning from me, deserting me, maddened me. I am not responsible for what I said. You must forgive me. But, oh my belovedest, you are mine! Don't try to deny it. We have belonged to each other for always. You know it. You feel it. I have seen the knowledge in your eyes, felt it flutter in your heart. Will you marry me, Tony Holiday? You shall be loved as no woman was ever loved. You shall be my queen. I will be true to you forever and ever, your slave, your mate. Tony, Tony, say yes. You must!"

But Tony drew back from him, frightened, repulsed, shocked, by the storm of his passion which shook him as mighty trees are shaken by tempests. She shrank from the hungry fires in his eyes, from the abandon and fierceness of his wooing. It was an alien, disturbing, dreadful thing to her.

"Don't," she implored. "You mustn't love me like that, Alan. You must not."

"How can I help it, sweetheart? I am no iceberg. I am a man and you are the one woman in the world for me. I love you--love you. I want you. I'm going to have you--make you mine--marry you, bell and book, what you will, so long as you are mine--mine--mine."

Tony set down her basket, clasped her hands behind her and stood looking straight up into his face.

"Listen, Alan. I cannot marry you. I couldn't, even if I loved you, and I don't think I do love you, though you fascinate me and, when we are dancing, I forget all the other things in you that I hate. I have been very foolish and maybe unkind to let it go on so far. I didn't quite know what I was doing. Girls don't know. That is why they play with men as they do. They don't mean to be cruel. They just don't know."

"But you know now, my Tony?" His dark, stormy face was very close to hers. Tony felt her heart leap but she did not flinch nor pull away this time.

"Yes, Alan, I know, in a way, at least. We mustn't go on like this. It is bad for us both. I'll tell Carlotta I am going home to-morrow."

"You want--to go away from me?" The haunting music of his voice, more moving in its hurt than in its mastery of mood, stirred Tony Holiday profoundly, but she steadied herself by a strong effort of will. She must not let him sweep her away from her moorings. She must not. She must remember Holiday Hill very hard.

"I have to, Alan," she said. "I am very sorry if I have hurt you, am hurting you. But I can't marry you. That is final. The sooner we end things the better."

"By God! It isn't final. It never will be so long as you and I are both alive. You will come to me of your own accord. You will love me. You do love me now. But you are letting the world come in between where it has no right to come. I tell you you are mine--mine!"

"No, no!" denied Tony.

"And I say yes, my love. You are my love. I have set my seal upon you. You can go away, back to your Hill, but you will not be happy without me. You will never forget me for a waking moment. You cannot. You are a part of me, forever."

There was something solemn, inexorable in Alan's tones. A strange fear clutched at Tony's heart. Was he right? Could she never forget him? Would he always be a part of her--forever? No, that was nonsense! How could it be true? How could he have set his seal upon her when he had never even kissed her? She would not let him hypnotize her into believing his prophecy.

She stooped mechanically to pick up her roses and remembered the story of Persephone gathering lilies in the vale of Enna and suddenly borne off by the coal black horses of Dis to the dark kingdom of the lower world. Was she Persephone? Had she eaten of the pomegranate seeds while she danced night after night in Alan

Massey's arms? No, she would not believe it. She was free. She would exile Alan Massey from her heart and life. She must.

This resolve was in her eyes as she lifted them to Alan's. The fire had died out of his now, and his face was gray and drawn in the sunshine. His mood had changed as his moods so often did swiftly.

"Forgive me, Tony," he said humbly. "I have troubled you, frightened you. I am sorry. You needn't go away. I will go. I don't want to spoil one moment of happiness for you. I never shall, except when the devil is in me. Please try to remember that. Say always, 'Alan loves me. No matter what he does or says, he loves me. His love is real, if nothing else about him is.' You do believe that, don't you, dearest?" he pleaded.

"I do, Alan. I have always believed it, I think, ever since that first night, though I have tried not to. I am very sorry though. Love--your kind of love is a fearful thing. I am afraid of it."

"It is fearful, but beautiful too--very beautiful--like fire. Did you ever think what a strange dual element fire is? It consumes--is a force of destruction. But it also purifies, burns out dross. Love is like that, my Tony. Mine for you may damn me forever, or it may take me to the very gate of Heaven. I don't know myself which it will be."

As he spoke there was a strange kind of illumination on his face, a look almost of spiritual exaltation. It awed Tony, bereft her of words. This was a new Alan Massey--an Alan Massey she had never seen before, and she found herself looking up instead of down at him.

He stooped and kissed her hand reverently, as a devotee might pay homage at the shrine of a saint.

"I shall not see you again until to-night, Tony. I am going into town. But I shall be back--for one more dance with you, heart's dearest. And then I promise I will go away and leave you tomorrow. You will dance with me, Tony--once? We shall have that one perfect thing to remember?"

Tony bowed assent. And in a moment she was alone with her roses.

That afternoon she shut herself in her room to write letters to the home people whom she had neglected badly of late. Every moment had been so full since she had come to Carlotta's. There had been so little time to write and when she had written it had given little of what she was really living and feeling--just the mere externals and not all of them, as she was very well aware. They would never understand her relation with Alan. They would disapprove, just as Dick had disapproved. Perhaps she did not understand, herself, why she had let herself get so deeply entangled in something which could not go on, something, which was the profoundest folly, if nothing worse.

The morning had crystallized her fear of the growing complication of the situation. She was glad Alan was going away, glad she had had the strength of will to deny him his will, glad that she could now--after to-night--come back into undisputed possession of the kingdom of herself. But in her heart she was gladder that there was to-night and that one last dance with Alan Massey before life became simple and sane and tame again, and Alan and his wild love passed out of it forever.

She finished her letters, which were not very satisfactory after all. How could one write real letters when one's pen was writing one thing and one's thoughts were darting hither and thither about very different business? She threw herself in the chaise longue, not yet ready to dress and go down to join the others. There was nobody there she cared to talk to, somehow. Alan was not there. Nobody else mattered. It had come to that.

Idly she picked up a volume of verse that lay beside her on the table and fluttered its pages, seeking something to meet her restless mood. Presently in her vagrant seeking she chanced upon a little poem--a poem she read and reread, twice, three times.

"For there is a flame that has blown too near, And there is a name that has grown too dear,   And there is a fear. And to the still hills and cool earth and far sky I make moan. The heart in my bosom is not my own! Oh, would I were free as the wind on wing! Love is a terrible thing!"

Tony laid the book face down upon the table, still open at the little verse. The shadows were growing long out there in the dusk. The late afternoon sun was pale honey color. A soft little breeze stirred the branches of a weeping willow tree and set them to swaying languorously. Unseen birds twittered happily among the shrubbery. A golden butterfly poised for a moment above the white holly hocks and then drifted off over the flaming scarlet poppies and was lost to sight.

It was all so beautiful, so serene. She felt that it should have come like a benediction, cooling the fever of her tired mind, but it did not. It could not even drive the words of the poem out of her head.

Oh, would I were free as the wind on wing! Love is a terrible thing!

CHAPTER XIII
BITTER FRUIT

From the North Station in Boston Alan Massey directed his course to a small cigar store on Atlantic Avenue. A black eyed Italian lad in attendance behind the counter looked up as he entered and surveyed him with grave scrutiny.

"I am Mr. Massey," announced Alan. "Mr. Roberts is expecting me. I wired."

"Jim's sick," said the boy briefly.

"I am sorry. I hope he is not too sick to see me."

"Naw, he'll see you. He wants to." The speaker motioned Alan to follow him to the rear of the store. Together they mounted some narrow stairs, passed through a hallway and into a bedroom, a disorderly, dingy, obviously man-kept affair. On the bed lay a large framed, exceedingly ugly looking man. His flesh was yellow and sagged loosely away from his big bones. The impression he gave was one of huge animal bulk, shriveling away in an unlovely manner, getting ready to disintegrate entirely. The man was sick undoubtedly. Possibly dying. He looked it.

The door shut with a soft click. The two men were alone.

"Hello, Jim." Alan approached the bed. "Bad as this? I am sorry." He spoke with the careless, easy friendliness he could assume when it suited him.

The man grinned, faintly, ironically. The grin did not lessen the ugliness of his face, rather accentuated it.

"It's not so bad," he drawled. "Nothing but death and what's that? I don't suffer much--not now. It's cancer, keeps gnawing away like a rat in the wall. By and by it will get up to my heart and then it's good-by Jim. I shan't care. What's life good for that a chap should cling to it like a barnacle on a rock?"

"We do though," said Alan Massey.

"Oh, yes, we do. It's the way we're made. We are always clinging to something, good or bad. Life, love, home, drink, power, money! Always something we are ready to sell our souls to get or keep. With you and me it was money. You sold your soul to me to keep money and I took it to get money."

He laughed raucously and Alan winced at the sound and cursed the morbid curiosity that had brought him to the bedside of this man who for three years past had held his own future in his dirty hand, or claimed to hold it. Alan Massey had paid, paid high for the privilege of not knowing things he did not wish to know.

"What kind of a trail had you struck when you wired me, Massey? I didn't know you were anxious for details about young John Massey's career I thought you preferred ignorance. It was what you bought of me."

"I know it was," groaned Alan, dropping into a creaking rocker beside the bed. "I am a fool. I admit it. But sometimes it seems to me I can't stand not knowing. I want to squeeze what you know out of you as you would squeeze a lemon until there was nothing left but bitter pulp. It is driving me mad."

The sick man eyed the speaker with a leer of malicious satisfaction. It was meat to his soul to see this lordly young aristocrat racked with misery and dread, to hold him in his power as a cat holds a mouse, which it can crush and crunch at any moment if it will. Alan Massey's mood filled Jim Roberts with exquisite enjoyment, enjoyment such as a gourmand feels on setting his teeth in some rare morsel of food.

"I know," he nodded. "It works like that often. They say a murderer can't keep away from the scene of his crime if he is left at large. There is an irresistible fascination to him about the spot where he damned his immortal soul."

"I'm not a criminal," snarled Alan. "Don't talk to me like that or you will never see another cent of my money."

"Money!" sneered the sick man. "What's that to me now? I've lost my taste for money. It is no good to me any more. I've got enough laid by to bury me and I can't take the rest with me. Your money is nothing to me, Alan Massey. But you'll pay still, in a different way. I am glad you came. It is doing me good."

Alan made a gesture of disgust and got to his feet, pacing to and fro, his face dark, his soul torn, between conflicting emotions.

"I'll be dead soon," went on the malicious, purring voice from the bed. "Don't begrudge me my last fling. When I am in my grave you will be safe. Nobody in the living world but me knows young John Massey's alive. You can keep your money then with perfect ease of mind until you get to where I am now and then,--maybe you will find out the money will comfort you no longer, that nothing but having a soul can get you over the river."

The younger man's march came to a halt by the bedside.

"You shan't die until you tell me what you know about John Massey," he said fiercely.

"You're a fool," said James Roberts. "What you don't know you are not responsible for--you can forget in a way. If you insist on hearing the whole story you will never be able to get away from it to your dying day. John Massey as an abstraction is one thing. John Massey as a live human being, whom you have cheated out of a name and a fortune, is another."

"I never cheated him of a name. You did that."

The man grunted.

"Right. That is on my bill. Lord knows, I wish it wasn't. Little enough did I ever get out of that particular piece of deviltry. I over-reached myself, was a darned little bit too smart. I held on to the boy, thinking I'd get more out of it later, and he slid out of my hands like an eel and I had nothing to show for it, until you came along and I saw a chance to make a new deal at your expense. You fell for it like a lamb to the slaughter. I'll never forget your face when I told you John Massey was alive and that I could produce him in a minute for the courts. If I had, your name would have been Dutch, young man. You'd never have gotten a look in on the money. You had the sense to see that. Old John died without a will. His grandson and not his grand-nephew was his heir provided anybody could dig up the fellow, and I was the boy that could do that. I proved that to you, Alan Massey."

"You proved nothing. You scared me into handing you over a whole lot of money, you blackmailing rascal, I admit that. But you didn't prove anything. You showed me the baby clothes you said John Massey wore when he was stolen. The name might easily enough have been stamped on the linen later. You showed me a silver rattle marked 'John Massey.' The inscription might also easily enough have been added later at a crook's convenience. You showed me some letters purporting to have been written by the woman who stole the child and was too much frightened by her crime to get the gains she planned to win from it. The letters, too, might easily have been forgery. The whole thing might have been a cock and bull story, fabricated by a rotten, clever mind like yours, to apply the money screw to me."

"True," chuckled Jim Roberts. "Quite true. I wondered at your credulity at the time."

"You rat! So it was all a fake, a trap?"

"You would like to believe that, wouldn't you? You would like to have a dying man's oath that there was nothing but a pack of lies to the whole thing, blackmail of the crudest, most unsupportable variety?"

Alan bent over the man, shook his fist in the evil, withered old face.

"Damn you, Jim Roberts! Was it a lie or was it not?"

"Keep your hands off me, Alan Massey. It was the truth. Sarah Nelson did steal the child just as I told you. She gave the child to me when she was dying a few months later. I'll give my oath on that if you like."

Alan brushed his hand across his forehead, and sat down again limply in the creaking rocker.

"Oh, you are willing to believe that again now, are you?" mocked Roberts.

"I've got to, I suppose. Go on. Tell me the rest. I've got to know. Did you really make a circus brat of John Massey and did he really run away from you? That is all you told me before, you remember."

"It was all you wanted to know. Besides," the man smiled his diabolical grin again, "there was a reason for going light on the details. At the time I held you up I hadn't any more idea than you had where John Massey was, nor whether he was even alive. It was the weak spot in my armor. But you were so panic stricken at the thought of having to give up your gentleman's fortune that you never looked at the hollowness of the thing. You could have bowled over my whole scheme in a minute by being honest and telling me to bring on your cousin, John Massey. But you didn't. You were only too afraid I would bring him on before you could buy me off. I knew I could count on your being blind and rotten. I knew my man."

"Then you don't know now whether John Massey is alive or not?" Alan asked after a pause during which he let the full irony of the man's confession sink into his heart and turn there like a knife in a wound.

"That is where you're dead wrong. I do know. I made it my business to find out. It was too important to have an invulnerable shield not to patch up the discrepancy as early as possible. It took me a year to get my facts and it cost a good chink of the filthy, but I got them. I not only know that John Massey is alive but I know where he is and what he is doing. I could send for him to-morrow, and cook your goose for you forever, young man."

He pulled himself up on one elbow to peer into Alan's gloomy face.

"I may do it yet," he added. "You needn't offer me hush money. It's no good to me, as I told you. I don't want money. I only want to pass the time until the reaper comes along. You'll grant that it would be amusing to me to watch the see-saw tip once more, to see you go down and your cousin John come up."

Alan was on his feet again now, striding nervously from door to window and back again. He had wanted to know. Now he knew. He had knowledge bitter as wormwood. The man had lied before. He was not lying now.

"What made you send that wire? Were you on the track, too, trying to find out on your own where your cousin is?"

"Not exactly. Lord knows I didn't want to know. But I had a queer hunch. Some coincidences bobbed up under my nose that I didn't like the looks of. I met a young man a few days ago that was about the age John would have been, a chap with a past, who had run away from a circus. The thing stuck in my crop, especially as there was a kind of shadowy resemblance between us that people noticed."

"That is interesting. And his name?"

"He goes under the name of Carson--Richard Carson."

Roberts nodded.

"The same. Good boy. You have succeeded in finding your cousin. Congratulations!" he cackled maliciously.

"Then it really is he?"

"Not a doubt of it. He was taken up by a family named Holiday in Dunbury, Massachusetts. They gave him a home, saw that he got some schooling, started him on a country newspaper. He was smart, took to books, got ahead, was promoted from one paper to another. He is on a New York daily now, making good still, I'm told. Does it tally?"

Alan bowed assent. It tallied all too well. The lad he had insulted, jeered at, hated with instinctive hate, was his cousin, John Massey, the third, whom he had told the other was quite dead. John Massey was very much alive and was the rightful heir to the fortune which Alan Massey was spending as the heavens had spent rain yesterday.

It was worse than that. If the other was no longer nameless, had the right to the same fine, old name that Alan himself bore, and had too often disgraced, the barrier between him and Tony Holiday was swept away. That was the bitterest drop in the cup. No wonder he hated Dick--hated him now with a cumulative, almost murderous intensity. He had mocked at the other, but how should he stand against him in fair field? It was he--Alan Massey--that was the outcast, his mother a woman of doubtful fame, himself a follower of false fires, his life ignoble, wayward, erratic, unclean? Would it not be John rather than Alan Massey Tony Holiday would choose, if she knew all? This ugly, venomous, sin-scarred old rascal held his fate in the hollow of his evil old hand.

The other was watching him narrowly, evidently striving to follow his thoughts.

"Well?" he asked. "Going to beat me at my own game, give your cousin his due?"

"No," curtly.

"Queer," mused the man. "A month ago I would have understood it. It would have seemed sensible enough to hold on to the cold cash at any risk. Now it looks different. Money is filthy stuff, man. It is what they put on dead eye-lids to keep them down. Sometimes we put it on our own living lids to keep us from seeing straight. You are sure the money's worth so much to you, Alan Massey?"

The man's eyes burned livid, like coals. It was a strange and rather sickening thing, Alan Massey thought, to hear him talk like this after having lived the rottenest kind of a life, sunk in slime for years.

"The money is nothing to me," he flung back. "Not now. I thought it was worth considerable when I drove that devilish bargain with you to keep it. It has been worse than nothing, if you care to know. It killed my art--the only decent thing about me--the only thing I had a right to take honest pride in. John Massey might have every penny of it to-morrow for all I care if that were all there were to it."

"What else is there?" probed the old man.

"None of your business," snarled Alan. Not for worlds would he have spoken Tony Holiday's name in this spot, under the baleful gleam of those dying eyes.

The man chuckled maliciously.

"You don't need to tell me, I know. There's always a woman in it when a man takes the path to Hell. Does she want money? Is that why you must hang on to the filthy stuff?"

"She doesn't want anything except what I can't give her, thanks to you and myself--the love of a decent man."

"I see. When we meet *the* woman we wish we'd sowed fewer wild oats. I went through that myself once. She was a white lily sort of girl and I--well, I'd gone the pace long before I met her. I wasn't fit to touch her and I knew it. I went down fast after that--nothing to keep me back. Old Shakespeare says something somewhere about our pleasant vices beings whips to goad us with. You and I can understand that, Alan Massey. We've both felt the lash."

Alan made an impatient gesture. He did not care to be lumped with this rotten piece of flesh lying there before him.

"I suppose you are wondering what my next move is," went on Roberts.

"I don't care."

"Oh yes, you do. You care a good deal. I can break you, Alan Massey, and you know it."

"Go ahead and break and be damned if you choose," raged Alan.

"Exactly. As I choose. And I can keep you dancing on some mighty hot grid-irons before I shuffle off. Don't forget that, Alan Massey. And there will be several months to dance yet, if the doctors aren't off their count."

"Suit yourself. Don't hurry about dying on my account," said Alan with ironical courtesy.

A few moments later he was on his way back to the station. His universe reeled. All he was sure was that he loved Tony Holiday and would fight to the last ditch to win and keep her and that she would be in his arms to-night for perhaps the last time. The rest was a hideous blur.

CHAPTER XIV
SHACKLES

The evening was a specially gala occasion, with a dinner dance on, the last big party before Tony went home to her Hill. The great ball room at Crest House had been decorated with a network of greenery and crimson rambler roses. A ruinous-priced, *de luxe* orchestra had been brought down from the city. The girls had saved their prettiest gowns and looked their rainbow loveliest for the crowning event.

Tony was wearing an exquisite white chiffon and silver creation, with silver slippers and a silver fillet binding her dark hair. Alan had sent her some wonderful orchids tied with silver ribbon, and these she wore; but no jewelry whatever, not even a ring. There was something particularly radiant about her young loveliness that night. The young men hovered about her like honey bees about a rose and at every dance they cut in and cut in until her white and silver seemed to be drifting from one pair of arms to another.

Tony was very gay and bountiful and impartial in her smiles and favors, but all the time she waited, knowing that presently would come the one dance to which there would be no cutting in, the dance that would make the others seem nothing but shadows.

By and by the hour struck. She saw Alan leave his place by the window where he had been moodily lounging, saw him come toward her, taller than any man in the room, distinguished--a king among the rest, it seemed to Tony, waiting, longing for his coming? yet half dreading it, too. For the sooner he came, the sooner it must all end. She was with Hal at the moment, waiting for the music to begin, but as Alan approached she turned to her companion with a quick appeal in her eyes and a warm flush on her cheeks.

"I am sorry, Hal," she said, low in his ear. "But this is Alan's. He is going away to-morrow. Forgive me."

Hal turned, stared at Alan Massey, turned back to Tony, bowed and moved away.

"Hanged if there isn't something magnificent about the fellow," he thought. "No matter how you detest him there is something about him that gets you. I wonder how far he has gone with Tony. Gee! It's a rotten combination. But Lordy! How they can dance--those two!"

Never as long as she lived was Tony Holiday to forget that dance with Alan Massey. As a musician pours himself into his violin, as a poet puts his soul into his sonnet, as a sculptor chisels his dream in marble, so her companion flung his passion and despair and imploring into his dancing. They forgot the others, forgot everything but themselves. They might have been dancing alone on the top of Olympus for all either knew or cared for the rest of the world.

It was Alan, not Tony, who brought it to an end, however. He whispered something in the girl's ear and their feet paused. In a moment he was holding open the French window for her to pass out into the night. The white and silver vanished like a cloud. Alan Massey followed. The window swung shut again. The music stopped abruptly as if now its inspiration had come to an end. A single note of a violin quivered off into silence after the others, like the breath of beauty itself passing.

Carlotta and her aunt happened to be standing near each other. The girl's eyes were troubled. She wished Alan had not come back at all from the city. She hoped he really intended to go away to-morrow as he had told her. More than all she hoped she was right in believing that Tony had refused to marry him. Like Dick, Carlotta had reverence for the Holiday tradition. She could not bear to think of Tony's marrying Alan. She felt woefully responsible for having brought the two together.

"Did you say he was going to-morrow?" asked her aunt.

Carlotta nodded.

"He won't go," prophesied Miss Cressy.

"Oh, yes. I think he will. I don't know for certain but I have an idea she refused him this morning."

"Ah, but that was this morning. Things look very different by star light. That child ought not to be out there with him. She is losing her head."

"Aunt Lottie! Alan is a gentleman," demurred Carlotta.

Miss Lottie smiled satirically. Her smile repeated Ted Holiday's verdict that some gentlemen were rotters.

"You forget, my dear, that I knew Alan Massey when you and Tony were in short petticoats and pigtails. You can't trust too much to his gentlemanliness."

"Of course, I know he isn't a saint," admitted Carlotta. "But you don't understand. It is real with Alan this time. He really cares. It isn't just--just the one thing."

"It is always the one thing with Alan Massey's kind. I know what I am talking about, Carlotta. He was a little in love with me once. I dare say we both thought it was different at the time. It wasn't. It was pretty much the same thing. Don't cherish any romantic notions about love, Carlotta. There isn't any love as you mean it."

"Oh yes, there is," denied Carlotta suddenly, a little fiercely. "There is love, but most of us aren't--aren't worthy of it. It is too big for us. That is why we get the cheap *little* stuff. It is all we are fit for."

Miss Carlotta stared at her niece. But before she could speak Hal Underwood had claimed the latter for a dance.

"H--m!" she mused looking after the two. "So even Carlotta isn't immune. I wonder who he was."

Meanwhile, out in the garden Tony and Alan had strayed over to the fountain, just as they had that first evening after that first dance.

"Tony, belovedest, let me speak. Listen to me just once more. You do love me. Don't lie to me with your lips when your eyes told me the truth in there. You are mine, mine, my beautiful, my love--all mine."

He drew her into his arms, not passionately but gently. It was his gentleness that conquered. A storm of unrestrained emotion would have driven her away from him, but his sudden quiet strength and tenderness melted her last reservation. She gave her lips unresisting to his kiss. And with that kiss, desire of freedom and all fear left her. For the moment, at least, love was all and enough.

"Tony, my belovedest," he whispered. "Say it just once. Tell me you love me." It was the old, old plea, but in Tony's ears it was immortally new.

"I love you, Alan. I didn't want to. I have fought it all along as you know. But it was no use. I do love you."

"My darling! And I love you. You don't know how I love you. It is like suddenly coming out into sunshine after having lived in a cave all my life. Will you marry me to-morrow, *carissima*?"

But she drew away from his arms at that.

"Alan, I can't marry you ever. I can only love you."

"Why not? You must, Tony!" The old masterfulness leaped into his voice.

"I cannot, Alan. You know why."

She lifted her eyes to his and in their clear depths he saw reflected his own willful, stained, undisciplined past. He bowed his head in real shame and remorse. Nothing stood between himself and Antoinette Holiday but himself. He had sown the wind. He reaped the whirlwind.

After a moment he looked up again. He made no pretence of misunderstanding her meaning.

"You couldn't forgive?" he pleaded brokenly. Gone was the royal-willed Alan Massey. Only a beggar in the dust remained.

"Yes, Alan. I could forgive. I do now. I think I can understand how such things can be in a man's life though it would break my heart to think Ted or Larry were like that. But you never had a chance. Nobody ever helped you to keep your eyes on the stars."

"They are there now," he groaned. "You are my star, Tony, and stars are very, very far away from the like of me," he echoed Carlotta's phrase.

For almost the first time in his life humility possessed him. Had he known it, it lifted him higher in Tony's eyes than all his arrogance and conceit of power had ever done.

Gently she slid her hand into his.

"I don't feel far away, Alan. I feel very near. But I can't marry you--not now anyway. You will have to prove to them all--to me, too--that you are a man a Holiday might be proud to marry. I could forget the past. I think I could persuade Uncle Phil and the rest to forget it, too. They are none of them self-righteous Puritans. They could understand, just as I understand, that a man might fall in battle and carry scars of defeat, but not be really conquered. Alan, tell me something. It isn't easy to ask but I must. Are the things I have to forget far back in the past or--nearer? I know they go back to Paris days, the days Miss Lottie belongs to. Oh, yes," as he started at that. "I guessed that. You mustn't blame her. She was merely trying to warn me. She meant it for my good, not to be spiteful and not because she still cares, though I think she does. And I know there are things that belong to the time after your mother died, and you didn't care what you did because you were so unhappy. But are they still nearer? How close are they, Alan?"

He shook his head despairingly.

"I wish I could lie to you, Tony. I can't. They are too close to be pleasant to remember. But they never will be again. I swear it. Can you believe it?"

"I shall have to believe it--be convinced of it before I could marry you. I can't marry you, not being certain of you, just because my heart beats fast when you come near me, because I love your voice and your kisses and would rather dance with you than to be sure of going to Heaven. Marriage is a world without end business. I can't rush into it blindfold. I won't."

"You don't love me as I love you or you couldn't reason so coldly about it," he reproached. "You would go blindfold anywhere--to Hell itself even, with me."

"I don't know, Alan. I could let myself go. While we were dancing in there I am afraid I would have been willing to go even as far as you say with you. But out here in the star-light I am back being myself. I want to make my life into something clean and sweet and fine. I don't want to let myself be driven to follow weak, selfish, rash impulses and do things that will hurt other people and myself. I don't want to make my people sorry. They are dearer than any happiness of my own. They would not let me marry you now, even if I wished it. If I did what you want and what maybe something in me wants too--run off and marry you tomorrow without their consent--it would break their hearts and mine, afterward when I had waked up to what I had done. Don't ask me, dear. I couldn't do it."

"But what will you do, Tony? Won't you marry me ever?" Alan's tone was helpless, desolate. He had run up against a power stronger than any he had ever wielded, a force which left him baffled.

"I don't know. It will depend upon you. A year from now, if you still want me and I am still free, if you can come to me and tell me you have lived for twelve months as a man who loves a woman ought to live, I will marry you if I love you enough; and I think--I am sure, I shall, for I love you very much this minute."

"A year! Tony, I can't wait a year for you. I want you now." Alan's tone was sharp with dismay. He was not used to waiting for what he desired. He had taken it on the instant, as a rule, and as a rule, his takings had been dust and ashes as soon as they were in his hands.

"You cannot have me, Alan. You can never have me unless you earn the right to win me--straight. Understand that once for all. I will not marry a weakling. I will marry--a conquerer--perhaps."

"You mean that, Tony?"

"Absolutely."

"Then, by God, I'll be a conquerer!" he boasted.

"I hope you will. Oh, my dear, my dear! It will break my heart if you fail. I love you." And suddenly Tony was clinging to him, just a woman who cared, who wanted her lover, even as he wanted her. But in a breath she pulled herself away. "Take me in, Alan, now," she said. "Kiss me once before we go. I shall not see you in the morning. This is really good-by."

Later, Carlotta, coming in to say goodnight to Tony, found the latter sitting in front of the mirror brushing out her abundant red-brown hair and noticed how very scarlet her friend's cheeks were and what a tell-tale shining glory there was in her eyes.

"It was a lovely party," announced Tony casually, unaware how much Carlotta had seen over her shoulder in the mirror.

"Tony, are you in love with Alan Massey?" demanded Carlotta.

Tony whirled around on the stool, her cheeks flying deeper crimson banners at this unexpected challenge.

"I am afraid I am, Carlotta," she admitted. "It is rather a mess, isn't it?"

Carlotta groaned and dropping into a chaise lounge encircled her knees with her arms, staring with troubled eyes at her guest.

"A mess? I should say it was--worse than a mess--a catastrophe. You know what Alan is--isn't--" She floundered off into silence.

"Oh, yes," said Tony, the more tranquil of the two. "I know what he is and isn't, better than most people, I think. I ought to. But I love him. I just discovered it to-night, or rather it is the first time I ever let myself look straight at the fact. I think I have known it from the beginning."

"But Tony! You won't marry him. You can't. Your people will never let you. They oughtn't to let you."

Tony shook back her wavy mane of hair, sent it billowing over her rose-colored satin kimono.

"It don't matter if the whole world won't let me. If I decide to marry Alan I shall do it."

"Tony!"

There was shocked consternation in Carlotta's tone and Tony relenting burst into a low, tremulous little laugh.

"Don't worry, Carlotta. I'm not so mad as I sound. I told Alan he would have to wait a year. He has to prove to me he is--worth loving."

"But you are engaged?" Carlotta was relieved, but not satisfied.

Tony shook her head.

"Absolutely not. We are both free as air--technically. If you were in love your-self you would know how much that amounts to by way of freedom."

Carlotta's golden head was bowed. She did not answer her friend's implication that she could not be expected to comprehend the delicate, invisible, omnipotent shackles of love.

"Don't tell anyone, Carlotta, please. It is our secret--Alan's and mine. Maybe it will always he a secret unless he--measures up."

"You are not going to tell your uncle?"

"There is nothing to tell yet."

"And I suppose this is the end of poor Dick."

"Don't be silly, Carlotta. Dick never said a word of love to me in his life."

"That doesn't mean he doesn't think 'em. You have convenient eyes, Tony dar-ling. You see only what you wish to see."

"I didn't want to see Alan's love. I tried dreadfully hard not to. But it set up a fire in my own house and blazed and smoked until I had to do something about it. See here, Carlotta. I'd like to ask you a question or two. You are not really going to marry Herbert Lathrop, are you?"

A queer little shadow, almost like a veil, passed over Carlotta's face at this counter charge.

"Why not?" she parried.

"You know why not. He is exactly what Hal Underwood calls him, a poor fish. He is as close to being a nonentity as anything I ever saw."

"Precisely why I selected him," drawled Carlotta. "I've got to marry somebody and poor Herbert hasn't a vice except his excess of virtue. We can't have another old maid in the family. Aunt Lottie is a shining example of what to avoid. I am not going to be 'Lottie the second' I have decided on that."

"As if you could," protested Tony indignantly.

"Oh, I could. You look at Aunt Lottie's pictures of fifteen years ago. She was just as pretty as I am. She had loads of lovers but somehow they all slipped through her fingers. She has been sex-starved. She ought to have married and had children. I don't want to be a hungry spinster. They are infernally miserable."

"Carlotta!" Tony was a little shocked at her friend's bluntness, a little puzzled as to what lay behind her arguments. "You don't have to be a hungry spinster. There are other men besides Herbert that want to marry you."

"Certainly. Some of them want to marry my money. Some of them want to marry my body. I grant you Herbert is a poor fish in some ways, but at least he wants to marry me, myself, which is more than the others do."

"That isn't true. Hal Underwood wants to marry you, yourself."

"Oh, Hal!" conceded Carlotta. "I forgot him for a moment. You are right. He is real--too real. I should hurt him marrying him and not caring enough. That is why a nonentity is preferable. It doesn't know what it is missing. Hal would know."

"But there is no reason why you shouldn't wait until you find somebody you could care for," persisted Tony.

"That is all you know about it, my dear. There is the best reason in the world. I found him--and lost him."

"Carlotta--is it Phil?"

Carlotta sprang up and went over to the window. She took the rose she had been wearing, in her hands and deliberately pulled it apart letting the petals drift one by one out into the night. Then she turned back to Tony.

"Don't ask questions, Tony. I am not going to talk." But she lingered a moment beside her friend. "You and I, Tony darling, don't seem to have very much luck in love," she murmured. "I hope you will be happy with Alan, if you do marry him. But happiness isn't exactly necessary. There are other things--" She broke off and began again. "There are other things in a man's life besides love. Somebody said that to me once and I believe it is true. But there isn't so much besides that matters much to a woman. I wish there were. I hate love." And pressing a rare kiss on her friend's cheek Carlotta vanished for the night.

Meanwhile Alan Massey smoked and thought and cursed the past that had him in its hateful toils. Like the guilty king in Hamlet, his soul, "struggling to be free" was "but the more engaged." He honestly desired to be worthy of Tony Holiday, to stand clear in her eyes, but he did not want it badly enough, to the "teeth and forehead of his faults to give in evidence." He did not want to bare the one worst plague spot of all and run the risk not only of losing Tony himself but perhaps also of clearing the way to her for his cousin, John Massey. Small wonder he smoked gall and wormwood in his cigarettes that night.

And far away in the heat and grime and din of the great city, Dick Carson the nameless, who was really John Massey and heir to a great fortune, sat dreaming over a girl's picture, telling himself that Tony must care a little to have gotten up in the silver gray of the morning to see him off so kindly. Happily for the dreamer's peace of mind he had no means of knowing that that very night, in the starlit garden by the sea, Tony Holiday had taken upon herself the mad and sad and glad bondage of love.

CHAPTER XV
ON THE EDGE OF THE PRECIPICE

Tony, getting off the train at Dunbury on Saturday, found her brothers waiting for her with the car, and the kiddies on the back seat, "for ballast" as Ted said. With one quick apprizing glance the girl took in the two young men.

Ted was brown and healthy looking, clear-eyed, steady-nerved, for once, without the inevitable cigarette in his mouth. He was oddly improved somehow, his sister thought, considering how short a time she had been away from the Hill. She noticed also that he drove the car much less recklessly than was his wont, took no chances on curves, slid by no vehicles at hair-breadth space, speeded not at all, and though he kept up a running fire of merry nonsense, had his eye on the road as he drove. So far so good. That spill out on the Florence road wasn't all loss, it seemed.

Larry was more baffling. He was always quiet. He was quieter than ever to-day. There was something in his gray eyes which spelled trouble, Tony thought. What was it? Was he worried about a case? Was Granny worse? Was Ted in some scrape? Something there certainly was on his mind. Tony was sure of that, though she could not conjecture what.

The Holidays had an almost uncanny way of understanding things about each other, things which sometimes never rose to the surface at all. Perhaps it was that they were so close together in sympathy that a kind of small telepathic signal registered automatically when anything was wrong with any of them. So far as her brothers were concerned Tony's intuition was all but infallible.

She found the family gift a shade disconcerting, a little later, when after her uncle kissed her he held her off at arm's length and studied her face. Tony's eyes fell beneath his questioning gaze. For almost the first time in her life she had a secret to keep from him if she could.

"What have they been doing to my little girl?" he asked. "They have taken away her sunshininess."

"Oh, no, they haven't," denied Tony quickly. "It is just that I am tired. We have been on the go all the time and kept scandalously late hours. I'll be all right as soon as I have caught up. I feel as if I could sleep for a century and any prince who has the effrontery to wake me up will fare badly."

She laughed, but even in her own ears the laughter did not sound quite natural and she was sure Uncle Phil thought the same, though he asked no more questions.

"It is like living in a palace being at Crest House," she went on. "I've played princess to my heart's content--been waited on and feted and flirted with until I'm tired to death of it all and want to be just plain Tony again."

She slid into her uncle's arms with a weary little sigh. It was good--oh so good--to have him again! She hadn't known she had missed him so until she felt the comfort of his presence. In his arms Alan Massey and all he stood for seemed very far away.

"Got letters for you this morning," announced Ted. "I forgot to give them to you." He fished the aforesaid letters out of his pocket and examined them before handing them over. "One is from Dick--the other"--he held the large square envelope off and squinted at it teasingly. "Some scrawl!" he commented. "Reckless display of ink and flourishes, I call it. Who's the party?"

Tony snatched the letters, her face rosy.

"Give me Dick's. I haven't heard from him but once since he went back to New York and that was just a card. Oh-h! Listen everybody. The Universal has accepted his story and wants him to do a whole series of them. Oh, isn't that just wonderful?"

Tony's old sparkles were back now. There were no reservations necessary here. Everybody knew and loved Dick and would be glad as she was herself in his success.

"Hail to Dicky Dumas!" she added, gaily waving the letter aloft. "I always knew he would get there. And that was the very story he read me. Wasn't it lucky I liked it really? If I hadn't, and it had turned out to be good, wouldn't it have been awful?"

Everybody laughed at that and perhaps nobody but the doctor noticed that the other letter in the unfamiliar handwriting was tucked away very quickly out of sight in her bag and no comments made.

It was not until Tony had gone the rounds of the household and greeted everyone from Granny down to Max that she read Alan's letter, as she sat curled up in the cretonned window seat, just as the little girl Tony had been wont to sit and devour love stories. This was a love story, too--her own and with a sadly complicated plot at that.

It was the first letter she had had from Alan and she found it very wonderful and exciting reading. It was brimming over, as might have been expected, with passionate lover's protests and extravagant endearments which Tony could not have imagined her Anglo-Saxon relatives or friends even conceiving, let alone putting on paper. But Alan was different. These things were no affectation with him, but natural as breathing, part and parcel of his personality. She could hear him now say "*carissima*" in that low, deep-cadenced, musical voice of his and the word seemed very sweet and beautiful to her as it sang in her heart and she read it in the dashing script upon the paper.

He was desolated without her, he wrote. Nothing was worth while. Nothing interested him. He was refusing all invitations, went nowhere. He just sat alone in the studio and dreamed about her or made sketches of her from memory. She was everywhere, all about him. She filled the studio with her voice, her laughter, her wonderful eyes. But oh, he was so lonely, so unutterably lonely without her. Must he really wait a whole year before he made her his? A year was twelve long, long months. Anything could happen in a year. One of them might die and the other would go frustrate and lonely forever, like a sad wind in the night.

Tony caught her breath quickly at that sentence. The poetry of it captivated her fancy, the dread of what it conjured clutched like cold hands at her heart. She wanted Alan now, wanted love now. Already those dear folks downstairs were beginning to seem like ghosts, she and Alan the only real people. What if he should die, what if something should happen to keep them forever apart, how could she bear it? How could she?

She turned back to her letter which had turned into an impassioned plea that she would never forsake him, no matter what happened, never drive him over the precipice like the Gadderene swine.

"You and your love are the only thing that can save me, dear heart," he wrote. "Remember that always. Without you I shall go down, down into blacker pits than I ever sank before. With you I shall come out into the light. I swear it. But oh, beloved, pray for me, if you know how to pray. I don't. I never had a god."

There were tears in Tony's eyes as she finished her lover's letter. His unwonted humility touched her as no arrogance could ever have done. His appeal to his desperate need moved her profoundly as such appeals will always move woman. It is an old tale and one oft repeated. Man crying out at a woman's feet, "Save me! Save me! Myself I cannot save!" Woman, believing, because she longs to believe it, that salvation lies in her power, taking on herself the all but impossible mission for love's high sake.

Tony Holiday believed, as all the million other women have believed since time began, that she could save her lover, loved him tenfold the more because he threw himself upon her mercy, came indeed perhaps to truly love him for the first time now with a kind of consecrated fervor which belonged all to the spirit even as the love that had come to her while they danced had belonged rather to the flesh.

*   *   *   *   *

And day by day Jim Roberts grew sicker and the gnawing thing crept up nearer to his heart. Day by day he gloated over the goading whips he brandished over Alan Massey's head, amused himself with the various developments it lay in his power to give to the situation as he passed out of life.

He wrote two letters from his sick bed. The first one was addressed to Dick Carson, telling the full story of his own and Alan Massey's share in the deliberate defraudment of that young man of his rightful name and estate. It pleased him to read and reread this letter and to reflect that when it was mailed Alan Massey would drink the full cup of disgrace and exposure while he who was infinitely guiltier would be sleeping very quietly in a cool grave where hate, nor vengeance, nor even pity could touch him.

The other letter, which like the first he kept unmailed, was a less honest and less incriminating letter, filled with plausible half truths, telling how he had just become aware at last through coming into possession of some old letters of the identity of the boy he had once had in his keeping and who had run away from him, an identity which he now hastened to reveal in the interests of tardy justice. The letter made no mention of Alan Massey nor of the unlovely bargain he had driven with that young man as the price of silence and the bliss of ignorance. It was addressed to the lawyers who handled the Massey estate.

Roberts had followed up various trails and discovered that Antoinette Holiday was the girl Massey loved, discovered through the bribing of a Crest House servant, that the young man they called Carson was also presumably in love with the girl whose family had befriended him so generously in his need. It was incredibly good he thought. He could hardly have thought out a more diabolically clever plot if he had tried. He could make Alan Massey writhe trebly, knowing these things.

Pursuing his malignant whim he wrote to Alan Massey and told him of the existence of the two letters, as yet unmailed, in his table drawer. He made it clear that one of the letters damned Alan Massey utterly while the other only robbed him of his ill-gotten fortune, made it clear also that he himself did not know which of the two would be mailed in the end, possibly he would decide it by a flip of a coin. Massey could only wait and see what happened.

"I suppose you think the girl is worth going to Hell for, even if the money isn't," he had written. "Maybe she is. Some women are, perhaps. But don't forget that if she loves you, you will be dragging her down there too. Pretty thought, isn't it? I don't mean any future-life business either. That's rot. I heard enough of that when I was a boy to sicken me of it forever. It is the here and now Hell a man pays for his sins with, and that is God's truth, Alan Massey."

And Alan, sitting in his luxurious studio reading the letter, crushed it in his hands and groaned aloud. He needed no commentary on the "here and now Hell" from Jim Roberts. He was living it those summer days if ever a man did.

It wasn't the money now. Alan told himself he no longer cared for that, hated it in fact. It was Tony now, all Tony, and the horrible fear lest Roberts betray him and shut the gates of Paradise upon him forever. Sometimes in his agony of fear he could almost have been glad to end it all with one shot of the silver-mounted automatic he kept always near, to beat Jim Roberts to the bliss of oblivion in the easiest way.

But Alan Massey had an incorrigible belief in his luck. Just as he had hoped, until he had all but believed, that his cousin John was as dead as he had told that very person he was, so now he hoped against all reason that he would be saved at the eleventh hour, that Roberts would go to his death carrying with him the secret that would destroy himself if it ceased to be a secret.

Those unmailed letters haunted him, however, day and night, so much so, in fact, that he took a journey to Boston one day and sought out the little cigar store again. But this time he had not mounted the stairs. His business was with the black-eyed boy. With one fifty dollar bill he bought the lad's promise to destroy the letters and the packet in Robert's drawer in the event of the latter's death; secured also the promise that if at any time before his death Roberts gave orders that either letter should be mailed, the boy would send the same not to the address on the envelope but to Alan Massey. If the boy kept faith with his pledges there would be another fifty coming to him after the death of the man. He bought the lad even as Roberts had once bought himself. It was a sickening transaction but it relieved his mind considerably and catered in a measure to that incorrigible hope within him.

But he paid a price too. Fifty miles away from Boston was Tony Holiday on her Heaven kissing hill. He was mad to go to her but dared not, lest this fresh corruption in some way betray itself to her clear gaze.

So he went back to New York without seeing her and Tony never knew he had been so near.

And that night Jim Roberts took an unexpected turn for the worse and died, foiled of that last highly anticipated spice of malice in flipping the coin that was to decide Alan Massey's fate.

In the end the boy had not had the courage to destroy the letters as he had promised to do. Instead he sent them both, together with the packet of evidence as to John Massey's identity, to Alan Massey.

The thing was in Alan's own hands at last. Nothing could save or destroy him but himself. And by a paradox his salvation depended upon his being strong enough to bring himself to ruin.

CHAPTER XVI
IN WHICH PHIL GETS HIS EYES OPENED

At home on her Hill Tony Holiday settled down more or less happily after her eventful sally into the great world. To the careless observer she was quite the same Tony who went down the Hill a few weeks earlier. If at times she was unusually quiet, had spells of sitting very still with folded hands and far away dreams in her eyes, if she crept away by herself to read the long letters that came so often, from many addresses but always in the same bold, beautiful script and to pen long answers to these; if she read more poetry than was her wont and sang love songs with a new, exquisite, but rather heart breaking timbre in her lovely contralto voice, no one paid much attention to these signs except possibly Doctor Philip who saw most things. He perceived regretfully that his little girl was slipping away from him, passing through some experience that was by no means all joy or contentment and which was making her grow up all too fast. But he said nothing, quietly bided the hour of confidence which he felt sure would come sooner or later.

Tony puzzled much over the complexities of life these days, puzzled over other things beside her own perverse romance. Carlotta too was much on her mind. She wished she could wave a magic wand and make things come right for these two friends of hers who were evidently made for each other as Hal had propounded. She wondered if Phil were as unhappy as Carlotta was and meant to find out in her own time and way.

She had seen almost nothing of him since her return to the Hill. He was working very hard in the store and never appeared at any of the little dances and picnics and teas with which the Dunbury younger set passed away the summer days and nights, and which Ted and the twins and usually Tony herself frequented. Larry never did. He hated things of that sort. But Phil was different. He had always liked fun and parties and had always been on hand and in great demand hitherto at every social function from a Ladies' Aid strawberry festival to a grand Masonic ball. It wasn't natural for Phil to shut himself out of things like that. It was a bad sign Tony thought.

At any rate she determined to find out for herself how the land lay if she could. Having occasion to do some shopping she marched down the Hill and presented herself at Stuart Lambert and Son's, demanding to be served by no less a person than Philip himself.

"I want a pair of black satin pumps with very frivolous heels," she announced. "Produce them this instant, slave." She smiled at Phil and he smiled back. He and Tony had always been the best of chums.

"Cannzy ones?" he laughed. "That's what one of our customers calls them."

And while he knelt before her with an array of shoe boxes around him, fitting a dainty slipper on Tony's pretty foot, Tony herself looked not at the slipper but at Philip, studying his face shrewdly. He looked older, graver. There was less laughter in his blue eyes, a grimmer line about his young mouth. Poor Phil! Evidently Carlotta wasn't the only one who was paying the price of too much loving. Tony made up her mind to rush in, though she knew it might be a case for angel hesitation.

"I've never given you a message Hal Underwood sent you," she observed irrelevantly.

Philip looked up surprised.

"Hal Underwood! What message did he send me? I hardly know him."

"He seemed to know you rather well. He told me to tell you to come down and marry Carlotta, that you were the only man that could keep her in order. That is too big, Phil. Try a smaller one." The speaker kicked off the offending slipper. Philip mechanically picked it up and replaced it in the box.

"That is rather a queer message," he commented. "I had an idea Underwood wanted to marry Carlotta himself. Try this." He reached for another pump. His eyes were lowered so Tony could not see them. She wished she could.

"He does," she said. "She won't have him."

"Is--is there--anybody she is likely to have?" The words jerked out as the young man groped for the shoe horn which was almost beside his hand but which apparently he did not see at all.

"I am afraid she is likely to take Herbert Lathrop unless somebody stops her by main force. Why don't you play Lochinvar yourself, Phil? You could."

Philip looked straight up at Tony then, the slipper forgotten in his hand.

"Tony, do you mean that?" he asked.

"I certainly do. Make her marry you, Phil. It is the only way with Carlotta."

"I don't want to *make* any girl marry me," he said.

"Oh, hang your silly pride, Phil Lambert! Carlotta wants to marry you I tell you though she would murder me if she knew I did tell you."

"Maybe she does. But she doesn't want to live in Dunbury. I've good reason to know that. We thrashed it out rather thoroughly on the top of Mount Tom last June. She hasn't changed her mind."

Tony sighed. She was afraid Phil was right. Carlotta hadn't changed her mind. Was it because she was afraid she might, that she was determining to marry Herbert?

"And you can't leave Dunbury?" she asked soberly.

Just at that moment Stuart Lambert approached, a tall fine looking man, with the same blue eyes and fresh coloring as his son and brown hair only slightly graying around the temples. He had an air of vigor and ageless youth. Indeed a stranger might easily have taken the two men for brothers instead of father and son.

"Hello, Tony, my dear," he greeted cordially. "It is good to see you round again. We have missed you. This boy of mine getting you what you want?"

"He is trying," smiled Tony. "A woman doesn't always know what she wants, Mr. Lambert. The store is wonderful since it was enlarged and I see lots of other improvements too." Her eyes swept her surroundings with sincere appreciation.

"Make your bow to Phil for all that. It is good to get fresh brains into a business. We old fogies need jerking out of our ruts."

The older man's eyes fell upon Phil's bowed head and Tony realized how much it meant to him to have his son with him at last, pulling shoulder to shoulder.

"New brains nothing!" protested Phil. "Dad's got me skinned going and coming for progressiveness. As for old fogies he's the youngest man I know. Make all your bows to him, Tony. It is where they belong." And Phil got to his feet and himself made a solemn obeisance in Stuart Lambert's direction.

Mr. Lambert chuckled.

"Phil was always a blarney," he said. "Don't know where he got it. Don't you believe a word he says, my dear." But Tony saw he was immensely pleased with Phil's tribute for all that. "How do you like the sign?" he asked.

"Fine. Looks good to me and I know it does to you, Mr. Lambert."

"Well, rather." The speaker rested his hand on Phil's shoulder a moment. "I tell you it *is* good, young lady, to have the son part added, worth waiting for. I'm mighty proud of that sign. Between you and me, Miss Tony, I'm proud of my son too."

"Who is blarneying now?" laughed Phil. "Go on with you, Dad. You are spoiling my sale."

The father chuckled again and moved away. Phil looked down at the girl.

"I think your question is answered. I can't leave Dunbury," he said.

"Then Carlotta ought to come to you."

"There are no oughts in Carlotta's bright lexicon. I don't blame her, Tony. Dunbury is a dead hole from most points of view. I am afraid she wouldn't be happy here. You wouldn't be yourself forever. Bet you are planning to get away right now."

Tony nodded ruefully.

"I suppose I am, Phil. The modern young woman isn't much to pin one's faith to I am afraid. Do I get another slipper? Or is one enough?"

Phil came back from his mental aberration with a start and a grin at his own expense.

"I am afraid I am not a very good salesman today," he apologized. "Honestly I do better usually but you hit me in a vulnerable spot."

"You do care for Carlotta then?" probed Tony.

"Care! I'm crazy over her. I'd go on my hands and knees to Crest House if I thought I could get her to marry me by doing it."

"You would much better go by train--the next one. That's my advice. Are you coming to Sue Emerson's dance? That is why I am buying slippers. You can dance with 'em if you'll come."

"Sorry. I don't go to dances any more."

"That is nonsense, Phil. It is the worst thing in the world for you to make a hermit of yourself. No girl's worth it. Besides there are other girls besides Carlotta."

Phil shook his head as he finished replacing Tony's trim brown oxfords.

"Unfortunately that isn't true for me," he said rising. "At present my world consists of myself bounded, north, south, east and west by Carlotta."

And Tony passing out under the sign of STUART LAMBERT AND SON a few minutes later sighed a little. Here was Carlotta with a real man for the taking and too stubborn and foolish to put out her hand and here was herself, Tony Holiday, tying herself all up in a strange snarl for the sake of somebody who wasn't a man at all as Holiday Hill standards ran. What queer creatures women were!

Other people besides Tony were inclined to score Phil's folly in making a hermit of himself. His sisters attacked him that very night on the subject of Sue Emerson's dance and accused him of being a "Grumpy Grandpa" and a grouch and various other uncomplimentary things when he announced that he wasn't going to attend the function.

"I'm the authentic T.B.M.," he parried from his perch on the porch railing. "I've cut out dancing."

"More idiot you!" retorted Charley promptly. "Mums, do tell Phil it is all nonsense making such an oyster in a shell of himself."

Mrs. Lambert smiled and looked up at her tall young son, looked rather hard for a moment.

"I think the twins are right, Phil," she said. "You are working too hard. You don't allow yourself any relaxation."

"Oh, yes I do. Only my idea of relaxation doesn't happen to coincide with the twins. Dancing in this sort of weather with your collar slumping and the perspiration rolling in tidal waves down your manly brow doesn't strike me as being a particularly desirable diversion."

"H-mp!" sniffed Charley. "You didn't object to dancing last summer when it was twice as hot. You went to a dance almost every night when Carlotta was visiting Tony. You know you did."

"I wasn't a member of the esteemed firm of Stuart Lambert and Son last summer. A lily of the field can afford to dance all night. I'm a working man I'd have you know."

"Well, I think you might come just this once to please us," joined in Clare, the other twin. "You are a gorgeous dancer, Phil. I'd rather have a one step with you than any man I know." Clare always beguiled where Charley bullied, a method much more successful in the long run as Charley sometimes grudgingly admitted after the fact.

Phil smiled now at pretty Clare and promised to think about it and the twins flew off across the street to visit with Tony and Ruth whom the whole Hill adored.

"Phil dear, aren't you happy?" asked Mrs. Lambert. "Have we asked too much of you expecting you to settle down at home with us?"

"Why yes, Mums. I'm all right." Phil left his post on the rail and dropped into a chair beside his mother. Perhaps he did it purposely lest she see too much. "Don't get notions in your head. I like living in Dunbury. I wouldn't live in a city for anything and I like being with Dad not to mention the rest of you."

Mrs. Lambert shifted her position also. She wanted to see her son's face; just as much as he didn't want her to see it.

"Possibly that is all so but you aren't happy for all that. You can't fool mother eyes, my dear."

Phil looked straight at her then with a little rueful smile.

"I reckon I can't," he admitted. "Very well then. I am not entirely happy but it is nobody's fault and nothing anybody can help."

"Philip, is it a girl?"

How they dread the *girl* in their sons' lives--these mothers! The very possibility of her in the abstract brings a shadow across the path.

"Yes, Mums, it is a girl."

Mrs. Lambert rose and went over to where her son sat, running her fingers through his hair as she had been wont to do when the little boy Phil was in trouble of any sort.

"I am very sorry, dear boy," she said. "It won't help to talk about it?"

"I am afraid not. Don't worry, Mums. It is just--well, it hurts a little just now that's all."

She kissed his forehead and went back to her chair. It hurt her to know her boy was being hurt, hurt her almost as much to know she could not help him, she must just let him close the door on his grief and bear it alone.

Yet she respected his reserve and loved him the better for it. Phil was like that always. He never cried out when he was hurt. She remembered how long ago the little boy Phil had come to her with a small finger just released from a slamming door that had crushed it unmercifully, the tears streaming down his cheeks but uttering no sound. She recalled another incident of years later, when the coach had been obliged to put some one else in Phil's place on the team the last minute because his sprained ankle had been bothering. She and Stuart had come on for the game. It had been a bitter disappointment to them all. To the boy it had been little short of a tragedy. But he had smiled bravely at her in spite of the trouble in his blue eyes. "Don't mind, Mums. It is all right," he had said steadily. "We've got to win. We can't risk my darned ankle's flopping. It's the bleachers for me. The game's the thing."

The game had always been the thing for Phil. Even in his blundering, willful boyhood he had played hard and played fair and taken defeat like a man when things had gone against him.

There was a moment's silence. Then Mrs. Lambert spoke again.

"Phil, I wish you would go to the dance with the girls. It will please them and be good for you. You can't shut yourself away from everything the way you are doing, if you are going to make Dunbury your home. Your father never has. He has always given himself freely to it, worked with it, played with it, made it a real part of himself. You mustn't start out by building a wall around yourself."

"Am I doing that, Mums?" Phil's voice was sober.

"I am afraid you are, Phil. It troubles your father. He was so disappointed when you wouldn't serve on the library committee. They were disappointed too. They didn't expect it of your father's son."

"I--I wasn't interested."

"No, you weren't interested. That was the trouble. You ought to have been. You have had your college training, the world of books has been thrown wide open for you. You come back here and aren't interested in seeing that others less fortunate get the right kind of books into their hands and heads. I don't want to preach, dear. But education isn't only a privilege. It is a responsibility."

"Maybe you are right, Mums. I didn't think of it that way. I just didn't want to bother. I was--well, I was thinking too much about myself I suppose."

"Youth is apt to. There were other things too. When they asked you to take charge of the Fourth of July pageant, to dig up Dunbury's past history and make it live for us again, your father and I both thought you would enjoy it. He was tremendously excited about it, full of ideas to help. But the project fell through because nobody would undertake the leadership. You were too busy. Every one was too busy."

"But, Mums, I was busy," Phil defended himself. "It is no end of a job to put things like that through properly."

"Most things worth doing are no end of a job. Your father would have taken it with all the rest he has on his hands and made a success of it. But he was hurt by your high handed refusal to have anything to do with it and he let it go, though you know having Fourth of July community celebrations is one of his dearest hobbies-- always has been since he used to fight so hard to get rid of the old, wretched noise, law breaking and rowdyism kind of village celebration you and the other young Dunbury vandals delighted in."

Phil flushed at that. The point went home. He remembered vividly his boyish self tearing reluctantly from Doctor Holiday's fireworks impelled by an unbearably guilty conscience to confess to Stuart Lambert that his own son had been a transgressor against the law. Boy as he was, he had gotten out of the interview with his father that night a glimpse into the ideal citizenship which Stuart Lambert preached and lived and worked for. He had understood a little then. He understood better now having stood beside his father man to man.

"I am sorry, Mums. I would have done the thing if I'd known Dad wanted me to. Why didn't he say so?"

Mrs. Lambert smiled.

"Dad doesn't say much about what he wants. You will have to learn to keep your eyes open and find out for yourself. I did."

"Any more black marks on my score? I may as well eat the whole darned pie at once." Phil's smile was humorous but his eyes were troubled. It was a bit hard when you had been thinking you had played your part fairly creditably to discover you had been fumbling your cues wretchedly all along.

"Only one other thing. We were both immensely disappointed when you wouldn't take the scout-mastership they offered you. Father believes tremendously in the movement. He thinks it is going to be the making of the next generation of men. He would have liked you to be a Scoutmaster and when you wouldn't he went on the Scout Troop Committee himself though he really could not spare the time."

"I see," said Phil. "I guess I've been pretty blind. Funny part of it is I really wanted to take the Scoutmaster job but I thought Dad would think it took too much of my time. Anything more?" he asked.

"Not a thing. Haven't you had quite enough of a lecture for once?" his mother smiled back.

"I reckon I needed it. Thank you, Mums. I'll turn over a new leaf if it isn't too late. I'll go to the dance and I'll ask them if there is still a place for me on the library committee and I'll start a troop of Scouts myself--another bunch I've had my eyes on for some time."

"That will please Dad very much. It pleases me too. Boys are very dear to my heart. I wonder if you can guess why, Philip, my son?"

"I wish I'd been a better son, Mums. Some chaps never seem to cause their-mothers any worry or heart ache. I wasn't that kind. I am afraid I am not even yet."

"No son is, dear, unless there is something wrong with him or the mother. Mothering means heart ache and worries, plus joy and pride and the joy and pride more than makes up for the rest. It has for me a hundred times over even when I had a rather bad little boy on my hands and now I have a man--a man I am glad and proud to call my son."

CHAPTER XVII
A WEDDING RING IT WAS HARD TO REMEMBER

It was a grilling hot August afternoon. The young Holidays were keeping cool as best they could out in the yard. Ruth lay in the canopied hammock against a background of a hedge of sweet peas, pink and white and lavender, looking rather like a dainty, frail little flower herself. Tony in cool white was seated on a scarlet Navajo blanket, leaning against the apple tree. Around her was a litter of magazines and an open box of bonbons. Ted was stretched at his ease on the grass, gazing sky-ward, a cigarette in his lips, enjoying well-earned rest after toil. Larry occupied the green garden bench in the lee, of the hammock. He was unsolaced either by candy or smoke and looked tired and not particularly happy. There were dark shadows under his gray eyes which betrayed that he was not getting the quota of sleep that healthy youth demands. His eyes were downcast now, apparently absorbed in con-templation of a belated dandelion at his feet.

"Ruth, why don't you come down to the dance with us tonight?" demanded Tony suddenly dropping her magazine. "You are well enough now and I know you would enjoy it. It is lovely down on the island where the pavilion is--all quiet and pine-woodsy. You needn't dance if you don't want to. You could just lie in the hammock and listen to the music and the water. We'd come and talk to you between dances so you wouldn't be lonesome. Do come."

"Oh, I couldn't." Ruth's voice was dismayed, her blue eyes filled with alarm at the suggestion.

"Why couldn't you?" persisted Tony. "You aren't going to just hide away forever are you? It is awfully foolish, isn't it, Larry?" she appealed to her brother.

He did not answer, but he did transfer his gaze from the dandelion to Ruth as if he were considering his sister's proposition.

"Sure, it's foolish," Ted replied for him, sitting up. "Come on down and dance the first foxtrot with me, sweetness. You'll like it. Honest you will, when you get started."

"Oh, I couldn't" reiterated Ruth.

"That is nonsense. Of course, you could," objected Tony. "It is just your notion, Ruthie. You have kept away from people so long you are scared. But you would get over that in a minute and truly it would be lots better for you. Tell her it would, Larry. She is your patient."

"I don't know whether it would or not," returned Larry in his deliberate way, which occasionally exasperated the swift-minded, impulsive Tony.

"Then you are a rotten doctor," she flung back. "I know better than that myself and Uncle Phil agrees with me. I asked him."

"Ruth's my patient, as you reminded me a moment ago. She isn't Uncle Phil's." There was an unusual touchiness in the young doctor's voice. He was not professionally aggressive as a rule.

"Well, I wouldn't be a know-it-all, if she is," snapped Tony. "Maybe Uncle Phil knows a thing or two more than you do yet. And anyway you are only a man and I am a girl and I know that girls need people and fun and dancing. It isn't good for anybody to hide away by herself. I believe you are keeping Ruth away from everybody on purpose."

The hot weather and other things were setting Tony's nerves a bit on edge. She

felt slightly belligerent and not precisely averse to picking a quarrel with her ag-
gravatingly quiet brother, if he gave her half an opening.

Larry flushed and scowled at that and ordered her sharply not to talk nonsense.
Whereupon Ted intervened.

"I'm all on your side, Tony. Of course it is bad for Ruth not to see anybody but
us. Any fool would know that. Dancing may be the very thing for her anyhow. You
can't tell till you try. Maybe when you are foxtrotting with me, goldilocks, you'll
remember how it seemed to have some other chap's arm around you. It might be
like laying a fuse."

"I'm glad you all know so much about my business," said Larry testily. "You
make me tired, both of you."

"Oh," begged Ruth, her blue eyes full of trouble. "Please, please, don't quarrel
about me."

"I beg your pardon," apologized Larry. "See here, would you be willing to try
it, just as an experiment? Would you go down there for a little while tonight with
us?"

The blue eyes met the gray ones.

"If you--wanted me to," faltered the blue-eyes.

"Would you mind it very much?" Larry leaned forward. His voice was low, solicitous. Tony, listening, resented it a little. She didn't see why Larry had to keep his
good manners for somebody outside the family. He might have spoken a little more
politely to herself, she thought. She had only been trying to be nice to Ruth.

"Not--if you would take care of me and not let people talk to me too much,"
Ruth answered the solicitous tone.

"I will," promised Larry. "You needn't talk to a soul if you don't want to. I'll
ward 'em off. And you can dance if you want to--one dance anyway."

"With me," announced Ted complacently from the grass. "My bid was in first.
Don't you forget, Miss Peaseblossom." Ted had a multitude of pet names for Ruth.
They slipped off his tongue easily, as water falling over a cliff.

"No, with me," said his brother shortly.

"Gee, I wish I were a doctor! It gives you a hideous advantage."

"But I haven't anything to wear," exclaimed Ruth, coming next to the really
sole and only supreme woman question.

"We'll fix that easy as easy," said Tony, amicable again now. "I've a darling blue organdy that will look sweet on you--just the color of your eyes. Don't you worry a minute, honey. Your fairy godmother will see to all that. All I ask is that you won't let that old ogre of an M.D. change his mind and say you can't go. It isn't good for Larry to obey him so meekly. He is getting to be a regular tyrant."

A moment later Doctor Holiday joined the group, dropped on the bench beside Larry and was informed by Tony that Ruth was to go on an adventure down the Hill; to Sue Emerson's dance in fact.

"Isn't that great?" she demanded.

"Superb," he teased. Then he smiled approval at Ruth. "Good idea, Larry," he added to his nephew. "Glad you thought of it."

"I didn't think of it. Tony did. You really approve?" The gray eyes were a little anxious. Larry was by no means a know-it-all doctor, as his sister accused him. He had too little rather than too much confidence in his own judgment in fact.

"I certainly do. Go to it, little lady. May be the best medicine in the world for you."

"Now you are talking," exulted Ted. "That's what Tony and I said and Larry wanted to execute us on the spot for daring to have an opinion at all."

"Scare you much to think of it?" Doctor Holiday asked Ruth, prudently ignoring this last sally.

"A good deal," sighed Ruth. "But I'll try not to be too much scared if Larry will go too and not let people ask questions."

The young doctor had long since become Larry to Ruth. It was too confusing talking about two Doctor Holidays. Everybody in Dunbury said Larry or Doctor Larry or at most, respectfully, Doctor Laurence.

"I'll let nobody talk to you but myself," said Larry.

"There you are!" flashed Tony. "You might just as well keep her penned up here in the yard. You want to keep her all to yourself."

She didn't mean anything in particular, only to be a little disagreeable, to pay Larry back for being so snappy. But to her amazement Ruth was suddenly blushing a lovely but startling blush and Larry was bending over to examine the hammock-hook in obvious confusion.

"Good gracious!" she thought in consternation. "Is that what's up? It can't be.

I'm just imagining it. Larry wouldn't fall in love with any one who wore a wedding ring. He mustn't."

But she knew in her heart that whether Larry must or must not he had. A thousand signs betrayed the truth now that her eyes were open. Poor Larry! No wonder he was cross and unlike himself. And Ruth was so sweet--just the girl for him. And poor Uncle Phil! She herself was hurting him dreadfully keeping her secret about Alan and nobody knew what Ted had up his sleeve under his cloak of incredible virtue. And now here was Larry with a worse complication still. Oh dear! Would the three of them ever stop getting into scrapes as long as they lived? It was bad enough when they were children. It was infinitely worse now they were grown up and the scrapes were so horribly serious.

"I suppose you can't tear yourself away from your studies to attend a mere dance?" Doctor Holiday was asking of his younger nephew with a twinkle in his eyes when Tony recovered enough to listen again.

Ted sent his cigarette stub careening off into the shrubbery and grinned back at his uncle, a grin half merry, half defiant.

"Like fun, I can't!" he ejaculated. "I'm a union man, I am. I've done my stunt for the day. If anybody thinks I'm going to stick my nose in between the covers of a book before nine A.M. tomorrow he has a whole orchard of brand new little thinks growing up to stub his toes on, that's all."

"So the student life doesn't improve with intimate acquaintance?" The doctor's voice was still teasing, but there was more than teasing behind his questions. He was really interested in his nephew's psychology.

"Not a da--ahem--darling bit. If I had my way every book in existence would be placed on a huge funeral pyre and conflagrated instantly. Moreover, it would be a criminal offence punishable by the death sentence for any person to bring another of the infernal nuisances into the world. That is my private opinion publicly expressed." So saying Ted picked himself up from the grass and sauntered off toward the house.

His uncle chuckled. He was sorry the boy did not take more cordially to books, since it looked as if there were a good two years of them ahead at the least. But he liked the honesty that would not pretend to anything it did not feel, and he liked even better the spirit that had kept the lad true to his pledge of honest work without a squirm or grumble through all these weeks of grilling summer weather when sustained effort of any sort, particularly mental effort, was undoubtedly a weariness and abomination to flesh and soul, to his restless, volatile, ease-addicted, liberty loving young ward. The boy had certainly shown more grit and grace than he had credited him with possessing.

The village clock struck six. Tony sprang up from her blanket and began to gather up her possessions.

"I never get over a scared, going-to-be-scolded feeling running down my spine when the clock strikes and I'm not ready for supper," she said. "Poor dear Granny! She certainly worked hard trying to make truly proper persons out of us wild Arabs. It isn't her fault if she didn't succeed, is it Larry?" She smiled at her brother--a smile that meant in Tony language "I am sorry I was cross. Let's make up."

He smiled back in the same spirit. He rose taking the rug and magazines from his sister's hand and walked with her toward the house.

Ruth sat up in her hammock and smoothed her disarrayed blonde hair.

"I am glad you are going down the Hill," said the doctor to her. "It is a fine idea, little lady. Do you lots of good."

"Doctor Holiday, I think I ought to go away," announced Ruth suddenly. "I am perfectly well now, and there is no reason why I should stay."

"Tired of us?"

"Oh no! I could never be that. I love it here and love all of you. But after all I am only a stranger."

"Not to us, Ruthie. Listen. I would like to explain how I feel about this, not from your point of view but from ours."

Tony would be going away soon. They needed a home daughter very much, needed Ruth particularly as she had such a wonderful way with the children, who adored her, and because Granny loved her so well, though she did not love many people who were not Holidays. And he and Larry needed her good fairy ministrations. They had not been unmindful, though perhaps manlike they had not expressed their appreciation of the way fresh flowers found their way to the offices daily, and they were kept from being snowed under by the newspapers of yester week. In short Doctor Holiday made it very clear that, if Ruth cared to stay she was wanted and needed very much in the House on the Hill. And Ruth touched and grateful and happy promised to remain.

"If you think it is all right--" she added with rather sudden blush, "for me to stay when I am married or not married and don't know which."

Whereupon Doctor Holiday, who happened not to observe the blush, remarked that he couldn't see what that had to do with it. Anyway she seemed like such a child to them that they hardly remembered the wedding ring at all.

Ruth blushed again at that and wished she dared confess that she was afraid the wedding ring had a good deal to do with the situation in the eyes of one Holiday at least. But she could not bring herself to speak the fatal word which might banish her from the dear Hill and from Larry, who had come to be even dearer.

A dozen times, while she was dressing for the dance later, Ruth felt like crying out to Tony in the next room that she could not go, that she dared not face strangers, that it was too hard. But she set her lips firmly and did nothing of the sort. Larry wanted her to do it. She wouldn't disappoint him if it killed her.

Oh dear! Why did she always have to do everything as a case, never just as a girl. She couldn't even be natural as a girl. She had to be maybe married. She hated the ring which seemed to her a symbol of bondage to a past that was dead and yet still clutched her with cold hands. She had a childish impulse to fling the ring out of the window where she could never--never see it again. If it wasn't for the ring--

She interrupted her own thoughts, blushing hotly again. She knew she had meant to go on, "If it were not for the ring she could marry Larry Holiday." She mustn't think about that. She must not forget the ring, nor let Larry forget it. She must not let him love her. It was a terrible thing she was doing. He was unhappy--dreadfully unhappy and it was all her fault. And by and by they would all see it. Tony had seen it today, she was almost sure. And Doctor Holiday would see it. He saw so much it was a wonder he had not seen it long before this. They would hate her for hurting Larry and spoiling his life. She could not bear to have them hate her when she loved them so and they had been so kind and good to her. She must go away. She must. Maybe Larry would forget her if she wasn't always there right under his eyes.

But how could she go? Doctor Philip would think it queer and ungrateful of her after she had promised to stay. How could she desert him and the children and dear Granny? And if she went what could she do? What use was she anyway but to be a trouble and a burden to everybody? It would have been better, much better, if Larry had left her to die in the wreck.

Why didn't Geoffrey Annersley come and get her, if there was a Geoffrey Annersley? She knew she would hate him, but she wished he would come for all that. Anything was better than making Larry suffer, making all the Holidays suffer through him. Oh why hadn't she died, why hadn't she?

But in her heart Ruth knew she did not want to die. She wanted to live. She wanted life and love and happiness and Larry Holiday.

And then Tony stood on the threshold, smiling friendly encouragement.

"Ready, hon? Oh, you look sweet! That blue is lovely for you. It never suited me at all. Blue is angel color and I have too much--well, of the other thing in my composition to wear it. Come on. The boys have been whistling impatience for half an hour and I don't want to scare Larry out of going. It is the first function he has condescended to attend in a blue moon."

On the porch Ted and Larry waited, two tall, sturdy, well-groomed, fine-looking youths, bearing the indefinable stamp of good birth and breeding, the inheritance of a long line of clean strong men and gentle women--the kind of thing not forged in one generation but in many.

They both rose as the girls appeared. Larry crossed over to Ruth. His quick gaze took in her nervousness and trouble of mind.

"Are you all right, Ruth? You mustn't let us bully you into going if you really don't want to."

"No, I am all right. I do want to--with you," she added softly.

"We'll all go over in the launch," announced Ted, but Larry interposed the fact that he and Ruth were going in the canoe. Ruth would get too tired if she got into a crowd.

"More professional graft," complained Ted. He was only joking but Tony with her sharpened sight knew that it was thin ice for Larry and suspected he had non-professional reasons for wanting Ruth alone in the canoe with him that night. Poor Larry! It was all a horrible tangle, just as her affair with Alan was.

It was a night made for lovers, still and starry. Soft little breezes came tiptoeing along the water from fragrant nooks ashore and stopped in their course to kiss Ruth's face as she lay content and lovely among the scarlet cushions, reading the eloquent message of Larry Holiday's gray eyes.

They did not talk much. They were both a little afraid of words. They felt as if they could go on riding in perfect safety along the edge of the precipice so long as neither looked over or admitted out loud that there was a precipice.

CHAPTER XVIII
A YOUNG MAN IN LOVE

The dance was well in progress when Larry and Ruth arrived. The latter was greeted cordially and not too impressively by gay little Sue Emerson, their hostess, and her friends. Ruth was ensconced comfortably in a big chair where she could watch the dancers and talk as much or little as she pleased. Everybody was so pleasant and natural and uncurious that she did not feel frightened or strange at all, and really enjoyed the little court she held between dances. Pretty girls and pleasant lads came to talk with her, the latter besieging her with invitations to dance which she refused so sweetly that they found the little Goldilocks more charming than ever for her very denial.

They rallied Larry however on his rigorous dragonship and finally Ruth herself dismissed him to dance with his hostess as a proper guest should. She never meant he must stick to her every moment anyway. That was absurd. He rose to obey reluctantly; but paused to ask if she wouldn't dance with him just once. No, she couldn't--didn't even know whether she could. He mustn't try to make her. And seeing she was in earnest, Larry left her. But Ted came skating down the floor to her and he begged for just one dance.

"Oh, I couldn't, Ted, truly I couldn't," she denied.

But obeying a sudden impulse Ted had swooped down upon her, picked her up and before she really knew what was happening she had slid into step with him and was whirling off down the floor in his arms.

"Didn't I tell you, sweetness?" he exulted. "Of course you can dance. What fairy can't? Tired?" He bent over to ask with the instinctive gentleness that was in all Holiday men.

Ruth shook her head. She was exhilarated, excited, tense, happy. She could dance--she could. It was as easy and natural as breathing. She did not want to stop. She wanted to go on and on. Then suddenly something snapped. They came opposite Sue and Larry. The former called a gay greeting and approval. Larry said nothing. His face was dead white, his gray eyes black with anger. Both Ted and Ruth saw and understood and the lilt went out of the dance for both of them.

"Oh Lord!" groaned Ted. "Now I've done it. I'm sorry, Ruth. I didn't suppose the old man would care. Don't see why he should it you are willing. Come on, just one more round before the music stops and we're both beheaded."

But Ruth shook her head. There was no more joy for her after that one glimpse of Larry's face.

"Take me to a seat, Ted, please. I'm tired."

He obeyed and she sank down in the chair, white and trembling, utterly exhausted. She was hurt and aching through and through. How could she? How could she have done that to Larry when he loved her so? How could she have let Ted make her dance with him when she had refused to dance with Larry? No wonder he was angry. It was terrible--cruel.

But he mustn't make a scene with Ted. He mustn't. She cast an apprehensive glance around the room. Larry was invisible. A forlornness came over her, a despair such as she had never experienced even in that dreadful time after the wreck when she realized she had forgotten everything. She felt as if she were sinking down, down in a fearful black sea and that there was no help for her anywhere. Larry had deserted her. Would he never come back?

In a minute Tony and the others were beside her, full of sympathetic questions. How had it seemed to dance again? Wasn't it great to find she could still do it? How had she dared to do it while Larry was off guard? Why wouldn't she, couldn't she dance with this one or that one if she could dance with Ted Holiday? But they were quick to see she was really tired and troubled and soon left her alone to Tony's ministrations.

"Ruth, what is the trouble? Where is Larry? And Ted is gone, too. What happened?" Tony's voice was anxious. She hadn't seen Larry's face, but she knew Larry and could guess at the rest.

"Ted made me dance with him. I didn't mean to. But when we got started I couldn't bear to stop, it was so wonderful to do it and to find I could. I--am afraid

Larry didn't like it."

"I presume he didn't," said Larry's sister drily. "Let him be angry if he wants to be such a silly. It was quite all right, Ruthie. Ted has just as much right to dance with you as Larry has."

"I am afraid Larry doesn't think so and I don't think so either."

Tony squeezed the other girl's hand.

"Never mind, honey. You mustn't take it like that. You are all of a tremble. Larry has a fearful temper, but he will hang on to it for your sake if for no other reason. He won't really quarrel with Ted. He never does any more. And he won't say a word to you."

"I'd rather he would," sighed Ruth. "You are all so good to me and I--am making a dreadful lot of trouble for you all the time, though I don't mean to and I love you so."

"It isn't your fault, Ruthie, not a single speck of it. Oh, yes. I mean just what you mean. Not simply Larry's being so foolish as to lose his temper about this little thing, but the whole big thing of your caring for each other. It is all hard and mixed up and troublesome; but you are not to blame, and Larry isn't to blame, and it will all come out right somehow. It has to."

As soon as Ted had assured himself that Ruth was all right in his sister's charge he had looked about for Larry. Sue was perched on a table eating marshmallows she had purloined from somewhere with Phil Lambert beside her, but there was no Larry to be seen.

Ted stepped outside the pavilion. He was honestly sorry his brother was hurt and angry. He realized too late that maybe he hadn't behaved quite fairly or wisely in capturing Ruth like that, though he hadn't meant any harm, and had had not the faintest idea Larry would really care, care enough to be angry as Ted had not seen him for many a long day. Larry's temper had once been one of the most active of the family skeletons. It had not risen easily, but when it did woe betide whatever or whomever it met in collision. By comparison with Larry's rare outbursts of rage Tony's frequent ebullitions were as summer zephyrs to whirlwinds.

But that was long past history. Larry had worked manfully to conquer his familiar demon and had so far succeeded that sunny Ted had all but forgotten the demon ever existed. But he remembered now, had remembered with consternation when he saw the black passion in the other's face as they met on the floor of the dance hall.

Puzzled and anxious he stared down the slope toward the water. Larry was just stepping into the canoe. Was he going home, leaving Ruth to the mercies of the rest of them, or was he just going off temporarily by himself to fight his temper to a finish as he had been accustomed to do long ago when he had learned to be afraid and ashamed of giving into it? Ted hesitated a moment, debating whether to call him back and get the row over, if row there was to be, or to let him get away by himself as he probably desired.

"Hang it! It's my fault. I can't let him go off like that. It just about kills him to take it out of himself that way. I'd rather he'd take it out of me."

With which conclusion Ted shot down the bank whistling softly the old Holiday Hill call, the one Dick had used that day on the campus to summon himself to the news that maybe Larry was killed.

Larry did not turn. Ted reached the shore with one stride.

"Larry," he called. "I say, Larry."

No answer. The older lad picked up the paddle, prepared grimly to push off, deaf, to all intents and purposes to the appeal in the younger one's voice.

But Ted Holiday was not an easily daunted person. With one flying leap he landed in the canoe, all but upsetting the craft in his sudden descent upon it.

The two youths faced each other. Larry was still white, and his sombre eyes blazed with half subdued fires. He looked anything but hospitable to advances, however well meant.

"Better quit," he advised slowly in a queer, quiet voice which Ted knew was quiet only because Larry was making it so by a mighty effort of will. "I'm not responsible just now. We'll both be sorry if you don't leave me alone."

"I won't quit, Larry. I can't. It was my fault. Confound it, old man! Please listen. I didn't mean to make you mad. Come ashore and punch my fool head if it will make you feel any better."

Still Larry said nothing, just sat hunched in a heap, running his fingers over the handle of the paddle. He no longer even looked at Ted. His mouth was set at its stubbornest.

Ted rushed on, desperately in earnest, entirely sincere in his willingness to undergo any punishment, himself, to help Larry.

"Honest, I didn't mean to make trouble," he pleaded. "I just picked her up and made her dance on impulse, though she told me she wouldn't and couldn't. I never thought for a minute you would care. Maybe it was a mean trick. I can see it might have looked so, but I didn't intend it that way. Gee, Larry! Say something. Don't swallow it all like that. Get it out of your system. I'd rather you'd give me a dozen black eyes than sit still and feel like the devil."

Larry looked up then. His face relaxed its sternness a little. Even the hottest blaze of wrath could not burn quite so fiercely when exposed to a generous penitence like his young brother's. He understood Ted was working hard not only to make peace but to spare himself the sharp battle with the demon which, as none knew better that Larry Holiday, did, indeed, half kill.

"Cut it, Ted," he ordered grimly. "'Nough said. I haven't the slightest desire to give you even one black eye at present, though I may as well admit if you had been in my hands five minutes ago something would have smashed."

"Don't I know it?" Ted grinned a little. "Gee, I thought my hour had struck!"

"What made you come after me then?"

Ted's grin faded.

"You know why I came, old man. You know I'd let you pommel my head off any time if it could help you anyhow. Besides it was my fault as I told you. I didn't mean to be mean. I'll do any penance you say."

Larry picked up the paddle.

"Your penance is to let me absolutely alone for fifteen minutes. You had better go ashore though. You will miss a lot of dances."

"Hang the dances! I'm staying."

Ted settled down among the cushions against which Ruth's blonde head had nestled a few hours ago. He took out his watch, struck a match, looked at the time, lit a cigarette with the same match, replaced the watch and relapsed into silence.

The canoe shot down the lake impelled by long, fierce strokes. Larry was working off the demon. Far away the rhythmic beat of dance music reached them faintly. Now and then a fish leaped and splashed or a bull frog bellowed his hoarse "Better go home" into the silence. Otherwise there was no sound save the steady ripple of the water under the canoe.

Presently Ted finished his cigarette, sent its still ruddy remains flashing off into the lake where it fell with a soft hiss, took out his watch again, lit another match, considered the time, subtracted gravely, looked up and announced "Time's up, Larry."

Larry laid down the paddle and a slow reluctant smile played around the corners of his mouth, though there was sharp distress still in his eyes. He loathed losing his temper like that. It sickened him, filled him with spiritual nausea, a profound disgust for himself and his mastering weakness.

"I've been a fool, kid," he admitted. "I'm all right now. You were a trump to stand by me. I appreciate it."

"Don't mention it," nonchalantly from Ted "Going back to the pavilion?"

His brother nodded, resumed the paddle and again the canoe shot through the waters, this time toward the music instead of away from it.

"I suppose you know why your dancing with Ruth made me go savage," said Larry after a few moments of silence.

"Damned if I do," said Ted cheerfully. "It doesn't matter. I don't need a glossary and appendix. Suit yourself as to the explanations. I put my foot in it. I've apologized. That is the end of it so far as I am concerned unless you want to say something more yourself. You don't have to you know."

"It was plain, fool movie stuff jealousy. That is the sum and substance of it. I'm in love with her. I couldn't stand her dancing with you when she had refused me. I could almost have killed you for a minute. I am ashamed but I couldn't help it. That is the way it was. Now--forget it, please."

Ted swallowed hard and pulled his forelock in genuine perturbation.

"Good Lord, Larry!" he blurted. "I--"

His brother held up an imperious warning hand.

"I said 'forget it.' Don't make me want to dump you now, after coming through the rest."

Ted saluted promptly.

"Ay, ay, sir! It's forgot. Only perhaps you'll let me apologize again, underscored, now I understand. Honest, I'm no end sorry, Larry."

The other nodded acceptance of the underscored apology and again silence had its way.

As they landed Ted fastened the canoe and for a moment the two brothers stood side by side in the starlight. Larry put out his hand. Ted took it. Their eyes met, said more than any words could have expressed.

"Thank you, Ted. You've been great--helped a lot."

Larry's voice was a little unsteady, his eyes were full of trouble and shame.

"Ought to, after starting the conflagration," said Ted. "I'll attend to the general explanations. You go to Ruth."

More than one person had wondered at the mysterious disappearance of the two Holidays. It is quite usual, and far from unexpected, when two young persons of the opposite sex drift off somewhere under the stars on a summer night without giving any particular account of themselves; but one scarcely looks for that sort of social--or unsocial--eccentricity from two youths, especially two brothers. Nobody but Ruth and Tony, and possibly shrewd-eyed Sue, suspected a quarrel, but everybody was curious and ready to burst into interrogation upon the simultaneous return of the two young men which was quite as sudden as their vanishing had been.

"Larry and I had a wager up," announced Ted to Sue in a perfectly clear, distinct voice which carried across the length of the small hall now that the music was silent. "He said he could paddle down to the point, current against him, faster than I could paddle back, current with me. We took a notion to try it out tonight. Please forgive us, Susanna, my dear. A Holiday is a creature of impulse you know."

Sue made a little face at the speaker. She was quite sure he was lying about the wager, but she was a good hostess and played up to his game.

"You don't deserve to be forgiven, either of you," she sniffed. "Especially Larry who never comes to parties and when he does has to go off and do a silly thing like that. Who won though? I will ask that." She smiled at Ted and he grinned back.

"Larry, of course. Give me a dance, Sue. I've got my second wind."

"Bless Ted!" thought Tony, listening to her brother's glib excuses. "Thank goodness he can lie like that. Larry never could." And as her eyes met Ted's a moment later when they passed each other in the maze of dancers he murmured "All right" in her ear and she was well content. Bless Ted, indeed!

Meanwhile Larry had gone, as Ted bade him, straight to Ruth. He bent over her tired little white face, an agony of remorse in his own.

"Ruth, forgive me. I'll never forgive myself."

"Don't, Larry. It is I who ought to be sorry and I am--oh so sorry--you don't know. Ted didn't mean any harm. I ought not to have let him do it. It was my fault."

"There was nobody at fault except me and my fool temper. I am desperately ashamed of myself Ruth. I've left you all alone all this time and I promised I wouldn't. You'll never trust me again and I don't deserve to be trusted. It doesn't do any good to say I am sorry. It can't undo what I did. I didn't dare stay and that's the fact. I didn't know what I'd do to Ted if he got in my way. I felt--murderous."

"Larry!"

"I know it sounds awful. It is awful. It is an old battle. I thought I'd won it, but I haven't. Don't look so scared though. Nothing happened. Ted came after me like the corking big-hearted kid he is and brought me to, in half the time I could have done it for myself. It is thanks to him I'm here now. But never mind that. It is only you that matters. Shall I take you home? I don't deserve it, but if you will let me it will show you forgive me a little bit anyway," he finished humbly.

"Don't look so dreadfully unhappy, Larry. It is over now, and of course I forgive you if you think there is anything to forgive. I'm so thankful you didn't quarrel with Ted. I was awfully worried and so was Tony. She watched the door every minute till you came back."

"I suppose so," groaned Larry. "I made one horrible mess of everything for you all. Are you ready to go?"

"I'd like to dance with you once first, Larry, if--if you would like to."

"Would I like to!" Larry's face lost its mantle of gloom, was sudden sunshine all over. "Will you really dance with me--after the rotten way I've behaved?"

"Of course, I will. I wanted to all the time, but I was afraid. But when Ted made me it all came back and I loved it, only it was you I wanted to dance with most. You know that, don't you, Larry, dear?" The last word was very low, scarcely more than a breath, but Larry heard it and it nearly undid him. A flood of long-pent endearments trembled on his lips. But Ruth held up a hand of warning.

"Don't, Larry. We mustn't spoil it. We've got to remember the ring."

"Damn the ring!" he exploded. "I beg your pardon." Larry was genuinely shocked at his own bad manners. "I don't know why I'm such a brute tonight. Let's dance."

And to the delight and relief of the younger Holidays, Larry and Ruth joined the dancers.

The dance over, they made their farewells. Larry guided Ruth down the slope, his arm around her ostensibly for her support, and helped her into the canoe. Once more they floated off over the quiet water, under the quiet stars. But their young hearts were anything but quiet. Their love was no longer an unacknowledged thing. Neither knew just what was to be done with it; but there it was in full sight, as both admitted in joy and trepidation and silence.

As Larry held open the door for her to step inside the quiet hall he bent over the girl a moment, taking both her hands in his. Then he drew away abruptly and bolted into the living room, leaving her to grope her way up stairs in the dark alone.

"I wonder," she murmured to herself later as she stood before her mirror shaking out her rippling golden locks from their confining net. "I wonder if it would have been so terrible if he had kissed me just that once. Sometimes I wish he weren't quite so--so Holidayish."

CHAPTER XIX
TWO HOLIDAYS MAKE CONFESSION

The next evening Doctor Holiday listened to a rather elaborate argument on the part of his older nephew in favor of the latter's leaving Dunbury immediately in pursuit of his specialist training that he had planned to go in for eventually.

"You are no longer contented here with me--with us?" questioned the older man when the younger had ended his exposition.

Larry's quick ear caught the faint hurt in his uncle's voice and hastened to deny the inference.

"It isn't that, Uncle Phil. I am perfectly satisfied--happier here with you that I would be anywhere else in the world. You have been wonderful to me. I am not such an ungrateful idiot as not to understand and appreciate what a start it has given me to have you and your name and work behind me. Only--maybe I've been under your wing long enough. Maybe I ought to stand on my feet."

Doctor Holiday studied the troubled young face opposite him. He was fairly certain that he wasn't getting the whole or the chief reasons which were behind this sudden proposition.

"Do you wish to go at once?" he asked. "Or will the first of the year be soon enough."

Larry flushed and fell to fumbling with a paper knife that lay on the desk.

"I--I meant to go right away," he stammered.

"Why?"

Larry was silent.

"I judge the evidence isn't all in," remarked the older doctor a little drily. "Am I going to hear the rest of it--the real reason for your decision to go just now?"

Still silence on Larry's part, the old obstinate set to his lips.

"Very well then. Suppose I take my turn. I think you haven't quite all the evidence yourself. Do you know Granny is dying?"

The paper knife fell with a click to the floor.

"Uncle Phil! No, I didn't know. Of course I knew it was coming but you mean--soon?"

"Yes, Larry, I mean soon. How soon no one can tell, but I should say three months would be too long to allow."

The boy brushed his hand across his eyes. He loved Granny. He had always seemed to understand her better than the others had and had been himself always the favorite. Moreover he was bound to her by a peculiar tie, having once saved her life, conquering his boyish fear to do so. It was hard to realize she was really going, that no one could save her now.

"I didn't know," he said again in a low voice.

"Ted will go back to college. I shall let Tony go to New York to study as she wishes, just as you had your chance. It isn't exactly the time for you to desert us, my boy."

"I won't, Uncle Phil. I'll stay."

"Thank you, son. I felt sure you wouldn't fail us. You never have. But I wish you felt as if you could tell me the other reason or reasons for going which you are keeping back. If it is they are stronger than the one I have given you for staying it is only fair that I should have them."

Larry's eyes fell. A slow flush swept his face, ran up to his very hair.

"My boy, is it Ruth?"

The gray eyes lifted, met the older man's grave gaze unfalteringly.

"Yes, Uncle Phil, it is Ruth. I thought you must have seen it before this. It seemed as if I were giving myself away, everything I did or didn't do."

"I have thought of it occasionally, but dismissed the idea as too fantastic. It hasn't been so obvious as it seemed to you no doubt. You have not made love to her?"

"Not in so many words. I might just as well have though. She knows. If it weren't for the ring--well, I think she would care too."

"I am very sorry, Larry. It looks like a bad business all round. Yet I can't see that you have much to blame yourself for. I withdraw my objections to your going away. If it seems best to you to go I haven't a word to say."

"I don't know whether it is best or not. I go round and round in circles trying to work it out. It seems cowardly to run away from it, particularly if I am needed here. A man ought not to pull up stakes just because things get a little hard. Besides Ruth would think she had driven me away. I know she would go herself if she guessed I was even thinking of going. And I couldn't stand that. I'd go to the north pole myself and stay forever before I would send her away from you all. I was so grateful to you for asking her to stay and making her feel she was needed. She was awfully touched and pleased. She told me last night."

The senior doctor considered, thought back to his talk with Ruth. Poor child! So that was what she had been trying to tell him. She had thought she ought to go away on Larry's account, just as he was thinking he ought to go on hers. Poor hapless youngsters caught in the mesh of circumstances! It was certainly a knotty problem.

"It isn't easy to say what is right and best to do," he said after a moment. "It is something you will have to decide for yourself. When you came to me you had decided it was best to go, had you not? Was there a specially urgent reason?"

Larry flushed again and related briefly the last night's unhappy incident.

"I'm horribly ashamed of the way I acted," he finished. "And the whole thing showed me I couldn't count on my self-control as I thought I could. I couldn't sleep last night, and I thought perhaps maybe the thing to do was to get out quick before I did any real damage. It doesn't matter about me. It is Ruth."

"Do you think you can stay on and keep a steady head for her sake and for ours?"

"I can, Uncle Phil. It is up to me to stick and I'll do it. Uncle Phil, how long must a woman in Ruth's position wait before she can legally marry?"

"Ruth's position is so unique that I doubt if there is any legal precedent for it. Ordinarily when the husband fails to put in appearance and the presumption is he is no longer living, the woman is considered free in the eyes of the law, after a certain number of years, varying I believe, in different states. With Ruth the affair doesn't seem to be a case of law at all. She is in a position which requires the utmost protection from those who love her as we do. The obligation is moral rather than legal. I wouldn't let my mind run on the marrying aspects of the case at present my boy."

"I--Uncle Phil, sometimes I think I'll just marry her anyway and let the rest of it take care of itself. There isn't any proof she is married--not the slightest shadow of proof," Larry argued with sudden heat.

His uncle's eyebrows went up. "Steady, Larry. A wedding ring is usually considered presumptive evidence of marriage."

"I don't care," flashed the boy, the tension of the past weeks suddenly snapping. "She loves me. I don't see what right anything has to come between us. What is a wedding ceremony when a man and woman belong to each other as we belong? Hanged if I don't think I'd be justified in marrying her tomorrow! There is nothing but a ring to prevent."

"There is a good deal more than a ring to prevent," said Doctor Holiday with some sternness. "What if you did do just that and her husband appeared in two months or six?"

"I don't believe she has a husband. If she had he would have come after her before this. We've waited. He's had time."

"You have waited scarcely two months, Larry. That is hardly enough time upon which to base finalities."

"What of it? I'm half crazy sometimes over the whole thing. I can't see things straight. I don't want to. I don't want anything but Ruth, whether she is married or not. I want her. Some day I'll ask her to go off with me and she will go. She will do anything I ask."

"Hold on, Larry lad. You are saying things you don't mean. You are the last man in the world to take advantage of a girl's defenseless position and her love for you to gratify your own selfish desires and perhaps wreck her life and your own."

Larry bit his lip, wheeled and went over to the window, staring out into the night. At last he turned back, white, but master of himself again.

"I beg your pardon, Uncle Phil. You are right. I was talking like a fool. Of course I'll do nothing of the kind. I won't do anything to harm Ruth anyway. I won't even make love to her--if I can help it," he qualified in a little lower tone.

"If you can't you had better go at once," said his uncle still a bit sternly. Then more gently. "I know you don't want to play the cad, Larry."

"I won't, Uncle Phil. I promise."

"Very well. I am satisfied with your word. Remember I am ready to help any way and if it gets too hard I'll make it easy at any time for you to go. But in the mean time we won't talk about it. The least said the better."

Larry nodded his assent to that and suddenly switched to another subject, asking his uncle what he knew about this Alan Massey with whom Tony was having such an extensive correspondence.

His uncle admitted that he didn't know much of anything about him, except that he was the inheritor of the rather famous Massey property and an artist of some repute.

"He has plenty of repute of other kinds," said Larry. "He is a thorough-going rotter, I infer. I made some inquiries from a chap who knows him. He has gone the pace and then some. It makes me sick to have Tony mixed up with a chap like that."

"You haven't said anything to her yourself?"

"No. Don't dare. It would only make it worse for me to tackle her. Neither she nor Ted will stand any interference from me. We are a cranky lot I am afraid. We all have what Dad used to call the family devil. So far as I know you are the only person on record that can manage him."

And Larry smiled rather shame-facedly at his uncle.

"I am afraid you will all three have to learn to manage your own particular familiar. Devils are rather personal property, Larry."

"Don't I know it? I got into mighty close range with mine last night, and just now for that matter. Anyway I am not prepared to do any preaching at anybody at present; but I would be awfully grateful to you if you will speak to Tony. Somebody has to. And you can do it a million times better than anyone else."

"Very well. I will see what I can do." And thus quietly Doctor Holiday accepted another burden on his broad shoulders.

The next day he found Tony on the porch reading one of the long letters which came to her so frequently in the now familiar, dashing script.

"Got a minute for me, niece o' mine?" he asked.

Tony slid Alan's letter back into its envelope and smiled up at her uncle.

"Dozens of them, nice uncle," she answered.

"It is getting well along in the summer and high time we decided a few things. Do you still want to go in for the stage business in the fall?"

"I want to very much, Uncle Phil, if you think it isn't too much like deserting Granny and the rest of you."

"No, you have earned it. I want you to go. I don't suppose because you haven't talked about Hempel's offer that it means you have forgotten it?"

"Indeed, I haven't forgotten it. For myself I would much rather get straight on the stage if I could and learn by doing it, but you would prefer to have me go to a regular dramatic school, wouldn't you?"

"Yes, Tony, I would. A year of preparation isn't a bit too much to get your bearings in before you take the grand plunge. I want you to be very sure that the stage is what you really want."

"I am sure of that already. I've been sure for ages. But I am perfectly willing to do the thing any way you want and I am more grateful than I can tell you that you are on my side about it. Are you going to tell Granny? It will about break her heart I am afraid." Tony's eyes were troubled. She did hate to hurt Granny; but on the other hand she couldn't wait forever to begin.

She did not see the shadow that crept over her uncle's face. Well he knew that long before Tony was before the footlights, Granny would be where prejudices and misunderstandings were no more; but he had no wish to mar the girl's happiness by betraying the truth just now.

"I think we are justified in indulging in a little camouflage there," he said. "We will tell Granny you are going to study art. Art covers a multitude of sins," he added with a lightness he was far from feeling. "One thing more, my dear. I have waited a good while to hear something about the young man who writes these voluminous letters.'" He nodded at the envelope in Tony's lap. "I like his writing; but I should like to know something about him,--himself."

Tony flushed and averted her eyes for a moment. Then she looked up frankly.

"I haven't said anything because I didn't know what to say. He is Alan Massey, the artist. I met him at Carlotta's. He wants to marry me."

"But you have not already accepted him?"

"No, I couldn't. He--he isn't the kind of man you would want me to marry. He is trying to be, for my sake though. I think he will succeed. I told him if he wanted to ask me again next summer I would tell him what my answer would be."

"He is on probation then?"

"Yes."

"And you care for him?"

"I--think so."

"You don't know it?"

"No, Uncle Phil. I don't. He cares so much for me--so terribly much. And I don't know whether I care enough or not. I should have to care a great deal to overlook what he has been and done. Maybe it wasn't anything but midsummer madness and his wonderful dancing. We danced almost every night until I sent him away. And when we danced we seemed to be just one person. Aside from his dancing he fascinated me. I couldn't forget him or ignore him. He was--is--different from any man I ever knew. I feel differently about him from what I ever felt about any other man. Maybe it is love. Maybe it isn't. I--I thought it was last month."

Doctor Holiday shook his head dubiously.

"And you are not so sure now?" he questioned.

"Not always," admitted Tony. "I didn't want to love him. I fought it with all my might. I didn't want to be bothered with love. I wanted to be happy and free and make a great success of my work. But after Alan came all those things didn't seem to matter. I am afraid it goes rather deep, Uncle Phil. Sometimes I think he means more to me than even you and Larry and Ted do. It is strange. It isn't kind or loyal or decent. But that is the way it is. I have to be honest, even if it hurts."

Her dark eyes were wistful and beseeched forgiveness as they sought her uncle's. He did not speak and she went on swiftly, earnestly.

"Please don't ask me to break off with him, Uncle Phil. I couldn't do it, not only because I care for him too much, but because it would be cruel to him. He has gotten out of his dark forest. I don't want to drive him back into it. And that is what it would mean if I deserted him now. I have to go on, no matter what you or Larry or any one thinks about it."

She had risen now and stood before her uncle earnestly pleading her lover's cause and her own.

"It isn't fair to condemn a man forever because he has made mistakes back in the past. We don't any of us know what we would have been like if things had been different. Larry and Ted are fine. I am proud of their clean record. It would be horrible if people said things about either of them such as they say about Alan. But Larry and Ted have every reason to be fine. They have had you and Dad and Grandfather Holiday and the rest of them to go by. They have lived all their lives in the Holiday tradition of what a man should be. Alan has had nobody, nothing. Nobody ever helped him to see the difference between right and wrong and why it mattered which you chose. He does see now. He is trying to begin all over again and begin right. And I'm going to stand by him. I have to--even if I have to go against you, Uncle Phil."

There was a quiver--almost a sob in Tony's voice Her uncle drew her into his arms.

"All right, little girl. It is not an easy thing to swallow. I hate to have your shining whiteness touch pitch even for a minute. No, wait, dear. I am not going to condemn your lover. If he is sincerely in earnest in trying to clean the slate, I have only respect for the effort. You are right about much of it. We can none of us afford to do over much judging. We are all sinners, more or less. And there are a million things to be taken into consideration before we may dare to sit in judgment upon any human being. It takes a God to do that. I am not going to ask you to give him up, or to stop writing or even seeing him. But I do want you to go slow. Marriage is a solemn thing. Don't wreck your life from pity or mistaken devotion. Better a heart-ache now than a life-long regret. Let your lover prove himself just as you have set him to do. A woman can't save a man. He has to save himself. But if he will save himself for love of her the chances are he will stay saved and his love is the real thing. I shall accept your decision. I shan't fight it in any way, whatever it is. All I ask is that you will wait the full year before you make any definite promise of marriage."

"I will," said Tony. "I meant to do that any way. I am not such a foolish child as maybe you have been thinking I was. I am pretty much grown up, Uncle Phil. And I have plenty of sense. It I hadn't--I should be married to Alan this minute."

He smiled a little sadly at that.

"Youth! Youth! Yes, Tony, I believe you have sense. Maybe I have under-estimated it. Any way I thank the good Lord for it. No more secrets? Everything clear?"

He lifted her face in his hands and looked down into her eyes with tender searching.

"Not a secret. I am very glad to have you know. We all feel better the moment we dump all our woes on you," she sighed.

He smiled and stroked her hair.

"I had much rather be a dumping ground than be shut out of the confidence of any one of you. That hurts. We all have to stand by Larry, just now. Not in words but in--well, we'll call it moral support. The poor lad needs it."

"Oh, Uncle Phil! Did he tell you or did you guess?"

"A little of both. The boy is in a bad hole, Tony. But he will keep out of the worst of the bog. He has grit and chivalry enough to pull through somehow. And maybe before many weeks the mystery will be cleared for better or worse. We can only hope for the best and hold on tight to Larry, and Ruth too, till they are out of the woods."

CHAPTER XX
A YOUNG MAN NOT FOR SALE

Philip Lambert was rather taken by surprise when Harrison Cressy appeared at the store one day late in August, announcing that he had come to talk business and practically commanding the young man to lunch with him that noon. It was Saturday and Phil had little time for idle conjecture, but he did wonder every now and then that morning what business Carlotta's father could possibly have with himself, and if by any chance Carlotta had sent him.

Later, seated in the dining-room of the Eagle Hotel, Dunbury's one hostelry, it seemed to Phil that his host was distinctly nervous, with considerably less than his usual brusque, dogmatic poise of manner.

Having left soup the waiter shuffled away with the congenial air of discouragement which belongs to his class, and Harrison Cressy got down to business in regard both to the soup and his mission in Dunbury. He was starting a branch brokerage concern in a small city just out of Boston. He needed a smart young man to put at the head of it. The smart young man would get a salary of five thousand a year, plus his commissions to start with. If he made good the salary would go up in proportion. In fact the sky would be the limit. He offered the post to Philip Lambert.

Phil laid down his soup spoon and stared at his companion. After a moment he remarked that it was rather unusual, to say the least, to offer a salary like that to an utter greenhorn in a business as technical as brokerage, and that he was afraid he was not in the least fitted for the position in question.

"That is my look out," snapped Mr. Cressy. "Do I look like a born fool, Philip Lambert? You don't suppose I am jumping in the dark do you? I have gone to some pains to look up your record in college. I found out you made good no matter what you attempted, on the gridiron, in the classroom, everywhere else. I've been picking men for years and I've gone on the principle that a man who makes good in one place will make good in another if he has sufficient incentive."

"I suppose the five thousand is to be considered in the light of an incentive," said Phil.

"It is five times the incentive and more than I had when I started out," grunted his host. "What more do you want?"

"Nothing. I don't want so much. I couldn't earn it. And in any case I cannot consider any change at present. I have gone in with my father."

"So I understood. But that is not a hard and fast arrangement. A young man like you has to look ahead. Your father won't stand in the way of your bettering yourself." Harrison Cressy spoke with conviction. Well he might. Though Philip had not known it his companion had spent an hour in earnest conversation with his father that morning. Harrison Cressy knew his ground there.

"Go ahead, Mr. Cressy," Stewart Lambert had said at the close of the interview. "You have my full permission to offer the position to the boy and he has my full permission to accept it. He is free to go tomorrow if he cares to. If it is for his happiness it is what his mother and I want."

But the younger Lambert was yet to be reckoned with.

"It is a hard and fast arrangement so far as I am concerned," he said quietly now. "Dad can fire me. I shan't fire myself."

Mr. Cressy made a savage lunge at a fly that had ventured to light on the sugar bowl, not knowing it was for the time being Millionaire Cressy's sugar bowl. He hated being balked, even temporarily. He had supposed the hardest sledding would be over when he had won the father's consent. He had authentic inside information that the son had stakes other than financial. He counted on youth's imperious urge to happiness. The lad had done without Carlotta for two months now. It had seemed probable he would be more amenable to reason in August than he had been in June. But it did not look like it just now.

"You are a darn fool, my young man," he gnarled.

"Very likely," said Phil Lambert, with the same quietness which had marked his father's speech earlier in the day. "If you had a son, Mr. Cressy, wouldn't you want him to be the same kind of a darn fool? Would you expect him to take French leave the first time somebody offered him more money?"

Harrison Cressy snorted, beckoned to the waiter his face purple with rage. Why in blankety blank blank et cetera, et cetera, didn't he bring the fish? Did he think they were there for the season? Philip did not know he had probed an old wound. The one great disappointment of Harrison Cressy's career was the fact that he had no son, or had had one for such a brief space of hours that he scarcely counted except as a pathetic might-have-been And even as Phil had said, so he would have wanted his son to behave. The boy was a man, every inch of him, just such a man as Harrison Gressy had coveted for his own.

"Hang the money part." he snapped back at Phil, after the interlude with the harrassed waiter. "Let's drop it."

"With all my heart," agreed Phil. "Considering the money part hanged what is left to the offer? Carlotta?"

Mr. Cressy dropped his fork with a resounding clatter to the floor and swore muttered monotonous oaths at the waiter for not being instantaneously on the spot to replace the implement.

"Young man," he said to Phil. "You are too devilish smart. Carlotta--is why I am here."

"So I imagined. Did she send you?"

"Great Scott, no! My life wouldn't be worth a brass nickel if she knew I was here."

"I am glad she didn't. I wouldn't like Carlotta to think I could be--bribed."

"She didn't. Carlotta has perfectly clear impressions as to where you stand. She gives you entire credit for being the blind, stubborn, pigheaded jack-ass that you are."

Phil grinned faintly at this accumulation of epithets, but his blue eyes had no mirth in them. The interview was beginning to be something of a strain. He wished it were over.

"That's good," he said. "Apparently we all know where we all stand. I have no illusions about Carlotta's view-point either. There is no reason I should have. I got it first hand."

"Don't be an idiot," ordered Mr. Cressy. "A woman can have as many view-points as there are days in the year, counting Sundays double. You have no more idea this minute where Carlotta stands than--than I have," he finished ignominiously, wiping his perspiring forehead with an imported linen handkerchief.

"Do you mind telling me just why you are here, if Carlotta didn't send you? I don't flatter myself you automatically selected me for your new post without some rather definite reason behind it."

"I came because I had a notion you were the best man for another job--a job that makes the whole brokerage business look like a game of jack-straws--the job of marrying my daughter Carlotta."

Phil stared. He had not expected Mr. Cressy to take this position. He had been ready enough to believe Carlotta's prophecy that her parent would raise a merry little row if she announced to him her intention of marrying that obscure individual, Philip Lambert, of Dunbury, Massachusetts. He thought that particular way of behavior on the parent's part not only probable but more or less justifiable, all things considered. He saw no reason now why Mr. Cressy should feel otherwise.

Harrison Cressy drained a deep draught of water, once more wiped his highly shining brow and leaned forward over the table toward his puzzled guest.

"You see, Philip," he went on using the young man's first name for the first time. "Carlotta is in love with you."

Philip flushed and his frank eyes betrayed that this, though not entirely new news, was not unwelcome to hear.

"In fact," continued Carlotta's father grimly, "she is so much in love with you she is going to marry another man."

The light went out of Phil's eyes at that, but he said nothing to this any more than he had to the preceding statement. He waited for the other man to get at what he wanted to say.

"I can't stand Carlotta's being miserable. I never could. It is why I am here, to see if I can't fix up a deal with you to straighten things out. I am in your hands, boy, at your mercy. I have the reputation of being hard as shingle nails. I'm soft as putty where the girl is concerned. It kills me by inches to have her unhappy."

"Is she--very unhappy?" Phil's voice was sober. He thought that he too was soft as putty, or softer where Carlotta was concerned. It made him sick all over to think of her being unhappy.

"She is--damnably unhappy." Harrison Cressy blew his nose with a sound as of a trumpet. "Here you," he bellowed at the waiter who was timidly approaching. "Is that our steak at last? Bring it here, quick and don't jibber. Are you deaf and dumb as well as paralyzed?"

The host attacked the steak with ferocity, slammed a generous section on a plate and fairly threw it at the young man opposite. Phil wasn't interested in steak. He scarcely looked at it. His eyes were on Mr. Cressy, his thoughts were on that gentleman's only daughter.

"I am sorry she is unhappy," he said. "I don't know how much you know about it all; but since you know so much I assume you also know that I care for Carlotta just as much as she cares for me, possibly more. I would marry her tomorrow if I could."

"For the Lord Harry's sake, do it then. I'll put up the money."

Phil's face hardened.

"That is precisely the rock that Carlotta and I split on, Mr. Cressy. She wanted to have you put up the money. I love Carlotta but I don't love her enough to let her or you--buy me."

The old man and the young faced each other across the table. There was a deadlock between them and both knew it.

"But this offer I've made you is a bona fide one. You'll make good. You will be worth the five thousand and more in no time. I know your kind. I told you I was a good picker. It isn't a question of buying. Can the movie stuff. It's a fair give and take."

"I have refused your offer, Mr. Cressy."

"You refused it before you knew Carlotta was eating her heart out for you. Doesn't that make any difference to you, my lad? You said you loved her," reproachfully.

A huge blue-bottle fly buzzed past the table, passed on to the window where it fluttered about aimlessly, bumping itself against the pane here and there. Mechanically Phil watched its gyrations. It was one of the hardest moments of his life.

"In one way it makes a great difference, Mr. Cressy," he answered slowly. "It breaks my heart to have her unhappy. But it wouldn't make her happy to have me do something I know isn't right or fair or wise. I know Carlotta. Maybe I know her better than you do; I know she doesn't want me that way."

"But you can't expect her to live in a hole like this, on a yearly income that is probably less than she spends in one month just for nothing much."

"I don't expect it," explained Phil patiently. "I've never blamed Carlotta for deciding against it. But there is no use going over it all. She and I had it out together. It is our affair, not yours, Mr. Cressy."

"Philip Lambert, did you ever see Carlotta cry?"

Phil winced. The shot went home.

"No. I'd hate to," he admitted.

"You would," seconded Harrison Cressy. "I hated it like the devil myself. She cried all over my new dress suit the other night."

Phil's heart was one gigantic ache. The thought of Carlotta in tears was almost unbearable. Carlotta--his Carlotta--was all sunshine and laughter.

"It was like this," went on Carlotta's parent. "Her aunt told me she was going to marry young Lathrop--old skin-flint tea-and-coffee Lathrop's son. I couldn't quite stomach it. The fellow's an ass, an unobjectionable ass, it is true, but with all the ear marks. I tackled Carlotta about it. She said she wasn't engaged but might be any minute. I said some fool thing about wanting her to be happy, and the next thing I knew she was in my arms crying like anything. I haven't seen her cry since she was a little tot. She has laughed her way through life always up to now. I couldn't bear it. I can't bear it now, even remembering it. I squeezed the story out of her, drop at a time, till I got pretty much the whole bucket full. I tell you, Phil Lambert, you've got to give in. I can't have her heart broken. You can't have her heart broken. God, man, it's your funeral too."

Phil felt very much as if it were his own funeral. But he did not speak. He couldn't. The other forged on, his big, mumbling bass mingled with the buzz of the blue-bottle in the window.

"I made up my mind something had to be done and done quick. I wasn't going to have my little girl run her head into the noose by marrying Lathrop when it was you she loved. I got busy, made inquiries about you as I said. I had to before I offered you the job naturally, but it was more than that. I had to find out whether you were the kind of man I wanted my Carlotta to marry. I found out, and came up here to put the proposition to you. I talked to your father first, by the way, and got his consent to go ahead with my plans."

"You went to my father!" There was concern and a trace of indignation in Phil's voice.

"Naturally I was playing to win. I had to hold all the trumps. I wanted your father on my side--had to have him in fact. He came without a murmur. He is a good sport. Said all he wanted was your happiness, same as all I wanted was Carlotta's. We quite understood each other."

Phil sat silent with down cast eyes on his almost untasted salad. He couldn't bear to think of his father's being attacked like that, hit with a lightning bolt out of a clear sky. The more he thought about it the more he resented it. Of course Dad would agree. He was a good sport as Mr. Cressy said. Rut that didn't make the thing any easier or more justifiable.

"Your father is willing. I want it. Carlotta wants it. You want it, yourself. Lord, boy, be honest. You know you do. You'll never regret giving in. Remember it is for Carlotta's happiness we are both looking for." There was an almost pleading note in

Harrison Cressy's voice--a note few men had heard. He was more used to command than to sue for what he desired.

Phil rose from the table. His face was a little white as he stood there, tall, quiet, perfectly master of himself and the situation. Even before the young man spoke Harrison Cressy knew he had failed.

"I am sorry, Mr. Cressy. If Carlotta wants happiness with me I am afraid she will have to come to Dunbury."

"You won't reconsider?"

"There is nothing to reconsider. There never was any question. I am sorry you even raised one in Dad's mind. You shouldn't have gone to him in the first place. You should have come to me. It was for me to settle."

"Highty, tighty!" fumed the exasperated magnate. "People don't tell me what I should and should not do. They do what I tell 'em."

"I don't," said Philip Lambert in much the same tone he had once said to Carlotta, "You can't have this." "I am sorry, Mr. Cressy. I don't want to be rude, or unkind or obstinate; but there are some things no man can decide for me. And there are some things I won't do even to win Carlotta."

Harrison Cressy's head drooped for a moment. He was beaten for once--beaten by a lad of twenty-three whose will was quite as strong as his own. The worst of it was he had never liked any young man in his life so well as he liked Philip Lambert at this minute, never so coveted any thing for his daughter Carlotta as he coveted her marriage with Philip Lambert.

"That is final, I suppose," he asked after a moment, looking up at the young man.

"Absolutely, Mr. Cressy. I am sorry."

Harrison Cressy lumbered to his feet.

"I am sorry too," he said, "damnably sorry for Carlotta and for myself. Will you shake hands with me, Philip? It is good to meet a man now and then."

CHAPTER XXI
HARRISON CRESSY REVERTS

Left to himself, Harrison Cressy discovered to his annoyance that there was no train out of Dunbury for two hours. That was the worst of these little one-horse towns. You might as well be dead as alive in 'em. By the time he had smoked his after-dinner cigar he felt as if he might as well be dead himself. He felt suddenly heavy, old, almost decrepit, though that morning when he had left Boston he had considered himself in the prime of life and vigor. Hang it! He was sixty-nine. A man was about done for at sixty-nine, all but ready to turn into his grave. And he without son or grandson. Lord! What a swindle life was anyway!

Well, there was no use sitting still groaning. He would get up and take a little walk until train time. Maybe it was his liver that made him feel so confoundedly rotten and no count. A little exercise would do him good.

Absentmindedly he noted, as he strolled down the elm-shaded streets, the neatness of the lawns, the gay flower beds, the hammocks and swings out under the trees as if people really lived out of doors here. There were animate evidences of the fact everywhere. Children played here and there in shady spaces under big trees. Pretty girls on wide, hospitable-looking porches chatted and drank lemonade and knitted. A lithe, red-haired lass in white played tennis on a smooth dirt court with a tall, clean looking youth. As Mr. Cressy passed the girl cried out, "Love all" and the millionaire smiled. It occurred to him it was not so hard to love all in a village like this. It was only in cities that you hated your neighbor and did him first lest you be done yourself.

He hadn't been loose in a country town like this for years. He had almost forgotten what they were like when you didn't shoot through them in a motor car, rushing always to get somewhere else. His casual saunter down the quiet street was oddly soothing to his nerves, awoke happy, yet half-sad memories.

He had met and loved Carlotta's mother in a country town. The lilacs had been in bloom and the orioles had stood sponsor for his first Sunday call. They had become engaged by the time the asters were out. The next lilac time they had been married. A third spring and the little Carlotta had come. They had both been disappointed at its not being a boy, but the little girl was a wonder, with hair as gold as buttercups, eyes like wood violets and a laugh that lilted and gurgled like the little brook down in the meadow.

And then, two years later, the boy had come, come and drifted off to some far place. It had been a bitter blow to Rose as well as to Harrison Cressy, especially as they said there never could be any more children. Rose grew frail, did not rally or regain her strength. They advised a sanitarium in the Adirondacks for her. She had gone, but it had been of no use. By the time they brought in the first gentians Rose had drifted off after her little son. Carlotta and her father were alone.

By this time Harrison Cressy had begun to show the authentic Midas touch. Only the little Carlotta stood between him and sheer, sordid money grubbing. And even she was an excuse for the getting of always more and more wealth. He told himself Carlotta should be a veritable princess, should go always clad in the finest, have of the best, be surrounded always by the most beautiful. She should know only joy and light and laughter.

Thinking these thoughts, Carlotta's father sighed. For now at last Carlotta wanted something he could not give her, was learning after twenty-two years of cloudless joy the bitter way of tears. Why hadn't that stubborn boy surrendered?

For that matter why didn't Carlotta surrender? This was a new idea to Harrison Cressy. All the time he had been talking to Philip Lambert he had been seeing Carlotta only in relation to Crest House and the Beacon Street mansion. But just now he had been recalling her mother under very different associations. Rose had been content with a tiny little cottage set in a green yard gay with bright old fashioned flowers. He and Rose had nested as happily as the orioles in the maples, especially after the gold-haired baby came. Was Carlotta so different from Rose? Was her happiness such a different kind of thing? Were women not pretty much alike at heart? Did they not want about the same things?

Carlotta loved this lad of hers as Rose had loved himself. Was it her own father who was cheating her out of happiness because he had taught her to believe that money and limousines and great houses and many servants and silken robes are happiness? If he had talked to her of other things, told her about her mother and the happy old days among the lilacs and orioles, with little but love to nest with, couldn't he have made her see things more truly, shown her that love was the main thing, that money could not buy happiness? One could not buy much of anything that was worth buying Harrison Cressy thought. One could purchase only the worthless. That was the everlasting failure of money.

He remembered the boy's, "I love Carlotta. But I don't love her enough to let her or you buy me." It was true. Neither he nor his daughter had been able to purchase the lad's integrity, his good faith, his ideals. And Harrison Cressy was thankful from the bottom of his heart that it was so.

He turned his steps back to the village and as he did so an oriole flashed out of the shrubbery near him, and passed like a flame out of sight among the trees. This was a good sign. Orioles had nested every year in the maple tree by the little white house where Carlotta had been born. Carlotta herself had always loved them. "Pretty, pretty, birdie!" she had been wont to call out. "Come, daddy, let's follow him and see where he goes."

He would go home and tell Carlotta all this, make her see that her happiness was in her own hands. No, it was the boy's story. If Carlotta would not follow the orioles and her own heart for Philip Lambert she would not for any argument of his.

By this time a distant puff of smoke gave evidence that the Boston train was already on its way, leaving Harrison Cressy in Dunbury. Not that he cared. He had business still to transact ere he departed, a new battle to fight. He walked with the firm elastic step of a youth back to town. What did it matter if you were sixty-nine when the best things of life were still ahead of you?

Accordingly Phil was a second time that day surprised by the unheralded arrival of Carlotta's father, a rather dusty, weary and limp-looking gentleman this time, but exuding a sort of benignant serenity that had not been there early in the day.

"Hello," greeted the millionaire blandly. "Missed my train--got to browsing round the town like an old billy goat. Not sorry though. It is a nice little town. Mind if I sit down? I'm a bit blown." And dropping on a stool Mr. Cressy fanned himself with his panama and grinned at Philip, a grin the young man could not quite fathom. What new trick had the clever old financier at the bottom of his mind? Phil hoped he had not got to go through the thing again. Once had been quite enough for one day.

"Let me send out for something cool to drink, Mr. Cressy. You must be horribly hot. It is warm in here, even with all the fans going. Hi, there, Tommy!" Philip summoned a freckled, red-haired youth from somewhere in the background. "Run over to Greene's and get a lemonade for this gentleman, will you?"

"Right, Mr. Phil." The boy saluted--an odd salute, Mr. Cressy noted. It was rendered with the right hand, the three middle fingers held up, the thumb bent over touching the nail of the little finger. The saluter stood very straight as he went through the ceremony and looked very serious about it. "Queer!" thought the onlooker. The messenger boys he knew did not behave like that when you gave them an order.

Philip excused himself to attend to a customer and in a moment the red-haired lad was back with a tall glass of lemonade clinking delightfully with ice. Mr. Cressy took it and set it down on the counter while he fumbled for his wallet and produced a dollar bill.

To his amazement the boy's grin faded, and he drew himself up with dignity.

"No, thank you, sir," he said to the proffered greenback. "I'm a Scout and Scouts don't take tips."

"What!" gasped Harrison Cressy. In all his life he did not recall meeting a boy who ever refused money before. He began to think there was something uncanny about this town of Dunbury. First a young man who could not be bought at any price. And now a boy who wouldn't take a tip for service rendered.

"I said I was a Scout," repeated the lad patiently. "And Scouts don't take tips. We are supposed to do one good turn every day, anyway, and I hadn't gotten mine in before. I'm only a Tenderfoot but I'm most ready for my second class tests. Mr. Phil's going to try me out in first aid as soon as he gets time."

"Mr. Phil! What's he got to do with it?" inquired Mr. Cressy, after a long, satisfying swig of lemonade.

"He is our Scout-master and a peach of a one too. He is going to take us on a hike tomorrow."

"Tomorrow? Tomorrow is Sunday, young man." The Methodist in Harrison Cressy rose to the surface.

"I know. We all go to church and Sunday school in the morning. Mr. Phil won't take us unless we do. But in the afternoon he thinks it is all right to go on a hike. We don't practise signaling and things like that, but we get in a lot of nature study. I can identify all my ten trees now and a whole lot more besides, and I've got a bird list of over sixty."

"You don't say so?" Harrison Cressy was plainly impressed. "So your Mr. Phil gives a good deal of time to that sort of thing, does he?" he added, his eyes seeking Philip Lambert in the distance.

"Should say he did. I guess he gives about all the time he has outside of the store. He's a dandy Scout-master. What he says goes, you betcher."

Remembering the scene at the luncheon table that day, Harrison Cressy thought it quite probable. What Philip had said had gone "you betcher" on that occasion with a vengeance. So young Lambert gave his off hours to business of this sort. Most of Carlotta's male friends gave most of theirs to polo, jazz, and chorus girls. He began to covet Philip more than ever for a possible, and he hoped probable, son-in-law.

It played into his purposes excellently that Philip on returning invited him to supper on the Hill that night. He wanted to meet the boy's people, especially the mother. Carlotta had told him once that Philip's mother was the most wonderful person in the world.

Seated at the long table in the Lambert dining-room Harrison Cressy enjoyed a meal such as his chef-ridden soul had almost forgotten could exist--a meal so simple yet so delectable that he dreamed of it for days afterward.

But the food, excellent as it was, was only a small part of the significance of the occasion. It was a revelation to the millionaire to know that a family could gather around the board like this and have such a thoroughly delightful time all round. There was gay talk and ready laughter, a fine flavor of old-fashioned courtesy and hospitality and good will in everything that was said or done.

The Lambert girls--the pretty twins and the younger, slim slip of a lassie, Elinor--were charming, fresh, natural, unspoiled, very different from and far more to his taste than most of the young women who came to Crest House--hot-house products, over-sophisticated, cynical, too familiar with rouge and cigarettes and the game of love and lure, huntresses more or less, the whole pack of them. It seemed girls could still be plain girls on this enchanted Hill--girls who would make wonderful wives some day for some lucky men.

But the mother! She was the secret of it all, quite as remarkable as Carlotta had said. She was extraordinarily well read, talked well on a dozen subjects as to which he was himself but vaguely informed, and she was evidently even more extraordinarily busy. There was talk of a Better Babies movement in which she was interested, of a Red Cross Chapter at which she had spent the afternoon, of a committee meeting of the local Woman's Club which was bringing a noted English poet-lecturer to town. There were Chatauqua plans in view, and a new children's reading room in the public library with a story-telling hour of which Clare was to be in charge. A hundred things indicated that Mrs. Lambert was by no means confined to the four walls of her home for interests and activities. Yet her home was exquisitely kept and she was a mother first of all. One could see that every moment. It was "Mums, this" and "Mums, that" from them all. The life of the home clearly pivoted about her.

Harrison Cressy found himself wishing that Carlotta could have known a motherhood like that. Rose had gone so soon. Carlotta had never known what she missed. Perhaps Mr. Cressy himself had not known until he saw Mrs. Lambert and realized what a mother might be. Poor Carlotta! He had given her a great deal. At least, until this, afternoon, he had thought he had. But he had never given her anything at all comparable to what this quiet village store-keeper and his wife had given to their son and daughters. He hadn't had it to give. He had been poor, after all, all along. Though he hadn't suspected it until now.

After supper Stuart Lambert had slipped quickly away, bidding his son stay up on the Hill a little longer with their guest. Phil had demurred, but had been quietly overruled and had acquiesced perforce. Poor Dad! There had not been a moment all day to relieve his mind about Mr. Cressy's offer. Not once had the father and son been alone. Phil was afraid his father was taking the thing a good deal to heart, and it worried him. He had counted on talking it over together as they went back to the store but his father had willed otherwise.

It was with Carlotta's father instead of his own that Philip talked first after all.

"See here, Philip," began Mr. Cressy as they descended the Hill in "Lizzie." "I went at this all wrong. So did Carlotta. I understand better now. I've been back in the past this afternoon, remembering what it means to live in the country and love and mate there in the good old-fashioned way as Carlotta's mother and I did.

It is what I want her to do with you. Do you get that, boy? I want her to come to Dunbury. I want her to have a piece of your mother. Carlotta never knew what it was to have a mother. It is mostly my fault she doesn't see any clearer. You mustn't blame her, lad."

"I don't," said Phil. "I love her."

"I know you do. And she loves you. Go to her. Make her see. Make her marry you and be happy."

Phil was silent, not because he was not moved by the older man's plea but because he was almost too moved to speak. It rather took his breath away to have Harrison Cressy on his side like this. It was almost too incredible, and yet there was no mistaking the sincerity in the other's words or on his face. Carlotta's father did want Carlotta to come to him on his Hill.

But would Carlotta want it? That was the question. For himself he sought no higher road to follow than the one where his father and mother had blazed the trail through fair weather and stormy these many years. But would Carlotta be content to travel so with him? He did not know. At any rate he could ask her, try once more to make her see, as her father put it.

He turned to his companion with a sober smile at this point in his reflections.

"Thank you, Mr. Cressy. I will try again and I know it is going to make a great deal of difference to Carlotta--and to me--to have you on my side. Perhaps she will see it differently this time. I--hope so."

"Lord, boy, so do I!" groaned Mr. Cressy. "You will come back to Crest House tomorrow with me?"

Phil hesitated, considered, shook his head.

"I'll come next Saturday. I can't get away tomorrow," he said.

"Why not? For the Lord's sake, boy, get it over!"

Phil smiled but shook his head. He too wanted to get it over. He could hardly wait to get to Carlotta, would have started that moment if he could have done so. But there were clear-cut reasons why he could not go tomorrow, obligations that held him fast in Dunbury.

"I can't go tomorrow because I have promised my boys a hike," he explained.

Harrison Cressy nearly exploded.

"Heavens, man! What does a parcel of kids amount to when it comes to getting you a wife? You can call off your hike, can't you?"

"I could, but it would be hard on a good many of them. They count on it a good deal. Some of them have given up other pleasures they might have had on account of it. Tommy has, for instance. His uncle asked him to go to Worcester with him in his car, and he refused because of his date with me. They are all bribed to church and Sunday School by the means. One of the things Scouting stands for is sticking to your job and your word. I don't think it is exactly up to the Scoutmaster to dodge his responsibilities when he preaches the other kind of thing. Of course, if it were a life and death matter, it would be different. It isn't. I have waited a good many weeks to see Carlotta. I can wait one more."

Harrison Cressy grunted. He hardly knew whether to fly into a rage with this extraordinary young man or to clap him on the back and tell him he liked him better and better every minute. He contented himself by repeating a remark he had made earlier in the day.

"You are a darn fool, young man." Then he added, half against his will, "But I like your darnfoolness, hang me if I don't!"

Phil had a strenuous two hours in the store with never a minute to get at his father. It was not until the last customer had departed, the last clerk fled away and the clock striking eleven that the father and son were alone.

Philip came over to where the older man stood. His heart smote him when he saw how utterly worn and weary the other looked, as if he had suddenly added a full ten years to his age since morning. His characteristic buoyancy seemed to have deserted him for once.

"Dad, I've not had a minute alone with you all day. I am sorry Mr. Cressy bothered you about that blue sky proposition of his. I never would have let him if I had known. Of course there was nothing in it. I didn't consider it for a minute."

Stuart Lambert smiled wearily and sat down on the counter.

"I am afraid you have given up more than we realized, Philip, in coming into the store. Mr. Cressy gave me a glimpse into things that I knew nothing about. You should have told us."

"There was nothing to tell. I've given up nothing that was mine. I told Carlotta all along she would have to come to me. I couldn't come to her. My whole life is here with you. It is what I have wanted ever since I had the sense to want anything but to enjoy my fool self. But even then I didn't appreciate what it would be like to be here with you. I couldn't, till I had tried it and found out first hand what kind of a man my dad was. I am absolutely satisfied. If Mr. Cressy had offered me a million a year I wouldn't have taken it. It wouldn't have been the slightest temptation even--" he smiled a little sadly--"even with Carlotta thrown in. I don't want to get Carlotta that way."

"You say you are satisfied, Philip. Maybe that is so. But you are not happy."

"I wasn't, just at first. I was a fool. I let the thing swamp me for awhile. Mums helped pull me out of the slough and since then I've been finding out that happiness is--well, a kind of by-product. Like the kingdom of heaven it doesn't come for observation. I have had about as much happiness here with you, and with Mums and the girls at home, and with my Scouts in the woods, as I deserve, maybe more. I'm going to try to get Carlotta. I haven't given up hope. I'm going down to Sea View next week to ask her again and maybe things will be different this time. Her father is on my side now, which is a great help. He has got the Holiday Hill viewpoint all at once. He wants Carlotta to come to me--us. So do I, with all my heart. But whether she does or doesn't, I am here with you as long as you want me, first last and all the time and glad to be. Please believe that, Dad, always."

Stuart Lambert rose.

"Philip, you don't know what it means to me to hear you say this." There was a little break in the older man's voice, the suggestion of pent emotion. "It nearly killed me to think I ought to give you up. You are sure you are not making too much of a sacrifice?"

"Dad! Please don't say that word to me. There isn't any sacrifice. It is what I want. I haven't been a very good son always. Even this summer I am afraid I haven't come up to all you expected of me, especially just at first when I was wrapped up in myself and my own concerns too much to see that doing a good job in the store was only a small part of what I was here in Dunbury to do. But anyway I am prouder than I can tell you to be your son and I am going to try my darndest to live up to the sign if you will let me stay on being the minor part of it."

He held out his hand and his father took it. There were tears in the older man's eyes. A moment later the store was dark as the two passed out shoulder to shoulder beneath the sign of STUART LAMBERT AND SON.

CHAPTER XXII
THE DUNBURY CURE

Harrison Cressy awoke next morning to the cheerful chirrup of robins and the pleasant far-off sound of church bells. He liked the bells. They sounded different in the country he thought. You couldn't hear them in the city anyway. There were too many noises to distract you. There was no Sabbath stillness in the city. For that matter there wasn't much Sabbath.

He got up out of bed and went and looked out of the window. There was a heavenly hush everywhere. It was still very early. It had been the Catholic bells ringing for mass that he had heard. The dew was a-dazzle on every grass blade. The robins hopped briskly about at their business of worm-gathering. The morning glories all in fresh bloom climbed cheerfully over the picket fence. He hadn't seen a morning glory in years. It set him dreaming again, took him back to his boyhood days.

If only Carlotta would be sensible and yield to the boy's wooing. Dunbury had cast a kind of spell upon him. He wanted his daughter to live here. He wanted to come here to visit her. In his imagination he saw himself coming to Carlotta's home--not too big a home--just big enough to live and grow in and raise babies in. He saw himself playing with Carlotta's little golden-haired violet-eyed daughters, and walking hand in hand with her small son Harrison, just such a sturdy, good-looking, wide-awake youngster as Philip Lambert had no doubt been. Harrison Cressy's mind dwelt fondly upon this grandson of his. That was a boy indeed!

Carlotta's son should not be permitted to grow up a money grubber. There would be money of course. One couldn't very well avoid that under the circumstances. The boy would be trained to the responsibilities of being Harrison Cressy's heir. But he should be taught to see things in their true values and proportions. He must not grow up money-blinded like Carlotta. He should know that money was good--very good. But he should know it was not the chief good, was never for an instant to be classed with the abiding things--the real things, not to be purchased at a price.

Mr. Cressy sighed a little at that point and crept back to bed. It occurred to him he would have to leave this latter part of his grandson's education to the Lambert side of the family. That was their business, just as the money part was his.

He fell asleep again and presently re-awoke in a kind of shivering panic. What if Carlotta would not marry Philip after all? What if it was too late already? What if his grandson turned out to be a second Herbert Lathrop, an unobjectionable, possibly even an objectionable ass. Perspiration beaded on the millionaire's brow. Why was that young idiot on the Hill waiting? What were young men made of nowadays? Didn't Philip Lambert know that you could lose a woman forever if you didn't jump lively? Hanged if he wouldn't call the boy this minute and tell him he just had to change his mind and go to Crest House that very morning without a moment's delay. Delay might be fatal. Harrison Cressy sat up in bed, fumbled for his slippers, shook his head gloomily and returned to his place under the covers.

It wasn't any use. He might as well give up. He couldn't make Philip Lambert do anything he did not want to do. He had tried it twice and failed ignominiously both times. He wouldn't tackle it again. The boy was stronger than he was. He had to lie back and let things take their course as best they might.

"Cheer up! Cheer up!" counseled the robins outside, but millionaire Cressy heeded not their injunctions. The balloon of his hopes lay pricked and flat in the dust.

He rose, dressed, breakfasted and discovered there was an eleven o'clock train for Boston. He discovered also that he hadn't the slightest wish to take it. He did not want to go to Boston. He did not want to go to Crest House. And very particularly and definitely he did not want to see his daughter Carlotta. Carlotta might ferret out his errand to Dunbury and be bitterly angry at his interference with her affairs. Even if she were not angry how could he meet her without telling her everything, including things that were the boy's right to tell? It was safer to stay away from Crest House entirely. That was it. He would telegraph Carlotta his gout was worse, that he had gone to the country to take a cure. He would be home Saturday.

Immensely heartened he dispatched the wire. By this time it was ten-thirty and the dew on the grass was all dry, the morning glories shut tight and the robins vanished. The church bells were ringing again however and Harrison Cressy decided to go to church, the white Methodist church on the common. He wouldn't meet any of the Hill people there. The Holidays were Episcopal, the Lamberts Unitarian--a loose, heterodox kind of creed that. He wished Phil were Methodist. It would have given him something to go by. Then he grinned a bit sheepishly at his own expense and shook his head. He had had the Methodist creed to go by himself and much good had it done him. Maybe it did not make so much difference what you believed. It was how you acted that mattered. Why that was Unitarianism itself, wasn't it? Queer. Maybe there was something in it after all.

Seated in the little church Harrison Cressy hardly listened to the preacher's droning voice. He followed his own trend of thought instead, recalling long-forgotten scriptural passages. "What shall it profit a man though he gain the whole world and lose his own soul?" was one of the recurring phrases. He applied it to Philip Lambert, applied it sadly to himself and with a shake of his head to his daughter, Carlotta. He remembered too the story of the rich young man. Had he made Carlotta as the rich young man, cumbered her with so many worldly possessions and standards that by his own hand he was keeping her out of the heaven of happiness she might have otherwise inherited? He feared so.

He bowed his head with the others but he did not pray. He could not. He was too unhappy. And yet who knows? Perhaps his unwonted clarity of vision and humility of soul were acceptable that morning in lieu of prayer to Sandalphou.

As he ate his solitary dinner his despondency grew upon him. He felt almost positive Philip would fail in his mission, that Carlotta would go her willful way to regret and disillusionment, and all these things gone irretrievably wrong would be at bottom his own fault.

Later he endeavored to distract himself from his dreary thoughts by discoursing with his neighbor on the veranda, a tall, grizzled, soldierly looking gentleman with shrewd but kind eyes and the brow of a scholar.

As they talked desultorily a group of khaki clad youngsters filed past, Philip Lambert among them, looking only an older and taller boy in their midst. The lads looked happy, alert, vigorous, were of clean, upstanding type, the pick of the town it seemed probable to Harrison Cressy who said as much to his companion.

The other smiled and shook his head.

"You are mistaken, sir," he said. "Three months ago most of those fellows were riffraff--the kind that hang around street corners smoking and indulging in loose

talk and profanity. Young Lambert, the chap with them, their Scout-master, picked
that kind from choice, turned down a respectable church-mothered bunch for this
one, left the other for a man who wanted an easier row to hoe. It was some stunt,
as the boys say. It took a man like Phil Lambert to put it through. He has the crowd
where he wants them now though. They would go through fire and water if he led
them and he is a born leader."

Harrison Cressy's eyes followed the departing group. Here was a new light on
his hoped-for son-in-law. So he picked "publicans-and-sinners" to eat with. Mr.
Cressy rather liked that. He hated snobs and pharisees, couldn't stomach either
brand.

"It means a good deal to a town like this when its college-bred boys come
back and lend a hand like that," the other man went on. "So many of them rush
off to the cities thinking there isn't scope enough for their ineffable wisdom and
surpassing talents in their own home town. A number of people prophesied that
young Lambert would do the same instead of settling down with his father as we
all wanted him to do. I wasn't much afraid of that myself. Phil has sense enough to
see rather straight usually. He did about that. And then the kickers put up a howl
that he had a swelled head, felt above the rest of Dunbury because he had a college
education and his father was getting to be one of the most prosperous men in town.
They complained he wouldn't go in for things the rest of the town was interested
in, kept to himself when he was out of the store. There were some grounds for the
kick I will admit. But it wasn't a month before he got his bearings, had his head out
of the clouds and was in the thick of everything. They swear by him now almost as
much as they do by his father which is saying a good deal for Dunbury has revolved
about Stuart Lambert for years. It is beginning to revolve about Stuart Lambert and
Son now. But I am boring you with all this. Phil happens to be rather a favorite of
mine."

"You know him well?" questioned Mr. Cressy.

"I ought to. I am Robert Caldwell, principal of the High School here. I've
known Phil since he was in knickerbockers and had him under my direct eye for
four years. He kept my eye sufficiently busy at that," he added with a smile. "There
wasn't much mischief that youngster and a neighbor of his, young Ted Holiday,
didn't get into. Maybe that is why he is such a success with the black sheep," he

added with a nod in the direction in which the khaki-clad lads had gone.

"H-mm," observed Mr. Cressy. "I am rather glad to hear all this. You see it happens that I came to Dunbury to offer Philip Lambert a position. My name's Cressy--Harrison Cressy," he explained.

His companion lifted his eye-brows a little dubiously.

"I see. I didn't know I was discussing a young man you knew well enough to offer a position to. May I ask if he accepted it?" "He did not," admitted Harrison Cressy grimly.

"Turned it down, eh?" The school man looked interested.

"Turned it down, man? He made the proposition look flatter than a last year's pan-cake and it was a mighty good proposition. At least I thought it was," the magnate added with a faint grin remembering all that went with that proposition.

Robert Caldwell smiled. He rather liked the idea of one of his boys making a proposition of millionaire Cressy's look like a last year's pan-cake. It was what he would have expected of Phil Lambert.

"I am sorry for you, Mr. Cressy," he said. "But I am glad for Dunbury. Philip is the kind we need right here."

"He is the kind we need right everywhere," grunted Mr. Cressy. "Only we can't get 'em. They aren't for sale."

"No," agreed Robert Caldwell. "They are not for sale. Ah, the Boston train must be in. There is the stage."

Mr. Cressy allowed his eyes to stray idly to the arriving bus and the descending passengers.

Suddenly he stiffened.

"Good Lord!" he ejaculated, an exclamation called forth by the fact that the last person to alight from the bus was a slim young person in a trim, tailored, navy blue suit and a tiny black velvet toque whose air bespoke Paris, a person with eyes which were precisely the color of violets which grow in the deepest woods.

A little later Harrison Cressy sat in a deep leather upholstered chair in his bedroom with his daughter Carlotta in his lap.

"Don't try to deceive me, Daddy darling," Carlotta was saying. "You were worried--dreadfully worried because your little Carlotta wept salt tears all over your shirt bosom. You thought that Carlotta must not be allowed to be unhappy. Wars, earthquakes, ship sinkings, wrecks--anything might be allowed to go on as usual but not Carlotta unhappy. You thought that, didn't you, Daddy darling?"

Daddy darling pleaded guilty.

"Of course you did, you old dear. The moment I knew you were in Dunbury I knew what you were up to. I understand perfectly how your mind works. I ought to. Mine works very much the same way. It is a simple three stage operation. First we decide we want a thing. Next we decide the surest, quickest way to get it and third--we get it. At least we usually do. We must do ourselves that much justice, must we not, Daddy darling?"

Daddy darling merely grunted.

"You came to Dunbury to tell Phil he had to marry me because I was in love with him and wanted to marry him. He couldn't very well marry me and keep on living in Dunbury because I wouldn't care to live in Dunbury. Therefore he would have to emigrate to a place I would care to live in and he couldn't very well do that unless he had a very considerable income because spending money was one of my favorite sports both indoor and outdoor and I wouldn't be happy if I didn't keep right on playing it to the limit. Therefore, again, the very simple solution of the whole thing was for you to offer Phil a suitable salary so that we could marry at once and live in the suitable place and say, 'Go to it. Bless you my children. Bring on your wedding bells--I mean bills. I'll foot 'em.' Put in the rough, that was the plan wasn't it, my dear parent?"

"Practically," admitted the dear parent with a wry grin. "How did you work it out so accurately?"

Carlotta made a face at him.

"I worked it out so accurately because it was all old stuff. The plan wasn't at all original with you. I drew the first draft of it myself last June up on the top of Mount Tom, took Phil up there on purpose indeed to exhibit it to him."

"Humph!" muttered Harrison Cressy.

"Unfortunately Phil didn't at all care for the exhibit because it happened that I had fallen in love with a man instead of a puppet. I could have told you coming to Dunbury was no earthly use if you had consulted me. Phil did not take to your plan, did he?"

"He did not."

"And he told you--he didn't care for me any more?" Carlotta's voice was suddenly a little low.

"He did not. In fact I gathered he was fair-to-middling fond of you still, in spite of your abominable behavior."

"Phil, didn't say I had behaved abominably Daddy. You know he didn't. He might think it but he wouldn't ever say it--not to you anyway."

"He didn't. That is my contribution and opinion. Carlotta, I wish to the Lord Harry you would marry Philip Lambert!"

Carlotta's lovely eyes flashed surprise and delight before she lowered them.

"But, Daddy," she said. "He hasn't got very much money. And it takes a great deal of money for me."

"You had better learn to get along with less then," snapped Harrison Cressy. "I tell you, Carlotta, money is nothing--the stupidest, most useless, rottenest stuff in the world."

Carlotta opened her eyes very wide.

"Is that what you thought when you came to Dunbury?" she asked gravely.

"No. It is what I have learned to think since I have been in Dunbury."

"But you--you wouldn't want me to live here?" probed Carlotta.

"My child, I would rather you would live here than any place in the whole world. I've traveled a million miles since I saw you last, been back in the past with your mother. Things look different to me now. I don't want what I did for you. At least what I want hasn't changed. That is the same always--your happiness. But I have changed my mind as to what makes for happiness."

"I am awfully glad, Daddy darling," sighed Carlotta snuggling closer in his arms. "Because I came up here on purpose to tell you that I've changed my mind too. If Dunbury is good for gout maybe--maybe it will be good for what ails me. Do you think it might, Daddy?" For answer he held her very tight.

"Do you mean it, child? Are you here to tell that lad of yours you are ready to come up his Hill to him?"

"If--if he still wants me," faltered Carlotta. "I'll have to find that out for myself. I'll know as soon as I see Phil. There won't anything have to be said. I am afraid there has been too much talking already. You shouldn't have told him I cried," reproachfully.

"How could I help it? That is, how the deuce did you know I did?" floundered the trapped parent.

"Daddy! You know you played on Phil's sympathy every way you could. It was awful. At least it would have been awful if you had bought him with my silly tears after you failed to buy him with your silly money. But he didn't give in even for a moment--even when you told him I cried, did he?"

"Not even then. But that doesn't mean he doesn't care. He--"

But Carlotta's hand was over his mouth at that. How much Phil cared she wanted to hear from nobody but from Phil himself.

Philip Lambert found a queer message waiting for him when he came in from his hike. Some mysterious person who would give no name had telephoned requesting him to be at the top of Sunset Hill at precisely seven o'clock to hear some important information which vitally concerned the firm of Stuart Lambert and Son.

"Sounds like a hoax of some sort," remarked Phil. "But Lizzie has been chafing at the bit all day in the garage and I don't mind a ride. Come on, Dad, let's see what this bunk means."

Stuart Lambert smiled assent. And at precisely seven o'clock when dusk was settling gently over the valley and the glory in the western sky was beginning to fade into pale heliotrope and rose tints Lizzie brought the two Lamberts to the crest of Sunset Hill where another car waited, a hired car from the Eagle garage.

From the tonneau of the other car Harrison Cressy stepped out, somewhat ponderously, followed by some one else, some one all in white with hair that shone pure gold even in the gathering twilight.

Phil made one leap and in another moment, before the eyes of his father and Carlotta's, not to mention the interested stare of the Eagle garage chauffeur, he swept his far-away princess into his arms. There was no need of anybody's trying to make Carlotta see. Love had opened her eyes. The two fathers smiled at each other, both a little glad and a little sad.

"Brother Lambert," said Mr. Cressy. "Suppose you and I ride down the hill. I rather think this spot belongs to the children."

"So it seems," agreed Stuart Lambert. "We will leave Lizzie for chaperone. I think there will be a moon later."

"Exactly. There always was a moon, I believe. It is quite customary."

As Stuart Lambert got out of the small car Philip and Carlotta came to him hand-in-hand like happy children.

Carlotta slipped away from Phil, put out both hands to his father. He took them with a happy smile.

"I have a good many daughters, my dear," he said. "But I have always wanted to welcome one more. Do you think you could take in another Dad?"

"I know I could," said Carlotta lifting her flower face to him for a daughterly kiss.

"Come, come! Where do I come in on this deal? Where is my son, I'd like to know?" demanded Mr. Cressy.

"Right here at your service--darnfoolness and all," said Phil holding out his hand.

"Don't rub it in," snapped Harrison Cressy, though he gripped the proffered hand hard. "Come on, Lambert. This is no place for us."

And the two fathers went down the hill in the hired car leaving Lizzie and the lovers in possession of the summit with the world which the moon was just turning to silver at their feet.

CHAPTER XXIII
SEPTEMBER CHANGES

When September came Carlotta, who had been ostensibly visiting Tony though spending a good deal of her time "in the moon with Phil" as she put it, departed for Crest House, carrying Philip with her "for inspection," as he dubbed it somewhat ruefully. He wasn't particularly enamored of the prospect of being passed upon by Carlotta's friends and relatives. It was rather incongruous when you came to think of it that the lovely Carlotta, who might have married any one in the world, should elect an obscure village store keeper for a husband. But Carlotta herself had no qualms. She was shrewd enough to know that with her father on her side no one would do much disapproving. And in any case she had no fear that any one even just looking at Phil would question her choice. Carlotta was not the woman to choose a man she would have to apologize for. Phil would hold his own with the best of them and she knew it. He was a man every inch of him, and what more could any woman ask?

Ted went up for his examinations and came back so soberly that the family held its composite breath and wondered in secret whether he could possibly have failed after all his really heroic effort. But presently the word came that he had not only not failed but had rather covered himself with glory. The Dean himself, an old friend of Doctor Holiday's, wrote expressing his congratulations and the hope that this performance of his nephew's was a pledge of better things in the future and that this fourth Holiday to pass through the college might yet reflect credit upon it and the Holiday name.

Ted himself emphatically disclaimed all praise whatsoever in the matter and cut short his uncle's attempt at expressing his appreciation not only of the successful finish of the examinations but the whole summer's hard work and steadiness.

"I am glad if you are satisfied, Uncle Phil," he said. "But there isn't any credit coming to me. It was the least I could do after making such a confounded mess of things. Let's forget it."

But Ted Holiday was not quite the same unthinking young barbarian in September that he had been in June. Nobody could work as he had worked that summer without gaining something in character and self-respect. Moreover, being constantly as he was with his brother and uncle, he would have been duller than he was not to get a "hunch," as he would have called it, of what it meant to be a Holiday of the authentic sort. Larry's example was particularly salutary. The younger Holiday could not help comparing his own weak-willed irresponsibility of conduct with the older one's quiet self-control and firmness of principle. Larry's love for Ruth was the real thing. Ted could see that, and it made his own random, ill-judged attraction to Madeline Taylor look crude and cheap if nothing worse. He hated to remember that affair in Cousin Emma's garden. He made up his mind there would be no more things like that to have to remember.

"You can tell old Bob Caldwell," he wrote from college to his uncle, "that he'll sport no more caddies and golf balls at my expense. Flunking is too damned expensive every way, saving your presence, Uncle Phil. No more of it for this child. But don't get it into your head I am a violently reformed character. I am nothing of the kind and don't want to be. If I see any signs of angel pin-feathers cropping out I'll shave 'em. I'd hate to be conspicuously virtuous. All the same if I have a few grains more sense than I had last year they are mostly to your credit. Fact is, Uncle Phil, you are a peach and I am just beginning to realize it, more fool I."

Tony also flitted from the Hill that September for her new work and life in the big city. Rather against her will she had ensconced herself in a Student Hostelry where Jean Lambert, Phil's older sister, had been living several years very happily, first as a student and later as a successful illustrator. Tony had objected that she did not want anything so "schooly," and that the very fact that Jean liked the Hostelry would be proof positive that she, Tony, would not like it. What she really wanted to do was either to have a studio of her own or accept Felice Norman's invitation to make her home with her. Mrs. Norman was a cousin of Tony's mother, a charming widow of wealth and wide social connections whom Tony had always adored and admired extravagantly. Just visiting her had always been like taking a trip to fairy land and to live with her--well, it would be just too wonderful, Tony thought. But Doctor Holiday had vetoed decidedly both these pleasant and impractical proposi-tions. Tony was far too young and pretty to live alone. That was out of the ques-tion. And he was scarcely more willing that she should go to Mrs. Norman, though he liked the latter very well and was glad that his niece would have her to go to in any emergency. He knew Tony, and knew that in such an environment as Mrs. Norman's home offered the girl would all but inevitably drift into being a gay little social butterfly and forget she ever came to the city to do serious work. Life with Mrs. Norman would be "too wonderful" indeed.

So Tony went to the Hostelry with the understanding that if after a few months' trial she really did dislike it as much as she declared she knew she would they would make other arrangements. But rather to her chagrin she found herself liking the place very much and enjoying the society of the other girls who were all in the city as she and Jean were, pursuing some art or other.

The dramatic school work was all she had hoped and more, stimulating, en-grossing, altogether delightful. She made friends easily as always, among teachers and pupils, slipped naturally here as in college into a position of leadership. Tony Holiday was a born queen.

She had plenty of outside diversion too. Cousin Felice was kind and delighted to pet and exhibit her pretty little kinswoman. There were fascinating glimpses into high society, delightful private dancing parties in gorgeous ball rooms, motor trips, gay theater parties in resplendent boxes, followed by suppers in brilliant restaurants--all the pomp and glitter of life that youth loves.

There were other no less genuinely happy occasions spent with Dick Carson, way up near the roof in the theaters and opera house or in queer, fascinating out-of-the-way foreign restaurants. The two had the jolliest kind of time together, always like two children at a picnic. Tony was very nice to Dick these days. He kept her from being too homesick for the Hill and anyway she felt a wee bit sorry for him because he did not know about Alan and those long letters which came so frequently from the retreat in the mountains where the latter was sketching. She knew she ought to tell Dick how far things had gone but somehow she couldn't quite drive herself to do it. She didn't want to hurt him. And she did not want to banish him from her life. She wanted him, needed him just where he was, at her feet, and never bothering her with any inconvenient demands or love-making. It was selfish but it was true. And in any case it would be soon enough to worry Dick when Alan came back to town.

And then without warning he was back, very much back. And with his return the pleasant nicely balanced, casual scheme of things which she had been following so contentedly was knocked sky high. She had to adjust herself to a new heaven and a new earth with Alan Massey the center of both. In her delight and intoxication at having her lover near her again, more fascinating and lover-like than ever, Tony lost her head a little, neglected her work, snubbed her friends, refused invitations from Dick and Cousin Felice, and indeed from everybody except Alan. She went everywhere with him, almost nowhere without him, spent her days and more of her nights than was at all prudent or proper in his absorbing society, had, in short, what she afterward described to Carlotta as a "perfect orgy of Alan."

At the end of ten days she called a halt, sat down and took honest account of herself and her proceedings and found that this sort of thing would not do. Alan was too expensive every way. She could not afford so much of him. Accordingly with her usual decision and frankness she explained the situation to him as she saw it and announced that henceforth she would see him only twice a week and not as often if she were especially busy.

To this ultimatum she kept rigidly in spite of her lover's protests and pleas and threats. She was inexorable. If Alan wanted to see her at all he must do it on her terms. He yielded perforce and was madder over her than ever, feted and worshiped and adored her inordinately when he was with her, deluged her with flowers and poetry and letters between times, called her up daily and nightly by telephone just to hear her voice, if he might not see her face.

So superficially Tony conquered. But she was not over-proud of her victory. She knew that whether she saw Alan or not he was always in the under-current of her thoughts and feelings. In the midst of other occupations she caught herself wondering whether he had written her, whether she would find his flowers when she got home, where he was, what he was doing, if he was thinking of her as she of him. She wanted him most irrationally when she forbade his coming to her. She looked forward to those few hours spent with him as the only time when she was fully alive, dreamed them over afterward, knew they meant a hundredfold more to her than those she spent with any other man or woman. She wore his flowers, pored over his long, beautiful, impassioned letters, devoured the books of poetry he sent her, danced with him as often and as long as she dared, gave her soul more and more into his keeping, the more so perhaps in that he was so tenderly reverential of her body, never even touching her lips with his, though his eyes often told a less moderate story.

The orgy over she was again doing well with her work at the school. She knew that. Her teachers praised her gifts and her progress. Without any vanity she could not help seeing that she was forging ahead of others who had started even with her, had more real talent perhaps than most of those with whom she worked and played. But she took no pride in these things. For equally clearly she saw that she was not doing half what she might have done, would have done, had there been no Alan Massey in the city and in her heart. She had a divided allegiance and a divided allegiance is a hard thing to live with as a daily companion.

But she would not have had it otherwise. Not for a moment did she ever wish to go back to those free days when love was but a name and the flame had not blown so dangerously near.

As for Alan Massey himself, he alternated between moods which were starry pinnacles of ecstasy and others which were bottomless pits of despair. He lived for two things only--his hours with Tony and his work. For he had begun to paint again, magnificently, furiously, with all his old power and a new almost godlike one added to it. As an artist it was his supreme hour. He painted as he had never painted before.

His love for Tony ran the whole gamut. He loved her passionately, found it exquisite torture to have her in his arms when they danced and to have still to bank the fires which consumed him and of which she only dimly guessed. He loved her humbly, worshipfully as a moth might look to a star. He loved her tenderly, protectingly, longed to shield her by his own might from all griefs, troubles and petty annoyances, to guard her day and night, lest any rough, unlovely or unseemly thing press near her shining sphere. He desired to wrap her about with a magic mantle of beauty and luxury and the quintessence of life, to keep her in a place apart as he kept his priceless collection of rubies and emeralds. He loved her jealously, was sick at the thought that some other man might be near her when he might not, might dance with her, covet her, kiss her. He hated all men because of her and particularly he hated with black hate the man whom he was wronging daily by his silence, his cousin, John Massey.

Beneath all this strange, sad welter of emotion deeper still in Alan Massey's heart lay the tragic conviction that he would never win Tony, that his own sins would somehow rise to strike at him like a snake out of the grass. He had lost faith in his luck, had lost it strangely enough when luck had laid at his feet that most desirable of all gifts, Jim Roberts' timely death.

In the House on the Hill, things were very quiet, missing the gay presence of the two younger Holidays and with those at home cumbered with cares and perplexity and grief.

Things were easier for Ruth than for Larry. It was less difficult for her to play the part of quiet friendship than for him, partly because her love was a much less tempestuous affair and partly because a woman nearly always plays a part of any kind with more facility than a man does. And Larry Holiday was temperamentally unfit to play any part whatsoever. He was a Yea-Yea and Nay-Nay person.

The simplicity of the girl's role was also very largely created by her lover's rigid self control. She took her cue from his quietness and felt that things could not be so bad after all. At least they were together. Neither had driven the other away from the Hill by any unconsidered act or word. Ruth had no idea that being with her under the tormenting circumstances was scarcely undivided happiness for poor Larry or that her peace of mind was more or less purchased at cost of his.

Larry kept the promise he had made to his uncle more literally than the latter had had any idea he would or could. He never sought out Ruth's society, was never alone with her if he could help it, never so much as touched her hand. Ruth being a very human and feminine little person sometimes wished he were not quite so consistently, "Holidayish" in his conduct. She missed the ardent gaze of those wonderful gray eyes which he now kept studiously averted from hers. Privately she thought it would not have mattered so fearfully if just once in a while he had forgotten the ring. Life was very, very drab when you never forgot and let yourself go the tiniest little bit. Child like little Ruth never guessed that a man like Larry Holiday does not dare let himself go the tiniest little bit, lest he go farther, far enough to regret.

Doctor Holiday watching in silence out of the tail of his eye understood better what was going on behind his nephew's quiet exterior demeanor, and wondered sometimes if it had not been a mistake to keep the boy bound to the wheel like that, if he should not rather have packed him off to the uttermost parts of the earth, far away from the little lady with the wedding ring who was so little married. And yet there was Granny, growing perceptibly weaker day by day, clinging pathetically to Larry's young strength. Poor Granny! And poor Larry! How little one could do for either!

Ruth's memory did not return. She remembered, or at least found familiar, books she had read, songs she must have sung, drifted into doing a hundred little simple everyday things she must have done before, since they came to her with no effort. She could sew and knit and play the piano exquisitely. But all this seemed rather a trick of the fingers than of the mind. The people, the places, the life that lay behind that crash on the Overland never returned to her consciousness for all her anxious struggle to get them back.

It began to look as if her husband, if she had one, were not going to claim her. No one claimed her. Not a single response came from all the extensive advertising which Larry still kept up in vain hope of success. Apparently no one had missed the little Goldilocks. Precious as she was none sought her.

In the meanwhile she was an undisguised angel visitant to the House on the

Hill. If in his kindly hospitality Doctor Holiday had stretched a point or two in the first place to make the little stranger feel at home the case was different now. She was needed, badly needed and she played the part of house daughter so sweetly and unselfishly that her presence among them was a double blessing to them all, except perhaps to poor Larry who loved her best of all.

CHAPTER XXIV
A PAST WHICH DID NOT STAY BURIED

Coming in from a lively game of tennis with Elsie Hathaway, his newest sweetheart, the Ancient History Prof's pretty daughter, Ted Holiday found awaiting him a letter from Madeline Taylor. He turned it over in his hands with a keen distaste for opening it, had indeed almost a mind to chuck it in the waste paper basket unread. Hang it all! Why had she written? He didn't want to hear from her, didn't want to be reminded of her existence. He wanted instead distinctly to forget there was a Madeline Taylor and that he had been fool enough to make love to her once. Nevertheless he opened the letter and pulled his forelock in perturbation as he read it.

She had quarrelled with her grandfather and he would not let her come back home. She was with Emma just now but she couldn't stay. Fred was behaving very nastily and he might tell Emma any day that she, Madeline, had to go. They were all against her. Everything was against a girl anyway. They never had a chance as a man did. She wished she had been killed when she had been thrown out of the car that night. It would have been much better for her than being as miserable as she was now. She often wished she was dead. But what she had written to Ted Holiday for was because she thought perhaps he could help her to find a job in the college town. She had to earn some money right away. She would do anything. She didn't care what and would be very grateful to Ted if he would or could help her to find work.

That was all. There was not a single personal note in the whole thing, no reference to their flirtation of the early summer except the one allusion to the accident, no attempt to revive such frail ties as had existed between them, no reproaches to

Ted for having broken these off so summarily. It was simply and exclusively a plea for help from one human being to another.

Ted thrust the letter soberly in his pocket and went off for a shower. But the thing went with him. He wished Madeline hadn't written, wished she hadn't besought his aid, wished most of all she hadn't been such a devilish good sport in it all. If she had whined, cast things up against him as she might have done, thrown herself in any way upon him, he could perhaps have ignored her and her plea. But she had done nothing of the sort. She was deucedly game now just as she had been the night of the smash. And by a queer trick of his mind her very gameness made Ted Holiday feel more quiet and responsible, a frame of mind he heartily resented. Hanged if he could see why it was his funeral! If that old Hottentot of a grandfather of hers chose to turn her out without a cent it wasn't his fault. For that matter he wasn't to blame for what Madeline herself had done. He didn't suppose the old man would have cut so rough without plenty of cause. Why did she have to bob up now and make him feel so darned rotten?

Unfortunately, even the briefest of episodes have a way of not erasing themselves as conveniently as most of us would like to have them. The thing was there and Ted Holiday had to look at it whether it made him feel "darned rotten" or not. He did not want to help the girl, did not even want to renew their acquaintance by even so much as a letter. The whole thing was an infernal nuisance. But infernal nuisance or not, he had to deal with it, could not funk it. He was a Holiday and no Holiday ever shirked obligations he himself had incurred. He was a Holiday and no Holiday ever let a woman ask for help, and not give It. By the time he was back from the shower Ted knew precisely where he stood. Perhaps he had known all along.

The next day he bestirred himself, went to Berry the florist who he happened to know was in need of a clerk, got the burly Irishman's consent to give the girl a job at excellent wages, right away, the sooner the better. Ted opened his mouth to ask for an advance of salary but thought better of it before the words came out. Madeline might not like to have anybody know she was up against it like that. He would have to see to that part of it himself somehow.

"You're a good customer, Mr. Holiday," the genial florist was saying. "I'm tickled to be obligin' ye and mesilf at the same time. Anything in the flower line, to-day, Mr. Holiday? Some roses now or violets? Got some Jim dandies just in. Beauties, I'm tellin' you. Want to see 'em?"

Ted hesitated. His exchecquer was low, very low. The first of the month was also far away--too far, considering all things. His bill at Berry's already passed the bounds of wisdom and the possibility of being paid in full out of the next month's allowance without horribly crippling the debtor. It was exceedingly annoying to have to forfeit that ten dollars to Uncle Phil every month for that darned automobile business which it seemed as if he never would get free of one way or another. He certainly ought not to buy any more flowers this month.

Still, there was the hop to-night. Elsie was going with him. He had run a race with three other applicants for the privilege of escorting her and being victor it behooved him to prove he appreciated his gains. He didn't want Elsie to think he was a tight-wad, or worse still suspect him of being broke. He fell, let Berry open the show case, debated seriously the respective merits of roses and violets, having reluctantly relinquished orchids as a little too ruinous even for a ruined young man.

"If they are for Miss Hathaway," murmured a pretty, sympathetic clerk in his ear, "Mr. Delany sent roses this morning and she likes violets best. I've heard her say so."

That settled it. Ted Holiday wasn't going to be beaten by a poor fish like Ned Delany. The violets were bought and duly charged along with those other too numerous items on Ted Holiday's account. Going home Ted wrote a cheerful, friendly letter to Madeline Taylor reporting his success in getting her a job and enclosing a check for twenty live dollars, "just to tide you over," he had put in lightly, forbearing to mention that the gift made his bank balance even lighter, so light in fact that it approached complete invisibility. He added that he was sorry things were in a mess for her but they would clear up soon, bound to, you know. And nix on the wish-I-were-dead-stuff! It was really a jolly old world as she would say herself when her luck turned. He remained hers sincerely and so forth.

This business off his mind, young Mr. Holiday felt highly relieved and pleased with himself and the world which was such a jolly old affair as he had just assured Madeline. Later he went to the hop and had a corking time, stayed till the last violin swooned off into silence, then sauntered with deliberate leisureliness toward Prof. Hathaway's house with Elsie on his arm. On the Prof's porch he had lingered as long as was prudent, perhaps a little longer, spooning discreetly the while as one may, even with an Ancient History Prof's daughter. There was nothing suggestive of Ancient History about Elsie. She was slim and young as the little new moon they had both nearly broken their necks to see over their right shoulders a few minutes before. Moreover she was exceedingly pretty and as provocative as the dickens. In the end Ted stole a saucy kiss and left her pretending to be as indignant as if a dozen other impudent youths had not done precisely the same thing since the opening of the college year. It was the lady's privilege to protest. Ted granted that, but neither was he much taken in by injured innocence airs. Elsie was quite as sophisticated as he was himself as he knew very well. No first kiss business for either of them, he reflected as he went whistling back to the frat house. It was all in the game and both knew it was nothing but a game which made it perfectly pleasant and harmless.

At the frat house he found a quiet little game of another sort in progress, slid in, took a hand, got interested, played until three A.M. and on quitting found himself in possession of some thirty odd dollars he had not had when he sat in. Considering his recent financial depression the thirty dollars was all to the good, covered Madeline's check and Elsie's violets. It was indeed a jolly old world if you treated it right and did not take it or yourself too seriously.

Inasmuch as playing cards for money was strictly against college rules and gambling had been the one vice of all vices the late Major Holiday had hated with unrelenting hate, it might be a satisfaction to record that the late Major's son took an uneasy conscience to bed that night, or rather that morning, but truth is truth and we are compelled to state that Ted Holiday did not suffer the faintest twinge of remorse and went to sleep the moment his head touched the pillow as peacefully as a guileless new born babe might have done.

Moreover when he woke the next morning at an unconscionably late hour he turned over, looked at the clock, grunted and grinned sleepily and lapsed off again into blissful oblivion, thereby cutting all his morning classes and generally submerging himself in the unregenerate ways of his graceless sophomoric year. He had never contracted to be conspicuously virtuous it will be recalled.

The next day he secured a suitable lodging place for Madeline in an inexpensive but respectable neighborhood and the day after that betook himself to the station to meet the girl herself. Ted never did things by halves. Having made up his mind to stand by he did it thoroughly, perhaps the more punctiliously because in his heart he loathed the whole business and wished he were well out of it.

For a moment as Madeline came toward him he hardly recognized her. She looked years older. The brilliancy of her beauty was curiously dimmed as an electric light might be dimmed inside a dusty globe. There were hard lines about her full lips and a sharp, driven look in her black eyes. The two had met in June on equal terms of blithe youth. Now, only a few months later, Ted was still a careless boy but Madeline Taylor had been forced into premature womanhood and wore on her haggard young face, the stamp of a woman's hard won wisdom.

To the girl Ted Holiday appeared more the bonny Prince Charming than ever only infinitely farther removed from her than he had seemed in those happy summer days which were a million years ago to all intents and purposes now. How good looking he was--how tall and clean and manly looking! Her heart gave a quick jump seeing him again after all these dreary months. But oh, she must be very careful--must never forget for a moment that things were very, very different now from what they were in June!

There was a moment's slightly embarrassed silence as they shook hands. Both were remembering all too vividly the scene in Cousin Emma's garden upon the occasion of their last meeting. It was Ted who first found tongue and announced casually that he was going to take her straight to the house of Mrs. Bascom, her landlady to be.

"She's a good sort," he added. "Mothery like you know. You'll like her."

Madeline did not answer. She couldn't. Something choked in her throat. The phrase, "mothery like" was almost too much for the girl who had never had a mother to remember and wanted one now as she never had wanted one in her life. Ted's kindness--the first she had received from any one these many days--touched her deeply. For the first time in months the tears brimmed up into her eyes as she followed her companion to the cab and let him help her in. As the door closed upon them Ted turned and faced the girl and seeing the tears put out his hand and touched hers gently.

"Don't worry, Madeline," he said. "Things are going to look up. And please don't cry," he pleaded earnestly.

She wiped away the tears and summoned a wan little smile to meet his.

"I won't," she said. "Crying is silly and won't help anything. It is just that I was awfully tired and your being so good to me upset me. You've always been good even--when I thought you weren't. I understand better now. And oh, Ted, you don't know how ashamed I am of the way I behaved that night! It was awful--my striking you like that. It made me sick to think of it afterward."

"It needn't have. If anybody has any call to be ashamed of that night it's yours truly. See here, Madeline, I've worried a lot about you though maybe you won't believe it because I didn't write or act as if I were sorry about things. I kept still because it seemed the straightest thing to do all round, but I did think a great deal about you, honest I did, and I've wondered millions of times if my darn-foolness set things going wrong for you. Did it, Madeline?" he demanded.

"No," she answered her gaze away from his out the cab window. "You mustn't worry, Ted, or blame yourself. It--it's all my fault--everything."

"It's good of you to let me out but I am not so sure I ought to be let out. I'd give a good deal this minute if I could go back and not take Uncle Phil's car that night." Ted leaned forward suddenly and for a startled instant Madeline thought he meant to kiss her. But nothing was farther from his wish or thought. It was the scar he was looking for. He had almost forgotten it, just as he had almost forgotten the episode it represented. But there it was on her forehead. Even in the gathering darkness it showed with perfect distinctness. "I hoped it had gone," he added. "But it is still there, isn't it?"

"The scar? Yes, it is still there." For a moment the ghost of a smile played about the girl's lips. "I've always liked it. I'd miss it if it went."

"Well, I don't like it. I hate it," groaned the boy. "Why, Madeline I might have killed you!"

"I know. Sometimes I wish it had come out so. It--it would have been better."

"Don't Madeline. That is an awful thing to say. Things can't be as bad as all that, you know they can't. By the way, can you tell me the whole business or would you rather not?"

The girl shivered.

"No. Don't ask me, Ted. It--it's too awful. Don't bother about me. You have done quite enough as it is. I am very grateful but truly I would rather you wouldn't have anything more to do with me. Just forget I am here."

And because this injunction was precisely in line with his own inclination Ted suspected its propriety and swung counterwise in true Ted fashion.

"I'll do just exactly as I please about that. I won't pester you but you needn't think I'm going to leave you all soul alone in a strange place when you are feeling rotten anyway. I'm pretty doggoned selfish but not quite that bad."

CHAPTER XXV
ALL THE WORLD'S A STAGE

Although Max Hempel had not openly sought out Tony Holiday he was entirely aware of her presence in the city and in the dramatic school. Whenever she played a role in the course of the latter's program he had his trusted aides on the spot to watch her, gauge her progress, report their finding to himself. Once or twice he had come himself, sat in a dark corner and kept his eye unblinking from first to last upon the girl.

In November it had seemed good to the school to revive The Killarney Rose, a play which ten years ago had had a phenomenal run and ended as it began with packed houses. It was past history now. Even the road companies had lapsed, and its name was all but forgotten by the fickle public which must and will have ever new sensations.

Hempel was glad the school had made this particular selection, doubly glad it had given Antoinette Holiday the title role. The play would show whether the girl was ready for his purposes as he had about decided she was. He would send Carol Clay to see her do the thing. Carol would know. Who better? It was she who created the original Rose.

Tony Holiday behind the scene on that momentous evening, on being informed that Carol Clay--the famous Carol Clay herself--the real Rose--was out there in a box, was paralyzed with fear, for the first time in her life, victim of genuine stage fright. She was cold. She was hot. She was one tremendous shake and shiver. She was a very lump of stone. The orchestra was already playing. In a moment her call would come and she was going to fail, fail miserably. And with Carol Clay there to see.

Some flowers and a card were brought in. The flowers were from Alan of course, great crimson roses. It was dear of him to send them. Later she would appreciate it. But just now not even Alan mattered. She glanced at the card which had come separately, was not with the flowers. It was Dick's. Hastily she read the pencil-written scrawl. "Am covering the Rose. Will be close up. See you after the show. Best o' luck and love."

Tony could almost have cried for joy over the message. Somehow the knowledge of Dick's nearness gave her back her self-possession. She had refused to let Alan come. His presence in the audience always distracted her, made her nervous. But Dick was different. It was almost like having Uncle Phil himself there. She wouldn't fail now. She couldn't. It was for the honor of the Hill.

A moment later, still clutching Dick's comforting card, she ran in on the stage, swinging her sun-bonnet from its green ribbons with hoydenish grace, chanting a gay little lilt of an Irish melody. Her fear had gone even as the dew might have disappeared at the kiss of the sun upon the Killarney greensward.

Almost at once she discovered Dick and sang a part of her song straight down at him. A little later she dared to let her eyes stray to the box where Carol Clay sat. The actress smiled and Tony smiled back and then forgot she was Tony, was henceforth only Rose of Killarney.

It was a winsome, old-timey sort of play, with an almost Barriesque charm and whimsicality to it. The witching little Rose laughed and danced and sang and flirted and wept and loved her way through it and in the end threw herself in the right lover's arms, presumably there to dwell happy forever after.

After the last curtain went down and she had smiled and bowed and kissed her hand to the kindly audience over and over Tony fled to the dressing room where she could still hear the intoxicating, delightful thunder of applause. It had come. She could act. She could. Oh! She couldn't live and be any happier.

But, after all she could stand a little more joy without coming to an untimely end, for there suddenly smiling at her from the threshold was Carol Clay congratulating her and telling her what a pleasure to-night's Rose had been to the Rose of yesterday. And before Tony could get her breath to do more than utter a rather shy and gasping word of gratitude, the actress had invited her to take tea with her on the next day and she had accepted and Carol Clay was gone.

It was in a wonderful world of dreams that Tony Holiday dwelt as she removed a little of her makeup, gave orders to have all her flowers sent to a near-by hospital, except Alan's, which she gathered up in her arms and drawing her velvet cloak around her, stepped out into the waiting-room.

But it was a world of rather alarming realities that she went into. There was Dick Carson waiting as she had bidden him to wait in the message she had sent him. And there was Alan Massey, unbidden and unexpected. And both these males with whom she had flirted unconscionably for weeks past were ominously belligerent of manner and countenance. She would have given anything to have had a wand to wave the two away, keep them from spoiling her perfect evening. But it was too late. The hour of reckoning which comes even to queens was here.

"Hello, you two," she greeted, putting on a brave front for all her sinking heart. She laid down the roses and gave a hand impartially to each. "Awfully glad to see you, Dicky. Alan, I thought I told you not to come. Were you here all the same?"

"I was. I told you so in my note. Didn't you get it? I sent it in with the roses." He nodded at the flowers she had just surrendered.

Dick's eyes shadowed. Massey had scored there. He had not thought of flowers. Indeed there had been no time to get any he had gotten the assignment so late. There had been quantities of other flowers, he knew. The usher had carried up tons of them it seemed to the popular Rose, but she carried only Alan Massey's home with her.

"I am sorry, Alan. I didn't see it. Maybe it was there; I didn't half look at the flowers. Your message did me so much good, Dicky. I was scared to death because they had just said Miss Clay was outside. And somehow when I knew you were there I felt all right again. I carried your card all through the first act and I know it was your wishing me the best o' luck that brought it."

She smiled at Dick and it was Alan's turn to glower. She had not looked at his roses, had not cared to look for his message; but she carried the other man's card, used it as a talisman. And she was glad. The other was there, but she had forbidden himself--Alan Massey--to come, had even reproached him for coming.

A group of actors passed through the reception room, calling gay goodnights and congratulations to Tony as they went and shooting glances of friendly curiosity at the two, tall frowning men between whom the vivacious Rose stood.

"Tony Holiday doesn't keep all her lovers on the stage," laughed the near-heroine as she was out of hearing. "Did you ever see two gentlemen that hated each other more cordially?"

"She is an arrant little flirt, isn't she, Micky?" The speaker challenged the Irish lover of the play who had had the luck to win the sweet, thorny little Killarney Rose in the end and to get a real, albeit a play kiss from the pretty little heroine, who as Tony Holiday as well as Rose was prone to make mischief in susceptible male hearts.

"She can have me any minute, on the stage or off," answered Micky promptly. "She's a winner. Got me going all right. Most forgot my lines she was so darned pretty."

Dick took advantage of the confusion of the interruption to get in his word.

"Will you come out with me for a bite somewhere, Tony. I won't keep you late, but there are some things I want to talk over with you."

Tony hesitated. She had caught the ominous flash of Alan's eyes. She was desperately afraid there would be a scene if she said yes to Dick now in Alan's hearing. The latter strode over to her instantly, and laid his hand with a proprietorial air on her arm. From this point of vantage he faced Dick insolently.

"Miss Holiday is going out with me," he asserted. "You--clear out."

The tone and manner even more than the words were deliberate insult. Dick's face went white. His mouth set tight. There was almost as ugly a look in his eyes as there was in Alan's. Tony had never seen him look like that and was frightened.

"I'll clear out when Miss Holiday asks me to and not before," he said in a significantly quiet voice. "Don't go too far, Mr. Massey. I have taken a good deal from you. There's a limit. Tony, I repeat my question. Will you go out with me to-night?"

Before Tony could speak Alan Massey's long right arm shot out in Dick's direction. Dick dodged the blow coolly.

"Hold on, Massey," he said. "I'm perfectly willing to smash your head any time it is convenient. Nothing would afford me greater pleasure in fact. But you will kindly keep from making trouble here. You can't get a woman's name mixed up with a cheap brawl such as you are trying to start. You know, it won't do."

Alan Massey's white face turned a shade whiter. His arm fell. He turned back to Tony, real anguish in his fire-shot eyes.

"I beg your pardon, Tony dearest," he bent over to say. "Carson is right. We'll fight it out elsewhere when you are not present. May I take you to the taxi? I have one waiting outside."

Another group of people passed through the vestibule, said goodnight and went on out to the street exit. It made Tony sick to think of what they would have seen if Dick had lost his self control as Alan had. She thought she had never liked Dick as she did that moment, never despised Alan Massey so utterly. Dick was a man. Alan was a spoiled child, a weakling, the slave of his passions. It was no thanks to him that her name was not already bandied about on people's lips, the name of a girl, about whom men came to fist blows like a Bowery movie scene. She was humiliated all over, enraged with Alan, enraged with herself for stooping to care for a man like that. She waited until they were absolutely alone again and then said what she had to say. She turned to face Alan directly.

"You may take me nowhere," she said. "I don't want to see you again as long as I live."

For an instant Alan stared at her, dazed, unable to grasp the force of what she was saying, the significance of her tone. As a matter of fact the artist in him had leaped to the surface, banished all other considerations. He had never seen Tony Holiday really angry before. She was magnificent with those flashing eyes and scarlet cheeks--a glorious little Fury--a Valkyrie. He would paint her like that. She was stupendous, the most vividly alive thing he had ever seen, like flame itself, in her flaming anger. Then it came over him what she had said.

"But, Tony," he pleaded, "my belovedest--"

He put out both hands in supplication, but Tony whirled away from them. She snatched the great bunch of red roses from the table, ran to the window, flung up the sash, hurled them out into the night. Then she turned back to Alan.

"Now go," she commanded, pointing with a small, inexorable hand to the door.

Alan Massey went.

Tony dropped in a chair, spent and trembling, all but in tears. The disagreeable scene, the piled up complex of emotions coming on top of the stress and strain of the play were almost too much for her. She was a quivering bundle of nerves and misery at the moment.

Dick came to her.

"Forgive me, Tony. I shouldn't have forced the issue maybe. But I couldn't stand any more from that cad."

"I am glad you did exactly what you did do, Dick, and I am more grateful than I can ever tell you for not letting Alan get you into a fight here in this place with all these people coming and going. I would never have gotten over it if anything like that had happened. It would have been terrible. I couldn't ever have looked any of them in the face again." She shivered and put her two hands over her eyes ashamed to the quick at the thought.

Dick sat down on the arm of her chair, one hand resting gently on the girl's shoulder.

"Don't cry, Tony," he begged. "I can't stand it. You needn't have worried. There wasn't any danger of anything like that happening. I care too much to let you in for anything of that sort. So does he for that matter. He saw it in a minute. He really wouldn't want to do you any harm anyway, Tony. Even I know that, and you must know it better than I."

Tony put down her hands, looked at Dick. "I suppose that is true," she sighed. "He does love me, Dick."

"He does, Tony. I wish he didn't. And I wish with all my heart I were sure you didn't love him."

Tony sighed again and her eyes fell.

"I wish--I were sure, too," she faltered.

Dick winced at that. He had no answer. What was there to say?

"I don't see why I should care. I don't see how I can care after to-night. He is horrid in lots of ways--a cad--just as you called him. I know Larry would feel just as you do and hate to have him come near me. Larry and I have almost quarreled about it now. He thinks Uncle Phil is all wrong not to forbid my seeing Alan at all. But Uncle Phil is too wise. He doesn't want to have me marry Alan any more than the rest of you do but he knows if he fights it it would put me on the other side in a minute and I'd do it, maybe, in spite of everybody."

"Tony, you aren't engaged to him?"

She shook her head.

"Not exactly. I am afraid I might as well be though. I said I didn't ever want to see him again, but I didn't mean it. I shall want to see him again by to-morrow. I always do no matter what he does. I always shall I am afraid. It is like that with me. I'm sorry, Dicky. I ought to have told you that before. I've been horrid not to, I know. Take me home now, please. I'm tired--awfully tired."

Going home in the cab neither spoke until just as they were within a few blocks of the Hostelry when Dick broke the silence.

"I am sorry all this had to happen to-night," he said. "Because, well, I am going away tomorrow."

"Going away! Dick! Where?" It was horribly selfish of her, Tony knew; but it didn't seem as if she could bear to have Dick go. It seemed as if the only thing that was stable in her reeling life would be gone if he went. If he went she would belong to Alan more and more. There would be nothing to hold her back. She was afraid. She clung to Dick. He alone of the whole city full of human beings was a symbol of Holiday Hill. With him gone it seemed to her as if she would be hopelessly adrift on perilous seas.

"To Mexico--Vera Cruz, I believe," he answered her question.

"Vera Cruz! Dick, you mustn't! It is awful down there now. Everybody says so." He smiled a little at that.

"It is because it is more or less awful that they are sending me," he said. "Journalism isn't much interested in placidity. A newspaper man has to be where things are happening fast and plenty. If things are hot down there so much the better. They will sizzle more in the copy."

"Dick! I can't have you go. I can't bear it." Tony's hand crept into his. "Something dreadful might happen to you," she wailed.

He pressed her hand, grateful for her real trouble about him and for her caring.

"Oh no, dear. Nothing dreadful will happen to me. You mustn't worry," he soothed.

"But I do. I shall. How can I help it? It is just as if Larry or Ted were going. It scares me."

Dick drew away his hand suddenly.

"For heaven's sake, Tony, please don't tell me again that I'm just like Larry and Ted to you. It is bad enough to know it without your rubbing it in all the time. I can't stand it--not to-night."

"Dick!" Tony was startled, taken aback by his tone. Dick rarely let himself go like that.

In a moment he was all contrition.

"Forgive me, Tony. I'm sorry I said that. I ought to be thankful you care that much, and I am. It is dear of you and I do appreciate it."

"Oh me!" sighed Tony. "Everything I do or say is wrong. I wish I did care the other way for you, Dicky dear. Truly I do. It would be so much nicer and simpler than caring for Alan," she added naively.

"Life isn't fixed nice and simple, Tony. At least it never has been for me."

"Oh, Dick! Everything has been horribly hard for you always, and I'm making it harder. I don't want to, Dicky dear. You know I don't. It is just that I can't help it."

"I know, Tony. You mustn't bother about me. I'm all right. Will you tell me just one thing though? If you hadn't cared for Massey--no I won't put it like that. If you had cared for me would my not having any name have made any difference?"

"Of course it wouldn't have made any difference, Dicky. What does a name matter? You are you and that is what I would care for--do care for. The rest doesn't matter. Besides, you are making a name for yourself."

"I am doing it under your name--the one you gave me."

"I am proud to have it used that way. Why wouldn't I be? It is honored. You have not only lived up to it as you promised Uncle Phil. You have made it stand for something fine. Your stories are splendid. You are going to be famous and I--Why, Dicky, just think, it will be my name you will take on up to the stars. Oh, we're here," as the cab jolted to a halt in front of the Hostelry.

The cabby flung open the door. Tony and Dick stepped out, went up the steps. In a moment they were alone in the dimly lit hall.

"Tony, would you mind letting me kiss you just once as you would Larry or Ted if one of them were going off on a long journey away from you?"

Dick's voice was humble, pleading. It touched Tony deeply, and sent the quick tears welling up into her eyes as she raised her face to his.

For a moment he held her close, kissed her on the cheek and then released her.

"Good-by, Tony. Thank you and God bless you," he said a little huskily as he let her go.

"Good-by, Dick." And then impulsively Tony put up her lips and kissed him, the first time he ever remembered a woman's lips touching his.

A second later the door closed upon him, shutting him out in the night. He dismissed the cab driver and walked blindly off, not knowing or caring in what direction he went. It was hours before he let himself into his lodging house. It seemed as if he could have girdled the earth on the strength of Tony Holiday's kiss. The next morning he was off for Mexico.

CHAPTER XXVI
THE KALEIDOSCOPE REVOLVES

Tony slept late next morning and when she did open her eyes they fell upon a huge florist box by the door and a special delivery letter on top of it. The maid had set the two in an hour ago and tiptoed away lest she waken the weary little sleeper.

Tony got up and opened the box. Roses--dozens of them, worth the price of a month's wages to many a worker in the city! Frail, exquisite, shell-pink beauties, with gold at their hearts! Tony adored roses but she almost hated these because it seemed to her Alan was bribing her forgiveness by playing upon her worship of their beauty and fragrance.

Still kneeling by the flowers she glanced at the clock. Ten-thirty! Dick was already miles away on his hateful journey, had gone sad and hopeless because she loved Alan Massey. Why did it have to be so? Why was love so perverse and unreasonable a thing? Alan was not worthy to touch Dick's hand, though in his arrogance he affected to despise the other. But it was Alan she loved, not Dick. There must be something wrong with her, dreadfully wrong that it should be so. After last night there could be no doubt of that.

She sat down on the floor, opened Alan's letter, despised herself for letting its author's spell creep over her anew with every word. It was an abject plea for mercy, for forgiveness, for restoration to favor. It had been a devil of jealousy that had possessed him, he had not known what he was doing. Surely she must know that he would not willingly harm or hurt or anger her in any way. He loved her too much. Carson had behaved like a man. Alan would apologize to him if the other man would accept the apology. It was Tony really who had driven him mad by being so much kinder to the other than to himself. She must realize what he was, not drive him too far.

"I am sending you roses," he ended. "Please don't throw them away as you did the others. Keep them and let them plead for me. And don't ah Tony, don't ever, ever say again what you said last night, that you never wanted to see me again! You don't mean it, I know. But don't say it. It kills me to hear you. If you throw me over I'll blow my brains out as sure as I am a living man this moment. But you won't, you cannot, Tony dearest. You will forgive me, stand by me, rotten as I am. You are mine. You love me. You won't push me down to Hell."

It was a cowardly letter Tony thought, a letter calculated to frighten her, bring her to subjection again as well as to gratify the writer's own Byronic instinct for pose. He had behaved badly. He acknowledged it but claimed forgiveness on the grounds of love, his love for her which had been goaded to mad jealousy by her thoughtless unkindness, her love for him which would not desert him no matter what he did.

But pose or not, Tony was obliged to admit there was some truth in it all. Perhaps it was all true-too true. Even if he did not resort to the pistol as he threatened he would find other means of slaying his soul if not his body if she forsook him now. She could not do it. As he said she loved him too well. She had gone too far in the path to turn back now.

Ah why, why had she let it go so far? Why had she not listened to Dick, to Uncle Phil, to Carlotta, even to Miss Lottie? They had all told her there was no happiness for her in loving Alan Massey. She knew it herself better than any of them could possibly know it. And yet she had to go on, for his sake, for her own because she loved him.

By this time she was no longer angry or resentful. She was just sorry--sorry for Alan--sorry for herself. She knew just as she had known all along that last night's incident would not really make any difference. It would be put away in time with all the other things she had to forgive. She had eaten her pomegranate seeds. She could not escape the dark kingdom. She did not wish to.

Later came violets from Dick which she put in a vase on her desk beside Uncle Phil's picture. But it was the fragrance and color of Alan's roses that filled the room, and presently she sat down and wrote her ill-behaved lover a sweet, forgiving little note. She was sorry if she had been unkind. She had not meant to be. As for what happened it was too late to worry about it now. They had best forget it, if they could. He couldn't very well apologize to Dick in person because he was already on his way to Mexico. There was no need of any penance. Of course she forgave him, knew he had not meant to hurt her, though he had horribly. If he cared to do so he might take her to dinner tomorrow night--somewhere where they could dance. And in conclusion she was always his, Tony Holiday.

Both Dick and Alan were driven out of her mind later that day by the delightful and exciting interview over the tea table with Carol Clay. Miss Clay was a charming hostess, drew the girl out without appearing to do so, got her to talk naturally about many things, her life with her father at army barracks, and with her uncle on her beloved Hill, of her friends and brothers, her college life, of books and plays. Plays took them to the Killarney Rose and once more Miss Clay expressed her pleasure in the girl's rendering of one of her own favorite roles.

"You acted as if you had been playing Rose all your life," she added with a smile.

"Maybe I have," said Tony. "Rose is--a good deal like me. Maybe that is why I loved playing her so."

"I shouldn't wonder. You are a real little actress, my dear. I wonder if you are ready to pay the price of it. It is bitterly hard work and it means giving up half the things women care for."

The speaker's lovely eyes shadowed a little. Tony wondered what Carol Clay had given up, was giving up for her art to bring that look into them.

"I am not afraid. I am willing to work. I love it. And I--I am willing to give up a good deal."

"Lovers?" smiled Miss Clay.

"Must I? I thought actresses always had lovers, at least worshipers. Can't I keep the lovers, Miss Clay?" There was a flash of mischief in Tony's eyes as she asked the important question.

"Better stick to worshipers. Lovers are risky. Husbands--fatal."

Tony laughed outright at that.

"I am willing to postpone the fatality," she murmured.

"I am glad to hear it for I lured you here to take you into a deep-laid plot. I suppose you did not suspect that it was Max Hempel who sent me to see you play Rose?"

"Mr. Hempel? I thought he had forgotten me."

"He never forgets any one in whom he is interested. He has had his eye on you ever since he saw you play Rosalind. He told me when he came back from that trip that I had a rival coming on."

"Oh, no!" Tony objected even in jest to such desecration.

"Oh, yes," smiled her hostess. "Max Hempel is a brutally frank person. He never spares one the truth, even the disagreeable truth. He has had his eye out for a new ingenue for a long time. Ingenues do get old--at least older you know."

"Not you," denied Tony.

"Even I, in time. I grant you not yet. It takes a degree of age and sophistication to play youth and innocence. We do it better as a rule at thirty than at twenty. We are far enough away from it to stand off and observe how it behaves and can imitate it better than if we still had it. That is one reason I was interested in your Rose last night. You played like a little girl as Rose should. You looked like a little girl. But you couldn't have given it that delightfully sure touch if you hadn't been a little bit grown up. Do you understand?"

Tony nodded.

"I think so. You see I am--a little bit grown up."

"Don't grow up any more. You are adorable as you are. But to business. Have you seen my Madge?"

"In the 'End of the Rainbow?' Yes, indeed. I love it. You like the part too, don't you? You play it as if you did."

"I do. I like it better than any I have had since Rose. Did it occur to you that you would like to play Madge yourself?"

Tony blushed ingenuously.

"Well, yes, it did," she admitted half shyly. "Of course, I knew I couldn't play it as you did. It takes years of experience and a real art like yours to do it like that, but I did think I'd like to try it and see what I could do."

Miss Clay nodded, well pleased.

"Of course you did. Why not? It is your kind of a role, just as Rose is. You and I are the same types. Mr. Hempel has said that all along, ever since he saw your Rosalind. But I won't keep you in suspense. The long and short of all this preliminary is--how would you like to be my understudy for Madge?"

"Oh, Miss Clay!" Tony gasped. "Do you think I could?"

"I know you could, my dear. I knew it all the time while I was watching you play Rose. Mr. Hempel has known it even longer. I went to see Rose to find out if there was a Madge in you. There is. I told Mr. Hempel so this morning. He is brewing his contracts now so be prepared. Will you try it?"

"I'd love to if you and Mr. Hempel think I can. I promised Uncle Phil I would take a year of the school work though. Will I have to drop that?"

"I think so--most of it at least. You would have to be at the rehearsals usually which are in the morning. You might have to play Madge quite often then. There are reasons why I have to be away a great deal just now." Again the shadow, darkened the star's eyes and a droop came to her mouth. "It isn't even so impossible that you would be called upon to play before the real Broadway audience in fact. Understudies sometimes do you know."

Miss Clay was smiling now, but the shadow in her eyes had not lifted Tony saw.

"I am particularly anxious to get a good understudy started in immediately," the actress continued. "The one I had was impossible, did not get the spirit of the thing at all. It is absolutely essential to have some one ready and at once. My little daughter is in a sanitarium dying with an incurable heart leakage. There will be a time--probably within the next two months--when I shall have to be away."

Tony put out her hand and let it rest upon the other woman's. There was compassion in her young eyes.

"I am so sorry," she said simply. "I didn't know you had a daughter. Of course, I did know you weren't really Miss Clay, that you were Mrs. Somebody, but I didn't think of your having children. Somehow we don't remember actresses may be mothers too."

"The actresses remember it--sometimes," said Miss Clay with a tremulous little smile. "It isn't easy to laugh when your heart is heavy, Miss Antoinette. It is all I can do to go on with 'Madge' sometimes. I just have to forget--make myself forget I am a mother and a wife. Captain Carey, my husband, is in the British Army. He is in Flanders now, or was when I last heard."

"Oh, I don't see how you can do it--play, I mean," sighed Tony aghast at this new picture the actress's words brought up.

"One learns, my dear. One has to. An actress is two distinct persons. One of her belongs to the public. The other is just a plain woman. Sometimes I feel as if I were far more the first than I am the second. There wouldn't be any more contracts if I were not. But never mind that. To come back to you. Mr. Hempel will send you a contract to-morrow. Will you sign it?"

"Yes, if Uncle Phil is willing. I'll wire him to-night. I am almost positive he will say yes. He is very reasonable and he will see what a wonderful, wonderful chance this is for me. I can't thank you enough, Miss Clay. It all takes my breath away. But I am grateful and so happy; you can't imagine it."

Miss Clay smiled and drew on her gloves. The interview was over.

"There is really nothing to thank me, for," she said. "The favor is on the other side. It is I who am lucky. The perfect understudy like a becoming hat is hard to find, but when found is absolutely beyond price. May I send you a pass for to-morrow night to the 'End of the Rainbow'? Perhaps you would like to see it again and play 'Madge' with me from a box. The pass will admit two. Bring one of the lovers if you like."

Tony wired her uncle that night. In the morning mail arrived Max Hempel's contract as Miss Clay had promised. Tony regarded it with superstitious awe. It was the first contract she had ever seen in her life, much less had offered for her signature. The terms were, generous--appallingly so it seemed to the girl who knew little of such things and was not inclined to over-rate her powers financially speaking. She wisely took the contract over to the school and got the manager's advice to "Go ahead."

"We've nothing comparable to offer you, Miss Tony. With Hempel and Miss Clay both behind you you are practically made. You are a lucky little lady. I know a dozen experienced actresses in this city who would give their best cigarette cases to be in your shoes."

Arrived home at the Hostelry, armed with this approval, Tony found her Uncle's answering wire bidding her do as she thought best and sending heartiest love and congratulations. Dear Uncle Phil!

And then she sat down and signed the impressive document that made her Carol Clay's understudy and a real wage-earning person.

All the afternoon she spent in long, delicious, dreamless slumber. At five she was wakened by the maid bringing a letter from Alan, a wonderful, extravagant lover-note such as only he could pen. Later she bathed and dressed, donning the white and silver gown she had worn the night when she had first admitted to Alan in Carlotta's garden that she loved him, first took his kisses. It was rather a sacred little gown to Tony, sacred to Alan and her own surrender to love. He called it her starlight dress and loved it especially because it brought out the springlike, virginal quality of her youth and loveliness as her other more sophisticated gowns did not. Tony wore it for Alan to-night, wanted him to think her lovely, to love her immensely. She wanted to taste all life's joy at once, have a perfect deluge of happiness. Youth must be served.

Alan, graceful for being forgiven so easily, fell in with her mood and was at his best, courtly, considerate, adoring. He exerted all the magic of his not inconsiderable charm to make Tony forget that other unfortunate night when he had appeared in other, less attractive colors. And Tony was ready enough to forget beneath his worshiping green eyes and under the spell of his wonderful voice. She meant to shut out the unwelcome guests of fear and doubt from her heart, let love alone have sway.

They dined at a gorgeous restaurant in a great hotel. Tony reveled in the splendor and richness of the setting, delighted in the flawless service, the perfection of the strange and delectable viands which Alan ordered for their consumption. Particularly she delighted in Alan himself and the way he fitted into the richness and luxury. It was his rightful setting. She could not imagine him in any of the shabby restaurants where she and Dick had often dined so contentedly. Alan was a born aristocrat, patrician of the patricians. His looks, his manner, everything about him betrayed it. Most of all it was revealed in the way the waiters scurried to do his bidding, bowed obsequiously before him, recognized him as the authentic master, lord of the purple.

"So Carson really has gone to Mexico," Alan murmured as they dallied over their salads, looking mostly into each other's eyes.

"Yes, he went yesterday. I hated to have him go. It is awfully disagreeable and dangerous down there they say. He might get a fever or get killed or something." Tony absent-mindedly nibbling a piece of roll already saw Dick in her mind's eye the victim of an assassin's blade.

"No such luck!" thought Alan Massey bitterly. The thought brought a flash of venom into his eyes which Tony unluckily caught.

"Alan! Why do you hate Dick so? He never did you any harm."

Tony Holiday did not know what outrageous injury Dick had done his cousin, Alan Massey.

Alan was already suavely master of himself, the venom expunged from his eyes.

"Why wouldn't I hate him, **Antoinetta mia**? You are half in love with him."

"I am not," denied Tony indignantly. "He is just like Lar--." She broke off abruptly, remembering Dick's flare of resentment at that familiar formula, remembering too the kiss she had given him in the dimly-lit hall in the Hostelry, the kiss which had not been precisely such a one as she would have given Larry.

Alan's face darkened again.

"Oh, yes, you are. You are blushing."

"I am not." Then putting her hands up to her face and feeling it warm she changed her tactics. "Well, what, if I am? I do care a lot about Dick. I found out the other night that I cared a whole lot more than I knew. It isn't like caring for Larry and Ted. It's different. For after all he isn't my brother--never was--never will be. I'm a wretched flirt, Alan. You know it as well as I do. I've let Dick keep on loving me, knowing all the time I didn't mean to marry him. And I'm not a bit sure I am going to marry you either."

"Tony!"

"Well, anyway not for a long, long time. I want to go on the stage. I can't put all of myself into my work and give it to you at the same time. I don't want to get married. I don't dare to. I don't dare even let myself care too much. I want to be free."

"You want to be loved."

"Of course. Every woman does."

Alan made an impatient gesture.

"I don't mean lip-worship. You are a woman, not a piece of statuary. Come on now. Let's dance."

They danced. In her lover's arms, their feet keeping time to the syncopated, stirring rhythms of the violins, their hearts beating to a mightier harmony of nature's own brewing, Tony Holiday was far from being a piece of statuary. She was all woman, a woman very much alive and very much in love.

Alan bent over her.

"Tony, belovedest. There are more things than art in the world," he said softly. "Don't you know it, feel it? There is life. And life is bigger than your work or mine. We're both artists, but we'll be bigger artists together. Marry me now. Don't make me wait. Don't make yourself wait. You want it as much as I do. Say yes, sweetheart," he implored.

Tony shook her head vehemently. She was afraid. She knew that just now all her dreams of success in her chosen art, all her love for the dear ones at home were as nothing in comparison with this greater thing which Alan called life and which she felt surging mightily within her. But she also knew that this way lay madness, disloyalty, regret. She must be strong, strong for Alan as well as for herself.

"Not yet," she whispered back. "Be patient, Alan. I love you, dear. Wait."

The music came to an end. Many eyes followed the two as they went back to their places at the table. They were incomparable artists. It was worth missing one's own dance to see them have theirs. Aside from his wonderful dancing and striking personality Alan was at all times a marked figure, attracting attention wherever he went and whatever he did. The public knew he had a superlative fortune which he spent magnificently as a prince, and that he had a superlative gift which for all they were aware he had flung wantonly away as soon as the money came into his hands. Moreover he was even more interesting because of his superlatively bad reputation which still followed him. The public would have found it hard to believe that at last Alan Massey was leading the most temperate and arduous of lives and devoting himself exclusively to one woman whom he treated as reverently as if she were a goddess. The gazes focussed upon Alan now inevitably included the girl with him, as lovely and young as spring itself.

"Who was she?" they asked each other. "What was a girl like that doing in Alan

Massey's society?" To most of the observers it meant but one thing, eventually if not now. Even the most cynical and world-hardened thought it a pity, and these would have been confounded if they could have heard just now his passionate plea for marriage. One did not associate marriage with Alan Massey. One had not associated it too much with his mother, one recalled.

CHAPTER XXVII
TROUBLED WATERS

Ted Holiday drifted into Berry's to buy floral offerings for the reigning goddess who chanced still to be pretty Elsie Hathaway. Things had gone on gayly since that night a month ago when he had stolen that impudent kiss beneath the crescent moon. Not that there was anything at all serious about the affair. College coquettes must have lovers, and Ted Holiday would not have been himself if there had not been a pretty sweetheart on hand.

By this time Ted had far outdistanced the other claimants for Elsie's favor. But the victory had come high. His bank account was again sadly humble in porportions and his bills at Berry's and at the candy shops were things not to be looked into too closely. Nevertheless he was in a gala humor that November morning. Aside from chronic financial complications things were going very well with him. He was working just hard enough to satisfy his newly-awakened common sense or conscience, or whatever it was that was operating. He was having a jolly good time with Elsie and basket ball and other things and college life didn't seem quite such a bore and burden as it had hitherto. Moreover Uncle Phil had just written that he would waive the ten dollar automobile tax for December in consideration of the approach of Christmas, possibly also in consideration of his nephew's fairly creditable showing on the new leaf of the ledger though he did not say so. In any case it was a jolly old world if anybody asked Ted Holiday that morning as he entered Berry's.

He made straight for Madeline as he invariably did. He was always friendly and gay and casual with her, always careful to let no one suspect he had ever known her any more intimately than at present--not because he cared on his own account-- Ted Holiday was no snob. But because he had sense to see it was better for Madeline herself.

He was genuinely sorry for the girl. He could not help seeing how her despondency grew upon her from week to week and that she appeared miserably sick as well as unhappy. She looked worse than usual to-day, he thought, white and heavy-eyed and unmistakably heavy-hearted. It troubled him to see her so. Ted had the kindest heart in the world and always wanted every one else to be as blithely content with life as he was himself. Accordingly now under cover of his purchase of chrysanthemums for Elsie he managed to get in a word in her ear.

"You look as if you needed cheering up a bit. How about the movies to-night? Charlie's on. He'll fix you."

"No, thank you, I couldn't." The girl's voice was also prudently low, and she busied herself with the flowers instead of looking at Ted as she spoke.

"Why not?" he challenged, always impelled to insistence by denial.

"Because I--" And then to Ted's consternation the flowers flew out of her hands, scattering in all directions, her face went chalky white and she fell forward in a heavy faint in Ted Holiday's arms.

Ted got her to a chair, ordered another clerk to get water and spirits of ammonia quick. His arm was still around her when Patrick Berry strayed in from the back room. Berry's eyes narrowed. He looked the girl over from head to foot, surveyed Ted Holiday also with sharp scrutiny and knitted brows. The clerk returned with water and dashed off for the ammonia as ordered. Madeline's eyes opened slowly, meeting Ted's anxious blue ones as he bent over her.

"Ted!" she gasped. "Oh, Ted!"

Her eyes closed again wearily. Berry's frown deepened. His best customer had hitherto in his hearing been invariably addressed by the girl as Mr. Holiday.

In a moment Madeline's eyes opened again and she almost pushed Ted away from her, shooting a frightened, deprecating glance at her employer as she did so.

"I--I am all right now," she said, rising unsteadily.

"You are nothing of the sort, Madeline," protested Ted, also forgetting caution in his concern. "You are sick. I'll get a taxi and take you home. Mr. Berry won't mind, will you Berry?" appealed the best customer, completely unaware of the queer, sharp look the florist was bending upon him.

"No, she'd better go," agreed Berry shortly. "I'll call a cab." He walked over to the telephone but paused, his hand on the receiver and looked back at Ted. "Where does she live?" he asked. "Do you know?"

"Forty-nine Cherry," returned Ted still unconsciously revelatory.

The big Irishman got his number and called the cab. The clerk came back with the ammonia and vanished with it into the back room. Berry walked over to where Ted stood.

"See here, Mr. Holiday," he said. "I don't often go out of my way to give college boys advice. Advice is about the one thing in the world nobody wants. But I'm going to give you a bit. I like you and I liked your brother before you. Here's the advice. Stick to the campus. Don't get mixed up with Cherry Street. You wanted the chrysanthemums sent to Miss Hathaway, didn't you?"

"I did." There was a flash in Ted's blue eyes. "Send 'em and send a dozen of your best roses to Miss Madeline Taylor, forty-nine Cherry and mind your business. There is the cab. Ready, Madeline?" As the girl appeared in the doorway with her coat and hat on. "I'll take you home."

"Oh, no, indeed, it isn't at all necessary," protested Madeline. "You have done quite enough as it is, Mr. Holiday. You mustn't bother." The speaker's tone was cool, almost cold and very formal. She did not know that Patrick Berry had heard that very different, fervid, "Ted! Oh, Ted!" if indeed she knew it had ever passed her lips as she came reluctantly back to the world of realities.

Ted held the door open for her. They passed out. But a moment later when Berry peered out the window he saw the cab going in one direction and his best customer strolling off in the other and nodded his satisfaction.

Sauntering along his nonchalant course, Madeline Taylor already half forgotten, Ted Holiday came face to face with old Doctor Hendricks, a rosy cheeked, white bearded, twinkling eyed Santa Claus sort of person who had known his father and uncle and brother and had pulled himself through various minor itises and sprains. Seeing the doctor reminded him of Madeline.

"Hello, Doc. Just the man I wanted to see. Want a job?"

"Got more jobs than I can tend to now, young man. Anything the matter with you? You look as tough as a two year old rooster."

The old man's small, kindly, shrewd eyes scanned the lad's face as he spoke.

"Smoking less, sleeping more, nerves steadier, working harder, playing the devil lighter," he gummed up silently with satisfaction. "Good, he'll come out a Holiday yet if we give him time."

"I am tough," Ted grinned back, all unconscious that he had been diagnosed in that flitting instant of time. "Never felt better in my life. Always agrees with me to be in training."

The old doctor nodded.

"I know. You young idiots will mind your coaches when you won't your fathers and your doctors. What about the job?"

"There's a girl I know who works at Berry's flower shop. I am afraid she is sick though she won't see a doctor. She fainted away just now while I was in the store, keeled over into my arms, scared me half out of my wits. I'm worried about her. I wish you would go and see her. She lives down on Cherry Street."

"H-m!" The doctor's eyes studied the boy's face again but with less complacency this time. Like Patrick Berry he thought a young Holiday would better stick to the campus, not run loose on Cherry Street.

"Know the girl well?" he queried.

Ted hesitated, flushed, looked unmistakably embarrassed.

"Yes, rather," he admitted. "I ran round with her quite a little the first of the summer. I got her the job at Berry's. Her grandfather, a pious old stick in the mud, turned her out of his house. She had to do something to earn her living. I hope she isn't going to be sick. It would be an awful mess. She can't have much saved up. Go and see her, will you, Doc? Forty-nine Cherry. Taylor is the name."

"H-m." The doctor made a note of these facts. "All right, I'll go. But you had better keep away from Cherry Street, young man. It is not the environment you belong in."

"Environment be--blessed!" said Ted. "Don't you begin on that sort of rot, please, Doc. Old Pat Berry's just been giving me a lecture on the same subject. You make me tired both of you. As if the girls on Cherry Street weren't as good any day as the ones on the campus, just because they work in shops and stores and the girls on the campus work--us," he concluded with a grin. "I'm not an infant that has to be kept in a Kiddie coop you know."

"Look out you don't land in a chicken coop," sniffed the doctor. "Very well, you young sinner. Don't listen to me if you don't want to. I know I might as well talk to the wind. You always were open to all the fool germs going, Ted Holiday. Some day you'll own the old Doc knew best."

"I wouldn't admit to being so hanged well up on the chicken-roost proposition myself if I were you," retorted Ted impudently. "So long. I'm much obliged for your kind favors all but the moral sentiments. You can have those back. You may need 'em to use over again."

So Ted went on his way, dropped in to see Elsie, had a cup of tea and innumerable small cakes, enjoyed a foxtrot to phonograph music with the rug rolled up out of the way, conversed amicably with the Ancient History Prof himself, who wasn't such a bad sort as Profs go and had the merit of being one of the few instructors who had not flunked Ted Holiday in his course the previous year.

The next morning Ted found a letter from Doctor Hendricks in his mail which he opened with some curiosity wondering what the old Doc could have to say. He read the communication through in silence and tucking it in his pocket walked out of the room as if he were in a dream, paying no attention to the question somebody called after him as he went. He went on to his classes but he hardly knew what was going on about him. His mind seemed to have stopped dead like a stop watch with the reading of the old doctor's letter.

He understood at last the full force of the trouble which engulfed Madeline Taylor and why she had said that it would have been better for her if that mad joy ride with him had ended life for her. The doctor had gone to her as he had promised and had extracted the whole miserable story. It seemed Madeline had married, or thought she had married, Willis Hubbard against her grandfather's express command, a few weeks after Ted had parted from her in Holyoke. In less than two months Hubbard had disappeared leaving behind him the ugly fact that he already had one wife living in Kansas City in spite of the pretense of a wedding ceremony which he had gone through with Madeline. Long since disillusioned but still having power and pride to suffer intensely the latter found herself in the tragic position of being-a wife and yet no wife. In her desperate plight she besought her grandfather's clemency and forgiveness but that rigid old covenanter had declared that even as she had made her bed in willful disobedience to his command so she should lie on it for all of him.

It was then that she had turned as a last resort to Ted Holiday though always hoping against hope that she could keep the real truth of her unhappy situation from him.

"It is a bad affair from beginning to end," wrote the doctor. "I'd like to break every rotten bone in that scoundrel's body but he has taken mighty good care to effect a complete disappearance. That kind is never willing to foot the bills for their own villainy. I am telling you the story in order to make it perfectly clear that you are to keep out of the business from now on. You have burned your fingers quite enough as it is I gather. Don't see the girl. Don't write her. Don't telephone her. Let her alone absolutely. Mind, these aren't polite requests. They are orders. And if you don't obey them I'll turn the whole thing over to your uncle double quick and I don't think you want me to do that. Don't worry about the girl. I'll look after her now and later when she is likely to need me more. But you keep hands off. That is flat--the girl's wish as well as my orders."

And this was what Ted Holiday had to carry about with him all that bleak day and a half sleepless, uneasy night. And in the morning he was summoned home to the House on the Hill. Granny was dying.

CHAPTER XXVIII
IN DARK PLACES

The House on the Hill was a strange place to Tony and Ted those November days, stranger than to the others who had walked day by day with the sense of the approaching shadow always with them. Death itself was an awesome and unaccustomed thing to them. They did not see how the others bore it so well, took it all so calmly. To make matters worse, Uncle Phil who never failed any one was stricken down with a bad case of influenza and was unable to leave his bed. This of course made Margery also practically *hors de combat*. The little folks spent most of their time across the street in motherly Mrs. Lambert's care. Upon Ned Holiday's children rested the chief burden of the hour.

Granny was rarely conscious and all three of her grandchildren coveted the sad privilege of being near her when these brief moments of lucidity came though Tony and Ted could not stand long periods of watching beside the still form as Larry could and did. It was Larry that she most often recognized. Sometimes though he was his father to her and she called him "Ned" in such tones of yearning tenderness that it nearly broke down his self control. Sometimes too he was Philip to her and this also was bitterly hard for Larry missed his uncle's support woefully in this dark hour. Ruth, Granny seemed to know, oftener indeed, than she did Tony to the latter's keen grief though she acknowledged the justice of the stab. For she had gone her selfish way leaving the stranger to play the loving granddaughter's part.

One night when the nurse was resting and Larry too had flung himself upon the couch in the living room to snatch a little much needed relaxation, leaving Ruth in charge of the sickroom, Ted drifted in and demanded to take his turn at the watch, giving Ruth a chance to sleep. She demurred at first, knowing how hard these vigils were for the restless, unhappy lad. But seeing he was really in earnest she yielded. As she passed out of the room her hand rested for a moment on the boy's bowed head. She had come to care a great deal for sunny, kind-hearted Teddy, loved him for himself and because she knew he loved Larry with deep devotion.

He looked up with a faint smile and gave her hand a squeeze.

"You are a darling, Ruthie," he murmured. "Don't know what we would ever do without you."

And then he was alone with death and his own somber thoughts. He could not get away from the memory of Madeline, could not help feeling with a terrible weight of responsibility that he was more than a little to blame for her plight. Whether he liked to think it or not he couldn't help knowing that the whole thing had started with that foolish joy ride with himself. Madeline had never risked her grandfather's displeasure till she risked it for him. She had never gone anywhere with Hubbard till she went because she was bitterly angry with himself because he had not kept his promise--a promise which never should have been made in the first place. And if he had not gone to Holyoke, hadn't behaved like an idiot that last night, hadn't deserted her like a selfish cad to save his own precious self--if none of these things had happened would Madeline still have gone to Hubbard? Perhaps. But in his heart Ted Holiday had a hateful conviction that she would not, that her wretchedness now was indirectly if not directly chargeable to his own folly. It was terrible that such little things should have such tremendous consequences but there it was.

All his life Ted Holiday had evaded responsibility and had found self extenu-ation the easiest thing in the world. But somehow all at once he seemed to have lost the power of letting himself off. He had no plea to offer even to himself except "guilty." Was he going to do as Doctor Hendricks commanded and let Madeline pay the price of her own folly alone or was he going to pay with her? The night was full of the question.

The quiet figure on the bed stirred. Instantly the boy had forgotten himself, remembered only Granny.

He bent over her.

"Granny, don't you know me? It's Teddy," he pleaded.

The white lips quivered into a faint smile. The frail hand on the cover lid groped vaguely for his.

"I know--Teddy," the lips formed slowly with an effort.

Ted kissed her, tears in his eyes.

"Be--a man, dear," the lips breathed softly. "Be--" and Granny was off again to a world of unconsciousness from which she had returned a moment to give her message to the grief stricken lad by her side.

To Ted in his overwrought condition the words were almost like a voice from heaven, a sacred command. To be a man meant to face the hardest thing he had ever had to face in his life. It meant marrying Madeline Taylor, not leaving her like a coward to pay by herself for something which he himself had helped to start. He rose softly and went to the window, staring out into the night. A few moments later he turned back wearing a strange uplifted sort of look, a look perhaps such, as Percival bore when he beheld the Grail.

Strange forces were at work in the House on the Hill that night. Ruth had gone to her room to rest as Ted bade her but she had not slept in spite of her intense weariness. She had almost lost the way of sleep latterly. She was always so afraid of not being near when Larry needed her. The night watches they had shared so often now had brought them very, very close to each other, made their love a very sacred as well as very strong thing.

Ruth knew that the time was near now when she would have to go away from the Hill. After Granny went there would be no excuse for staying on. If she did not go Larry would. Ruth knew that very well and did not intend the latter should happen.

She had laid her plans well. She would go and take a secretarial course some-where. She had made inquiries and found that there was always demand for secre-taries and that the training did not take so long as other professional education did. She could sell her rings and live on the money they brought her until she was self supporting. She did not want to dispose of her pearls if she could help it. She wanted to hold on to them as the link to her lost past. Yes, she would leave the Hill. It was quite the right thing to do.

But oh, what a hard thing it was! She did not see how she was ever going to face life alone under such hard, queer conditions without Doctor Philip, without dear Mrs. Margery and the children, without Larry, especially without Larry. For that matter what would Larry do without her? He needed her so, loved her so much. Poor Larry!

And suddenly Ruth sat up in bed. As clearly as if he had been in the room with her she heard Larry's voice calling to her. She sprang up and threw a dark blue satin negligee around her, went out of the room, down the stairs, seeming to know by an infallible instinct where her lover was.

On the threshold of the living room she paused. Larry was pacing the floor nervously, his face drawn and gray in the dim light of the flickering gas. Seeing her he made a swift stride in her direction, took both her hands in his.

"Ruth, why did you come?" There was an odd tension in his voice.

"You called me, didn't you? I thought you did." Her eyes were wondering. "I heard you say 'Ruth' as plain as anything."

He shook his head.

"No, I didn't call you out loud. Maybe I did with my heart though. I wanted you so."

He dropped her hands as abruptly as he had taken them.

"Ruth, I've got to marry you. I can't go on like this. I've tried to fight it, to be patient and hang on to myself as Uncle Phil wanted me to. But I can't go on. I'm done."

He flung himself into a chair. His head went down on the table. The clock ticked quietly on the mantel. What was Death upstairs to Time? What were Youth and Love and Grief down here? These things were merely eddies in the great tide of Eternity.

For a moment Ruth stood very still. Then she went over and laid a hand on the bowed head, the hand that wore the wedding ring.

"Larry, Larry dear," she said softly. "Don't give up like that. It breaks my heart." There was a faint tremor in her voice, a hint of tears not far off.

He lifted his head, the strain of his long self mastering wearing thin almost to the breaking point at last, for once all but at the mercy of the dominant emotion which possessed him, his love for the girl at his side who stood so close he could feel her breathing, got the faint violet fragrance of her. And yet he must not so much as touch her hand.

The clock struck three, solemn, inexorable strokes. Ruth and Larry and the clock seemed the only living things in the quiet house. Larry brushed his hand over his eyes, got to his feet.

"Ruth, will you marry me?"

"Yes, Larry."

The shock of her quiet consent brought Larry back a little to realities.

"Wait, Ruth. Don't agree too soon. Do you realize what it means to marry me? You may be married already. Your husband may return and find you living-- illegally--with me."

"I know," said Ruth steadily. "There must be something wrong with me, Larry. I can't seem to care. I can't seem to make myself feel as if I belonged to any one else except to you. I don't think I do belong to any one else. I was born over in the wreck. I was born yours. You saved me. I would have died if you hadn't gotten me out from under the beams and worked over and brought me back to life when ev-- erybody else gave me up as dead. I wouldn't have been alive for my husband if you hadn't saved me. I am yours, Larry. If you want me to marry you I will. If you want me--any way--I am yours. I love you."

"Ruth!"

Larry drew her into his arms and kissed her--the first time he had ever kissed any girl in his life except his sister. She lay in his arms, her fragrant pale gold hair brushing his cheek. He kissed her over and over passionately, almost roughly in the storm of his emotion suddenly unpent. Then he was Larry Holiday again. He pushed her gently from him, remorse in his gray eyes.

"Forgive me, Ruth. It's all wrong. I'm all wrong. We can't do it. I shouldn't have kissed you. I shouldn't have touched you--shouldn't have let you come to me like this. You must go now, dear. I am sorry."

Ruth faced him in silence a moment then bowed her head, turned and walked away to the door meekly like a chidden child. Her loosened hair fell like a golden shower over her shoulders. It was all Larry could do to keep from going after her, taking her in his arms again. But he stood grimly planted by the table, gripping its edge as if to keep himself anchored. He dared not stir one inch toward that childish figure in the dark robe.

On the threshold Ruth turned, flung back her hair and looked back at him. There was a kind of fearless exaltation and pride on her lovely young face and in her shining eyes.

"I don't know whether you are right or wrong, Larry, or rather when you are right and when you are wrong. It is all mixed up. It seems as if it must be right to care or we wouldn't be doing it so hard, as if God couldn't let us love like this if he didn't mean we should be happy together, belong to each other. Why should He make love if He didn't want lovers to be happy?"

It was an argument as old as the garden of Eden but to Ruth and Larry it was as if it were being pronounced for the first time for themselves, here in the dead of night, in the old House on the Hill, as they felt themselves drawn to each other by the all but irresistible impulse of their mutual love.

"Maybe," went on Ruth, "I forgot my morals along with the rest I forgot. I don't seem to care very much about right and wrong to-night. You called me. I heard you and I came. I am here." Her lovely, proud little head was thrown back, her eyes still shining with that fearless elation.

"Ruth! Don't, dear. You don't know what you are saying. I've got to care about right and wrong for both of us. Please go. I--I can't stand it."

He left his post by the table then came forward and held open the door for her. She passed out, went up the stairs, her hair falling in a wave of gold down to her waist. She did not turn back.

Larry waited at the foot of the stairs until he heard the door of her room close upon her and then he too went up, to Granny's room. Ted met him at the threshold in a panic of fear and grief.

"Larry--I think--oh--" and Ted bolted unable to finish what he had begun to say or to linger on that threshold of death.

The nurse was bending over Madame Holiday forcing some brandy between the blue lips. Larry was by the bedside in an instant. The nurse stepped back with a sad little shake of the head. There was nothing she could do and she knew it, knew also there was nothing the young doctor could do professionally. He knelt, chafed the cold hands. The pale lips quivered a little, the glazed eyes opened for a second.

"Ned--Larry--give Philip love--" That was all. The eyes closed. There was a little flutter of passing breath. Granny was gone.

It was two days after Granny's funeral. Ted had gone back to college. Tony would leave for New York on the morrow. Life cannot wait on death. It must go on its course as inevitably as a river must go its way to the sea.

Yet to Tony it seemed sad and heartless that it should be so. She was troubled by her selfishness, first to Granny living and now to Granny dead. She said as much to her uncle sorrowfully.

"It isn't really heartless or unkind," he comforted her. "We have to go on with our work. We can't lay it down or scamp it just because dear Granny's work is done. It is no more wrong for you to go back to your play than it is for me to go back to my doctoring."

"I know," sighed Tony. "But I can't help feeling remorseful. I had so much time and Granny had so little and yet I wasn't willing to give her even a little of mine. I would have if I had known though. I knew I was selfish but I didn't know how selfish. I wish you had told me, Uncle Phil. Why didn't you? You told Ruth. You let her help. Why wouldn't you let me?" she half reproached.

"I tried to do what was best for us all. I wanted to find a reason for keeping Ruth with us and I did not think then and I don't think now that it was right or necessary to keep you back for the little comfort it could have brought to Granny. You must not worry, dear child. The blame if there is any is mine. I know you would have stayed if I had let you."

Back in college Ted sorted out his personal letters from the sheaf of bills. Among them was one from Madeline Taylor, presumably the answer to the one Ted had written her from the House on the Hill. He stared at the envelope, dreading to open it. He was too horribly afraid of what it might contain. Suddenly he threw the letter down on the table and his head went down on top of it.

"I can't do it," he groaned. "I can't. I won't. It's too hard."

But in a moment his head popped up again fiercely.

"Confound you!" he muttered. "You can and you will. You've got to. You've made your bed. Now lie on it." And he opened the letter.

"I can't tell you," wrote the girl, "how your letter touched me. Don't think I don't understand that it isn't because you love me or really want to marry me that you are asking me to do it. It is all the finer and more wonderful because you don't and couldn't, ever. You had nothing to gain--everything to lose. Yet you offered it all as if it were the most ordinary gift in the world instead of the biggest.

"Of course, I can't let you sacrifice yourself like that for me. Did you really think I would? I wouldn't let you be dragged down into my life even if you loved me which you don't. Some day you will want to marry a girl--not somebody like me--but your own kind and you can go to her clean because you never hurt me, never did me anything but good ever. You lifted me up always. But there must have been something still stronger that pulled me down. I couldn't stay up. I was never your kind though I loved you just as much as if I were. Forgive my saying it just this once. It will be the last time. This is really good-by. Thank you over and over for everything,

"Madeline."

A mist blurred Ted Holiday's eyes as he finished the letter. He was free. The black winged vulture thing which had hovered over him for days was gone. By and by he would be thankful for his deliverance but just now there was room only in his chivalrous boy's heart for one overmastering emotion, pity for the girl and her needlessly wrecked life. What a hopeless mess the whole thing was! And what could he do to help her since she would not take what he had offered in all sincerity? He must think out a way somehow.

CHAPTER XXIX
THE PEDIGREE OF PEARLS

"Where is Larry?" asked Doctor Holiday a few days later coming into the dining room at supper time. "I haven't seen him all the afternoon."

Margery dropped into her chair with a tired little sigh.

"There is a note from him at your place. I think he has gone out of town. John told me he took him to the three ten train."

"H--m!" mused the doctor. "Where is Ruth?" he looked up to ask.

"Ruth went to Boston at noon. At least so Bertha tells me." Bertha was the maid. "She did not say good-by to me. I thought possibly she had to you!"

Her husband shook his head, perplexed and troubled.

"Dear Uncle Phil," ran Larry's message.

"Ruth has gone to Boston. She left a letter for me saying good-by and asking me to say good-by to the rest of you for her. Said she would write as soon as she had an address and that no one was to worry about her. She would be quite all right and thought it was best not to bother us by telling us about her plans until she was settled."

"Of course I am going after her. I don't know where she is but I'll find her. I've got to, especially as I was the one who drove her away. I broke my promise to you. I did make love to her and asked her to marry me the night Granny died. She said she would and then of course I said she couldn't and we've not seen each other alone since so I don't know what she thinks now. I don't know anything except that I'm half crazy."

"I know it is horribly selfish to go off and leave you like this when you need me especially. Please forgive me. I'll be back as soon as I can or send Ruth or we'll both come. And don't worry. I'm not going to do anything rash or wrong or anything that will hurt you or Ruth. I am sorry about the other night. I didn't mean to smash up like that."

The doctor handed the letter over to his wife.

"Why didn't he wait until he had her address? How can he possibly find her in a city like Boston with not the slightest thing to go on?"

Doctor Holiday smiled wearily.

"Wait! Do you see Larry waiting when Ruth is out of his sight? My dear, don't you know Larry is the maddest of the three when he gets under way?"

"The maddest and the finest. Don't worry, Phil. He is all right. He won't do anything rash just as he tells you."

"You can't trust a man in love, especially a young idiot who waited a full quarter century to get the disease for the first time. But you are right. I'd trust him anywhere, more rather than less because of that confession of his. I've wondered that he didn't break his promise long before this. He is only human and his restraint has been pretty nearly super-human. I don't believe he would have smashed up now as he calls it if his nerves hadn't been strained about to the limit by taking all the responsibility for Granny at the end. It was terrible for the poor lad."

"It was terrible for you too, Phil. Larry isn't the only one who has suffered. I do wish those foolish youngsters could have waited a little and not thrown a new anxiety on you just now. But I suppose we can't blame them under the circumstances. Isn't it strange, dear? Except for the children sleeping up in the nursery you and I are absolutely alone for the first time since I came to the House on the Hill."

He nodded a little sadly. His father was gone long since and now Granny too. And Ned's children were all grown up, would perhaps none of them ever come again in the old way. Their wings were strong enough now to make strange flights.

"We've filled your life rather full, Margery mine," he said. "I hope there are easier days ahead."

"I don't want any happier ones," said Margery as she slipped her hand into his.

The next few days were a perfect nightmare to Larry. Naturally he found no trace of Ruth, did not know indeed under what name she had chosen to go. The city had swallowed her up and the saddest part of it was she had wanted to be swallowed, to get away from himself. She had gone for his sake he knew, because he had told her he could endure things no longer. She had taken him at his word and vanished utterly. For all her gentleness and docility Ruth had tremendous fortitude. She had taken this hard, rash step alone in the dark for love's sake, just as she was ready that unforgettable night to take that rasher step with him to marriage or something less than marriage had he permitted it. She would have preferred to marry him, not to bother with abstractions of right and wrong, to take happiness as it offered but since he would not have it so she had lost herself.

Despair, remorse, anxiety, loneliness held him-in thrall while he roamed the streets of the old city, almost hopeless now of finding her but still doggedly persistent in his search. Another man under such a strain of mind and body would have gone on a stupendous thought drowning carouse. Larry Holiday had no such refuge in his misery. He took it straight without recourse to anaesthetic of any sort. And on the fourth day when he had been about to give up in defeat and go home to the Hill to wait for word of Ruth a crack of light dawned.

Chancing to be strolling absent mindedly across the Gardens he ran into a college classmate of his, one Gary Eldridge, who shook his hand with crushing grip and announced that it was a funny thing Larry's bobbing up like that because he had been hearing the latter's name pretty consecutively all the previous afternoon on the lips of the daintiest little blonde beauty it had been his luck to behold in many a moon, a regular Greuze girl in fact, eyes and all.

Naturally there was no escape for Eldridge after that. Larry Holiday grabbed him firmly and demanded to know if he had seen Ruth Annersley and if he had and knew where she was to tell him everything quick. It was important.

Considering Larry Holiday's haggard face and tense voice Eldridge admitted the importance and spun his yarn. No, he did not know where Ruth Annersley was nor if the Greuze girl was Ruth Annersley at all. He did know the person he meant was in the possession of the famous Farringdon pearls, a fact immensely interesting to Fitch and Larrabee, the jewelers in whose employ he was.

"Your Ruth Annersley or Farringdon or whoever she is brought the pearls in to our place yesterday to have them appraised. You can bet we sat up and took notice. We didn't know they had left Australia but here they were right under our noses absolutely unmistakable, one of the finest sets of matched pearls in the world. You Holidays are so hanged smart. I wonder it didn't occur to you to bring 'em to us anyway. We're the boys that can tell you who's who in the lapidary world. Pearls have pedigrees, my dear fellow, quite as faithfully recorded as those of prize pigs."

Larry thumped his cranium disgustedly. It did seem ridiculous now that the very simple expedient of going to the master jewelers for information had not struck any of them. But it hadn't and that was the end of it. He made Eldridge sit down in the Gardens then and there however to tell him all he knew about the pearls but first and most important did the other have any idea where the owner of the pearls was? He had none. The girl was coming in again in a few days to hear the result of a cable they had sent to Australia where the pearls had been the last Larrabee and Fitch knew. She had left no address. Eldridge rather thought she hadn't cared to be found. Larry bit his lip at that and groaned inwardly. He too was afraid it was only too true, and it was all his fault.

This was the story of the pearls as his friend briefly outlined it for Larry Holiday's benefit. The Farringdon pearls had originally belonged to a Lady Jane Farringdon of Farringdon Court, England. They had been the gift of a rejected lover who had gone to Africa to drown his disappointment and had died there after having sent the pearls home to the woman he had loved fruitlessly and who was by this time the wife of another man, her distant cousin Sir James Farringdon. At her death Lady Jane had given the pearls to her oldest son for his bride when he should have one. He too had died however before he had attained to the bride. The pearls went to his younger brother Roderick a sheep raiser in Australia who had amassed a fortune and discarded the title. The sheep raiser married an Australian girl and gave her the pearls. They had two children, a girl and a boy. Roderick was since deceased. Possibly his wife also was dead. They had cabled to find out details. But it looked as if the little blonde lady who possessed the pearls although she did not know where she got them was in all probability the daughter of Roderick Farringdon, the granddaughter of the famous beauty, Lady Jane. She was probably also a great heiress. The sheep raiser and his father-in-law had both been reported to be wallowing in money. "Oh boy!" Eldridge had ended significantly.

"But if Ruth is a person of so much importance why did they let her travel so far alone with those valuable pearls in her possession? Why haven't they looked her up? I suppose she told you about the wreck and--the rest of it?"

"She did, sang the praises of the family of Holiday in a thousand keys. Your advertisements were all on the Annersley track you see and they would all be out on the Farringdon one. The paths didn't happen to cross I suppose."

"You don't know anything about, Geoffrey Annersley do you?" Larry asked anxiously.

"Not a thing. We are jewelers not detectives or clairvoyants. It is only the pearls we are up on and we've evidently slipped a cog on them. We should have known when they came to the States but we didn't."

"I'll cable the American consul at Australia myself. It's the first real clue we have had--the rest has been working in the dark. The first thing though is to find Ruth." And Larry Holiday looked so very determined and capable of doing anything he set out to do that Gary Eldridge grinned a little.

"Wonderful what falling in love will do for a chap," he reflected. "Used to think old Larry was rather a slow poke but he seems to have developed into some whirlwind. Don't wonder considering what a little peach the girl is. Hope the good Lord has seen fit to recall Geoffrey Annersley to his heaven if he really did marry her."

Aloud he promised to telephone Larry the moment the owner of the pearls crossed the threshold of Larrabee and Fitch and to hold her by main force if necessary until Larry could get there. In the meantime he suggested that she had seemed awfully interested in the Australia part of the story and it was very possible she had gone to the--

"Library." Larry took the words out of his mouth and bolted without any formality of farewell into the nearest subway entrance.

His friend gazed after him.

"And this is Larry Holiday who used to flee if a skirt fluttered in his direction," he murmured. "Ah well, it takes us differently. But it gets us all sooner or later."

Larry's luck had turned at last. In the reading room of the Public Library he discovered a familiar blonde head bent over a book. He strode to the secluded corner where she sat "reading up" on Australia.

"Ruth!" Larry tried to speak quietly though he felt like raising the echoes of the sacred scholarly precincts.

The reader looked up startled, wondering. Her face lit with quick delight.

"Larry, oh Larry, I'm finding myself," she whispered breathlessly.

"I'm glad but I'm gladder that I'm finding--yourself. Come on outside sweetheart. I want to shout. I can't whisper and I won't. I'll get us both put out if you won't come peaceably."

"I'll come," said Ruth meekly.

Outside in the corridor she raised blue eyes to gray ones.

"I didn't mean you to find me--yet," she sighed.

"So I should judge. I didn't think a mite of a fairy girl like you could be so cruel. Some day I'll exact full penance for all you've made me suffer but just now we'll waive that and go over to the Plaza and have a high tea and talk. But first I'm going to kiss you. I don't care if people are looking. All Boston can look if it likes. I'm going to do it."

But it was only a scrub woman and not all Boston who witnessed that kiss, and she paid no attention to the performance. Even had she seen it is hardly probable that she would have been vastly startled at the sight. She was a very old woman and more than likely she had seen such sights before. Perhaps she had even been kissed by a man herself, once upon a time. We hope so.

The next day Larry and Ruth came home to the Hill, radiantly happy and full of their strange adventures. Ruth was wearing an immensely becoming new dark blue velvet suit, squirrel furs and a new hat which to Margery's shrewd feminine eyes betrayed a cost all out of proportion to its minuteness. She was looking exquisitely lovely in her new finery. Scant wonder Larry could not keep his eyes off of her. Margery and Philip were something in the same state.

"On the strength of my being an heiress maybe Larry thought I might afford some new clothes," Ruth confessed. "Of course he paid for them--temporarily," she had added with a charming blush and a side long, deprecating glance at Doctor Holiday, senior. She did not want him to disapprove of her for letting Larry buy her pretty clothes nor blame Larry for doing it.

But he only laughed and remarked that he would have gone shopping with her himself if he had any idea the results would be so satisfactory.

It was only when he was alone with Margery that he shook his head.

"Those crazy children behave as if everything were quite all right and as if they could run right out any minute and get married. She doesn't even wear her ring any more and they both appear to think the fact it presumably represents can be disposed of as summarily."

"Let them alone," advised his wife. "They are all right. It won't do them a bit of harm to let themselves go a bit. Larry does his worshiping with his eyes and maybe with his tongue when they are alone. I don't blame him. She is a perfect darling. And it is much better for him not to pretend he doesn't care when we all know he does tremendously. It was crushing it all back that made him so miserable and smash up as he wrote you. I don't believe he smashed very irretrievably anyway. He is too much of a Holiday."

The doctor smiled a little grimly.

"You honor us, my dear. Even Holidays are men!"

"Thank heaven," said Margery.

CHAPTER XXX
THE FIERY FURNACE

A few days after the return of Larry and Ruth to the Hill Doctor Holiday found among his mail an official looking document bearing the seal of the college which Ted attended and which was also his own and Larry's alma mater. He opened it carelessly supposing it to be an alumni appeal of some sort but as his-eyes ran down the typed sheet his face grew grave and his lips set in a tight line. The communication was from the president and informed its recipient that his nephew Edward Holiday was expelled from the college on the confessed charge of gambling.

"We are particularly sorry to be obliged to take this action," wrote the president, "inasmuch as Edward has shown recently a marked improvement both in class-room work and general conduct which has gone far to eradicate the unfortunate impression made by the lawlessness of his earlier career. But we cannot overlook so flagrant an offense and are regretfully forced to make an example of the offender. As you know gambling is strictly against the rules of the institution and your nephew played deliberately for high stakes as he admits and made a considerable sum of money--three hundred dollars to be precise--which he disposed of immediately for what purpose he refuses to tell. Again regretting," et cetera, et cetera, the letter closed.

But there was also a hand written postscript and an enclosure.

The postscript ran as follows:

"As a personal friend and not as the president of the college I am sending on the enclosed which may or may not be of importance. A young girl, Madeline Taylor by name, of Florence, Massachusetts, who has until recently been employed in Berry's flower shop, was found dead this morning with the gas jet fully turned on, the inference being clearly suicide. A short time ago a servant from the lodging house where the dead girl resided came to me with a letter addressed to your nephew. It seems Miss Taylor had given the girl the letter to mail the previous evening and had indeed made a considerable point of its being mailed. Nevertheless the girl had forgotten to do so and the next day was too frightened to do it fearing the thing might have some connection with the suicide. She meant to give it to Ted in person but finding him out decided at the last moment to deliver it to me instead. I am sending the letter to you, as I received it, unopened, and have not and shall not mention the incident to any one else. I should prefer and am sure that you will also wish that your nephew's name shall not be associated in any way with the dead girl's. Frankly I don't believe the thing contains any dynamite whatever but I would rather you handled the thing instead of myself.

"Believe me, my dear Holiday, I am heartily sick, and sorry over the whole matter of Ted's expulsion. If we had not had his own word for it I should not have believed him guilty. Even now I have a feeling that there was more behind the thing than we got, something perhaps more to his credit than he was willing to tell."

Philip Holiday picked up the enclosed letter addressed to Ted and looked at it as dubiously as if indeed it might have contained dynamite. The scrawling handwriting was painfully familiar. And the mention of Florence as the dead girl's home was disagreeably corroborating evidence. What indeed was behind it all?

Steeling his will he tore open the sealed envelope. Save for a folded slip of paper it was quite empty. The folded slip was a check for three hundred dollars made payable to Madeline Taylor and signed with Ted Holiday's name.

Here was dynamite and to spare for Doctor Holiday. Beside the uneasy questions this development conjured the catastrophe of the boy's expulsion took second place. And yet he forced himself not to judge until he had heard Ted's own story. What was love for if it could not find faith in time of need?

He said nothing to any one, even his wife, of the president's letter and that disconcerting check which evidently represented the results of the boy's law breaking. All day he looked for a letter from Ted himself and hoped against hope that he would appear in person. His anxiety grew as he heard nothing. What had become of the boy? Where had he betaken himself with his shame and trouble? How grave was his trouble? It was a bad day for Philip Holiday and a worse night.

But the morning brought a letter from his nephew, mailed ominously enough from a railway post office in northern Vermont. The doctor tore it open with hands that trembled a little. One thing at least he was certain of. However bad the story the lad had to tell it would be the truth. He could count on that.

"Dear Uncle Phil--" it ran. "By the time you get this I shall be over the border and enlisted, I hope, with the Canadians. I am horribly sorry to knife you like this and go off without saying good-by and leaving such a mess behind but truly it is the best thing I could do for the rest of you as well as myself.

"They will write you from college and tell you I am fired--for gambling. But they won't tell you the whole story because they don't know it. I couldn't tell them. It concerned somebody else besides myself. But you have a right to know everything and I am going to tell it to you and there won't be anything shaved off or tacked on to save my face either. It will be straight stuff on my honor as a Holiday which means as much to me as it does to you and Larry whether you believe it or not."

Then followed a straightforward account of events from the first ill-judged pick-up on the train and the all but fatal joy ride to the equally ill-judged kisses in Cousin Emma's garden.

"I hate like the mischief to put such things down on paper," wrote the boy, "but I said I'd tell the whole thing and I will, even if it does come out hard, so you will know it isn't any worse than it is. It is bad enough I'll admit, I hadn't any business to make fool love to her when I really didn't care a picayune. And I hadn't any business to be there in Holyoke at all when you thought I was at Hal's. I did go to Hal's but I only stayed two days. The rest of the time I was with Madeline and knew I was going to be when I left the Hill. That part can't look any worse to you than it does to me. It was a low-down trick to play on you when you had been so white about the car and everything. But I did it and I can't undo it. I can only say I am sorry. I did try afterward to make up a little bit by keeping my word about the studying. Maybe you'll let that count a little on the other side of the ledger. Lord knows I need anything I can get there. It is little enough, more shame to me!"

Then followed the events of the immediately preceding months from Madeline Taylor's arrival in the college town on to the stunning revelation of old Doctor Hendricks' letter.

"You don't know how the thing made me feel. I couldn't help feeling more or less responsible. For after all I did start the thing and though Madeline was always too good a sport to blame me I knew and I am sure she knew that she wouldn't have taken up with Hubbard if I hadn't left her in the lurch just when she had gotten to care a whole lot too much for me. Besides I couldn't help thinking what it would have been like if Tony had been caught in a trap like that. It didn't seem to me I could stand off and let her go to smash alone though I could see Doc Hendricks had common sense on his side when he ordered me to keep out of the whole business.

"I had all this on my mind when I came home that last time when Granny was dying. I had it lodged in my head that it was up to me to straighten things out by marrying Madeline myself though I hated the idea like death and destruction and I knew it would about kill the rest of you. I wrote and asked her to marry me that night after Granny went. She wouldn't do it. It wasn't because she didn't love me either. I guess it was rather because she did that she wouldn't. She wouldn't pull me down in the quick sands with her. Whatever you may think of what she was and did you will have to admit that she was magnificent about this. She might have saved herself at my expense and she wouldn't. Remember that, Uncle Phil, and don't judge her about the rest."

Doctor Holiday ceased reading a moment and gazed into the fire. By the measure of his full realization of what such a marriage would have meant to his young nephew he paid homage to the girl in her fine courage in refusing to take advantage of a chivalrous boy's impulsive generosity even though it left her the terrible alternative which later she had taken. And he thought with a tender little smile that there was something also rather magnificent about a lad who would offer himself thus voluntarily and knowingly a living sacrifice for "dear Honor's sake." He went back to the letter.

"But I still felt I had to do something to help though she wouldn't accept the way I first offered. I knew she needed money badly as she wasn't able to work and I wanted to give her some of mine. I knew I had plenty or would have next spring when I came of age. But I was sure you wouldn't let me have any of it now without knowing why and Larry wouldn't lend me any either, sight unseen. I wouldn't have blamed either of you for refusing. I haven't deserved to be taken on trust.

"The only other way I knew of to get money quick was to play for it. I have fool's luck always at cards. Last year I played a lot for money. Larry knew and rowed me like the devil for it last spring. No wonder. He knew how Dad hated it. So did I. I'd heard him rave on the subject often enough. But I did it just the same as I did a good many other things I am not very proud to remember now. But I haven't done it this year--at least only a few times. Once I played when I'd sent Madeline all the money I had for her traveling expenses and once or twice beside I did it on my own account because I was so darned sick of toeing a chalk mark I had to go on a tangent or bust. I am not excusing it. I am not excusing anything. I am just telling the truth.

"Anyhow the other night I played again in good earnest. There were quite a number of fellows in the game and we all got a bit excited and plunged more than we meant to especially myself and Ned Delany who was out to get me if he could. He hates me like the seven year itch anyway because I caught him cheating at cards once and said so right out in meeting. I had absolutely incredible luck. I guess the devil or the angels were on my side. I swept everything, made about three hundred dollars in all. The fellows paid up and I banked the stuff and mailed Madeline a check for the whole amount the first thing. I don't know what would have happened if I had lost instead of winning. I didn't think about that. A true gambler never does I reckon.

"But I want to say right here and now, Uncle Phil, that I am through with the business. The other night sickened me of gambling for good and all. Even Dad couldn't have hated it any more than I do this minute. It is rotten for a man, kills his nerves and his morals and his common sense. I'm done. I'll never make another penny that way as long as I live. But I'm not sorry I did it this once no matter how hard I'm paying for it. If I had it to do over again I'd do precisely the same thing. I wonder if you can understand that, Uncle Phil, or whether you'll think I'm just plain unregenerate.

"I thought then I was finished with the business but as a matter of fact I was just starting on it. Somebody turned state's evidence. I imagine it was Delany though I don't know. Anyhow somebody wrote the president an anonymous letter telling him there was a lot of gambling going on and I was one of the worst offenders, and thoughtfully suggested the old boy should ask me how much I made the other night and what I did with it. Of course that finished me off. I was called before the board and put through a holy inquisition. Gee! They piled up not only the gambling business but all the other things I'd done and left undone for two years and a half and dumped the whole avalanche on my head at once. Whew! It was fierce. I am not saying I didn't deserve it. I did, if not for this particular thing for a million other times when I've gone scot-free.

"They tried to squeeze out of me who the other men involved were but I wouldn't tell. I could have had a neat little come back on Delany if I had chosen but I don't play the game that way and I reckon he knew it and banked on my holding my tongue. I'd rather stand alone and take what was coming to me and I got it too good and plenty. They tried to make me tell what I did with the money. That riled me. It was none of their business and I told 'em so. Anyway I couldn't have told even if it would have done me any good on Madeline's account. I wouldn't drag her into it.

"Finally they dismissed me and said they would let me know later what they would do about my case. But there wasn't any doubt in my mind what they were going to do nor in theirs either, I'll bet. I was damned. They had to fire me--couldn't help it when I was caught with the goods under their very noses. I think a good many of them wished I hadn't been caught, that they could have let me off some way, particularly Prof. Hathaway. He put out his hand and patted my shoulder when I went out and I knew he was mighty sorry. He has been awfully decent to me always especially since I have been playing round with his daughter Elsie this fall and I guess it made him feel bad to have me turn out such a black sheep. I wished I could tell him the whole story but I couldn't. I just had to let him think it was as bad as it looked.

"I had hardly gotten back into the Frat house when I was called to the telephone. It was Madeline. She thanked me for sending her the money but said she was sending the check back as she didn't need it, had found a way out of her difficulties. She was going on a long, long journey in fact, and wouldn't see me again. Said she wanted to say good-by and wish me all kinds of luck and thank me for what she was pleased to call my goodness to her. And then she hung up before I could ask any questions or get it through my head what she meant by her long, long journey. My brain wasn't working very lively after what I'd been through over there at the board meeting anyway and I was too wrapped up in my own troubles to bother much about hers at the moment, selfish brute that I am.

"But the next morning I understood all right. She had found her way out and no mistake, just turned on the gas and let herself go. She was dead when they found her. I don't blame her, Uncle Phil. It was too hard for her. She couldn't go through with it. Life had been too hard for her from the beginning. She never had half a chance. And in the end we killed her between us, her pious old psalm singing hypocrite of a grandfather, the rotter who ruined her, and myself, the prince of fools.

"I went to see her with the old Doc. And, Uncle Phil, she was beautiful. Not even Granny looked more peaceful and happy than she did lying there dead with the little smile on her lips as if she were having a pleasant dream. But the scar was there on her forehead--the scar I put there. I've got a scar of my own too. It doesn't show on the surface but it is there for all that and always will be. I shan't talk about it but I'll never forget as long as I live that part of the debt she paid was mine. It is *mea culpa* for me always so far as she is concerned.

"Her grandfather arrived while I was there. If ever there was a man broken, mind and body and spirit he was. I couldn't help feeling sorry for him. Of the two I would much rather have been Madeline lying there dead than that poor old chap living with her death on his conscience.

"Later I got my official notice from the board. I was fired. I wanted to get out of college. I'm out for better or worse. Uncle Phil, don't think I don't care. I know how terribly you are going to be hurt and that it will be just about the finish of poor old Larry. I am not very proud of it myself--being catapulted out in disgrace where the rest of you left trailing clouds of glory. It isn't only what I have done just now. It is all the things I have done and haven't done before that has smashed me in the end--my fool attitude of have a good time and damn the expense. I didn't pay at the time. I am paying now compound interest accumulated. Worst of it is the rest of you will have to pay with me. You told me once we couldn't live to ourselves alone. I didn't understand then. I do now. I am guilty but you have to suffer with me for my mistakes. It is that that hurts worst of all.

"You have been wonderful to me always, had oceans of patience when I disappointed you and hurt you and worried you over and over again. And now here is this last, worst thing of all to forgive. Can you do it, Uncle Phil? Please try. And please don't worry about me, nor let the others. I'll come through all right. And if I don't I am not afraid of death. I have found out there are lots of worse things in the world. I haven't any pipe dreams about coming out a hero of any sort but I do mean to come out the kind of a man you won't be ashamed of and to try my darnedest to live up a little bit to the Holiday specifications. Again, dear Uncle Phil, please forgive me if you can and write as soon as I can send an address." Then a brief postscript. "The check Madeline sent back never got to me. If it is forwarded to the Hill please send it or rather its equivalent to the president. I wouldn't touch the money with a ten foot pole. I never wanted it for myself but only for Madeline and she is beyond needing anything any of us can give her now."

CHAPTER XXXI
THE MOVING FINGER CONTINUES TO WRITE

Having read and reread the boy's letter Doctor Holiday sat long with it in his hand staring into the fire. Poor Teddy for whom life had hitherto been one grand and glorious festival! He was getting the other, the seamy side of things, at last with a vengeance. Knowing with the sure intuition of love how deeply the boy was suffering and how sincerely he repented his blunders the doctor felt far more compassion than condemnation for his nephew. The fineness and the folly of the thing were so inextricably confused that there was little use trying to separate the two even if he had cared to judge the lad which he did not, being content with the boy's own judgment of himself. Bad as the gambling business was and deeply as he regretted the expulsion from college the doctor could not help seeing that there was some extenuation for Ted's conduct, that he had in the main kept faith with himself, paid generously, far more than he owed, and traveling through the fiery furnace had somehow managed to come out unscathed, his soul intact. After all could one ask much more?

It was considerably harder for Larry to accept the situation philosophically than it was for the senior doctor's more tolerant and mature mind. Larry loved Ted as he loved no one else in the world not perhaps even excepting Ruth. But he loved the Holiday name too with a fine, high pride and it was a bitter dose to swallow to have his younger brother "catapulted in disgrace," as Ted himself put it, out of the college which he himself so loved and honored. He was inclined to resent what looked in retrospect as entirely unnecessary and uncalled for generosity on Ted's part.

"Nobody but Ted would ever have thought of doing such a fool thing," he groaned. "Why didn't he pull out in the first place as Hendricks wanted him to? He would have been entirely justified."

But the older man smiled and shook his head.

"Some people could have done it, not Ted," he said. "Ted isn't built that way. He never deserted anybody in trouble in his life. I don't believe he ever will. We can't expect him to have behaved differently in this one affair just because we would have liked it better so. I am not sure but we would be wrong and he right in any case."

"Maybe. But it is a horrible mess. I can't get over the injustice of the poor kid's paying so hard when he was just trying to do the decent, hard, right thing."

"You have it less straight than Ted has, Larry. He knows he is paying not for what he did and thought right but for what he did and knew was wrong. You can't feel worse than I do about it. I would give anything I have to save Ted from the torture he is going through, has been going through alone for days. But I would rather he learned his lesson thoroughly now, suffering more than he deserves than have him suffer too little and fall worse next time. No matter how badly we feel for him I think it is up to us not to try to dilute his penitence and to leave a generous share of the blame where he puts it himself--on his own shoulders."

"I suppose you are right, Uncle Phil," sighed Larry. "You usually are. But it's like having a piece taken right out of me to have him go off like that. And the Canadians are the very devil of fighters. Always in the thick of things."

"That is where Ted would want to be, Larry. Let us not cross that bridge until we have to. As he says himself there are worse things than death anyway."

"I know. Marrying the girl would have been worse. She was rather magnificent, wasn't she, just as he says, not saving herself when she might have at his expense?"

"I think she was. I am almost glad the poor child is where she can suffer no more at the hands of men."

The next day came a wire from Ted announcing his acceptance in the Canadian army and giving his address in the training camp.

The doctor answered at once, writing a long, cheerful letter full of home news especially the interesting developments in Ruth's romantic story. It was only at the end that he referred to the big thing that had to be faced between them.

"I am not going to say a word that will add in any way to the burden you are already carrying, Teddy, my lad. You know how sadly disappointed we all are in your having to leave college this way but I understand and sympathize fully with your reasons for doing what you did. Even though I can't approve of the thing itself. I haven't a single reproach to offer. You have had a harsh lesson. Learn it so well that you will never bring yourself or the rest of us to such pain and shame again. Keep your scar. I should be sorry to think you were so callous that you could pass through an experience like that without carrying off an indelible mark from it. But it isn't going to ruin your life. On the contrary it is going to make a man of you, is doing that already if I may judge from the spirit of your letter which goes far to atone for the rest. The forgiveness is yours always, son, seventy times seven if need be. Never doubt it. We shall miss you very much. I wonder if you know how dear to us you are, Teddy lad. But we aren't going to borrow trouble of the future. We shall say instead God speed. May he watch over you wherever you are and bring you safe back to us in His good time!"

And Ted reading the letter later in the Canadian training camp was not ashamed of the tears that came stinging up in his eyes. He was woefully homesick, wanted the home people, especially Uncle Phil desperately. But the message from the Hill brought strength and comfort as well as heart ache.

"Dear Uncle Phil," he thought. "I will make it up to him somehow. I will. He shan't ever have to be ashamed of me again."

And so Ted Holiday girded on manhood along with his khaki and his Sam Browne belt and started bravely up out of the pit which his own willful folly had dug for him.

Tony was not told the full story of her brother's fiasco. She only knew that he had left college for some reason or other and had taken French leave for the Canadian training camp. She was relieved to discover that even in Larry's stern eyes the escapade, whatever it was, had not apparently been a very damaging one and accepted thankfully her uncle's assurance that there was nothing at all to worry about and that Ted was no doubt very much better off where he was than if he had stayed in college.

As for the going to war part small blame had she for Ted in that. She knew well it was precisely what she would have done herself in his case and teemed with pride in her bonny, reckless, beloved soldier brother.

She had small time to think much about anybody's affairs beside her own just now. Any day now might come the word that little Cecilia had gone and that Tony

Holiday would take her place on the Broadway stage as a real star if only for a brief space of twinkling.

She saw very little even of Alan. He was tremendously busy and seemed, oddly enough, to be drawing a little away from her, to be less jealously exacting of her time and attention. It was not that he cared less, rather more, Tony thought. His strange, tragic eyes rested hungrily upon her whenever they were together and it seemed as if he would drink deep of her youth and loveliness and joy, a draught deep enough to last a long, long time, through days of parching thirst to follow. He was very gentle, very quiet, very loveable, very tender. His stormy mood seemed to have passed over leaving a great weariness in its wake.

A very passion of creation was upon him. Seeing the canvases that flowered into beauty beneath his hand Tony felt very small and humble, knew that by comparison with her lover's genius her own facile gifts were but as a firefly's glow to the light of a flaming torch. He was of the masters. She saw that and was proud and glad and awed by the fact. But she saw also that the artist was consuming himself by the very fire of his own genius and the knowledge troubled her though she saw no way to check or prevent the holocaust if such it was.

Sometimes she was afraid. She knew that she would never be happy in the every day way with Alan. Happiness did not grow in his sunless garden. Married to him she would enter dark forests which were not her natural environment. But it did not matter. She loved him. She came always back to that. She was his, would always be his no matter what happened. She was bound by the past, caught in its meshes forever.

And then suddenly a new turn of the wheel took place. Word came just before Christmas that Dick Carson was very ill, dying perhaps down in Mexico, stricken with a malarial fever.

A few moments after Tony received this stunning news Alan Massey's card was brought to her. She went down to the reception room, gave him a limp cold little hand in greeting and asked if he minded going out with her. She had to talk with him. She couldn't talk here.

Alan did not mind. A little later they were walking riverward toward a brilliant orange sky, against which the Soldiers' and Sailors' Monument loomed gray and majestic. It was bitter cold. A stinging wind lashed the girl's skirts around her and bit into her cheeks. But somehow she welcomed the physical discomfort. It matched her mood.

Then the story came out. Dick was sick, very sick, going to die maybe and she, Tony Holiday couldn't stand it.

Alan listened in tense silence. So Dick Carson might be going to be so unexpectedly obliging as to die after all. If he had known how to pray he would have done it, beseeched whatever gods there were to let the thing come to an end at last, offered any bribe within his power if they would set him free from his bondage by disposing of his cousin.

But there beside him clinging to his arm was Tony Holiday aquiver with grief for this same cousin. He saw that there were tears on her cheeks, tears that the icy wind turned instantly to frosted silver. And suddenly a new power was invoked-- the power of love.

"Tony, darling, don't cry," he beseeched. "I--can't stand it. He--he won't die."

And then and there a miracle took place. Alan Massey who had never prayed in his life was praying to some God, somewhere to save John Massey for Tony because she loved him and his dying would hurt her. Tony must not be hurt. Any God could see that. It must not be permitted.

Tony put up her hand and brushed away the frosted silver drops.

"No, he isn't going to die. I'm not going to let him. I'm going to Mexico to save him."

Alan stopped short, pulling her to a halt beside him.

"Tony, you can't," he gasped, too astonished for a moment even to be angry.

"I can and I am going to," she defied him.

"But my dear, I tell you, you can't. It would be madness. Your uncle wouldn't let you. I won't let you."

"You can't stop me. Nobody can stop me. I'm going. Dick shan't die alone. He shan't."

"Tony, do you love him?"

"I don't know. I don't want to talk about love--your kind. I do love him one way with all my heart. I wish it were the way I love you. I'd go down and marry him if I did. Maybe I'll marry him anyway. I would in a minute if it would save him."

"Tony!" Alan's face was dead white, his green eyes savage. "You promised to stick to me through everything. Where is your Holiday honor that you can talk like that about marrying another man?" Maddened, he branished his words like whips, caring little whether they hurt or not.

"I can't help it, Alan. I am sorry if I am hurting you. But I can't think about anybody but Dick just now."

"Forgive me, sweetheart. I know you didn't mean it, what you said about marrying him and you didn't mean it about going to Mexico. You know you can't. It is no place for a woman like you."

"If Dick is there dying, it *is* the place for me. I love you, Alan. But there are some things that go even deeper, things that have their very roots in me, the things that belong to the Hill. And Dick is a very big part of them, sometimes I think he is the biggest part of all. I have to go to him. Please don't try to stop me. It will only make us both unhappy if you try."

A bitter blast struck their faces with the force of a blow. Tony shivered.

"Let's go back. I'm cold--so dreadfully cold," she moaned clinging to his arm.

They turned in silence. There was nothing to say. The sunset glory had faded now. Only a pale, cold mauve tint was left where the flame had blazed. A star or two had come out. The river flowed sinister black, showing white humps of foam here and there.

At the Hostelry Jean Lambert met them in the hall.

"Tony, where have you been? We have been trying everywhere to locate you. Cecilia died this afternoon. You have to take Miss Clay's place tonight."

Tony's face went white. She leaned against the wall trembling.

"I forgot--I forgot about the play. I can't go to Mexico. Oh, what shall I do? What shall I do?"

CHAPTER XXXII
DWELLERS IN DREAMS

The last curtain had gone down on the "End of the Rainbow" and Tony Holiday had made an undeniable hit, caught the popular fancy by her young charm and vivid personality and fresh talents to such a degree that for the moment at least even its idol of many seasons, Carol Clay, was forgotten. The new arriving star filled the whole firmament. Broadway was ready to worship at a new shrine.

But Broadway did not know that there were two Tony Holidays that night, the happy Tony who had taken its fickle, composite heart by storm and the other Tony half distracted by grief and trapped bewilderment. Tony had willed to exile that second self before she stepped out behind the foot lights. She knew if she did not she never could play Madge as Madge had the right to be played. For her own sake, for Max Hempel's sake because he believed in her, for Carol Clay's sake because Tony loved her, she meant to forget everything but Madge for those few hours. Later she would remember that Dick was dying in Mexico, that she had hurt Alan cruelly that afternoon, that she had a sad and vexed problem to solve to which there seemed no solution. These things must wait. And they had waited but they came crowding back upon her the moment the play was over and she saw Alan waiting for her in the little room off the wings.

He rose to meet her and oblivious of curious eyes about them drew her into his arms and kissed her. And Tony utterly miserable in a daze of conflicting emotions nestled in his embrace unresisting for a second, not caring any more than Alan himself what any one saw or thought upon seeing.

"You were wonderful, belovedest," he whispered. "I never saw them go madder over anybody, not even Carol herself."

Tony glowed all over at his praise and begged that they might drive a little in the park before they went home. She had to think. She couldn't think in the Hostelry. It stifled her. Nothing loath Alan acquiesced, hailed a cab and gave the necessary orders. For a moment they rode in silence Tony relaxing for the first time in many hours in the comfort of her lover's presence, his arm around her. Things were hard, terribly hard but you could not feel utterly disconsolate when the man you loved best in all the world was there right beside you looking at you with eyes that told you how much you were beloved in return.

"Tony, dear, I am going to surprise you," he said suddenly breaking the silence. "I have decided to go to Mexico."

"To go to Mexico! Alan! Why?"

Tony drew away from her companion to study his face, with amazement on her own.

"To find Carson and look after him. Why else?"

"But your exhibition? You can't go away now, Alan, even if I would let you go to Dick that way."

"Oh, yes I can. The arrangements are all made. Van Slyke can handle the last stages of the thing far better than I can. I loathe hanging round and hearing the fools rant about my stuff and wonder what the devil I meant by this or that or if I didn't mean anything. I am infinitely better off three thousand miles away."

"But even so--I don't want to hurt you or act as if I didn't appreciate what you are offering to do--but you hate Dick. I don't see how you could help him."

"I don't hate him any more, Tony. At least I don't think I do. At any rate whether I do or don't won't make the slightest bit of difference. I shall look after him as well as your uncle or your brothers would--better perhaps because I know Mexico well and how to get things done down there. I know how to get things done in most places."

"Oh, I know. I have often thought you must have magic at your command the way people fly to do your bidding. It is startling but it is awfully convenient."

"Money magic mostly," he retorted grimly.

"Partly, not mostly. You are a born potentate. You must have been a sultan or a pashaw or something in some previous incarnation. I don't care what you are if you will find Dick and see that he gets well. Alan, don't you think--couldn't I--wouldn't it be better--if I went too?"

There was a sudden gleam in Alan's eyes. The hour was his. He could take advantage of the situation, of the girl's anxiety for his cousin, her love for himself while it was at high tide as it was at this over stimulated hour of excitement. He could marry her. And once the rite was spoken--not John Massey--not all Holiday Hill combined could take her from him. She would be his and his alone to the end. Tony was ripe for madness to-night, overwrought, ready to take any wild leap in the dark with him. He could make her his. He felt the intoxicating truth quiver in the touch of her hand, read it in her eager, dark eyes lifted to his for his answer.

Alan Massey was unused to putting away temptation but this, perhaps the biggest and blackest that had ever assailed him he put by.

"No, dear I'll go alone," he said. "You will just have to trust me, Tony. I swear

I'll do everything in the world that can be done for Carson. Let us have just one dance though. I should like it to remember--in Mexico."

Tony hesitated. It was very late. The Hostelry would ill approve of her going anywhere to dance at such an hour. It ill approved of Alan Massey any way. Still--

"I am going to-morrow. It is our last chance," he pleaded. "Just one dance, *carissima*. It may have to last--a long, long time."

And Tony yielded. After all they could not treat this night as if it were like all the other nights in the calendar. They had the right to their one more hour of happiness before Alan went away. They had the right to this one last dance.

The one dance turned into many before they were through. It seemed to both as if they dared not stop lest somehow love and happiness should stop too with the end of the music. They danced on and on "divinely" as Alan had once called it. Tony thought the rest of his prophecy was fulfilled at last, that they also loved each other divinely, as no man or woman had ever loved since time began.

But at last this too had to come to an end as perfect moments must in this finite world and Alan and Tony went out of the brilliantly lighted restaurant into white whirls of snow. For a storm had started while they had been inside and was now well in progress. All too soon the cab deposited them at the Hostelry. In the dimly lit hall Alan drew the girl into his arms and kissed her passionately then suddenly almost flung her from him, muttered a curt good-by and before Tony hardly realized he was going, was gone, swallowed up in the night and storm. Alone Tony put her hands over her hot cheeks. So this was love. It was terrible, but oh--it was wonderful too.

Soberly after a moment she went to change the damning OUT opposite her name in the hall bulletin just as the clock struck the shocking hour of three. But lo there was no damning OUT visible, only a meek and proper IN after her name. For all the bulletin proclaimed Antoinette Holiday might have been for hours wrapt in innocent slumber instead of speeding away the wee' sma' hours in a public restaurant in the arms of a lover at whom Madame Grundy and her allies looked awry. Somebody had tampered with the thing to save Tony a reprimand or worse. But who? Jean? No, certainly not Jean. Jean's conscience was as inelastic as a yard stick. Whoever had committed the charitable act of mendacity it couldn't have been Jean.

But when Tony opened her own door and switched on the light there was Jean curled up asleep in the big arm chair. The sudden flare of light roused the sleeper and she sat up blinking.

"Wherever have you been, Tony? I have been worried to death about you. I've been home from the theater for hours. I couldn't think what had happened to you."

"I am sorry you worried. You needn't have. I was with Alan, of course."

"Tony, people say dreadful things about Mr. Massey. Aren't you ever afraid of him yourself?" Jean surveyed the younger girl with troubled eyes.

Tony flung off her cloak impatiently.

"Of course I am not afraid. People don't know him when they say such things about him. You needn't ever worry, Jean. I am safer with Alan than with any one else in the world. I'd know that to-night if I never knew it before. We were dancing. I knew it was late but I didn't care. I wouldn't have missed those dances if they had told me I had to pack my trunk and leave to-morrow." Thus spoke the rebel always ready to fly out like a Jack-in-the box from under the lid in Tony Holiday.

"They won't," said Jean in a queer, compressed little voice.

"Jean! Was it you that fixed that bulletin?"

"Yes, it was. I know it wasn't a nice thing to do but I didn't want them to scold you just now when you were so worried about Dick and everything. I thought you would be in most any minute any way and I waited up myself to tell you how I loved the play and how proud I was of you. Then when you didn't come for so long I got really scared and then I fell asleep and--"

Tony came over and stopped the older girl's words with a kiss.

"You are a sweet peach, Jean Lambert, and I am awfully grateful to you for straining your conscience like that for my sake and awfully sorry I worried you. I am afraid I always do worry good, sensible, proper people. I'm made that way, mad north north west like Hamlet," she added whimsically. "Maybe we Holidays are all mad that much, excepting Uncle Phil of course. He's all that keeps the rest of us on the track of sanity at all. But Alan is madder still. Jean, he is going to Mexico to take care of Dick."

"Mr. Massey is going to Mexico to take care of Dick!" Jean' stared. "Why, Tony--I thought--"

"Naturally. So did I. Who wouldn't think him the last person in the world to do a thing like that? But he is going and it is his idea not mine. I wanted to go too but he wouldn't let me," she added.

Jean gasped.

"Tony! You would have married him when your uncle--when everybody doesn't want you to?"

To Jean Lambert's well ordered, carefully fenced in mind such wild mental leaps as Tony Holiday's were almost too much to contemplate. But worse was to come.

"Married him! Oh, I don't know. I didn't think about that. I would just have gone with him. There wouldn't have been time to get a license. Of course I couldn't though on account of the play."

Jean gasped again. If it hadn't been for the play this astounding young person before her would have gone gallivanting off with one man to whom she was not married to the bedside, thousands of miles away, of another man to whom she was also not married. Such simplicity of mental processes surpassed any complexity Jean Lambert could possibly conceive.

"Alan wouldn't let me," repeated the astounding Tony. "I suppose it is better so. By to-morrow I will probably agree with him. When the wind is southerly I know a hawk from a handsaw too. But the wind isn't southerly to-night. It wasn't when I was dancing nor afterward," she added with a flaming color in her cheeks remembering that moment in the Hostelry hall when wisdom had mattered very little to her in comparison with love. "Oh, Jean, what if something dreadful should happen to him down there! I can't let him go. I can't. But Dick mustn't die alone either. Oh, what shall I do? What shall I do?"

And suddenly Tony threw herself face down on the bed sobbing great, heart rending sobs, but whether she was crying for Dick or Alan or herself or all three Jean was unable to decipher. Perhaps Tony did not know herself.

The next morning when Tony awoke Alan had already left for his long journey, but a great box full of roses told her she had been his last thought. One by one she lifted them out of the box--great, gorgeous, blood red beauties, royal, Tony thought, like the royal lover who had sent them. The only message with the flowers was a bit of verse, a poem of Tagore's whom Alan loved and had taught Tony to love too.

You are the evening cloud floating in the sky of
  my dreams.
I paint you and fashion you with my love longings.
You are my own, my own, Dweller in my endless
  dreams!

Your feet are rosy-red with the glow of my heart's
  desire, Gleaner of my sunset songs!
Your lips are bitter-sweet with the taste of my wine
  of pain.
You are my own, my own, Dweller in my lonesome
  dreams!

With the shadow of my passion have I darkened
  your eyes, Haunter of the depth of my gaze!
I have caught you and wrapt you, my love, in the
  net of my music.
You are my own, my own, Dweller in my deathless
  dreams!

As she read the exquisite lines Antoinette Holiday knew it was all true. The poet might have written his poem for her and Alan. Her lips were indeed bitter-sweet with the taste of his wine of pain, her eyes were darkened by his shadows. He had caught her and wrapt her in the net of his love, which was a kind of music in itself--a music one danced to. She was his, dweller in his dreams as he was always to dwell in hers. It was fate.

CHAPTER XXXIII
WAITING FOR THE END OF THE STORY

At home on the Hill Ruth's affairs developed slowly. It was in time ascertained from Australia that the Farringdon pearls had come to America in the possession of Miss Farringdon who was named Elinor Ruth, daughter of Roderick and Esther Farringdon, both deceased. What had become of her and her pearls no one knew. Grave fears had been entertained as to the girl's safety because of her prolonged silence and the utter failure of all the advertising for her which had gone on in English and American papers. She had come to America to join an aunt, one Mrs. Robert Wright, widow of a New York broker, but it had been later ascertained that Mrs. Wright had left for England before her niece could have reached her and had subsequently died having caught a fever while engaged in nursing in a military hospital. Roderick Farringdon, the brother of Elinor Ruth, an aviator in His Majesty's service, was reported missing, believed to be dead or in a German prison somewhere. The lawyers in charge of the huge business interests of the two young Farringdons were in grave distress because of their inability to locate either of the owners and begged that if Doctor Laurence Holiday knew anything of the whereabouts of Miss Farringdon that he would communicate without delay with them.

So far so good. Granted that Ruth was presumably Elinor Ruth Farringdon of Australia. Was she or was she not married? There had been no opportunity in the cables to make inquiry about one Geoffrey Annersley though Larry had put that important question first in his letter to the consul which as yet had received no answer. The lawyers stated that when Miss Farringdon had left Australia she was not married but unsubstantiated rumors had reached them from San Francisco hinting at her possible marriage there.

All this failed to stir Ruth's dormant memory in any degree. There was nothing to do but wait until further information should be forthcoming.

Not unnaturally these facts had a somewhat different effect upon the two individuals most concerned. Ruth was frankly elated over the whole thing and found it by no means impossible to believe that she was a princess in disguise though she had played Cinderella contentedly enough.

On the strength of her presumable princessship she had gone on another excursion to Boston carrying the Lambert twins with her this time and had returned laden with all manner of feminine fripperies. She had an exquisite taste and made unerringly for the softest and finest of fabrics, the hats with an "air," the dresses that were the simplest, the most ravishing and it must be admitted also the most extravagant. If she remembered nothing else Ruth remembered how to spend royally.

She had consulted the senior doctor before making the splendid plunge. She did not want to have Larry buy her anything more and she didn't want Doctor Philip and Margery to think her stark mad to go behaving like a princess before the princess purse was actually in her hands. But she had to have pretty things, a lot of them, had to have them quick. Did the doctor mind very much advancing her some money? He could keep her rings as security.

He had laughed indulgently and declared as the rings and the pearls too for that matter were in his possession in the safe deposit box he should worry. He also told her to go ahead and be as "princessy" as she liked. He would take the risk. Whereupon he placed a generous sum of money at her account in a Boston bank and sent her away with his blessing and an amused smile at the femininity of females. And Ruth had gone and played princess to her heart's content. But there was little enough of heart's content in any of it for poor Larry. Day by day it seemed to him he could see his fairy girl slipping away from him. Ruth was a great lady and heiress. Who was Larry Holiday to take advantage of the fact that circumstances had almost thrown her into his willing arms?

Moreover the information afforded as to Roderick Farringdon had put a new idea into his head. Roderick was reported "missing." Was it not possible that Geoffrey Annersley might be in the same category? Missing men sometimes stayed missing in war time but sometimes also they returned as from the dead from enemy prisons or long illnesses. What if this should be the case with the man who was presumably Ruth's husband? Certainly it put out of the question, if there ever had been a question in Larry's mind, his own right to marry the girl he loved until they knew absolutely that the way was clear.

Considering these things it was not strange that the new year found Larry Holiday in heavy mood, morose, silent, curt and unresponsive even to his uncle, inclined at times to snap even at his beloved little Goldilocks whose shining new happiness exasperated him because he could not share it. Of course he repented in sack cloth and ashes afterward, but repentance did not prevent other offenses and altogether the young doctor was ill to live with during those harrassed January days.

It was not only Ruth. Larry could not take Ted's going with the quiet fortitude with which his uncle met it. Those early weeks of nineteen hundred and seventeen were black ones for many. The grim Moloch War demanded more and ever more victims. Thousands of gay, brave, high spirited lads like Ted were mown down daily by shrapnel and machine gun or sent twisted and writhing to still more hideous death in the unspeakable horror of noxious gases. It was all so unnecessary--so senseless. Larry Holiday whose life was dedicated to the healing and saving of men's bodies hated with bitter hate this opposing force which was all for destruction and which held the groaning world in its relentless grip. It would not have been so bad he thought if the Moloch would have been content to take merely the old, the life weary, the diseased, the vile. Not so. It demanded the young, the strong, the clean and gallant hearted, took their bodies, maimed and tortured them, killed them sooner or later, hurled them undiscriminatingly into the bottomless pit of death.

To Larry it all came back to Ted. Ted was the embodiment, the symbol of the rest. He was the young, the strong, the clean and gallant hearted--the youth of the world, a vain sacrifice to the cruel blindness of a so called civilization which would not learn the futility of war and all the ways of war.

So while Ruth bought pretty clothes and basked in happy anticipations which for her took the place of memories, poor Larry walked in dark places and saw no single ray of light.

One afternoon he was summoned to the telephone to receive the word that there was a telegram for him at the office. It was Dunbury's informal habit to telephone messages of this sort to the recipient instead of delivering them in person. Larry took the repeated word in silence. A question evidently followed from the other end.

"Yes, I got it," Larry snapped back and threw the receiver back in place with vicious energy. His uncle who had happened to be near looked up to ask a question but the young doctor was already out of the room leaving only the slam of the door in his wake. A few moments later the older man saw the younger start off down the Hill in the car at a speed which was not unlike Ted's at his worst before the smash on the Florence road. Evidently Larry was on the war path. Why?

The afternoon wore on. Larry did not return. His uncle began to be seriously disturbed. A patient with whom the junior doctor had had an appointment came and waited and finally went away somewhat indignant in spite of all efforts to soothe her not unnatural wrath. Worse and worse! Larry never failed his appointments, met every obligation invariably as punctiliously as if for professional purposes he was operated by clock work.

At supper time Phil Lambert dropped in with the wire which had already been reported to Larry and which the company with the same informality already mentioned had asked him to deliver. Doctor Holiday was tempted to read it but refrained. Surely the boy would be home soon.

The evening meal was rather a silent one. Ruth was wearing a charming dark blue velvet gown which Larry especially liked. The doctor guessed that she had dressed particularly for her lover and was sadly disappointed when he failed to put in his appearance. She drooped perceptibly and her blue eyes were wistful.

An hour later when the three, Margery, her husband, and Ruth, were sitting quietly engaged in reading in the living room they heard the sound of the returning car. All three were distinctly conscious of an involuntary breath of relief which permeated the room. Nobody had said a word but every one of them had been filled with foreboding.

Presently Larry entered with the yellow envelope in his hand. He was pale and very tired looking but obviously entirely in command of himself whatever had been the case earlier in the day. He crossed the room to where his uncle sat and handed him the telegram.

"Please read it aloud," he said. "It--it concerns all of us."

The older doctor complied with the request.

Arrive Dunbury January 18 nine forty A.M. So ran the brief though pregnant message. It was signed *Captain Geoffrey Annersley*.

The color went out of Ruth's face as she heard the name. She put her hands over her eyes and uttered a little moan. Then abruptly she dropped her hands, the color came surging back into her cheeks and she ran to Larry, fairly throwing herself into his arms.

"I don't want to see him. Don't let him come. I hate him. I don't want to be Elinor Farringdon. I want to be just Ruth--Ruth Holiday," she whispered the last in Larry's ear, her head on his shoulder.

Larry kissed her for the first time before the others, then meeting his uncle's grave eyes he put her gently from him and walked over to the door. On the threshold he turned and faced them all.

"Uncle Phil--Aunt Margery, help Ruth. I can't." And the door closed upon him.

Philip and Margery did their best to obey his parting injunction but it was not an easy task. Ruth was possessed by a very panic of dread of Geoffrey Annersley and an even more difficult to deal with flood of love for Larry Holiday.

"I don't want anybody but Larry," she wailed over and over. "It is Larry I love. I don't love Geoffrey Annersley. I won't let him be my husband. I don't want anybody but Larry."

In vain they tried to comfort her, entreat her to wait until to-morrow before she gave up. Perhaps Geoffrey Annersley wasn't her husband. Perhaps everything was quite all right. She must try to have patience and not let herself get sick worrying in advance.

"He *is* my husband," she suddenly announced with startling conviction. "I remember his putting the ring on my finger. I remember his saying 'You've got to wear it. It is the only thing to do. You must.' I remember what he looks like--almost. He is tall and he has a scar on his cheek --here." She patted her own face feverishly to show the spot. "He made me wear the ring and I didn't want to. I didn't want to. Oh, don't let me remember. Don't let me," she implored.

At this point the doctor took things in his own hands. The child was obviously beginning to remember. The shock of the man's coming had snapped something in her brain. They must not let things come back too disastrously fast. He packed her off to bed with a stiff dose of nerve quieting medicine. Margery sat with her arms tight around the forlorn little sufferer and presently the dreary sobbing ceased and the girl drifted off to exhausted sleep, nature's kindest panacea for all human ills.

Meanwhile the doctor sought out Larry. He found him in the office apparently completely absorbed in the perusal of a medical magazine. He looked up quickly as the older man entered and answered the question in his eyes giving assurance that Ruth was quite all right, would soon be asleep if she was not already. He made no mention of that disconcerting flash of memory. Sufficient unto the day was the trouble thereof.

He came over and laid a kindly, encouraging hand on the boy's shoulder.

"Keep up heart a little longer," he said. "By tomorrow you will know where you stand and that will be something, no matter which way it turns."

"I should say it would," groaned Larry. "I'm sick of being in a labyrinth. Even the worst can't be much worse than not knowing. You don't know how tough it has been, Uncle Phil."

"I can make a fairly good guess at it, my boy. I've seen and understood more than you realize perhaps. You have put up a magnificent fight, son. And you are the boy who once told me he was a coward."

"I am afraid I still am, Uncle Phil,--sometimes."

"We all are, Larry, cowards in our hearts, but that does not matter so long as the yellow streak doesn't get into our acts. You have not let that happen I think."

Larry was silent. He was remembering that night when Ruth had come to him. He wasn't very proud of the memory. He wondered if his uncle guessed how near the yellow streak had come to the surface on that occasion.

"I don't deserve as much credit as you are giving me," he said humbly. "There have been times--at least one time--" He broke off.

"You would have been less than a man if there had not been, Larry. I understand all that. But on the whole you know and I know that you have a clean slate to show. Don't let yourself get morbid worrying about things you might have done and didn't. They don't worry me. They needn't worry you. Forget it."

"Uncle Phil! You are great the way you always clear away the fogs. But my clean slate is a great deal thanks to you. I don't know where I would have landed if you hadn't held me back, not so much by what you said as what you are. Ted isn't the only one who has learned to appreciate what a pillar of strength we all have in you. However this comes out I shan't forget what you did for me, are doing all the time."

"Thank you, Larry. It is good to hear things like that though I think you underestimate your own strength. I am thankful if I have helped in any degree. I have felt futile enough. We all have. At any rate the strain is about over. The telegram must have been a knock down blow though. Where were you this afternoon?"

"I don't know. I just drove like the devil--anywhere. Did you worry? I am sorry. Good Lord! I cut my appointment with Mrs. Blake, didn't I? I never thought of it until this minute. Gee! I am worse than Ted. Used to think I had some balance but evidently I am a plain nut. I'm disgusted with myself and I should think you would be more disgusted with me." The boy looked up at his uncle with eyes that were full of shamed compunction.

But the latter smiled back consolingly.

"Don't worry. There are worse things in the world than cutting an appointment for good and sufficient reasons. You will get back your balance when things get normal again. I have no complaint to make anyway. You have kept up the professional end splendidly until now. What you need is a good long vacation and I am going to pack you off on one at the earliest opportunity. Do you want me to meet Captain Annersley for you tomorrow?" he switched off to ask.

Larry shook his head.

"No, I'll meet him myself, thank you. It is my job. I am not going to flunk it. If he is Ruth's husband I am going to be the first to shake hands with him."

CHAPTER XXXIV
IN WHICH TWO MASSEYS MEET IN MEXICO

And while things were moving toward their crisis for Larry and Ruth another drama was progressing more or less swiftly to its conclusion down in Vera Cruz. Alan Massey had found his cousin in a wretched, vermin haunted shack, nursed in haphazard fashion by a slovenly, ignorant half-breed woman under the ostensible professional care of a mercenary, incompetent, drunken Mexican doctor who cared little enough whether the dog of an American lived or died so long as he himself continued to get the generous checks from a certain newspaper in New York City. The doctor held the credulity of the men who mailed those checks in fine contempt and proceeded to feather his nest valiantly while his good luck continued, going on many a glorious spree at the paper's expense while Dick Carson went down every day deeper into the valley of the shadow of death.

With the coming of Alan Massey however a new era began. Alan was apt to leave transformation of one sort or another in his wake. It was not merely his money magic though he wielded that magnificently as was his habit and predilection, spent Mexican dollars with a superb disregard of their value which won from the natives a respect akin to awe and wrought miracles wherever the golden flow touched. But there was more than money magic to Alan Massey's performance in Vera Cruz. There was also the magic of his dominating, magnetic personality. He was a born master and every one high or low who crossed his path recognized his rightful ascendency and hastened to obey his royal will.

His first step was to get the sick man transferred from the filthy hovel in which he found him to clean, comfortable quarters in an ancient adobe palace, screened, airy, spacious. The second step was to secure the services of two competent and high priced nurses from Mexico City, one an American, the other an English woman, both experienced, intrepid, efficient. The third step taken simultaneously with the other two was to dismiss the man who masqueraded as a physician though he was nothing in reality but a cheap charlatan fattening himself at the expense of weakness and disease. The man had been inclined to make trouble at first about his unceremonious discharge. He had no mind to lose without a protest such a convenient source of unearned increment as those checks represented. He had intended to get in many another good carouse before the sick man died or got well as nature willed. But a single interview with Alan Massey sufficed to lay his objections to leaving the case. In concise and forcible language couched in perfect Spanish Alan had made it clear that if the so-called doctor came near his victim again he would be shot down like a dog and if Carson died he would in any case be tried for man slaughter and hanged on the spot. The last point had been further punctuated by an expressive gesture on the speaker's part, pointing to his own throat accompanied by a significant little gurgling sound. The gesture and the gurgle had been convincing. The man surrendered the case in some haste. He did not at all care for the style of conversation indulged in by this tall, unsmiling, green-eyed man. Consequently he immediately evaporated to all intents and purposes and was seen no more. The new physician put in charge was a different breed entirely, a man who had the authentic gift and passion for healing which the born doctor always possesses, be he Christian or heathen, gypsy herb mixer or ten thousand dollar specialist. Alan explained to this man precisely what was required of him, explained in the same forcible, concise, perfect Spanish that had banished the other so completely. His job was to cure the sick man. If he succeeded there would be a generous remuneration. If he failed through no fault of his there would still be fair remuneration though nothing like what would be his in case of complete recovery. If he failed through negligence-- and here the expressive gesture and the gurgle were repeated--. The sentence had not needed completion. The matter was sufficiently elucidated. The man was a born healer as has been recorded but even if he had not been he would still have felt obliged to move heaven and earth so far as in him lay to cure Dick Carson. Alan Massey's manner was persuasive. One did one's best to satisfy a person who spoke such Spanish and made such ominous gestures. One did as one was commanded. One dared do no other.

As for the servants whom Alan rallied to his standard they were slaves rather than servants. They recognized in him their preordained master, were wax to his hands, mats to his feet. They obeyed his word as obsequiously, faithfully and un-questioningly as if he could by a clap of his lordly hands banish them to strange deaths.

They talked in low tones about him among themselves behind his back. This was no American they said. No American could command as this green-eyed one commanded. No American had such gift of tongues, such gestures, such picturesque and varied and awesome oaths. No American carried small bright flashing daggers such as he carried in his inner pockets, nor did Americans talk glibly as he talked of weird poisons, not every day drugs, but marvelous, death dealing concoctions done up in lustrous jewel-like capsules or diluted in sparkling, insidious gorgeous hued fluids. The man was too wise--altogether too wise to be an American. He had traveled much, knew strange secrets. They rather thought he knew black art. Certainly he knew more of the arts of healing than the doctor himself. There was nothing he did not know, the green-eyed one. It was best to obey him.

And while Alan Massey's various arts operated Dick Carson passed through a series of mental and physical evolutions and came slowly back to consciousness of what was going on.

At first he was too close to the hinterland to know or care as to what was happening here, though he did vaguely sense that he had left the lower levels of Hell and was traversing a milder purgatorial region. He did not question Alan's presence or recognize him. Alan was at first simply another of those distrusted foreigners whose point of view and character he comprehended as little as he did their jibbering tongues.

Gradually however this one man seemed to stand out from the others and finally took upon himself a name and an entity. By and by, Dick thought, when he wasn't so infernally-tired as he was just now he would wonder why Alan Massey was here and would try to recall why he had disliked him so, some time a million years ago or so. He did not dislike him now. He was too weak to dislike anybody in any case but he was beginning to connect Alan vaguely but surely with the superior cleanliness and comfort and care with which he was now surrounded. He knew now that he had been sick, very sick and that he was getting better, knew that before long he would find himself asking questions. Even now his eyes followed Alan Massey as the latter came and went with an ever more insistent wonderment though he had not yet the force of will or body to voice that pursuing question as to why Alan Massey was here apparently taking charge of his own slow return to health and consciousness.

Meanwhile Alan wired Tony Holiday every day as to his patient's condition though he wrote not at all and said nothing in his wires of himself. Letters from Tony were now beginning to arrive, letters full of eager gratitude and love for Alan and concern for Dick.

And one day Dick's mind got suddenly very clear. He was alone with the nurse at the time, the sympathetic American one whom he liked better and was less afraid of than he was of the stolid, inexorable British lady. And he began to ask questions, many questions and very definite ones. He knew at last precisely what it was he wanted to know.

He got a good deal of information though by no means all he sought. He found out that he had been taken desperately ill, that he had been summarily removed from his lodging place because of the owner's superstitious dread of contagion into the miserable little thatch roofed hut in which he had nearly died thanks to the mal-practice of the rascally, drunken doctor and the ignorant half-breed nurse. He learned how Alan Massey had suddenly appeared and taken things in his own hands, discovered that in a nutshell the fact was he owed his life to the other-man. But why? That was what he had to find out from Alan Massey himself.

The next day when Alan came in and the nurse went out he asked his question.

"That is easy," said Alan grimly. "I came on Tony's account."

Dick winced. Of course that was it. Tony had sent Massey. He was here as her emissary, naturally, no doubt as her accepted lover. It was kind. Tony was always kind but he wished she had not done it. He did not want to have his life saved by the man who was going to marry Tony Holiday. He rather thought he did not want his life saved anyway by anybody. He wished they hadn't done it.

"I--I am much obliged to you and to Tony," he said a little stiffly. "I fear it--it was hardly worth the effort." His eyes closed wearily.

"Tony didn't send me though," observed Alan Massey as if he had read the other's thought. "I sent myself."

Dick's eyes opened.

"That is odd if it is true," he said slowly.

Alan dropped into a chair near the bed.

"It is odd," he admitted. "But it happens to be true. It came about simply enough. When Tony heard you were sick she went crazy, swore she was coming down here in spite of us all to take care of you. Then Miss Clay's child died and she had to go on the boards. You can imagine what it meant to her--the two things coming at once. She played that night--swept everything as you'd know she would--got 'em all at her feet."

Dick nodded, a faint flash of pleasure in his eyes. Down and out as he was he could still be glad to hear of Tony's triumph.

"She wanted to come to you," went on Alan. "She let me come instead because she couldn't. I came for--for her sake."

Dick nodded.

"Naturally--for her sake," he said. "I could hardly have expected you to come for mine. I would hardly have expected it in any case."

"I would hardly have expected it of myself," acknowledged Alan with a wry smile. "But I've had rather a jolly time at your expense. I've always enjoyed working miracles and if you could have seen yourself the way you were when I got here you would think there was a magic in it somehow."

"I evidently owe you a great deal, Mr. Massey. I am grateful or at least I presume I shall be later. Just now I feel a little--dumb."

"My dear fellow, nothing would please me better than to have you continue dumb on that subject. I did this thing as I've done most things in my life to please myself. I don't want your thanks. I would like a little of your liking though. You and I are likely to see quite a bit of each other these next few weeks. Could you manage to forget the past and call a kind of truce for a while? You have a good deal to forgive me--perhaps more than you know. If you would be willing to let the little I have done down here--and mind you I don't want to magnify that part--wipe off the slate I should be glad. Could you manage it, Carson?"

"It looks as if it hardly could be magnified," said Dick with sudden heartiness. "I spoke grudgingly just now I am afraid. Please overlook it. I am more than grateful for all you have done and more than glad to be friends if you want it. I don't hate you. How could I when you have saved my life and anyway I never hated you as you used to hate me. I've often wondered why you did, especially at first before you knew how much I cared for Tony. And even that shouldn't have made you hate me because--you won."

"Never mind why I hated you. I don't any more. Will you shake hands with me, Carson, so we can begin again?"

Dick pulled himself weakly up on the pillow. Their hands met.

"Hang it, Massey," Dick said. "I am afraid I am going to like you. I've heard you were hypnotic. I believe on my soul you came down here to make me like you? Did you?"

But Alan only smiled his ironic, noncommital smile and remarked it was time for the invalid to take a nap. He had had enough conversation for the first attempt.

Dick soon drifted off to sleep but Alan Massey prowled the streets of the Mexican city far into the night, with tireless, driven feet. The demons were after him again.

And far away in another city whose bright lights glow all night Tony Holiday was still playing Madge to packed houses, happy in her triumph but with heart very pitiful for her beloved Miss Clay whose sorrow and continued illness had made possible the fruition of her own eager hopes. Tony was sadly lonely without Alan, thought of him far more often and with deeper affection even than she had while she had him at her beck and call in the city, loved him with a new kind of love for his generous kindness to Dick. She made up her mind that he had cleared the shield forever by this splendid act and saw no reason why she should keep him any longer on probation. Surely she knew by this time that he was a man even a Holiday might be proud to marry.

She wrote this decision to her uncle and asked to be relieved from her promise.

"I am sorry," she wrote, "if you cannot approve but I cannot help it. I love him and I am going to be engaged to him as soon as he comes back to New York if he wants it. I am afraid I would have married him and gone to Mexico with him, given up the play and broken my promise to you, if he would have let me. It goes that far and deep with me.

"People are crazy over his pictures. The exhibition came off last week and they say he is one of the greatest living painters with a wonderful future ahead of him. I am so proud and happy. He is fine everyway now, has really sloughed off the past just as he promised he would. So please, dear Uncle Phil, forgive me if I do what you don't want me to. I have to marry him. In my heart I am married to him already."

And this was the letter Philip Holiday found at his place at breakfast on the morning of the day Geoffrey Annersley was expected. He read it gravely. Rash, loving, generous-hearted Tony. Where was she going? Ah well, she was no longer a child to be protected from the storm and stress of life. She was a woman grown, woman enough to love and to be loved greatly, to sacrifice and suffer if need be for love's mighty sake. She must go her way as Ted had gone his, as their father had gone his before them. He could only pray that she was right in her faith that for love of her Alan Massey had been born anew.

His own deep affection for Ned's children seemed at the moment a sadly powerless thing. He had coveted the best things of life for them, happy, normal ways of peace and gentle living. Yet here was Ted at twenty already lived through an experience, tragic enough to leave its scarlet mark for all the rest of his life and even now on the verge of voluntarily entering a terrific conflict from which few returned alive and none came back unchanged. Here was Tony taking upon herself the thraldom of a love, which try as he would Philip Holiday could not see in any other light but as at best a cataclysmic risk. And at this very hour Larry might be learning that the desire of his heart was dust and ashes, his hope a vain thing, himself an exile henceforth from the things that round out a man's life, make it full and rich and satisfying.

And yet thinking of the three Philip Holiday found one clear ray of comfort. With all their vagaries, their rash impulsions, their willful blindness, their recklessness, they had each run splendidly true to type. Not one of the three had failed in the things that really count. He had faith that none of them ever would. They might blunder egregiously, suffer immeasurably, pay extravagantly, but they would each keep that vital spirit which they had in common, untarnished and undaunted, an unconquerable thing.

CHAPTER XXXV
GEOFFREY ANNERSLEY ARRIVES

There were few passengers alighting from the south bound train from Canada. Larry Holiday had no difficulty in picking out Geoffrey Annersley among these, a tall young man, wearing the British uniform and supporting himself with a walking stick. His face was lean and bronzed and lined, the face of a man who has seen things which kill youth and laughter and yet a serene face too as if its owner had found that after all nothing mattered very much if you looked it square in the eye.

Larry went to the stranger at once.

"Captain Annersley?" he asked. "I am Laurence Holiday."

The captain set down his bag, leaned on his stick, deliberately scrutinized the other man. Larry returned the look frankly. They were of nearly the same age but any one seeing them would have set the Englishman as at least five years the senior of the young doctor. Geoffrey Annersley had been trained in a stern school. A man does not wear a captain's bars and four wound stripes for nothing.

Then the Englishman held out his hand with a pleasant and unexpectedly boyish smile.

"So you are Larry," he said. "Your brother sent me to you."

"Ted! You have seen him?" For a minute Larry forgot who Geoffrey Annersley was, forgot Ruth, forgot himself, remembered only Ted and gave his guest a heartier handshake than he had willed for his "Kid" brother's sake.

"Yes, I was with him day before yesterday and the night before that. He was looking jolly well and sent all kinds of greetings to you all. See here, Doctor Holiday, I have no end of things to say to you. Can we go somewhere and talk?"

"My car is outside. You will come up to the house will you not? We are all expecting you." Larry tried hard to keep his voice quiet and emotionless. Not for anything would he have had this gallant soldier suspect how his knees were trembling.

"Delighted," bowed the captain suavely and permitted Larry to take his bag and lead the way to the car. Nothing more was said until the two men were seated and the car had left the station yard.

"I am afraid I should have made my wire a bit more explicit," observed the captain turning to Larry. "My wife says I am too parsimonious with my words in telegrams--a British trait possibly." He spoke deliberately and his keen eyes studied his companion's face as he made the casual remark which set Larry's brain reeling. "See here, Holiday, I'm a blunt brute. I don't know how to break things gently to people. But I am here to tell you if you care to know that Elinor Ruth Farringdon is no more married than you are unless she is married to you. That was her mother's wedding ring. Lord, man, do you always drive a car like this? I've been all but killed once this year and I don't care to repeat the experiment."

Larry grinned, flushed, apologized and moderated the speed of his motor. He wondered that he could drive at all. He felt strangely light as if he were stripped of his body and were nothing but spirit.

"Do you mind if we drive about a bit and talk things over before I see Elinor--Ruth, as you call her? I'm funking that a little though I've been trying ever since your brother told me the story to get used to the idea of her being, well not quite right, you know. But I can't stick it somehow."

"She is all right, perfectly normal every way except that she had forgotten things." Larry's voice was faintly indignant. He resented anybody's implying that Ruth was queer, unbalanced in any way. She wasn't. She was absolutely sane, as sane as Captain Annersley himself, considerably more sane than Larry Holiday could take oath he was at this moment.

"Good heavens! Isn't that enough?" groaned Annersley almost equally indignant. "You forget or rather you don't know all she has forgotten. I know. I was brought up with her. Her father was my uncle and guardian. We played together, had the same tutor, rode the same ponies, got into the same jolly old scrapes. Why, Elinor's like my own sister, man. I can't swallow her forgetting me and her brother Rod and all the rest as easily as you seem to do. It--well, it's the limit as you say in the states." The captain wiped his forehead on which great drops of perspiration stood in spite of the January chill in the air. There was agitation, suppressed vehemence in his tone.

"I suppose it is natural that you should feel that way." Larry spoke thoughtfully as he turned the car away from the Hill in response to his guest's request that he be permitted to postpone meeting Elinor Ruth Farringdon a little while. "The remembering part hasn't bothered me so much. Maybe I wasn't very keen on having her remember. Maybe I was afraid she would remember too much," he added coloring a little.

The frown on his companion's stern young face melted at that. The frank, boyish smile appeared again. He liked Larry Holiday none the less for his lack of pretense. He understood all that. The younger Holiday had taken pains to make things perfectly clear to him. He knew precisely what the young doctor was afraid of and why in case Elinor Farringdon's memory returned.

"My uncle thinks and I think too that her memory will come back now that it has the external stimulus to waken it," Larry continued. "I shouldn't be surprised if seeing you would give the necessary impetus. In fact I am counting on that very thing happening, hoping for it with all my might. That was one of the reasons I was glad to have you come. Please believe that I should have been glad even if your coming had made her remember she was your wife. Of course her recovery is the main thing. The rest is--a side issue."

"A jolly important side issue I take it for her and for you. I'm not a stranger, Doctor Holiday. I am Elinor Ruth Farringdon's cousin, in her brother's absence I represent her family and in that capacity I would like to say before I am a minute older that what you and the rest of you Holidays have done for Elinor passes anything I know of for sheer fineness and generosity. I'm not a man of words. War would have knocked them out of me if I had been but when I remember that you not only saved Elinor's life but took care of her afterward when she apparently hadn't a friend in the world--well, there isn't anything I can say but thank you and tell you that if there is ever anything I can do in return for you or yours you have only to ask. Neither Elinor nor I can ever repay you. It is the sort of thing that is--unpayable." And again the captain wiped his perspiring brow. He was deeply moved and emotion went hard with his Anglo-Saxon temperament.

"We did nothing but what anybody would have been glad to do. If there are any thanks coming they are chiefly due to my uncle and his wife. But we don't any of us want thanks. We love Ruth. Please forget the rest. We would rather you would."

The captain nodded quick approval. He had been told Americans were boasters, given to Big-Itis. But either people got the Americans wrong or these Holidays were an exception to the general run. He remembered that other young Holiday whom he had met rather intimately in the Canadian camp. There had been no side there either. His modesty had been one of his chief charms. And here was the brother quietly putting aside credit for a course of conduct which was simply immense in its quixotic generosity. He liked these Holidays. There was something rather magnificent about their simplicity--something almost British he thought.

"That is all very well," he made answer. "I won't talk about it if you prefer but you will pardon me if I don't forget that you saved my cousin's life and looked after her when she was in a desperately unhappy situation and her own people seemed to have utterly deserted her. And I consider my running into your brother at camp one of the sheerest pieces of good luck I've had these many days on all counts."

"How did it happen?" asked Larry.

"I was doing some recruiting work in the vicinity and they asked me to say a few words to the lads in training. I did. Your brother was there and lost no time in getting in touch with me when he heard who I was. And jolly pleased I was to hear his story--all of it."

The speaker smiled at his companion.

"I mean that, Larry Holiday. Elinor and I were kid sweethearts. We used to swear we were going to get married when we grew up. That was when she was eight and I a man of twelve or so. I gave her the locket which made some of the trouble as a sort of hostage for the future. We called her Ruth in those days. It was her own fancy to change it to Elinor later. She thought it more grown up and dignified I remember. Then I went back to England to school. I didn't see her again until we were both grown up and then I married her best friend with her blessing and approval. But that is another story. Just now I am trying to tell you that I am ready to congratulate my cousin with all my heart if it happens that you want to marry her as your brother seems to think."

"There is no doubt about what I want," said Larry grimly. "Whether it is what she wants is another matter. We haven't been exactly in a position to discuss marriage."

"I understand. I'm beastly sorry to have been such an infernal dog in the manger unwittingly. The only thing I can do to make, up is to give my blessing and wish you best of luck in your wooing. Shall we shake on it, Larry Holiday, and on the friendship I hope you and I are going to have?"

And with a cordial man to man grip there was cemented a friendship which was to last as long as they both lived.

To relate briefly the links of the story some of which Larry Holiday now heard as the car sped over the smooth, frost hardened roads which the open winter had left unusually snowless and clean. Geoffrey Annersley had been going his careless, happy go lucky way as an Oxford undergraduate when the sudden firing of a far off shot had startled the world and made war the one inevitable fact. The young man had enlisted promptly and had been in practically continuous service of one sort or another ever since. He had gone through desperate fighting, been four times wounded, and was now at last definitely eliminated from active service by a semi-paralyzed leg, the result of his last visit to "Blighty." He had been invalided the previous spring and had been sent to Australia on a recruiting mission. Here he had renewed his acquaintance with his cousins whom he had not seen for years and promptly fell in love with and married pretty Nancy Hallinger, his cousin Elinor's chum.

The speedy wooing accomplished as well as the recruiting job which was dispatched equally expeditiously and thoroughly Geoffrey prepared to return to France to get in some more good work against the Huns while his wife planned to enter Red Cross service as a nurse for which she had been in training for some time. Roderick had entered the Australian air service and was already in Flanders where he had the reputation of being one of the youngest and most reckless aviators flying which was saying considerable.

It was imperative that some arrangement be made for Elinor who obviously could not be left alone in Sydney. It was decided in family conclave that she should go to America and accept the often proffered hospitality of her aunt for a time at least. A cable to this effect had been dispatched to Mrs. Wright which as later appeared never reached that lady as she was already on her way to England and died there shortly after.

Geoffrey had been exceedingly reluctant to have his young cousin take the long journey alone though she had laughed at his fears and his wife had abetted her in her disregard of possible disastrous consequences, telling him that women no longer required wrapping in tissue paper. The war had changed all that.

At his insistence however Ruth had finally consented to wear her mother's wedding ring as a sort of shadowy protection. He had an idea that the small gold band, being presumptive evidence of an existing male guardian somewhere in the offing might serve to keep away the ill intentioned or over bold from his lovely little heiress cousin about whom he worried to no small degree.

They had gone their separate ways, he to the fierce fighting of May, nineteen hundred and sixteen, she to her long journey and subsequent strange adventures. At first no one had thought it unnatural that they heard nothing from Elinor. Letters went easily astray those days. Geoffrey was weeks without news even from his wife and poor Roderick was by this time beyond communication of any kind, his name labeled with that saddest of all tags--missing. It was not until Geoffrey was out of commission with that last worst knock out, lying insensible, more dead than alive in a hospital "somewhere in France" that the others began to realize that Elinor had vanished utterly from the ken of all who knew her. Some one who knew her by sight had chanced to see her in California and had noted the wedding ring, hence the "unsubstantiated rumor" of her marriage in San Francisco, a rumor which Nancy half frantic over her husband's desperate illness was the only person who was in a position to explain.

When Geoffrey came slowly back to the land of the living it was to learn that his cousin Roderick was still reported missing and that Elinor was even more sadly and mysteriously vanished from the face of the earth in spite of all effort to discover her fate. It had been a tragic coming back for the sick man. But an Englishman is hard to down and gradually he got back health and a degree of hope and happiness. There would be no more fighting for him but the War Department assured him there were plenty of other ways in which he could serve the cause and he had readily placed himself at their disposal for the recruiting work in which he had already demonstrated his power to success in Australia.

Which brings us to the Canadian training camp and Ted Holiday. Captain Annersley had been asked as he had told Larry to speak to the boys. He had done so, given a little straight talk of what lay ahead of them and what they were fighting for, bade them get in a few extra licks for him since he was out of it for good, done for, "crocked." In conclusion he had begged them give the Huns hell. It was all he asked of them and from the look of them he jolly well knew they would do it.

While he was speaking he was aware all the time of a tall, blue-eyed youth who stood leaning against a post with a kind of nonchalant grace. The boy's pose had been indolent but his eyes had been wide awake, earnest, responsive. Little by little the captain found himself talking directly to the lad. What he was saying might be over the heads of some of them but not this chap's. He got you as the Americans say. He had the vision, would go wherever the speaker could take him. One saw that.

Afterwards the boy had sought out the recruiter to ask if by any chance he knew a girl named Elinor Ruth Farringdon. It had been rather a tremendous moment for both of them. Each had plenty to say that the other wanted to hear. But the full story had to wait. Corporal Holiday couldn't run around loose even talking to a distinguished British officer. There would have to be special dispensation for that and special dispensations take time in an army world. It would be forthcoming however--to-morrow.

In the meantime Geoffrey Annersley had heard enough to want to know a great deal more and thought he might as well make some inquiries on his own. He wanted to find out who these American Holidays were, one of whom had apparently saved his cousin Elinor's life and all of whom had, one concluded, been amazingly kind to her though the blue-eyed boy had gracefully made light of that side of the thing in the brief synopsis of events he had had time to give to the Englishman. The captain had taken a fancy to the narrator and was not averse to beginning his investigation as to the Holiday family with the young corporal himself.

Accordingly he tackled the boy's commanding officer, a young colonel with whom he chanced to be dining. The colonel was willing to talk and Geoffrey Annersley discovered that young Holiday was rather by way of being a top-notcher. He had enlisted as a private only a short time ago but had been shot speedily into his corporalship. Time pressed. Officers were needed. The boy was officer stuff. He wouldn't stay a corporal. If all went well he would go over as a sergeant.

"We put him through though, just at first handled him rather nasty," the colonel admitted with a reminiscent twinkle. "We do put the Americans through somehow, though it isn't that we have any grudge against 'em. We haven't. We like 'em--most of 'em and we have to admit it's rather decent of them to be here at all when they don't have to. All the same we give 'em an extra twist of the discipline crank on general principles just to see what they are made of. We found out mighty quick with this youngster. He took it all and came back for more with a 'sir,' and a salute and a devilish debonair, you-can't-down-me kind of grin that would have disarmed a Turk."

"He doesn't look precisely meek to me," Annersley had said remembering the answering flash he had caught in those blue eyes when he was begging the boys to get in an extra lick against the Huns for his sake.

"Meek nothing! He has more spirit than any cub we've had to get into shape this many a moon. It isn't that. It is just that he has the right idea, had it from the start however he came by it. You know what it is, captain. It is obedience, first, last and all the time, the will to be willed. A soldier's job is to do what he is told whether he likes it or not, whether it is his job or not, whether it makes sense or not, whether he gets his orders from a man he looks up to and respects or whether he gets them from a low down cur that he knows perfectly well isn't fit to black his boots--none of that makes any difference. It is up to him to do what he is told and he does it without a kick if he's wise. Young Holiday is wise. He'd had his medicine sometime. One sees that. I don't know why he dropped down on us like a shooting star the way he did, some college fiasco I understand. He doesn't talk about himself or his affairs though he is a frank outspoken youngster in other ways. But there was a look in his eyes when he came to us that most boys of twenty don't have, thank the Lord! And it is that look or what is behind it that has made him ace high here. That boy struck bottom somewhere and struck it hard. I'll bet my best belt on that."

This interested Geoffrey Annersley. He thought he understood what the colonel meant. There was something in Ted Holiday's eyes which betrayed that he had already been under fire somehow. He had seen it himself.

"He is as smart as they make 'em," went on the colonel. "Quick as a flash to think and to see and to act, never loses his head. And he's a wonder with the men, jollies 'em along when they are grousing or homesick, sets 'em grinning from ear to ear when they are down-hearted, has a pat on the shoulder for this one and a jeer for that one. Old and young they are all crazy about him. They'd go anywhere he led. I tell you he's the stuff that will take 'em over the top and make the boches feel cold in the pit of their fat tumtums when they see him coming. Lord, but the uselessness of it though! He'll get killed. His kind always does. They are always in front. They are made that way. Can't help it. Sometimes they do come through though." The colonel flashed a quick admiring glance at his guest who had also been the kind that was always in front and yet had somehow by the grace of something come through in spite of the hazards he had run and the deaths he had all but died. "You are a living witness to that little fact," he added. "Lord love us! It's all in the game anyway and a man can die but once."

The next day Corporal Holiday was given a brief leave of absence from camp at the request of the distinguished British officer. Together the two went over the strange story of Elinor Ruth Farringdon and the Holidays' connection with the later chapters thereof. They decided not to write to the Hill as Annersley was planning to go to Boston next day whence he was to return soon to England his mission accomplished, and could easily stop over in Dunbury on his way and set things right in person, perhaps even by his personal presence renew Ruth's memory of things she had forgotten.

All through the pleasant dinner hour Ted kept wishing he could get the captain to talking about himself and his battle experiences and had no idea at all that he himself was being shrewdly studied as they talked. "Good breeding, good blood-quality," the captain summed up. "If he is a fair sample of young America then young America is a bit of all right." And if he is a fair sample of the Holiday family then Elinor had indeed fallen into the best of hands. Praise be! He wondered more than once what the young-corporal's own story was, what was the nature of the fiasco which had driven him into the Canadian training camp and what was behind that unboyish look which came now and then into his boyish eyes.

Later during the intimate evening over their cigarettes both had their curiosity gratified. Captain Annersley was moved to relate some of his hair breadth escapes and thrilling moments to an alert and hero worshiping listener. And later still Ted too waxed autobiographical in response to some clever baiting of which he was entirely unaware though he did wonder afterward how he had happened to tell the thing he had kept most secret to an entire stranger. It was an immense relief to the boy to talk it all out. It would never haunt him again in quite the same way now he had once broken the barriers of his reserve. Geoffrey Annersley served his purpose for Ted as well as Larry Holiday.

Annersley was immensely interested in the confession. It matched very well he thought with that other story of a gallant young Holiday to whom his cousin Elinor owed so much in more than one way. They were a queer lot these Holidays. They had the courage of their convictions and tilted at windmills right valiantly it seemed.

And then he fell to talking straight talk to Ted Holiday, saying things that only a man who has lived deeply can say with any effect. He urged the boy not to worry about that smash of his. It was past history, over and done with. He must look ahead not back and be thankful he had come out as well as he had.

"There is just one other thing I want to say," he added. "You think you have had your lesson. Maybe it is enough but you'll find it a jolly lot easier to slip up over there than it is at home. You lose your sense of values when there is death and damnation going all around you, get to feeling you have a right to take anything that comes your way to even it up. Anyway I felt that way until I met the girl I wanted to marry. Then the rest looked almighty different. I've given Nancy the best I had to give but it wasn't good enough. She deserved more than I could give her. That is plain speaking, Holiday. Men say war excuses justify anything. It doesn't do anything of the sort. Some day you will be wanting to marry a girl yourself. Don't let anything happen in this next year over there that you will regret for a life-time. That is a queer preachment and I'm a jolly rotten preacher. But somehow I felt I had to say it. You can remember it or forget it as you like."

Ted lit another cigarette, looked up straight into Geoffrey Annersley's war lined face.

"Thank you," he said. "I think I'll remember it. Anyway I appreciate your saying it to me that way."

The subject dropped then, went back to war and how men feel on the edge of death, of the unimportance of death anyway.

CHAPTER XXXVI
THE PAST AND FUTURE MEET

Larry knocked at Ruth's door. It opened and a wan and pathetically droop-ing little figure stood before him. Ever since she had been awake Ruth, had been haunted by that unwelcome bit of memory illumination which had come the night before. No wonder she drooped and scarcely dared to lift her eyes to her lover's face. But in a moment he had her in his arms, a performance which banished the droop and brought a lovely color back into the pale cheeks.

"Larry, oh Larry, is it all right? I'm not his wife? He didn't marry me?"

Larry kissed her.

"He didn't marry you. Nobody's going to marry you but me. No, I didn't mean to say that now. Forget it, sweetheart. You are free, and if you want to say so I'll let you go. If you don't want--"

"But I do want," she interrupted. "I want Larry Holiday and he is all I want. Why won't you ever, ever believe I love you? I do, more than anything in the world."

"You darling! Will you marry me? I shouldn't have asked you that other time. I hadn't the right. But I have now. Will you, Ruth? I want you so. And I've waited so long."

"Listen to me, Larry Holiday." Ruth held up a small warning forefinger. "I'll marry you if you will promise never, never to be cross to me again. I have shed quarts of tears because you were so unkind and--faithless. I ought to make you do some terrible penance for thinking the money or anything but you mattered to me. Not even the wedding ring mattered. I told you so but still you wouldn't believe."

Larry shook his head remorsefully.

"Rub it in, sweetheart, if you must. I deserve it. But don't you think I have had purgatory enough because I didn't dare believe to punish me for anything? As for the rest I know I've been behaving like a brute. I've a devil of a disposition and I've been half crazy anyway. Not that that is any excuse. But I'll behave myself in the future. Honest I will, Ruthie. All you have to do is to lift this small finger of yours--"

He indicated the digit by a loverly kiss "and I'll be as meek and lowly as--as an ash can," he finished prosaically.

Ruth's happy laughter rang out at this and she put up her lips for a kiss.

"I'll remember," she said. "You're not a brute, Larry. You're a darling and I love you--oh immensely and I'll marry you just as quick as ever I can and we'll be so happy you won't ever remember you have a disposition."

Another interim occurred, an interim occupied by things which are nobody's business and which anybody who has ever been in love can supply ad lib by exercise of memory and imagination. Then hand in hand the two went down to where Geoffrey Annersley waited to bring back the past to Elinor Farringdon.

"Does he know me?" queried Ruth as they descended.

"He surely does. He knows all there is to know about you, Miss Elinor Ruth Farringdon. He ought to. He is your cousin and he married your best friend, Nan--"

"Wait!" cried Ruth excitedly, "it's coming back. He married Nancy Hollinger and she gave me some San Francisco addresses of some friends of hers just before I sailed. They were in that envelope. I threw away the addresses when I left San Francisco and tucked my tickets into it. Why, Larry, I'm remembering--really remembering," she stopped short on the stairs to exclaim in a startled incredulous tone.

"Of course you are remembering, sweetheart," echoed Larry happily. "Come on down and remember the rest with Annersley's help. He is some cousin. You'd better be prepared to be horribly proud of him. He is a captain and wears all kinds of honorable and distinguished dingle dangles and decorations as well as a romantic limp and a magnificent gash on his cheek which he evidently didn't get shaving."

Larry jested because he knew Ruth was growing nervous. He could feel her tremble against his arm. He was more than a little anxious as to the outcome of the thing itself. The shock and the strain of meeting Geoffrey Annersley were going to be rather an ordeal he knew.

They entered the living room and paused on the threshold, Larry's arm still around the girl. Doctor Holiday and the captain both rose. The latter limped gallantly toward Ruth who stared at him an instant and then flung herself away from Larry into the other man's arms.

"Geoff! Geoff!" she cried.

For a moment nothing more was said then Ruth drew herself away.

"Geoffrey Annersley, why did you ever, ever make me wear that horrid ring?" she demanded reproachfully. "Larry and I could have married each other months ago if you hadn't. It was the silliest idea anyway and it's all your fault--everything."

He laughed at that, a, big whole-souled hearty laugh that came from the depths of him.

"That sounds natural," he said. "Every scrape you ever enticed me into as a kid was always my fault somehow. Are you real, Elinor? I can't help thinking I am seeing a ghost. Do you really remember me?" anxiously.

"Of course I remember you. Listen, Geoff. Listen hard."

And unexpectedly Ruth pursed her pretty lips and whistled a merry, lilting bar of melody.

"By Jove!" exulted the captain. "That does sound like old times."

"Don't tell me I don't remember," she flashed back happy and excited beyond measure at playing this new remembering game. "That was our special call, yours and Rod's and mine. Oh Rod!" And at that all the joy went out of the eager, flushed face. She went back into her cousin's arms again, sobbing in heart breaking fashion. The turning tide of memory had brought back wreckage of grief as well as joy. In Geoffrey Annersley's arms Ruth mourned her brother's loss for the first time. Larry sent his uncle a quick look and went out of the room. The older doctor followed. Ruth and her cousin were left alone to pick up the dropped threads of the past.

They all met again at luncheon however, Ruth rosy cheeked, excited and red-eyed but on the whole none the worse for her journey back into the land of forgotten things. As Larry had hoped the external stimulus of actually seeing and hearing somebody out of that other life was enough to start the train. What she did not yet remember Geoffrey supplied and little by little the past took on shape and substance and Elinor Ruth Farringdon became once more a normal human being with a past as well as a present which was dazzlingly delightful, save for the one dark blur of her dear Rod's unknown fate.

In the course of the conversation at table Geoffrey addressed his cousin as Elinor and was promptly informed that she wasn't Elinor and was Ruth and that he was to call her by that name or run the risk of being disapproved of very heartily.

He laughed, amused at this.

"Now I know you are real," he said. "It is exactly the tone you used when you issued the contrary command and by Jove almost the same words except for the reversed titles. 'Don't call me Ruth, Geoff,'" he mimicked. "'I am not going to be Ruth any more. I am going to be Elinor. It is a much prettier name.'"

"Well, I don't think so now," retorted Ruth. "I've changed my mind again. I think Ruth is the nicest name there is because--well--" She blushed adorably and looked across the table at the young doctor, "because Larry likes it," she completed half defiantly.

"Is that meant to be an official publishing of the bans?" teased her cousin when the laugh that Ruth's naive confession had raised subsided leaving Larry as well as Ruth a little hot of cheek.

"If you want to call it that," said Ruth. "Larry, I think you might say something, not leave me everything to do myself. Tell them we are engaged and are going to be married--"

"To-morrow," put in Larry suddenly pushing back his chair and going over to stand behind Ruth, a hand on either shoulder, facing the others gallantly if obviously also embarrassedly over her shyly bent blonde head.

The blonde head went up at that, and was shaken very decidedly.

"No indeed. That isn't right at all," she objected. "Don't listen to him anybody. It isn't going to be tomorrow. I've got to have a wedding dress and it takes at least a week to dream a wedding dress when it is the only time you ever intend to be married. I have all the other things--everything I need down to the last hair pin and powder puff. That's why I went to Boston. I knew I was going to want pretty clothes quick. I told Doctor Holiday so." She sent a charming, half merry, half deprecating smile at the older doctor who smiled back.

"She most assuredly did," he corroborated. "I never suspected it was part of a deep laid plot however. I thought it was just femininity cropping out after a dull season. How was I to know it was because you were planning to run off with my assistant that you wanted all the gay plumage?" he teased.

Ruth made a dainty little grimace at that.

"That isn't a fair way to put it," she declared. "If I had been planning to run away with Larry or he with me we would have done it months ago, plumage or no plumage. I wanted to but he wouldn't anyway," she confessed. "I like this way much, much better though. I don't want to be married anywhere except right here in the heart of the House on the Hill."

She slipped out of her chair and away from Larry's hands at that and went over to where Doctor Philip sat.

"May we?" she asked like a child asking permission to run out and play.

"It is what we all want more than anything in the world, dear child," he said. "You belong with Larry in our hearts as well as in the heart of the House. You know that, don't you?"

"I know you are the dearest man that ever was, not even excepting Larry. And I am going to kiss you, Uncle Phil, so there. I can call you that now, can't I? I've always wanted to." And fitting the deed to the word Ruth bent over and gave Doctor Philip a fluttering little butterfly kiss.

They rose from the table at that and Ruth was bidden go off to her room and get a long rest after her too exciting morning. Larry soberly repaired to the office and received patients and prescribed gravely for them just as if his inner self were not executing wild fandangoes of joy. Perhaps his patients did get a few waves of his happiness however for there was not one of them who did not leave the office with greater hope and strength and courage than he brought there.

"The young doctor's getting to be a lot like his uncle," one of them said to his wife later. "Just the very touch of his hand made me feel better today, sort of toned up as if I had had an electrical treatment. Queer how human beings can shoot sparks sometimes."

Not so queer. Larry Holiday had just been himself electrified by love and joy. No wonder he had new power that day and was a better healer than he had ever been before.

In the living room Doctor Philip and Captain Annersley held converse. The captain expressed his opinion that Ruth should go at once to Australia.

"If her brother is dead as we have every reason to fear, Elinor--Ruth--is the sole owner of an immense amount of property. The lawyers are about crazy trying to keep things going without either Roderick or Ruth. They have been begging me to come out and take charge of things for months but I haven't been able to see my way clear owing to one thing or another. Somebody will have to go at once and of course it should be Ruth."

"How would it do for her and Laurence both to go?"

"Magnificent. I was hoping you would think that was a feasible project. They will be glad to have a man to represent the family. My cousin knows nothing about the business end of the thing. She has always approached it exclusively from the spending side. Do you think your nephew would care to settle there?"

"Possibly," said the Doctor. "That will develop later. They will have to work that out for themselves. I am rather sorry he is going to marry a girl with so much money but I suppose it cannot be helped."

"Some people wouldn't look at it that way, Doctor Holiday," grinned the captain. "But I am prepared to accept the fact that you Holidays are in a class by yourselves. We have always been afraid that Elinor would be a victim of some miserable fortune hunter. I can't tell you what a relief it is to have her marry a man like your nephew. I am only sorry he had to go through such a punishing period of suspense waiting for his happiness. Since there wasn't really the slightest obstacle I rather wish he had cut his scruples and married her long ago."

"I don't agreed with you, Captain Annersley.. They are neither of them worse off for waiting and being absolutely sure that this is what they both want. If he had taken the risk and married her when he knew he hadn't the full right to do it he would have been miserable and made her more so. Larry is an odd chap. There is a morbid streak in him. He wouldn't have forgiven himself if he had done it. And losing his own self-respect would have been the worst thing that could have happened to him. No amount of actual legality could have made up for starting out on a spiritually illegal basis. We Holidays have to keep on moderately good terms with ourselves to be happy," he added with a quiet smile.

"I suppose you are right," admitted the Englishman. "Anyway the thing is straight and clear now. He has earned every bit of happiness that is coming to him and I hope it is going to be a great deal. My own sense of indebtness for all you Holidays have done for Ruth is enormous. I wish there were some way of making adequate returns for it all. But it is too big to be repaid. I may be able to keep an eye on your other nephew when he gets over. I certainly should like to. I don't know when I've taken such a fancy to a lad. My word he is a ripping sort."

"Ted?" Doctor Holiday smiled a little. "Well, yes, I suppose he is what you Britishers call ripping. It has been rather ripping in another sense being his guardian sometimes."

"I judge so by his own account of himself. Yoxi mustn't let that smash of his worry you. He'll find something over there that will be worth a hundred times what any college can give him, and as for the rest half the lads of mettle in the world come to earth with a jolt over a girl sooner or later and they don't all rise up out of the dust as clean as he did by, a long shot."

"So he told you about that affair? You must have gotten under his skin rather surprisingly Ted doesn't talk much about himself and I fancy he hasn't talked about that thing at all to any one. It went deep."

"I know. He shows that in a hundred ways. But it hasn't crushed him or made him reckless. It simply steadied him and I infer he needed some steadying."

Doctor Holiday nodded assent to that and asked if he thought the boy was doing well up there.

"Not a doubt of it," said the Englishman heartily. And he added a brief synopsis of the things that the colonel had said in regard to his youngest corporal.

"That is rather astonishing," remarked Doctor Holiday. "Obedience hasn't ever been one of Ted's strong points. In fact he has been a rebel always."

"Most boys are until they perceive that there is sense instead of tyranny in law. Your nephew has had that knocked into him rather hard and he is all the better for it tough as it was in the process. He is making good up there. He will make good over seas. He is a born leader--a better leader of men than his brother would be though maybe Larry is finer stuff. I don't know."

"They are very different but I like to think they are both rather fine stuff. Maybe that is my partial view but I am a bit proud of them both, Ted as well as Larry."

"You have every reason," approved the captain heartily. "I have seen a good many splendid lads in the last four years and these two measure up in a way which is an eye opener to me. In my stupid insular prejudice maybe I had fallen to thinking that the particular quality that marks them both was a distinctly British affair. Apparently you can breed it in America too. I'm glad to see it and to own it. And may I say one other thing, Doctor Holiday? I have the D.S.C. and a lot of other junk like that but I'd surrender every bit of it this minute gladly if I thought that I would ever have a son that would worship me the way those lads of yours worship you. It is an honor any man might well covet."

CHAPTER XXXVII
ALAN MASSEY LOSES HIMSELF

While Ruth and Larry steered their storm tossed craft of love into smooth haven at last; while Ted came into his own in the Canadian training camp and Tony played Broadway to her heart's content, the two Masseys down in Mexico drifted into a strange pact of friendship.

Had there been no other ministrations offered save those of creature comfort alone Dick would have had cause to be immensely grateful to Alan Massey. To good food, good nursing and material comfort the young man reacted quickly for he was a healthy young animal and had no bad habits to militate against recovery.

But there was more than creature comfort in Alan's service. Without the latter's presence loneliness, homesickness and heartache would have gnawed at the younger man retarding his physical gains. With Alan Massey life even on a sick bed took on fascinating colors like a prism in sunlight.

For the sick lad's delectation Alan spun long thrilling tales, many of them based on personal experience in his wide travels in many lands. He was a magnificent raconteur and Dick propped up among his pillows drank it all in, listening like another Desdemona to strange moving accidents of fire and flood which his scribbling soul recognized as superb copy.

Often too Alan read from books, called in the masters of the pen to set the listener's eager mind atravel through wondrous, unexplored worlds. Best of all perhaps were the twilight hours when Alan quoted long passages of poetry from memory, lending to the magic of the poet's art his own magic of voice and intonation. These were wonderful moments to Dick, moments he was never to forget. He drank deep of the soul vintage which the other man offered him out of the abundance of his experience as a life long pilgrim in the service of beauty.

It was a curious relation--this growing friendship between the two men. In some respects they were as master and pupil, in others were as man and man, friend and friend, almost brother and brother. When Alan Massey gave at all he gave magnificently without stint or reservation. He did now. And when he willed to conquer he seldom if ever failed. He did not now. He won, won first his cousin's liking, respect, and gratitude and finally his loyal friendship and something else that was akin to reverence.

Tony Holiday's name was seldom mentioned between the two. Perhaps they feared that with the name of the girl they both loved there might return also the old antagonistic forces which had already wrought too much havoc. Both sincerely desired peace and amity and therefore the woman who held both their hearts in her keeping was almost banished from the talk of the sick room though she was far from forgotten by either.

So things went on. In time Dick was judged by the physician well enough to take the long journey back to New York. Alan secured the tickets, made all the arrangements, permitting Dick not so much as the lifting of a finger in his own behalf. And just then came Tony Holiday's letter to Alan telling him she was his whenever he wanted her since he had cleared the shield forever in her eyes by what he had done for Dick. She trusted him, knew he would not ask her to marry him unless he was quite free morally and every other way to ask her. She wanted him, could not be surer of his love or her own if she waited a dozen years. He meant more to her than her work, more than her beloved freedom more even than Holiday Hill itself although she felt that she was not so much deserting the Hill as bringing Alan to it. The others would learn to love him too. They must, because she loved him so much! But even if they did not she had made her choice. She belonged to him first of all.

"But think, dear," she finished. "Think well before you take me. Don't come to me at all unless you can come free, with nothing on your soul that is going to prevent your being happy with me. I shall ask no questions if you come. I trust you to decide right for us both because you lave me in the high way as well as all the other ways."

Alan took this letter of Tony's out into the night, walked with it through flaming valleys of hell. She was his. Of her own free will she had given herself to him, placed him higher in her heart at last than even her sacred Hill. And yet after all the Hill stood between them, in the challenge she flung at him. She was his to take if he could come free. She left the decision to him. She trusted him.

Good God! Why should he hesitate to take what she was willing to give? He had atoned, saved his cousin's life, lived decently, honorably as he had promised, kept faith with Tony herself when he might perhaps have won her on baser terms than he had made himself keep to because he loved her as she said "in the high way as well as all the other ways." He would contrive some way of giving his cousin back the money. He did not want it. He only wanted Tony and her love. Why in the name of all the devils should he who had sinned all his life, head up and eyes open, balk at this one sin, the negative sin of mere silence, when it would give him what he wanted more than all the world? What was he afraid of? The answer he would not let himself discover. He was afraid of Tony Holiday's clear eyes but he was more afraid of something else--his own soul which somehow Tony had created by loving and believing in him.

All the next day, the day before they were to leave on the northern journey, Alan behaved as if all the devils of hell which he had invoked were with him. The old mocking bitterness of tongue was back, an even more savage light than Dick remembered that night of their quarrel was in his green eyes. The man was suddenly acidulated as if he had over night suffered a chemical transformation which had affected both mind and body. A wild beast tortured, evil, ready to pounce, looked out of his drawn, white face.

Dick wondered greatly what had caused the strange reaction and seeing the other was suffering tremendously for some reason or other unexplained and perhaps inexplicable was profoundly sorry. His friendship for the man who had saved his life was altogether too strong and deep to be shaken by this temporary lapse into brutality which he had known all along was there although held miraculously in abeyance these many weeks. The man was a genius, with all the temperamental fluctuations of mood which are comprehensible and forgivable in a genius. Dick did not begrudge the other any relief he might find in his debauch of ill humor, was more than willing he should work it off on his humble self if it could do any good though he would be immensely relieved when the old friendly Alan came back.

Twilight descended. Dick turned from the mirror after a critical survey of his own lean, fever parched, yellow countenance.

"Lord! I look like a peanut," he commenced disgustedly. "I say, Massey, when we get back to New York I think I should choke anybody if I were you who dared to say we looked alike. One must draw the line somewhere at what constitutes a permissible insult." He grinned whimsically at his own expense, turned back to the mirror. "Upon my word, though, I believe it is true. We do look alike. I never saw it until this minute. Funny things--resemblances."

"This isn't so funny," drawled Alan. "We had the same great grandfather."

Dick whirled about staring at the other man as if he thought him suddenly gone mad.

"What! What do you know about my great grandfather? Do you know who I am?"

"I do. You are John Massey, old John's grandson, the chap I told you once was dead and decently buried. I hoped it was true at the time but it wasn't a week before I knew it was a lie. I found out John Massey was alive and that he was going under the name of Dick Carson. Do you wonder I hated you?"

Dick sat down, his face white. He looked and was utterly dazed.

"I don't understand," he said. "Do you mind explaining? It--it is a little hard to get all at once."

And then Alan Massey told the story that no living being save himself knew. He spared himself nothing, apologised for nothing, expressed no regret, asked for no palliation of judgment, forgiveness or even understanding. Quietly, apparently without emotion, he gave back to the other man the birthright he had robbed him of by his selfish and dishonorable connivance with a wicked old man now beyond the power of any vengeance or penalty. Dick Carson was no longer nameless but as he listened tensely to his cousin's revelations he almost found it in his heart to wish he were. It was too terrible to have won his name at such a cost. As he listened, watching Alan's eyes burn in the dusk in strange contrast to his cool, liquid, studiously tranquil voice, Dick remembered a line Alan himself had read him only the other day, "Hell, the shadow of a soul on fire," the Persian phrased it. Watching, Dick Carson saw before him a sadder thing, a soul which had once been on fire and was now but gray ashes. The flame had blazed up, scorched and blackened its path. It was over now, burnt out. At thirty-three Alan Massey was through, had lived his life, had given up. The younger man saw this with a pang which had no reactive thought of self, only compassion for the other.

"That is all, I think," said Alan at last. "I have all the proofs of your identity with me. I never could destroy them somehow though I have meant to over and over again. On the same principle I suppose that the sinning monk sears the sign of the cross on his breast though he makes no outward confession to the world and means to make none. I never meant to make mine. I don't know why I am doing it now. Or rather I do. I couldn't marry Tony with this thing between us. I tried to think I could, that I'd made up to you by saving your life, that I was free to take my happiness with her because I loved her and she loved me. And she does love me. She wrote me yesterday she would marry me whenever I wished. I could have had her. But I couldn't take her that way. I couldn't have made her happy. She would have read the thing in my soul. She is too clean and honest and true herself not to feel the presence of the other thing when it came near her. I have tried to tell myself love was enough, that it would make up to her for the rest. It isn't enough. You can't build life or happiness except on the quarry stuff they keep on Holiday Hill, right, honor, decency. You know that. Tony forgave my past. I believe she is generous enough to forgive even this and go on with me. But I shan't ask her. I won't let her. I--I've given her up with the rest."

The speaker came over to where Dick sat, silent, stunned.

"Enough of that. I have no wish to appeal to you in any way. The next move is yours. You can act as you please. You can brand me as a criminal if you choose. It is what I am, guilty in the eyes of the law as well as in my own eyes and yours. I am not pleading innocence. I am pleading unqualified guilt. Understand that clearly. I knew what I was doing when I did it. I have known ever since. I've never been blind to the rottenness of the thing. At first I did it for the money because I was afraid of poverty and honest work. And then I went on with it for Tony, because I loved her and wouldn't give her up to you. Now I've given up the last ditch. The name is yours and the money is yours and if you can win Tony she is yours. I'm out of the face for good and all. But we have to settle just how the thing is going to be done. And that is for you to say."

"I wish I needn't do anything about it," said Dick slowly after a moment. "I don't want the money. I am almost afraid of it. It seems accursed somehow considering what it did to you. Even the name I don't seem to care so much about just now thought I have wanted a name as I have never wanted anything else in the world except Tony. It was mostly for her I wanted it. See here, Alan, why can't we make a compromise? You say Roberts wrote two letters and you have both. Why can't we destroy the one and send the other to the lawyers, the one that lets you out? It is nobody's business but ours. We can say that the letter has just fallen into your hands with the other proof that I am the John Massey that was stolen. That would straighten the thing out for you. I've no desire to brand you in any way. Why should I after all I owe you? You have made up a million times by saving my life and by the way you have given the thing over now. Anyway one doesn't exact payment from one's friends. And you are my friend, Alan. You offered me friendship. I took it--was proud to take it. I am proud now, prouder than ever."

And rising Dick Carson who was no longer Dick Carson but John Massey held out his hand to the man who had wronged him so bitterly. The paraquet in the corner jibbered harshly. Thunder rumbled heavily outside. An eerily vivid flash of lightning dispelled for a moment the gloom of the dusk as the two men clasped hands.

"John Massey!" Alan's voice with its deep cello quality was vibrant with emotion. "You don't know what that means to me. Men have called me many things but few have ever called me friend except in lip service for what they thought they could get out of it. And from you--well, I can only say, I thank you."

"We are the only Masseys. We ought to stand together," said Dick simply.

Alan smiled though the room was too dark for Dick to see.

"We can't stand together. I have forfeited the right. You chose the high road long ago and I chose the other. We have both to abide by our choices. We can't change those things at will. Spare me the public revelation if you care to. I shall be glad for Tony's sake. For myself it doesn't matter much. I don't expect to cross your path or hers again. I am going to lose myself. Maybe some day you will win her. She will be worth the winning. But don't hurry her if you want to win. She will have to get over me first and that will take time."

"She will never get over you, Alan. I know her. Things go deep with her. They do with all the Holidays. You shan't lose yourself. There is no need of it. Tony loves you. You must stay and make her happy. You can now you are free. She need never know the worst of this any more than the rest of the world need know. We can divide the money. It is the only way I am willing to have any of it."

Alan shook his head.

"We can divide nothing, not the money and not Tony's love. I told you I was giving it all up. You cannot stop me. No man has ever stopped me from doing what

I willed to do. I have a letter or two to write now and so I'll leave you. I am glad you don't hate me, John Massey. Shall we shake hands once more and then--good-night?"

Their hands met again. A sharp glare of lightning lit the room with ominous brilliancy for a moment. The paraquet screamed raucously. And then the door closed on Alan Massey.

An hour later a servant brought word to Dick that an American was below waiting to speak to him. He descended with the card in his hand. The name was unfamiliar, Arthur Hallock of Chicago, mining engineer.

The stranger stood in the hall waiting while Dick came down the stairs. He was obviously ill at ease.

"I am Hallock," announced the visitor. "You are Richard Carson?"

Dick nodded. Already the name was beginning to sound strange on his ears. In one hour he had gotten oddly accustomed to knowing that he was John Massey. And no longer needed Tony's name, dear as it was.

"I am sorry to be the bearer of ill news, Mr. Carson," the stranger proceeded. "You have a friend named Alan Massey living here with you?"

Again Dick nodded. He was apprehensive at the mention of Alan's name.

"There was a riot down there." The speaker pointed down the street. "A fuss over an American flag some dirty German dog had spit at. It didn't take long to start a life sized row. We are all spoiling for a chance to stick a few of the pigs our-selves whether we're technically at war or not. A lot of us collected, your friend Massey among the rest. I remember particularly when he joined the mob because he was so much taller than the rest of us and came strolling in as if he was going to an afternoon tea instead of getting into an international mess with nearly all the contracting parties drunk and disorderly. There was a good deal of excitement and confusion. I don't believe anybody knows just what happened but a drunken Mexi-can drew a dagger somewhere in the mix up and let it fly indiscriminate like. We all scattered like mischief when we saw the thing flash. Nobody cares much for that kind of plaything at close range. But Massey didn't move. It got him, clean in the heart. He couldn't have suffered a second. It was all over in a breath. He fell and the mob made itself scarce. Another fellow and I were the first to get to him but there wasn't anything to do but look in his pockets and find out who he was. We found his name on a card with this address and your name scribbled on it in pencil. I say, Mr. Carson, I am horribly sorry," suddenly perceiving Dick's white face. "You care a lot, don't you?"

"I care a lot," said Dick woodenly. "He was my cousin and--my best friend."

"I am sorry," repeated the young engineer. "Mr. Carson, there is something else I feel as if I had to say though I shan't say it to any one else. Massey might have dodged with the rest of us. He saw it coming just as we did. He waited for it and I saw him smile as it came--a queer smile at that. Maybe I'm mistaken but I have a hunch he wanted that dagger to find him. That was why he smiled."

"I think you are entirely right, Mr. Hallock," said Dick. "I haven't any doubt but that was why he smiled. He would smile just that way. Where --where is he?" Dick brushed his hands across his eyes as he asked the question. He had never felt so desolate, so utterly alone in his life.

"They are bringing him here. Shall I stay? Can I help anyway?"

Dick shook his head sadly.

"Thank you. I don't think there is anything any one can do. I--I wish there was."

A little later Alan Massey's dead body lay in austere dignity in the house in which he had saved his cousin's life and given him back his name and fortune together with the right to win the girl he himself had loved so well. The smile was still on his face and a strange serenity of expression was there too. He slept well at last. He had lost himself as he had proclaimed his intent to do and in losing had found himself. One could not look upon that calm white sculptured face without feeling that. Alan Massey had died a victor undaunted, a master of fate to the end.

CHAPTER XXXVIII
THE SONG IN THE NIGHT

Tony Holiday sat in the dressing room waiting her cue to go on the stage. It was only a rehearsal however. Miss Clay was back now and Tony was once more the humble understudy though with a heart full of happy knowledge of what it is like to be a real actress with a doting public at her feet.

While she waited she picked up a newspaper and carelessly scanned its pages. Suddenly to the amazement and consternation of the other girl who was dressing in the same room she uttered a sharp little cry and for the first time in her healthy young life slid to the floor in a merciful faint. Her frightened companion called for help instantly and it was only a moment before Tony's brown eyes opened and she pulled herself up from the couch where they had laid her. But she would not speak or tell them what had happened and it was only when they had gotten her off in a cab with a motherly, big hearted woman who played shrew's and villainess' parts always on the stage but was the one person of the whole cast to whom every one turned in time of trouble that the rest searched the paper for the clew to the thing which had made Tony look like death itself. It was not far to seek. Tony looked like death because Alan Massey was dead.

They all knew Alan Massey and knew that he and Tony Holiday were intimate friends, perhaps even betrothed. More than one of them had seen and remembered how he had kissed her before them all on the night of Tony's first Broadway triumph and some of them had wondered why he had not been seen since with her. So he had been in Mexico and now he was dead, his heart pierced by a Mexican dagger. And Tony--Tony of the gay tongue and the quick laughter--had the dagger gone into her heart too? It looked so. The "End of the Rainbow" cast felt very sad and sober that day. They loved Tony and just now she was not an actress to them but a girl who had loved a man, a man who was dead.

Jean Lambert telegraphed at once for Doctor Holiday to come to Tony who was in a bad way. She wouldn't talk. She wouldn't eat. She did not sleep. She did not cry. Jean thought if she cried her grief would not have been so pitiful to behold. It was the stony, white silence of her that was intolerable to witness.

In her uncle's arms Tony's terrible calm gave way and she sobbed herself to utter weariness and finally to sleep. But even to him she would not talk much about Alan. He had not known Alan. He had never understood--never would understand now how wonderful, how lovable, how splendid her lover had been. For several days she was kept in bed and the doctor hardly left her. It was a hard time for him as well as his stricken niece. Even their love for each other did not serve to lighten the pain to any great extent. It was not the same sorrow they had. Doctor Holiday was suffering because his little girl suffered. Tony was suffering because she loved

Alan Massey who would never come to her again. Neither could entirely share the grief of the other. Alan Massey was between them still.

Finally Dick came and was able to give what Doctor Philip could not. He could sing Alan's praises, tell her how wonderful he had been, how generous and kind. He could share her grief as no one else could because he had learned to love Alan Massey almost as well as she did herself.

Dick talked freely of Alan, told her of the strange discovery which they had made that he and Alan were cousins and that he himself was John Massey, the kidnapped baby whom he had been so sorry for when he had looked up the Massey story at the time of the old man's death. Dick was not an apt liar but he lied gallantly now for Alan's sake and for Tony's. He told her that it was only since Alan had been in Mexico that he had known who his cousin was and had immediately possessed the other of the facts and turned over to him the proofs of his identity as John Massey.

It was a good lie, well conceived and well delivered but the liar had not reckoned on that fatal Holiday gift of intuition. Tony listened to the story, shut her eyes and thought hard for a moment. Then she opened her eyes again and looked straight at Dick.

"That is not the truth," she said. "Alan knew before he went to Mexico. He knew long before. That was the other ghost--the one he could not lay. Don't lie to me. I know."

And then yielding to her command Dick began again and told her the truth, serving Alan's memory well by the relation. One thing only he kept back. After all he had no proof that the young engineer had been right in his conjecture that Alan had wanted the dagger to find him. There was no need of hurting Tony with that.

"Dick--I can't call you John yet. I can't even think about you to-night though I am so thankful to have you back safe and well. I can't be glad yet for you. I can't remember any one but Alan. You will forgive me, I know. But tell me. It was a terrible thing he did to you. Do you forgive him really?" The girl's deep shadowed eyes searched the young man's face, challenging him to speak the truth and only that.

He met the challenge willingly. He had nothing to conceal here. Tony might read him through and through and she would find in him neither hate nor rancor, nor condemnation.

"Of course I forgive him, Tony. He did a terrible thing to me you say. He did a much more terrible thing to himself. And he made up for everything over and over by what he did for me in Mexico. He might have let me die. I should have died if he had not come. There is no doubt in the world of that. He could not have done more if he had been my own brother. He meant me to like him. He did more. He made me love him. He was my friend. We parted as friends with a handshake which was his good-by though I didn't know it."

It was a fatal speech. Too late Dick realized it as he saw Tony's face.

"Dick, he meant to let himself get killed. I've thought so all along and now I know you think so too."

"I didn't mean to let that out. Maybe I am mistaken. We shall never know. But I believe he was not sorry to let the dagger get him. He had given up everything else. It wasn't so hard for him to give up the one thing more--the thing he didn't want anyway--life. Life wasn't much to him after he gave you up, Tony. His love was the biggest thing about him. I love you myself but I am not ashamed to say that his love was a bigger thing than mine every way, finer, more magnificent, the love of a genius whereas mine is just the love of an every day man. It was love that saved him."

"Dick, do you believe that the real Alan is dust--nothing but dust down in a grave?" demanded Tony suddenly.

"No, Tony, I don't. I can't. The essence of what was best in him is alive somewhere. I know it. It must be. His love for you--for all beauty--they couldn't die, dear. They were big enough to be immortal."

"And his dancing," sighed Tony. "His dancing couldn't die. It had a soul."

If she had not been sure already that Alan had meant to go out of her life even if he had not meant to go to his death when he left New York she would have been convinced a little later. Alan's Japanese servant brought two gifts to her from his honorable master according to his honorable master's orders should he not return from his journey. His honorable master being unfortunately dead his unworthy servant laid the gifts at Mees Holiday's honorable feet. Whereupon the bearer had departed as quietly as death itself might come.

One of the gifts was a picture, a painting which Tony had seen, and which was she thought the most beautiful of all his beautiful creations. Its sheer loveliness would have hurt her even if it had had no other significance and it did have a very real message.

At first sight the whole scene seemed enveloped in translucent, silver mist. As one looked more closely however there was revealed the figure of a man, black clad in pilgrim guise, kneeling on the verge of a precipitous cliff which rose out of a seemingly bottomless abyss of terrific blackness. Though in posture of prayer the pilgrim's head was lifted and his face wore an expression of rapt adoration. Above a film of fog in the heavens stretched a clear space of deep blue black sky in which hung a single luminous star. From the star a line of golden light of unearthly radiance descended and finding its way to the uplifted transfigured face of the kneeling pilgrim ended there.

Tony Holiday understood, got the message as clearly as if Alan himself stood beside her to interpret it. She knew that he was telling her through the picture that she had saved his soul, kept him out of the abyss, that to the end she was what he had so often called her--his star.

With tear blinded eyes she turned from the canvas to the little silver box which the servant had placed in her hands together with a sealed envelope. In the box was a gorgeous, unset ruby, the gem of Alan's collection as Tony well knew having worshiped often at its shrine. It lay there now against the austere purity of its white satin background--the symbol of imperishable passion.

Reverently Tony closed the little box and opened the sealed envelope dreading yet longing to know its contents. Alan had sent her no word of farewell, had not written to her that night before he went out into the storm to meet his death, had made no response to the letter she herself had written offering herself and her love and faith for his taking. At first these things had hurt her. But these gifts of his were beginning to make her understand his silence. Selfish and spectacular all his life at his death Alan Massey had been surpassingly generous and simple. He had chosen to bequeath his love to her not as an obsession and a bondage but as an elemental thing like light and air.

The message in the envelope was in its way as impersonal as the ruby had been but Tony found it more hauntingly personal than she had ever found his most impassioned love letter. Once more the words were couched in the symbol tongue of the poet in India--in only two sentences, but sentences so poignant that they stamped themselves forever on Tony Holiday's mind as they stood out from the paper in Alan's beautiful, striking handwriting.

"When the lighted lamp is brought into the room
  I shall go. And then perhaps you will listen to the night, and
  hear my song when I am silent."

The lines were dated on that unforgettable night when Tony had played Broadway and danced her last dance with her royal lover. So he had known even then that he was giving her up. Realizing this Tony realized as she never had before the high quality of his love. She could guess a little of what that night had meant to him, how passionately he must have desired to win through to the full fruition of his love before he gave her up for all the rest of time. And she herself had been mad that night Tony remembered. Ah well! He had been strong for them both. And now their love would always stay upon the high levels, never descend to the ways of earth. There would never be anything to regret, though Tony loving her lover's memory as she did that moment was not so sure but she regretted that most of all.

Yet tragic as Alan's death was and bitterly and sincerely as she mourned his loss Tony could see that he had after all chosen the happiest way out for himself as well as for her and his cousin. It was not hard to forgive a dead lover with a generous act of renunciation his last deed. It would have been far less easy to forgive a living lover with such a stain upon his life. Even though he tried to wash it away by his surrender and she by her forgiveness the stain would have remained ineradicable. There would always have been a barrier between them for all his effort and her own.

And his love would ill have borne denial or frustration. Without her he would have gone down into dark pits if he had gone on living. Perhaps he had known and feared this himself, willing to prevent it at any cost. Perhaps he had known that so long as he lived she, Tony, would never have been entirely her own again. His bondage would have been upon her even if he never saw her again. Perhaps he had elected death most of all for this reason, had loved her well enough to set her free. He had told her once that love was twofold, a force of destruction and damnation but also a force of purification and salvation. Alan had loved her greatly, perhaps in the end his love had taken him in his own words "to the gate of Heaven." Tony did not know but she thought if there really was a God he would understand and forgive the soul of Alan Massey for that last splendid sacrifice of his in the name of love.

And whatever happened Tony Holiday knew that she would bear forever the mark of Alan Massey's stormy, strange, and in the end all-beautiful love. Perhaps some day the lighted lamp might be brought in. She did not know, would not attempt to prophesy about that. She did not know that she would always listen to the night for Alan Massey's sake and hear his song though he was silent forever.

The next day Richard Carson officially disappeared from the world and John Massey appeared in his place. The papers made rather a striking story of his romantic history and its startling denouement which had come they said through the death bed confessions of the man Roberts which had only just reached the older Massey's hands, strangely enough on the eve of his own tragic death, which was again related to make the tale a little more of a thriller. That was all the world knew, was ever to know for the Holidays and John Massey kept the dead man's secret well.

And the grass grew green on Alan Massey's grave. The sun and dew and rain laid tender fingers upon it and great crimson and gold hearted roses strewed their fragrant petals upon it year by year. The stars he had loved so well shone down upon the lonely spot where his body slept quiet at last after the torment of his brief and stormy life. But otherwise, as John Massey and Tony Holiday believed, his undefeated spirit fared on splendidly in its divine quest of beauty.

CHAPTER XXXIX
IN WHICH THE TALE ENDS IN THE
HOUSE ON THE HILL

The winter had at last decided to recapture its forsaken role of the Snow King. For two days and as many nights the air had been one swirl of snow which shut out earth and sky. But on the third morning the Hill woke to a dazzling world of cloudless blue and trackless white. A resplendent bride-like day it was and fitly so for before sundown the old House on the Hill was to know another bride. Elinor Ruth Farringdon's affairs required her immediate attention in Australia and she was leaving to-night for that far away island which was again now dear to her heart as the home of her happy childhood, the memory of which had now all returned after months of strange obliteration. But she would not go as Elinor Ruth Farringdon. That name was to be shed as absolutely as her recollection of it had once been shed. She would go as Mrs. Laurence Holiday with a real wedding ring all her own and a real husband also all her own by her side.

There were to be no guests outside the family except for the Lamberts, Carlotta and Dick--John Massey, as they were now trying to learn to call him. The wedding was to be very quiet not only because of Granny but because they were all very pitiful of Tony's still fresh grief, the more so because she bore it so bravely and quietly, anxious lest she cast any shadow upon the happiness of the others, especially that of Larry and Ruth. In any case a quiet wedding would have been the choice of the two who were most concerned. They wanted only their near and dear about them when they took upon themselves the rites which were to unite them for the rest of their two lives.

Aside from Tony's sorrow the only two regrets which marred the household joy that bride white day were Ted's absence and imminent departure for France and that other even soberer remembrance of that other gallant young soldier, Ruth's brother Roderick of whom no news had come, though Ruth insisted that Rod wasn't dead, that he would came back just as her vivid memory of him had returned.

And it happened that her faith was rewarded and on the very day of days when one drop more of happiness made the cup fairly spill over. Larry was summoned to the telephone just as he had been once before on a certain memorable occasion to be told that a cabled message awaited him. The message was from Geoffrey Annersley and bore besides his love and congratulations the wonderful news that Roderick Farringdon had escaped from a German prison camp and was safe in England.

Ruth shed many happy tears over this best of all bridal gifts, not enough to dim the shining blue of her eyes but enough to give them a lovely, misty tenderness which made her sweeter than ever Larry thought, and who should have magic eyes if not a bridegroom?

A little later came Carlotta and Dick, the latter well and strong again but thin and pale and rather sober. Tony loved him for grieving for Alan as she knew he did. He too had known and loved the dead man and understood him perhaps better than she had herself. For after all no man and woman can ever fully understand each other especially if they are in love. So many faint nuances of doubt and fear and pride and passion and jealousy are forever drifting between lovers obscuring clarity of vision.

Carlotta was prettier than ever with a new sweetness and womanliness which her love had wrought in her during the year. People who had known her mother said she was growing daily more like Rose though always before they had traced a greater resemblance to the other side of the house, to her Aunt Lottie particularly. She and Philip were to be married in the spring. "When the orioles come" Carlotta had said remembering her father's story of that other brief mating.

Tony and Carlotta slipped away from the others to talk by themselves. Carlotta too had known and liked Alan and to all such Tony clung just now.

"He was so different at the end," she said to her friend. "I wish you could have known him that way--so dear and gentle and wonderful. He kept his promise everyway, lived absolutely straight and clean and fine."

"He did it for you, Tony. He never could have done it for himself. He wouldn't have thought it worth while. Don't tell me if you don't want to but I have guessed a good many things since I knew about Dick and I have wondered if he wasn't rather glad--to get killed."

"Yes, Dick thinks and I think too that he let the dagger find him. I have always called him my royal lover. His death was the most royal part of all."

Carlotta was silent. She hoped that somewhere Alan was finding the happiness he seemed always to have missed on earth. Then seeing her friend's lovely eyes with the heavy shadow in them where there had been only sunshine before her heart rebelled. Poor Tony! Why must she suffer like this? She was so young. Was life really over for her? For Carlotta in her own happiness life and love were synonymous terms. Something of what was in her mind she said to her friend.

"I don't know," confessed Tony. "It is too soon to tell. Just now Alan fills every nook and cranny of me. I can't think of any other man or imagine myself loving anybody else as I loved him. But I am a very much alive person. I don't believe I shall give myself to death forever. Alan himself wouldn't want it so. A part of me will always be his but there are other margins of me that Alan never touched and these maybe I shall give to some one else when the time comes."

"Does that mean Dick--John Massey?"

"Maybe. Maybe not. I have told him not to speak of love for a long, long time. We must both be free. He is going to France as a war correspondent next week."

"Don't you hate to have him go?"

"Yes, I do. But I can't be selfish enough to keep him hanging round me forever on the slim chance that some time I shall be willing to marry him. He is too fine to be treated like that. He wants to go overseas unless I will marry him now and I can't do that. It is better that we should be apart for a while. As for me I have my work and I am going to plunge into it as deep and hard as I can. I am not going to be unhappy. You can't be unhappy when you love your work as I love mine. Don't be sorry for me, Carlotta. I am not sorry for myself. Even if I never loved again and never was loved I should still have had enough for a life time. It is more than many women have, more than I deserve."

The bride white day wore on to twilight and as the clock struck the hour of five Ruth Farringdon came down the broad oak staircase clad in the shining splendor of the bridal gown she had "dreamed," wearing her grandmother's pearls and the lace veil which Larry's lovely mother had worn as Ned Holiday's bride long and long ago. At the foot of the stairs Larry waited and took her hand. Eric and Hester flanking the living room door pushed aside the curtains for the two who still hand in hand walked past the children into the room where the others were assembled. Gravely and brimming with importance the guard of honor followed, the latter bearing the bride's bouquet, the former squeezing the wedding ring in his small fist. Ruth took her place beside the senior doctor. The minister opened his mouth to proceed with the ceremony, shut it again with a little gasp.

For suddenly the curtains were swept aside again, this time with a breezier and less stately sweep and Ted Holiday in uniform and sergeant's regalia plunged into the room, a thinner, browner, taller Ted, with a new kind of dignity about him but withal the same blue-eyed lad with the old heart warming smile, still always Teddy the beloved.

"Don't mind me," he announced. "Please go on." And he slipped into a place beside Tony drawing her hand in his with a warm pressure as he did so.

They went on. Laurence LaRue Holiday and Elinor Ruth Farringdon were made man and wife till death did them part. The old clock on the mantel which had looked down on these two on a less happy occasion looked on still, ticking away calmly, telling no tales and asking no questions. What was a marriage more or less to time?

The ceremony over it was the newly arrived sergeant rather than the bride and groom who was the center of attraction and none were better pleased than Larry and Ruth to have it so.

It was a flying visit on Ted's part. He had managed to secure a last minute leave just before sailing from Montreal at which place he had to report the day after to-morrow.

"So let's eat, drink, and be merry," he finished his explanation gayly. "But first, please, Larry, may I kiss the bride?"

"Go to it," laughed his brother. "I'm so hanged glad to see you Kid, I've half a mind to kiss you myself."

Needing no further urging Ted availed himself of the proffered privilege and kissed the bride, not once but three times, once on each rosy cheek, and last full on her pretty mouth itself.

"There!" he announced standing off to survey her, both her hands still in his possession. "I've always wanted to do that and now I've done it. I feel better."

Everybody laughed at that not because what he said was so very amusing as because their hearts were so full of joy to have the irrepressible youngest Holiday at home again after the long anxious weeks of his absence.

Under cover of the laugh he whispered in Ruth's ear, "Gee! But I'm glad you are all right again, sweetness. And your Geoffrey Annersley is some peach of a cousin, I'm telling you, though I'm confoundedly glad he decided he was married to somebody else and left the coast clear for Larry."

He squeezed her hand again, a pressure which meant more than his words as Ruth knew and then he turned to Larry. The hands of the two brothers met and each looked into the other's face, for once unashamed of the emotion that mastered them. Characteristically Ted was the first to recover speech.

"Larry, dear old chap, I wish I could tell you how happy I am that it has come out so ripping right for you and Ruth. You deserve all the luck and love in the world. I only wish mother and dad could be here now. Maybe they are. I believe they must know somehow. Dad seems awfully close to me lately especially since I've been in this war business." Then seeing Larry's face shadow he added, "And you mustn't worry about me, old man. I am going to come through and it is all right anyway whatever happens. You know yourself death isn't so much--not such a horrible calamity as we talk as if it were."

"I know. But it is horribly hard to reconcile myself to your going. I can't seem to make up my mind to accept it especially as you needn't have gone."

"Don't let that part bother you. The old U.S.A. will be in it herself before you know it and then I'd have gone anyway. Nothing would have kept me. What is the odds? I am glad to be getting in on the front row myself. I am going to be all right I tell you. Going to have a bully time and when we have the Germans jolly well licked I'm coming home and find me as pretty a wife as Ruth if there is one to be found in America and marry her quick as lightning."

Larry smiled at that. It was so like Ted it was good to hear. And irrationally enough he found himself more than a little reassured and comforted because the other lad declared he was going to be all right and have a bully time and come back safe when the job was done.

"And I say, Larry." Ted's voice was soberer now. "I have always wanted to tell you how I appreciated your standing by me so magnificently in that horrible mess of mine. I wouldn't have blamed you if you had felt like throwing me over for life after my being such a tarnation idiot and disgracing the family like that. I'll never forget how white you and Uncle Phil both were about it every way and maybe you won't believe it but there'll never be anything like that again. There are some things I'm through with--at least if I'm not I'm even more of a fool than I think I am."

"Don't, Ted. I haven't been such a model of virtue and wisdom that I can afford to sit in judgment on you. I've learned a few things myself this year and I am not so cock sure in my views as I was by a long shot. Anyway you have more than made up by what you have done since and what you are going to do over there. Let's forget the rest and just remember that we are both Holidays, and it is up to both of us to measure up to Dad and Uncle Phil, far as we can."

"Some stunt, what?" Thus Ted flippantly mixed his familiar American and newly acquired British vernacular. "You are dead right, Larry. I am afraid I'm doomed to land some nine miles or so below the mark but I'm going to make a stab at it anyway."

Later there was a gala dinner party, an occasion almost as gay as that Round Table banquet over eight years ago had been when Dick Carson had been formally inducted into the order and Doctor Holiday had announced that he was going to marry Miss Margery. And as before there was laughter and gay talk and teasing, affectionate jest and prophecy mingled with the toasting.

There were toasts to the reigning bride and groom, Larry and Ruth, to the coming bride and groom Philip and Carlotta, to Tony, the understudy that was, the star that was to be; to Dick Carson that had been, John Massey that was, foreign correspondent, and future famous author. There was a particularly stirring toast to Sergeant Ted who would some day be returning to his native shore at least a captain if not a major with all kinds of adventures and honors to his credit. Everybody smiled gallantly over this toast. Not one of them would let a shadow of grief or dread for Teddy the beloved cloud this one happy home evening of his before he left the Hill perhaps forever. The Holidays were like that.

And then Larry on his feet raised his hand for silence.

"Last and best of all," he said, "I give you--the Head of the House of Holiday-- the best friend and the finest man I know--Uncle Phil!"

Larry smiled down at his uncle as he spoke but there was deep feeling in his fine gray eyes. Better than any one else he knew how much of his present happiness he owed to that good friend and fine man Philip Holiday.

The whole table rose to this toast except the doctor, even to the small Eric and Hester who had no idea what it was all about but found it all very exciting and delightful and beautifully grown up. As they drank the toast Ted's free hand rested with affectionate pressure on his uncle's and Tony on the other side set down her glass and squeezed his hand instead. They too were trying to tell him that what Larry had spoken in his own behalf was true for them also. They wanted to have him know how much he meant to them and how much they wanted to do and be for his dear sake.

Perhaps Philip Holiday won his order of distinguished service then and there. At any rate with his own children and Ned's around him, with the wife of his heart smiling down at him from across the table with proud, happy, tear wet eyes, the

Head of the House of Holiday was content.

THE END

The Codes Of Hammurabi And Moses
W. W. Davies

The discovery of the Hammurabi Code is one of the greatest achievements of archaeology, and is of paramount interest, not only to the student of the Bible, but also to all those interested in ancient history...

Religion   **ISBN:** *1-59462-338-4*

QTY

Pages:132
MSRP $12.95

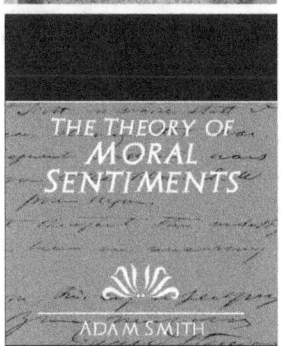

The Theory of Moral Sentiments
Adam Smith

This work from 1749. contains original theories of conscience amd moral judgment and it is the foundation for systemof morals.

Philosophy **ISBN:** *1-59462-777-0*

QTY

Pages:536
MSRP $19.95

Jessica's First Prayer
Hesba Stretton

In a screened and secluded corner of one of the many railway-bridges which span the streets of London there could be seen a few years ago, from five o'clock every morning until half past eight, a tidily set-out coffee-stall, consisting of a trestle and board, upon which stood two large tin cans, with a small fire of charcoal burning under each so as to keep the coffee boiling during the early hours of the morning when the work-people were thronging into the city on their way to their daily toil...

QTY

Pages:84

Childrens   **ISBN:** *1-59462-373-2*

MSRP $9.95

My Life and Work
Henry Ford

Henry Ford revolutionized the world with his implementation of mass production for the Model T automobile. Gain valuable business insight into his life and work with his own auto-biography... "We have only started on our development of our country we have not as yet, with all our talk of wonderful progress, done more than scratch the surface. The progress has been wonderful enough but..."

QTY

Pages:300

Biographies/   **ISBN:** *1-59462-198-5*

MSRP $21.95

The Art of Cross-Examination
Francis Wellman

QTY

I presume it is the experience of every author, after his first book is published upon an important subject, to be almost overwhelmed with a wealth of ideas and illustrations which could readily have been included in his book, and which to his own mind, at least, seem to make a second edition inevitable. Such certainly was the case with me; and when the first edition had reached its sixth impression in five months, I rejoiced to learn that it seemed to my publishers that the book had met with a sufficiently favorable reception to justify a second and considerably enlarged edition. ..

Pages:412

Reference   ISBN: *1-59462-647-2*   *MSRP $19.95*

On the Duty of Civil Disobedience
Henry David Thoreau

QTY

Thoreau wrote his famous essay, On the Duty of Civil Disobedience, as a protest against an unjust but popular war and the immoral but popular institution of slave-owning. He did more than write—he declined to pay his taxes, and was hauled off to gaol in consequence. Who can say how much this refusal of his hastened the end of the war and of slavery ?

Law   ISBN: *1-59462-747-9*   **Pages:48**

MSRP $7.45

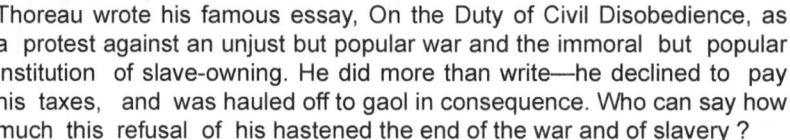

Dream Psychology Psychoanalysis for Beginners
Sigmund Freud

QTY

Sigmund Freud, born Sigismund Schlomo Freud (May 6, 1856 - September 23, 1939), was a Jewish-Austrian neurologist and psychiatrist who co-founded the psychoanalytic school of psychology. Freud is best known for his theories of the unconscious mind, especially involving the mechanism of repression; his redefinition of sexual desire as mobile and directed towards a wide variety of objects; and his therapeutic techniques, especially his understanding of transference in the therapeutic relationship and the presumed value of dreams as sources of insight into unconscious desires.

Pages:196

Psychology   ISBN: *1-59462-905-6*   *MSRP $15.45*

The Miracle of Right Thought
Orison Swett Marden

QTY

Believe with all of your heart that you will do what you were made to do. When the mind has once formed the habit of holding cheerful, happy, prosperous pictures, it will not be easy to form the opposite habit. It does not matter how improbable or how far away this realization may see, or how dark the prospects may be, if we visualize them as best we can, as vividly as possible, hold tenaciously to them and vigorously struggle to attain them, they will gradually become actualized, realized in the life. But a desire, a longing without endeavor, a yearning abandoned or held indifferently will vanish without realization.

Pages:360

Self Help   ISBN: *1-59462-644-8*   *MSRP $25.45*

QTY

The Rosicrucian Cosmo-Conception Mystic Christianity *by Max Heindel* ISBN: *1-59462-188-8* **$38.95**
The Rosicrucian Cosmo-conception is not dogmatic, neither does it appeal to any other authority than the reason of the student. It is: not controversial, but is: sent forth in the, hope that it may help to clear... New Age/Religion Pages 646

Abandonment To Divine Providence *by Jean-Pierre de Caussade* ISBN: *1-59462-228-0* **$25.95**
"The Rev. Jean Pierre de Caussade was one of the most remarkable spiritual writers of the Society of Jesus in France in the 18th Century. His death took place at Toulouse in 1751. His works have gone through many editions and have been republished... Inspirational/Religion Pages 400

Mental Chemistry *by Charles Haanel* ISBN: *1-59462-192-6* **$23.95**
Mental Chemistry allows the change of material conditions by combining and appropriately utilizing the power of the mind. Much like applied chemistry creates something new and unique out of careful combinations of chemicals the mastery of mental chemistry... New Age Pages 354

The Letters of Robert Browning and Elizabeth Barret Barrett 1845-1846 vol II ISBN: *1-59462-193-4* **$35.95**
by Robert Browning and Elizabeth Barrett Biographies Pages 596

Gleanings In Genesis (volume I) *by Arthur W. Pink* ISBN: *1-59462-130-6* **$27.45**
Appropriately has Genesis been termed "the seed plot of the Bible" for in it we have, in germ form, almost all of the great doctrines which are afterwards fully developed in the books of Scripture which follow... Religion/Inspirational Pages 420

The Master Key *by L. W. de Laurence* ISBN: *1-59462-001-6* **$30.95**
In no branch of human knowledge has there been a more lively increase of the spirit of research during the past few years than in the study of Psychology, Concentration and Mental Discipline. The requests for authentic lessons in Thought Control, Mental Discipline and... New Age/Business Pages 422

The Lesser Key Of Solomon Goetia *by L. W. de Laurence* ISBN: *1-59462-092-X* **$9.95**
This translation of the first book of the "Lernegton" which is now for the first time made accessible to students of Talismanic Magic was done, after careful collation and edition, from numerous Ancient Manuscripts in Hebrew, Latin, and French... New Age/Occult Pages 92

Rubaiyat Of Omar Khayyam *by Edward Fitzgerald* ISBN:*1-59462-332-5* **$13.95**
Edward Fitzgerald, whom the world has already learned, in spite of his own efforts to remain within the shadow of anonymity, to look upon as one of the rarest poets of the century, was born at Bredfield, in Suffolk, on the 31st of March, 1809. He was the third son of John Purcell... Music Pages 172

Ancient Law *by Henry Maine* ISBN: *1-59462-128-4* **$29.95**
The chief object of the following pages is to indicate some of the earliest ideas of mankind, as they are reflected in Ancient Law, and to point out the relation of those ideas to modern thought. Religiom/History Pages 452

Far-Away Stories *by William J. Locke* ISBN: *1-59462-129-2* **$19.45**
"Good wine needs no bush,' but a collection of mixed vintages does. And this book is just such a collection. Some of the stories I do not want to remain buried for ever in the museum files of dead magazine-numbers an author's not unpardonable vanity..." Fiction Pages 272

Life of David Crockett *by David Crockett* ISBN: *1-59462-250-7* **$27.45**
"Colonel David Crockett was one of the most remarkable men of the times in which he lived. Born in humble life, but gifted with a strong will, an indomitable courage, and unremitting perseverance... Biographies/New Age Pages 424

Lip-Reading *by Edward Nitchie* ISBN: *1-59462-206-X* **$25.95**
Edward B. Nitchie, founder of the New York School for the Hard of Hearing, now the Nitchie School of Lip-Reading, Inc, wrote "LIP-READING Principles and Practice". The development and perfecting of this meritorious work on lip-reading was an undertaking... How-to Pages 400

A Handbook of Suggestive Therapeutics, Applied Hypnotism, Psychic Science ISBN: *1-59462-214-0* **$24.95**
by Henry Munro Health/New Age/Health/Self-help Pages 376

A Doll's House: and Two Other Plays *by Henrik Ibsen* ISBN: *1-59462-112-8* **$19.95**
Henrik Ibsen created this classic when in revolutionary 1848 Rome. Introducing some striking concepts in playwriting for the realist genre, this play has been studied the world over. Fiction/Classics/Plays 308

The Light of Asia *by sir Edwin Arnold* ISBN: *1-59462-204-3* **$13.95**
In this poetic masterpiece, Edwin Arnold describes the life and teachings of Buddha. The man who was to become known as Buddha to the world was born as Prince Gautama of India but he rejected the worldly riches and abandoned the reigns of power when... Religion/History/Biographies Pages 170

The Complete Works of Guy de Maupassant *by Guy de Maupassant* ISBN: *1-59462-157-8* **$16.95**
"For days and days, nights and nights, I had dreamed of that first kiss which was to consecrate our engagement, and I knew not on what spot I should put my lips..." Fiction/Classics Pages 240

The Art of Cross-Examination *by Francis L. Wellman* ISBN: *1-59462-309-0* **$26.95**
Written by a renowned trial lawyer, Wellman imparts his experience and uses case studies to explain how to use psychology to extract desired information through questioning. How-to/Science/Reference Pages 408

Answered or Unanswered? *by Louisa Vaughan* ISBN: *1-59462-248-5* **$10.95**
Miracles of Faith in China Religion Pages 112

The Edinburgh Lectures on Mental Science (1909) *by Thomas* ISBN: *1-59462-008-3* **$11.95**
This book contains the substance of a course of lectures recently given by the writer in the Queen Street Hail, Edinburgh. Its purpose is to indicate the Natural Principles governing the relation between Mental Action and Material Conditions... New Age/Psychology Pages 148

Ayesha *by H. Rider Haggard* ISBN: *1-59462-301-5* **$24.95**
Verily and indeed it is the unexpected that happens! Probably if there was one person upon the earth from whom the Editor of this, and of a certain previous history, did not expect to hear again... Classics Pages 380

Ayala's Angel *by Anthony Trollope* ISBN: *1-59462-352-X* **$29.95**
The two girls were both pretty, but Lucy who was twenty-one who supposed to be simple and comparatively unattractive, whereas Ayala was credited, as her Bombwhat romantic name might show, with poetic charm and a taste for romance. Ayala when her father died was nineteen... Fiction Pages 484

The American Commonwealth *by James Bryce* ISBN: *1-59462-286-8* **$34.45**
An interpretation of American democratic political theory. It examines political mechanics and society from the perspective of Scotsman James Bryce Politics Pages 572

Stories of the Pilgrims *by Margaret P. Pumphrey* ISBN: *1-59462-116-0* **$17.95**
This book explores pilgrims religious oppression in England as well as their escape to Holland and eventual crossing to America on the Mayflower, and their early days in New England... History Pages 268

QTY

The Fasting Cure *by Sinclair Upton*   ISBN: *1-59462-222-1*   **$13.95**
In the Cosmopolitan Magazine for May, 1910, and in the Contemporary Review (London) for April, 1910, I published an article dealing with my experiences in fasting. I have written a great many magazine articles, but never one which attracted so much attention... New Age/Self Help/Health Pages 164

Hebrew Astrology *by Sepharial*   ISBN: *1-59462-308-2*   **$13.45**
In these days of advanced thinking it is a matter of common observation that we have left many of the old landmarks behind and that we are now pressing forward to greater heights and to a wider horizon than that which represented the mind-content of our progenitors... Astrology Pages 144

Thought Vibration or The Law of Attraction in the Thought World
by William Walker Atkinson   ISBN: *1-59462-127-6*   **$12.95**
Psychology/Religion Pages 144

Optimism *by Helen Keller*   ISBN: *1-59462-108-X*   **$15.95**
Helen Keller was blind, deaf, and mute since 19 months old, yet famously learned how to overcome these handicaps, communicate with the world, and spread her lectures promoting optimism. An inspiring read for everyone... Biographies/Inspirational Pages 84

Sara Crewe *by Frances Burnett*   ISBN: *1-59462-360-0*   **$9.45**
In the first place, Miss Minchin lived in London. Her home was a large, dull, tall one, in a large, dull square, where all the houses were alike, and all the sparrows were alike, and where all the door-knockers made the same heavy sound... Childrens/Classic Pages 88

The Autobiography of Benjamin Franklin *by Benjamin Franklin*   ISBN: *1-59462-135-7*   **$24.95**
The Autobiography of Benjamin Franklin has probably been more extensively read than any other American historical work, and no other book of its kind has had such ups and downs of fortune. Franklin lived for many years in England, where he was agent... Biographies/History Pages 332

Name	
Email	
Telephone	
Address	
City, State ZIP	

☐ **Credit Card**   ☐ **Check / Money Order**

Credit Card Number	
Expiration Date	
Signature	

Please Mail to: Book Jungle
PO Box 2226
Champaign, IL 61825
or Fax to: 630-214-0564

ORDERING INFORMATION

web*: www.bookjungle.com*
email*: sales@bookjungle.com*
fax*: 630-214-0564*
mail*: Book Jungle PO Box 2226 Champaign, IL 61825*
or PayPal *to sales@bookjungle.com*

Please contact us for bulk discounts

DIRECT-ORDER TERMS

**20% Discount if You Order
Two or More Books**
Free Domestic Shipping!
Accepted: Master Card, Visa,
Discover, American Express

www.ingramcontent.com/pod-product-compliance
Lightning Source LLC
Chambersburg PA
CBHW081145020726
47504CB00009B/2003